# Hardly a Husband

Jarrod, fifth Marquess of Shepherdston, gets the shock of his life when childhood friend Sarah Eckersley approaches him with a tempting proposition. The daughter of the village rector, Sarah is desperate for money and has decided that being a courtesan is her only hope. And she wants Jarrod's help in the art of seduction.

As the leader of the Free Fellows League, Jarrod is wary of a marriage trap. He agrees only to help Sarah find a husband—but soon finds himself bristling at the thought of any other man touching her. Unable to abandon a friend in need, Jarrod reluctantly offers Sarah a marriage of convenience, in which he will be hardly a husband—until his heart decides otherwise . . .

**"Historical romance fans are fortunate to have a treasure like Rebecca Hagan Lee."**                    —*Affaire de Coeur*

Don't miss the first two novels of the Free Fellows League

## Barely a Bride
## Merely a Groom

or

The Marquess of Templeston's Heirs Trilogy

*Once a Mistress*
*Ever a Princess*
*Always a Lady*

*Turn the page for more acclaim for Rebecca Hagan Lee . . .*

# Hardly a Husband

Rebecca Hagan Lee

BERKLEY SENSATION, NEW YORK

**THE BERKLEY PUBLISHING GROUP**
**Published by the Penguin Group**
**Penguin Group (USA) Inc.**
**375 Hudson Street, New York, New York 10014, USA**
Penguin Group (Canada), 10 Alcorn Avenue, Toronto, Ontario M4V 3B2, Canada
(a division of Pearson Penguin Canada Inc.)
Penguin Books Ltd., 80 Strand, London WC2R 0RL, England
Penguin Group Ireland, 25 St. Stephen's Green, Dublin 2, Ireland (a division of Penguin Books Ltd.)
Penguin Group (Australia), 250 Camberwell Road, Camberwell, Victoria 3124, Australia
(a division of Pearson Australia Group Pty. Ltd.)
Penguin Books India Pvt. Ltd., 11 Community Centre, Panchsheel Park, New Delhi—110 017, India
Penguin Group (NZ), Cnr. Airborne and Rosedale Roads, Albany, Auckland 1310, New Zealand
(a division of Pearson New Zealand Ltd.)
Penguin Books (South Africa) (Pty.) Ltd., 24 Sturdee Avenue, Rosebank, Johannesburg 2196, South
Africa

Penguin Books Ltd., Registered Offices: 80 Strand, London WC2R 0RL, England

This is a work of fiction. Names, characters, places, and incidents either are the product of the author's
imagination or are used fictitiously, and any resemblance to actual persons, living or dead, business establishments, events, or locales is entirely coincidental.

HARDLY A HUSBAND

A Berkley Sensation Book / published by arrangement with the author

PRINTING HISTORY
Berkley Sensation edition / October 2004

ISBN: 0-425-19879-0

BERKLEY® SENSATION
Berkley Sensation Books are published by The Berkley Publishing Group,
a division of Penguin Group (USA) Inc.,
375 Hudson Street, New York, New York 10014.
BERKLEY SENSATION and the "B" design
are trademarks belonging to Penguin Group (USA) Inc.

PRINTED IN THE UNITED STATES OF AMERICA

10  9  8  7  6  5  4  3  2  1

*For my friend Dena M. Russell,*
*who wanted Jarrod's story*
*and who always knows just when to call.*
*With love*

## Official Charter of the Free Fellows League

On this, the seventh day of January in the year of Our Lord 1793, we, the sons and heirs to the oldest and most esteemed titles and finest families of England and Scotland, do found and charter our own Free Fellows League.

The Free Fellows League is dedicated to the proposition that sons and heirs to great titles and fortunes, who are duty bound to marry in order to beget future sons and heirs, should be allowed to avoid the inevitable leg-shackling to a female for as long as possible in order to fight the French and become England's greatest heroes.

As charter members of the Free Fellows League, we agree that:

1) We shall only agree to marry when we've no other choice or when we're old. (No sooner than our thirtieth year.)

2) We shall agree to pay each of our fellow Free Fellows the sum of five hundred pounds sterling should any of us marry before we reach our thirtieth year.

3) We shall never darken the doors of any establishments that cater to "Marriage Mart" mamas or their desperate daughters unless forced to do so. Nor shall we frequent the homes of any relatives, friends, or acquaintances that seek to match us up with prospective brides.

4) When compelled to marry, we agree that we shall only marry suitable ladies from suitable families with fortunes equal to or greater than our own.

5) We shall never be encumbered by sentiment known as love or succumb to female wiles or tears.

6) We shall sacrifice ourselves on the altar of duty in order to beget our heirs, but we shall take no pleasure in the task. We shall look upon the act in the same manner as medicine that must be swallowed.

7) We shall install our wives in country houses and keep separate establishments nearby or in London.

8) We shall drink and ride and hunt, and consort with our boon companions whenever we are pleased to do so.

9) We shall not allow the females who share our names to dictate to us in any manner. We shall put our feet upon tables and sofas and the seats of chairs if we so choose and allow our hounds to sit upon the furnishings and roam our houses at will.

10) We shall give our first loyalty and our undying friend-ship to England and our brothers and fellow members of the Free Fellows League.

Signed (in blood) and sealed by:

*The Right Honorable Griffin Abernathy, 17th Viscount Abernathy, aged nine years and two months, eldest son of and heir apparent to the 16th Earl of Weymouth.*

*The Right Honorable Colin McElreath, 27th Viscount Grantham, aged nine years and five months, eldest son of and heir apparent to the 9th Earl of McElreath.*

*The Right Honorable Jarrod Shepherdston, 22nd Earl of Westmore, aged ten years and three months, eldest son of and heir apparent to the 4th Marquess of Shepherdston.*

*League member added on this seventh day of January in the year of Our Lord 1812:*

*Daniel, 9th Duke of Sussex, aged six and twenty years and eight months.*

*League member added on this seventh day of January in the year of Our Lord 1813:*

*Jonathan Manners, 11th Earl of Barclay, aged six and twenty years and ten months.*

*Alexander Courtland, 2nd Marquess of Courtland, aged five and twenty years and one month.*

# Prologue

*Two are better than one; because they have a good reward for their labor. For if they fall, the one will lift up his fellow: but woe to him that is alone when he falleth; for he hath not another to help him up. Again, if two lie together, then they have heat: but how can one be warm alone? And if one prevail against him, two shall withstand him; and a threefold cord is not quickly broken.*

*—Hebrew Bible, Ecclesiastes 4:9–12*

KNIGHTSGUILD SCHOOL FOR GENTLEMEN
*January 1794*

"*Our Father who art in heaven, thank you for this horrid* hell-hole of a school and for old Norworthy who runs it. Thank you for the canings and for the forfeiture of the puddings I've suffered since I came here. Thank you for the Marquess and Marchioness of Shepherdston, my father and mother, who've never agreed upon anything except that I am, as my father's heir, a necessity, about which something must be done so that they need not be bothered overmuch by my presence. And thank you ever so much for giving Esme Kelverton's father the power to break the betrothal between Esme and Colin. I know his doing so broke Colin's heart, but if Lord Kelverton had not taken such a drastic measure, I would not have discovered Colin crying and he would not have punched me in the nose and called me a 'bloody, rich English lord who ought to mind his own business.' And if Colin had not punched me in the nose, I would not have had to blacken his eye and Griffin would not have taken it upon himself to separate us and received a split lip for his efforts. The three of us would not have been sent to Norworthy or received a caning before the whole assembly. If these things had not happened, there would be no Free Fellows League and I would not have Colin and Griffin as my friends. The Free Fellows League is celebrating our first anniversary, so thank you, Heavenly Father, for providing me with friends—at last.

"And thank you, Father, for making me the oldest and for giving me a higher rank so that Colin and Griffin would naturally look to me for leadership—despite the fact that I am only nine months older, have no experience leading friends or companions of any sort, and would rather have a lower rank and parents who love me the way Lord and Lady Weymouth love Griffin and the way Lady McElreath, and when he's not gaming and drinking, Lord McElreath, love Colin. Guide me, Heavenly Father, and grant me the strength to always do what's right, to be the leader my brothers in blood expect me to be, to use the League so that we may become the greatest heroes England (and Scotland) have ever known and make it possible for good to always triumph over evil. Above all, please make it so that I never disappoint Colin or Griffin or cause them to regret choosing me to be their friend. Amen.

"Oh, and Heavenly Father, if you're still listening, thank you for Jonathan Manners who sleeps in the cot next to mine and cries for his nanny every night. I grumble about it. But I don't really mind. He's only seven so it's only natural for him to whine and fret. And I suppose it's only natural for him to plague me with his constant questions and by trying to tag along. Griffin and Colin are assigned to the other dormitory and although I try to comfort him, I am secretly thankful for Manners's wailing. His crying prevents me from feeling alone in the darkness. So, Heavenly Father, I'm not asking you to stop Manners from crying if that's what it takes for him to learn to endure life here at Knightsguild, but it will be quite all right by me if you'll let him know that while I don't want him hanging on to my coattails at every turn, I'll protect him from the monsters he fears are hiding under our cots. In the name of the Father, the Son, and the Holy Ghost, this is Jarrod Shepherdston saying thank you, good night, and amen."

# Chapter 1

*All is flux, nothing stays still.*

—*Heraclitus, c. 540–c. 480 B.C.*

"Good-bye, Miss Eckersley. And you, Lady Dunbridge."

"Wait, please!" Sarah Eckersley stood with her aunt beside the front gate feverishly tugging on the drawstrings of her reticule as the Reverend Tinsley, his wife, and children bade them farewell.

The reverend pretended not to hear her as he waved good-bye, then shepherded his wife and children inside before resolutely closing the front door, shutting Sarah out.

"I forgot to give you the key. . . ." Sarah withdrew the brass door key.

"Don't worry about it," Lady Dunbridge advised, fastening a leash on her little spaniel, Precious, as they walked to the front gate. "He may be a rector, but he doesn't appear to know that charity begins at home."

"We don't need their charity," Sarah said. "Nor do we need to be accused of stealing the front door key." She took a step forward. "I should go give it to them."

"After the way they treated you?" Sarah's aunt was outraged. "After the way they shoved our belongings onto the front lawn? And tried to steal Precious? *And* Budgie. Hang it on the gate," she suggested. "They'll find it."

Sarah hesitated. "Someone else might find it first."

"So what?" Lady Dunbridge dismissed her niece's concern. "It isn't as if anyone in Helford Green locks their doors anyway. Unless a desperate highwayman or a gang of sneak thieves finds its way here, you can be certain the reverend and his family will be safe. Callous, but safe."

"I've never seen anyone get so angry so quickly," Sarah said. "Certainly not a man of the cloth. I don't know how you managed to calm him. He appeared almost pleasant by the time I arrived with Squire Perkins."

"The only reason I was able to calm him was because I told him you would be returning with your father's close friend the magistrate, who wouldn't tolerate your mistreatment by anyone," Lady Dunbridge explained, patiently waiting while Precious squatted beside the wrought-iron fence.

"His pleasant demeanor was merely an act for Squire Perkins's benefit," Sarah concluded.

"Precisely."

"Then I don't suppose it will matter if I *do* leave the front door key hanging on the front gate." Ignoring a lifetime of her father's sermons about the meek inheriting the earth and turning the other cheek, Sarah took a deep breath and hung the brass key on the center point of the wrought-iron gate. "Besides, what self-respecting thief would bother with a rectory when Shepherdston Hall is just down the way?"

"My point exactly," Lady Dunbridge agreed.

The sleepy little village of Helford Green was three miles off the main road. Sarah had never heard of any type of crime in the community and she doubted the rectory would present much of a target for would-be thieves. Not when magnificent Shepherdston Hall sat between the village and the main road.

Sarah smiled for the first time since Reverend Tinsley and his family had arrived at the rectory without warning, entering the front door and descending like biblical locusts, where they immediately began laying claim to the things they wanted and casting aside everything they didn't without regard to the rectory's current residents.

Sarah had watched in horror as one of the Tinsley daughters shot past her. Precious, Aunt Etta's little spaniel, began to bark as the little girl ran past her basket, through the parlor, and up the stairs where she headed for Sarah's bedroom.

"Pippa, you mustn't run up the stairs," her mother had scolded.

But Pippa already had.

Sarah bounded up the stairs after her with the child's mother close on her heels. They arrived just as the little girl announced, "This shall be my room," and grabbed hold of Budgie's cage, pulling it off the stand before exclaiming, "Oh, look, Mama, what a darling little bird! I believe I shall keep him and name him Admiral Nelson."

Sarah hadn't realized how ferocious she could be until she'd snatched the birdcage out of the child's hand and held it out of reach. "*I* believe he already has a name and an owner. His name is Budgie and he belongs to me."

"Does not," the child insisted, reaching for the birdcage. "Mama says the land and the rectory and everything in it is ours. Admiral Nelson is mine!"

"Your mother is in error," Sarah said firmly, meeting the mother's gaze over the child's head.

"Make her give me Admiral Nelson!" the child screeched at the top of her lungs. "He's mine! I want him!"

"Ouch!" Sarah looked down to find that Pippa had sunk her teeth into the flesh of her arm.

"Now, Pippa . . ." the child's mother soothed. "We mustn't bite."

Pippa paid her mother no heed. She was preparing another assault on Sarah's arm when Sarah stopped her with a look and a promise. "Bite me again and I shall bite you back." She grinned at Pippa. "And unlike you, I have all my teeth and they're much bigger and stronger than yours."

"You wouldn't dare!" Pippa retorted.

"Try me," Sarah challenged.

"Now, Pippa, be a good girl and I'll speak to the lady about the budgie. . . ."

"Admiral Nelson!" Pippa wailed.

"Very well. Admiral Nelson." Pippa's mother patted her daughter on the head before turning her attention to Sarah. "You must be Miss Eckersley."

"Yes," Sarah acknowledged over Pippa's screaming demands for Admiral Nelson. "I must be."

"I'm Reverend Tinsley's wife and this is our youngest daughter, Pippa." Mrs. Tinsley introduced herself and her daughter, then added, "Pippa is high-spirited. But I'm sure she'll quiet down if you'll allow her to hold Admiral Nelson."

Mrs. Tinsley was a rather thin woman of average height, with pale blonde hair, a longish face, and a poor complexion. Her only remarkable features were the dark blue color of her eyes and the long elegant fingers of the hand she extended toward the birdcage.

"No doubt, she would," Sarah answered. "But then Budgie and I will start screaming."

Mrs. Tinsley's blue eyes shot daggers at Sarah as Sarah refused to relinquish Budgie's cage. "Lord Dunbridge and Bishop Fulton warned us that you and Lord Dunbridge's aunt by marriage might still be in residence."

"Why shouldn't we be in residence?" Sarah met the other woman's furious gaze without flinching. "Since this is our home and neither Lord Dunbridge nor the bishop saw fit to warn us that you might be descending"—Sarah refrained from adding, *like a scourge of locusts*—"upon it."

"Oh, but my dear Miss Eckersley, the bishop awarded my husband, Reverend Tinsley, with the Helford Green living a fortnight ago. We would have been here sooner, but it's taken us that long to remove our things from our former vicarage in Bristol."

"Bristol?" Sarah was surprised. "How is it that a vicar in Bristol succeeds to a rectory in Bedfordshire?"

"There's a family connection, and of course, Bishop Fulton ordained the reverend."

"Of course," Sarah echoed.

"But that's neither here nor there, since we've finally succeeded to an acceptable living. The village is perfectly charming and I'm sure I'll have the rectory put to rights in no time at all." She smiled at Sarah. "We're moving in today."

"There's nothing in the rectory that needs putting to rights," Sarah told her. "And I'm afraid you cannot move into the rectory until we move out and we have not moved out."

Mrs. Tinsley glowered at Sarah. "The rectory and everything in it has been awarded to us. My husband is to be inducted to the living tomorrow. You, your aunt, and your personal possessions *will* be out this afternoon."

Sarah straightened to her full height and glowered back. "While it's true that the Helford Green rectory was once a collation to be presented by the bishops, that's no longer the case. The Church sold the benefice to the Dunbridge family during my grandfather's time. Lord Dunbridge is the patron of it and the magistrate guaranteed that my aunt and I would have thirty days from the date of notification of the awarding of the living to vacate. We've received no such notification."

"The magistrate is the civil authority." Reverend Tinsley entered Sarah's already crowded bedchamber without consideration or permission and came to stand beside his wife and daughter. "The church and the rectory are houses of God and as such, they come under the province of divine law. Since civil authority on this matter binds neither the church, nor the bishop, nor me, we were not required to send notification. The magistrate erred in guaranteeing you thirty days' notice."

"Lord Dunbridge *is* bound by civil authority," Sarah retorted. "He owns the living, but he cannot award it until the magistrate clears the way for him to do so."

"He already has," the reverend replied. "By temporarily ceding his ownership of it back to the Church in order that the bishop might present the living to me."

"He can't."

"He did." The reverend gave Sarah a beatific smile that suggested the Lord and his army of angels was on his side. "This parish is much too important to allow it to continue without a rector. Lord Dunbridge and the bishop sought to hurry things along by relieving the magistrate of his duty in this matter. The rectory is my home now and your moving has already begun." He nodded toward the window.

Sarah glanced out it to find half a dozen workmen carrying cartons of her father's clothing and personal belongings out of the rectory and onto the lawn.

"I think it would be best if you and your aunt gather your possessions as quickly and as quietly as possible and depart for London before the afternoon slips away. I have a sermon to write and we've a great deal to accomplish today before we can see ourselves comfortably settled. You and Lady Dunbridge are impeding our progress. Besides, I'm sure you've no wish to be traveling the main road alone after dark."

Sarah frowned. "Depart for London? Why should we depart for London?"

"Your betrothed is in London for the season. . . ."

"My *betrothed?*"

"Yes, of course. Lord Dunbridge." Reverend Tinsley smiled once again. "When he said that you and his aunt would be joining him, I assumed London was where he meant."

Sarah was beginning to understand how Lord Dunbridge and the Reverend Tinsley had circumvented the magistrate's authority. The magistrate would do his best to protect the unmarried daughter and sister-in-law of the Reverend Eckersley, but he would never question a viscount's authority over his betrothed or his aunt by marriage. Reginald Blanchard, the current Lord Dunbridge, had lied to the magistrate and been rewarded with a means to an end. He wanted Sarah and his late uncle's widow out of the rectory and at his mercy. "Lord Dunbridge told you he and I were betrothed?"

"Yes." The clergyman frowned, seeming to experience

misgivings about evicting her and her aunt for the first time
since he'd arrived. "He assured me of it. He said you and
your aunt—his aunt by marriage—would be residing with
him during the London season and that you and he would
be wed at the end of it. If I have mistaken what he told me,
I shall be happy to offer you a position here."

"You want to offer us positions here?" Sarah wasn't
sure she'd heard him correctly.

"I wish to offer *you* a position," he said.

"What about my aunt?" Sarah asked.

"We've no need of your aunt," he replied. "Besides, she
can claim a home with Lord Dunbridge. The position I'm
offering is for you alone, Miss Eckersley."

Sarah frowned. "What sort of position?"

"Mrs. Tinsley and I require a qualified governess for our
children."

"You're asking me to be governess to your children?"

He nodded and smiled. "Yes, of course, at twelve
pounds annual, plus room and board. You would have to
vacate this room, of course." He glanced around the bedchamber. "And claim the little room in the attic, but you
would join our household as governess to Polly, Pippa, and
Paul." He patted Pippa on the head in much the same way
as Sarah had watched Mrs. Tinsley do earlier.

Pippa beamed up at her father.

"I can tell Pippa adores you already."

"Pippa *abhors* me already," Sarah said. "And the feeling
is mutual."

The reverend gasped. "How dare you?"

"How dare you?" Sarah shot back. "How dare you displace me—the daughter of a fellow clergyman—from my
home without so much as a word of condolence or the
courtesy of a note informing me that you were about to do
so? How dare you cart my father's possessions from his
room to the front gate without a single expression of re-
morse or apology? And how dare you suggest that I remove
myself to London to live with a man with whom I am

barely acquainted, then offer me a position as governess to your horridly ill-mannered children in the same breath?"

"Get out." Reverend Tinsley was so angry his entire body vibrated with the effort to keep his temper in check. "Get out of my house."

"*Your* house, Mr. Tinsley?" Sarah queried. "Don't you mean *God's* house?"

"Get out." The good reverend came within a hairsbreadth of shaking her, but managed to retain control of his senses. "Now." His face was crimson and his body stiff with suppressed rage. "Gather your personal items and leave before I instruct the laborers to escort you and your baggage out." Opening the door to her wardrobe, Reverend Tinsley removed an armload of Sarah's dresses, then opened the window and tossed them out. He stared down at the heap of pastel muslins with an expression of deep satisfaction on his face. "There now," he told Sarah. "That should help speed the packing process and get you on your way."

Mrs. Tinsley stood gape-mouthed as her husband gathered another armload of Sarah's clothing and threw it out the window and Pippa began wailing for Admiral Nelson once again.

"Sarah?" Lady Dunbridge stood in the doorway with Precious in her arms. "Reverend Tinsley? What on earth is going on in here?" Precious growled a low, throaty warning and Lady Dunbridge held her higher, out of reach of the Tinsleys' little boy, who had grabbed a fistful of Lady Dunbridge's skirts. "Why are you throwing Sarah's garments out the window? Why has this ill-mannered child laid claim to my spaniel and why does that one keep screaming for Admiral Nelson?"

"The reverend is demonstrating from whom his daughter and his son get their charming manners," Sarah offered, snagging Budgie's cage stand before Pippa could knock it to the floor.

"What?" Lady Dunbridge cried in outrage.

"Take him!" Sarah thrust Budgie's cage and stand into her aunt's arms. "Save him from a fate worse than death. Take him before *she*"—she nodded toward Pippa—"claims him and names him Admiral Nelson. I'll save whatever else I can manage."

Struggling to hold a squirming, growling King Charles spaniel and a parakeet in a cage, Lady Dunbridge took one look at the reverend's crimson face and thrust Budgie's cage and stand back at Sarah. "You take him and go. *I'll* save whatever else I can manage."

"But . . ."

"Go, Sarah, before your clothes and everything else you own are scattered all across Helford Green."

Sarah had left the rectory and gone straight to the magistrate.

Nimrod Perkins, the magistrate, a tall, rotund man with dark brown eyes, a head full of thick black hair, and a perpetual smile, met Sarah at his front door.

"The new rector and his family has arrived," Sarah announced without preamble.

"I heard," the magistrate told her. "I was on my way there."

"To do what?" Sarah asked. "Watch as he removes me from my home? You guaranteed we would have thirty days' notice *after* the living was awarded."

"I know I did, Miss Eckersley, but when Lord Dunbridge temporarily ceded the living back to the Church, the matter was taken out of my hands."

"That is no excuse," Sarah protested. "*You* were charged with the responsibility of looking out for me and for Lady Dunbridge. We trusted you."

"There was nothing I could do," he said. "Bishop Fulton and Lord Dunbridge assured me that you and Lady Dunbridge would be removing to London. They assured me that you and Lady Dunbridge would not be evicted, but would have ample time to move out of the rectory."

"They lied."

The magistrate gasped. "Miss Eckersley, one should not

accuse a viscount and a bishop of lying. Especially when one is speaking to a magistrate."

"We are being evicted," Sarah said.

"What?"

"Go to the rectory and see for yourself," she advised. "Reverend Tinsley is tossing my clothing and all our personal belongings out the window onto the lawn even as we speak." She stared at the magistrate who had failed to protect her, then held up Budgie's cage. "I barely managed to save my budgerigar from a similar fate."

"Does Lord Dunbridge know about this?" Squire Perkins asked. "Surely he wouldn't allow his betrothed and his aunt by marriage to be evicted from the rectory he owns?"

"Of course he knows about it," Sarah replied. "He arranged to temporarily cede the living to the Church so his hands would be clean. So he can bemoan the fact that there was nothing he could do to prevent our eviction. So he could force us into accepting his hospitality."

"But he's your betrothed," the magistrate insisted.

"He's *not* my betrothed." Sarah's voice vibrated with anger and frustration. "He never formally asked my father for my hand, he simply mentioned the possibility. Papa refused to consider it. And so did I. Believe me when I tell you that I am not going to marry Lord Dunbridge."

After Sarah's father died, Viscount Dunbridge had tried again. This time, he had spoken directly to Sarah, informing her that he intended to have her as his wife at the end of the season. Sarah had flatly rejected his offer, refusing to consider the possibility, but apparently Reggie hadn't been persuaded that she meant it.

"You have to marry someone," Squire Perkins told her. "It might as well be a young, wealthy viscount with connections to your family. Come, Miss Eckersley, surely you see the advantages to that? It's a perfect match."

"There's nothing perfect about it," Sarah pronounced. "And I won't consider it."

"You are an unmarried female with no male relation to look out for you except Lord Dunbridge."

"He is related to my maternal aunt through her marriage to his uncle," Sarah clarified. "He's no relation to me."

"All the better," the magistrate said. "And as I've been charged with the duty of finding a husband or guardian for you . . ."

"You've already shown yourself to be negligent in your duty." Sarah all but stomped her foot in objection. "I'll find my own husband or guardian."

Squire Perkins took exception to her tone. "And you've already shown yourself to be incapable of finding a husband."

"Not incapable," Sarah corrected. "Just unwilling."

"Incapable or unwilling, you've had two unsuccessful seasons, Miss Eckersley. Do you wish to be permanently on the shelf?"

"I do if the only alternative is marriage to Reggie Blanchard."

"You don't mean that."

"I do mean it," Sarah retorted. "Lord Dunbridge is evicting me from my home! He lied to you and a bishop in order to accomplish it. And you expect me to want to marry him? To think he's a perfect match?"

"If he's evicting you from your home, he ought to provide you with another one," the magistrate stubbornly insisted. "And indeed, he promised to do just that. The viscount wants to marry you. That's something to think about, Miss Eckersley. You may not have many more opportunities to catch a suitable husband."

"That's all the more reason you should allow me one more chance before you decide I should become the next Viscountess Dunbridge," Sarah told him. "You owe me that much consideration for failing to protect me otherwise."

Squire Perkins puffed up like an adder in surprise at having Miss Eckersley speak so forthrightly and at having her accuse him of not performing his duty. But he acknowledged the truth in her words. He had been her father's friend and as the local magistrate, he had been charged with the duty of looking out for Miss Eckersley and Lady Dunbridge's interests. He *had* assured them that they would be given ample opportunity to relocate, but he had allowed Viscount Dunbridge and Bishop Fulton to persuade him otherwise without consulting either of the ladies. However much he hated to admit it, Squire Perkins did owe Miss Eckersley some concessions for having failed her. "All right," he declared at last, "I'll grant you thirty days in which to find a husband or a guardian for yourself or I will find one for you."

"Thirty days *in London during the season*," Sarah amended.

"The *first* thirty days of the London season," he concluded.

Sarah offered him her hand. "Agreed."

Squire Perkins accepted her hand and shook it in a firm businesslike manner. "Agreed."

"Thank you, Squire Perkins." Sarah gave the magistrate a beautiful smile. "Now, if you would be so kind as to put our agreement in writing . . ."

He had grumbled about it, but the magistrate had put their verbal agreement in writing, had it signed, witnessed, and sealed, and had handed it over to Sarah. Squire Perkins had also summoned Mr. Birdwell, the village coachman, and hired him to take them back to the rectory.

Together Sarah, Aunt Etta, Squire Perkins, and Mr. Birdwell had loaded Mr. Birdwell's coach with traveling trunks full of clothing and Sarah's mother's china, books and papers that had belonged to her father, a cloth doll, a diary, and small keepsakes of happier days that had been deposited in heaps by the front gate.

When they had fitted Budgie and everything else they could fit into Mr. Birdwell's coach, Sarah hired the coach and workmen who had brought the Tinsley family from Bristol to load the remainder of her and Lady Dunbridge's personal possessions and small furniture onto the coach and deliver it to Ibbetson's Hotel in London.

"Come, Sarah." Lady Dunbridge opened the front gate. She smiled as the brass door key jangled against the painted wrought iron, then took her niece by the arm and led her through the gate and down the walkway. "Mr. Birdwell is waiting. It's time to go."

Sarah hesitated. She had been so bold at the magistrate's house, so full of righteous indignation, and so sure of herself, but suddenly, all she felt was lost. She looked back over her shoulder at the closed front door of the rectory, smelled the fragrance of the early blooming roses growing beside it and the scent of the mint in the garden wafting on the breeze, and was filled with trepidation. "I was born here," Sarah whispered, her voice quivering with emotion. "It's the only home I've ever known. I can't leave." She turned to her aunt with tears in her eyes. "All my memories are here."

"No, my dear," Lady Dunbridge said. "Your memories are in your heart and in your head." She led Sarah to the coach. "The rectory is just the place where they were made. And it will always be here."

"But it won't be the same."

"No, it won't," Lady Dunbridge agreed. "But, my dear, nothing ever stays the same. Things must change in order to grow and survive. *We* must change in order to grow and survive."

"What shall we do in London?" Sarah asked as she climbed into the coach and settled onto the seat.

"We start over," Lady Dunbridge replied matter-of-factly, settling herself and Precious onto the seat. "We begin again and build another life for ourselves."

"How?"

"By doing what we should have done years ago," Lady Dunbridge answered. "By finding you a husband and a home of your own."

"Then you'd better pray for a miracle," Sarah told her. "Because I've only got thirty days to convince the man of my dreams that I'm the woman of his."

## Chapter 2

❧

*Be bold, be bold, and everywhere Be bold.*
—*Edmund Spenser, 1553–1599*

"*Be bold.*" *Sarah took a deep breath and released it* slowly, attempting to calm her racing heart. "Be bold and everywhere be bold."

On the road to London, Sarah realized that they needed more than a miracle. They needed a plan of action. It had taken Sarah most of the journey to devise one, and another few hours following their arrival to convince Mr. Birdwell to stay on in London as their personal driver, and several days of reading the society pages and gossip columns to obtain the information she needed in order to proceed.

But her plan was decidedly unconventional and since it was best that Aunt Etta not know the details, Sarah had spent much of the night lying awake, listening for the snoring that signaled her aunt's deep slumber, waiting to begin. And now, it was time to put her plan into action and pray that the object of her plan would willingly comply with her request.

Slipping silently out of the bed she shared with her aunt, Sarah shoved her feet into her slippers, pulled her heavy black traveling cloak on over her nightgown, tiptoed across the room, and carefully made her way down the main corridor to the back of the hotel, where she negotiated the stairs at the rear of the hotel as quickly as she could. A few yards beyond the back entrance, Mr. Birdwell waited to take her on the boldest and possibly the most foolish adventure she had ever undertaken.

Mr. Birdwell had argued against Sarah's traveling through the streets of town alone and had threatened to go to Aunt Etta with his concerns, but Sarah had stopped him with a threat of her own. If Mr. Birdwell wouldn't agree to drive her to her late-night appointment, Sarah promised to hire a public conveyance to do so. She didn't like forcing Mr. Birdwell's hand, but she had no choice. It was one thing to allow a young lady to traverse London alone at night in a coach driven by a longtime friend of the family and something else entirely to allow her to hire a public hack. Mr. Birdwell could guarantee that no harm would befall her in his carriage, but the same couldn't be said about a hack hired off the street. Sarah knew Mr. Birdwell would never allow her to take that sort of risk. Whether he agreed with her or not, the village coachman would drive her wherever she needed to go and never say a word to worry Aunt Etta.

Clutching the lapels of her cloak tightly in one hand, Sarah flipped the hood over her hair with her other hand, opened the back door, and groaned in dismay. "Oh, no."

The gentle spring rain that had persisted throughout the day and into the night had become a torrent. Her velvet cloak offered little protection against the pouring rain and her slippers afforded none at all against the puddles forming on the cobblestones as Sarah darted from the rear of the hotel, across the wet cobblestones to the mews and the shelter of Mr. Birdwell's coach.

"I could have waited at the back door," Mr. Birdwell told her as he held out his hand to assist her into the coach.

Sarah shook her head. "Our habits are well known here, Mr. Birdwell. I didn't want to risk having anyone inquire as to why you were waiting with the coach when Aunt Etta had retired for the night."

The coachman eyed her velvet traveling cape. "But now you're soaked to the skin."

"Not quite," Sarah told him, fighting to control the chattering of her teeth as she settled onto the cushions. "Just damp around the edges."

But Mr. Birdwell knew better. He handed her a thick wool lap robe, then reached for the brass pan in the floor of the coach. "Wrap this around you while I freshen the coals in the warming pan."

Sarah unfolded the wool blanket and settled it over her wet cloak. "I don't need the warming pan, Mr. Birdwell," she said. "I'm in a bit of a hurry and the blanket is quite sufficient."

Mr. Birdwell left the warming pan where it was, tucked the ends of the blanket around Sarah's feet, then closed the door. "Are you sure you still want to do this, miss?"

"I'm not sure of anything," Sarah admitted, "except that I have to do this."

"All right then, miss." Mr. Birdwell acknowledged her decision with a tip of his hat. He had known Sarah all her life. He didn't need to understand the nature of her venture to understand her determination to see it through to the end. "Rap on the ceiling if you change your mind," he instructed. "And I'll turn this coach around and we'll come back and join Lady Dunbridge in a good night's sleep."

"Thank you," she whispered.

Mr. Birdwell frowned. "Don't be thanking me, miss, for doing something that goes against my grain. As a matter of fact, I don't look forward to driving you around the city this time of night. And the only reason I'm doing it is because I know that look of determination on your face and because I know that you must have a very good reason for doing what you're doing." He leaned into the coach and looked Sarah in the eye. "What *are* you doing, miss?"

Sarah returned his gaze steadily. "I'm waiting for you."

The coachman heaved a sigh as he climbed up to his seat, released the brake, and lifted the ribbons. "Where to, miss?"

"Mayfair."

Mr. Birdwell wasn't sure he'd heard her correctly. "Mayfair, miss?"

"Yes, Mr. Birdwell," Sarah confirmed. "Mayfair. Drop me off on Park Lane."

"Where on Park Lane?"

"The beginning," she replied. "I'll walk from there."

"In this weather?" The coachman was stunned. "I'll do no such thing."

"Yes, you will, Mr. Birdwell." Sarah's firm tone of voice brooked no argument. "Because I'd rather you not draw attention to my presence by pulling up to the house."

"Where shall I wait?"

"You're not to wait," she said. "You're to return here immediately."

"I can't do that, miss."

"Yes, you can, Mr. Birdwell."

"How will you get back?"

Sarah gave the coachman what she hoped was a reassuring smile. "By coach. Through the park. And I suggest you use the same route, Mr. Birdwell. It's quicker."

*Jarrod, fifth Marquess of Shepherdston, looked up* from the stack of deciphered messages he was reading as his butler, Henderson, entered the study of his Park Lane town house. "I beg pardon for disturbing you, sir."

"What are you doing up?" Jarrod asked. "I may be cursed with the inability to sleep, but the staff needn't suffer with me. I thought everyone retired for the night hours ago."

"We did, sir, but I got up to answer the door. You have a visitor."

Jarrod glanced at the clock on the mantel and lifted an

eyebrow in query. He had been so engrossed in his work that he hadn't heard the front bell. "At this hour?"

Henderson nodded.

It was nearly four o'clock in the morning and although the hour was still early by the ton's standards, it was much too late to be paying a social call . . . unless one of the Free Fellows needed him. "Lord Grantham or either one of His Graces?"

"Neither, milord," Henderson replied.

"Then who?"

"I'm afraid I cannot tell you, sir," Henderson answered.

"Why not?" Jarrod demanded.

Henderson met his employer's disapproving gaze without flinching. "The young female wouldn't give her name."

"What young female?"

"The one dripping water upon the drawing room rug, sir," Henderson replied. "I would have refused her entrance," he explained, "but the forward creature insisted you were expecting her. Are we expecting a visitor this evening, sir?"

Jarrod frowned. "No, we are not."

"Shall I send her packing, sir?"

Jarrod glanced at the rivulets of rain on the window. "In this weather?" He sighed, then raked his fingers through his hair and stretched his aching shoulders before collecting his ciphers from the surface of the desk and locking them in the top drawer. "No, let's find out who she is and what she wants. Send her in."

Henderson raised an eyebrow but he didn't voice his opinion on the unusual turn of events. Unattended females did not pay calls on gentlemen and most certainly did not turn up on unsuspecting gentlemen's doorsteps.

Jarrod walked over to the drinks table, poured himself a glass of whisky, then moved to the fireplace and stoked the embers. If she was dripping water on the carpet, she'd be cold.

Henderson opened the study door and announced the visitor. "The female, milord."

Jarrod pursed his lips, then turned to face his visitor. The figure in the hooded black cape was tall and slim and, from the looks of it, soaked to the skin. "Good evening. Won't you come in and warm yourself by the fire?"

She walked over to the fireplace. Steam rose from the fabric of her cape as she neared it. "Thank you, milord."

Her voice was soft, deeply provocative, and hauntingly familiar. Jarrod took a sip of his drink, trying to recall where he'd heard it before, then suddenly remembered his manners. "Would you like something to eat? Drink?"

She gave him a mysterious smile. "It's kind of you to offer, milord, but I'm not a woman of the street—yet."

"Pardon me," he said. "But you have me at a disadvantage."

"I hope so," she breathed, flipping back her hood to reveal her face and her hair. "But I'm afraid it's rather unlikely. I don't think you've ever been at a disadvantage, Jays."

# Chapter 3

*When a woman wants a man and lusts after him, the lover need not bother to conjure up opportunities, for she will find more in an hour than we men could think of in a century.*

—*Pierre de Bourdeille, Abbé de Brantôme, c. 1530–1614*

"*Sarah.*" Only one person had ever had the temerity to call him Jays. He breathed her name as his heart began to beat in staccato rhythm. He hadn't seen her since Lady Harralson's ball last season. And he'd been trying to put her out of his mind ever since. Theirs had been a brief encounter—an exchange of conversation and one dance—yet Jarrod still vividly recalled each detail. Jarrod had accompanied Colin to Lady Harralson's. He had been standing near the refreshment table watching Gillian Davies—the same Gillian who was now Colin's bride—when someone spoke.

"Why didn't you ask her to dance?"

Jarrod had turned at the sound of the softly spoken question and discovered a pretty, brown-eyed redhead looking up at him. "Whom?"

"Gillian," she answered. "Gillian Davies, the woman dancing with Lord Grantham. The woman at whom you've been staring for the better part of a quarter hour."

"Davies?" Jarrod had asked, frowning in concentration. "Any relation to—"

The young woman nodded. "Baron Carter Davies is her father. And despite the fact that her father is richer than

Croesus, Gillian is quite nice. Unfortunately, she seems to be in disgrace."

Jarrod lifted his eyebrow. "Oh?"

"Yes," she answered, lowering her voice to make certain no one could overhear. "The story is that she's been visiting relatives in the country for the past month. But there's a nasty rumor circulating around town that she wasn't in the country at all, but that she eloped to Scotland with a bounder who left her there."

"Do you believe the story or the rumor?" he asked, staring at Gillian Davies once again.

She hesitated, chewing her bottom lip for a moment. "I find it difficult to believe that Gillian would ever do anything to disgrace her family. But then again, no one goes to visit relatives in the country at the beginning of the season." She looked up at him. "I'm sure it's just a rumor. I'm sure Gillian's reputation is beyond reproach." Her voice quavered. "She'll make you a wonderful marchioness."

Jarrod whipped around, focusing his full attention on the young woman standing at his side. "What makes you think I'm interested in making Miss Davies my marchioness?"

"Because you're the Marquess of Shepherdston and because you've been staring at her most of the evening."

"I only noticed her because she wasn't dancing," Jarrod answered honestly.

"And you were trying to summon the courage to ask her to dance with you. . . ."

"Not at all," he argued.

She arched one pale reddish blonde brow in disbelief. "Then you're staring at Gillian because she's beautiful."

Jarrod frowned. He wasn't accustomed to being contradicted and his brown eyes flashed fire as he turned his gaze on her. "Not true."

"Gillian *isn't* beautiful?" she asked hopefully.

Jarrod shook his head. "She's quite beautiful, but so are a great many other ladies here tonight. I noticed Miss Davies because I found it strange that she wasn't dancing."

"Lucky Gillian," the young woman muttered. "Because *I* haven't been dancing, Jarrod, and you didn't pay me the slightest bit of attention until I spoke to you."

She'd broken the rules of etiquette by speaking to him and by daring to call him by his given name. But Sarah had always been good at breaking rules and that daring finally captured his full attention.

"Are we acquainted?" he remembered asking.

She presented him with a mysterious smile. "I'm well acquainted with you, my lord. But apparently, you are unable to say the same." She looked him up and down, and then gave him a dismissive glance. "I apologize for interrupting your search for a marchioness, *Jays.* And when you dance with her, please, give my best to Gillian."

Jarrod frowned as she turned to walk away. Only one person in the world had ever had the temerity to call him Jays. And she had been a scrawny, knock-kneed, flame-haired, precocious five-year-old girl named Sarah Eckersley. "Sarah? Is it you?"

She turned on her heels and beamed at him. "All grown up and in the flesh."

Jarrod had eyed the creamy expanse of flesh displayed above the fashionably squared neck of her evening gown and agreed. She had certainly grown up and, from the looks of it, quite beautifully. The shockingly bright orange-colored hair she'd despaired of as a child had darkened over the years, mellowing into the soft, rich color of burnished copper, and the freckles that dotted her pale skin had all but disappeared, leaving a scant few paler freckles to decorate the bridge of her nose. Only her eyes were the same. He should have recognized them if nothing else, for Sarah Eckersley's big, almond-shaped eyes had always been more gold than brown and had always seemed much too large for her face. Years ago, she had been a funny little kitten with full-grown cat eyes. But now, it seemed, the kitten had filled out and grown into a breathtakingly lovely queen. "How long has it been?"

"Long enough for you to forget about me and look for someone else."

His breath caught in his throat. "Sarah, I'm not—"

"Looking?" Her eyes sparkled with mischief. "I beg to differ, Jays."

It took a moment for Jarrod to recover his speech. "It's not what you suppose. I'm not interested in dancing with Gillian Davies or in making her my marchioness."

"Why not?" she demanded.

"I don't happen to be in the market for a wife," he answered.

"Then, what are you doing here?"

He shrugged. "Would you believe I came to dance?"

She didn't believe it for a moment. "You don't appear to be dancing."

Jarrod grinned at her. "Only because you haven't asked me to."

They had danced one dance and Jarrod still recalled the sight of her in the gold ball gown with the square neckline that bared her neck and shoulders and had showed her figure off to perfection, still smelled the scent of her perfume in her skin and in her hair, could still feel his hand at her waist and the brush of her body against his.

During the past year, Sarah's image had popped into his brain at the most inopportune times, but Jarrod never dreamed the real Sarah would appear in his study in the middle of the night. Like this.

"What the devil are you doing here? Alone? At this time of morning?" Jarrod couldn't stop staring at her. Her plump lips were tinged with blue from the cold and her long red hair was wet and plastered to her head, but she was as lovely as he remembered.

"You're a hard man to catch, Jays." Sarah Eckersley stared up at him, fascinated by the wedge of dark curly hair peeking out from beneath the open front of his shirt and the velvet dressing gown he wore over it. "I read about the Duchess of Sussex's ball in the papers and I came at a time I hoped I might find you at home. Alone." She left the fireplace and moved closer to him. "You are alone, aren't you, Jays?" Sarah reached up, removed the glass of whisky from his hand, and took a sip from the same place his lips had touched.

Her provocative gesture took him by surprise. When had she learned to do that? Who had taught her to appreciate fine whisky? Jarrod narrowed his gaze at her and sucked in a breath as a certain part of his anatomy came to life, pressing against the buttons of his breeches in a powerful bid to be free of the constraints of the fabric. Reaching down, he automatically tightened the belt of his robe in an effort to conceal the evidence of his arousal. "Except for the twenty or so employees in this household and you, I am quite alone."

Sarah took another sip of his whisky, then handed it back to him. "Somehow, I don't think their presence makes much difference," she said. "I think you're always quite alone."

"Oh?" Jarrod arched an elegant eyebrow. "Have you come all the way from Helford Green to discuss my solitary state of affairs?"

"No." She shook her head. "I've come all the way from Helford Green for lessons."

"Lessons?" He was puzzled. "In what?"

"Seduction."

Jarrod choked on a mouthful of whisky and set the glass aside. "From whom?"

"You, of course."

Jarrod coughed again. "Sarah, be serious," he began, as soon as he'd recovered well enough to speak.

"I'm very serious," she told him. "I need to learn the art of seduction and I came to the most seductive man I know for lessons."

"Lessons for what purpose?" Jarrod didn't know whether to be insulted or flattered. Flattered that Sarah found him seductive or insulted because she thought he would agree to give her lessons on the subject.

"I'm not a beauty. . . ."

Jarrod frowned. When had she gotten the notion that she wasn't a beauty?

"I don't possess a fortune or a great family name or even a dowry to offer a man," she said. "All I have is my body." Sarah reached up and unfastened her cape, then let it fall to the floor. "I need to learn how to use it."

Jarrod caught his breath. Sarah Eckersley, the rector's daughter from Helford Green, had come to him wearing nothing more than a white lawn nightgown beneath her cape. And he had never seen anything more lovely. He leaned closer, until his lips were only inches away from hers. "Forgive me if I'm reading this the wrong way, but are you here because you're in the market for a husband?"

Sarah tossed her hair over her shoulder, then reached up and put her arms around his neck. "I'm here for lessons, Jays." She focused her gaze on his lips. "You can start by teaching me to kiss."

"I'll kiss you," he said, leaning close enough to detect the hint of whisky on her breath as he inhaled the air she exhaled. Jarrod closed his eyes. He'd kiss her. Quite thoroughly. Not because she had audaciously demanded that he do so, but because he suddenly felt an overwhelming desire to press himself against her, to taste the whisky on her lips, and to satisfy his curiosity. Because he'd wanted to kiss her the last time he'd seen her and hadn't done so. And because he wasn't noble enough to pass up a second opportunity and resist temptation when it arrived in so intriguing a fashion. "But I'm not going to marry you."

"I don't recall asking you to," Sarah replied. "At least, not since I turned ten or so . . ."

Jarrod stared at her, openmouthed.

Sarah placed her index finger beneath his chin and pushed upward. "Don't look so stunned, Jays," she said softly. "It's all right. I'm not a little girl anymore. I don't expect you to marry me."

"Why not?" he asked, slightly affronted. Over the years, he'd grown quite accustomed to Sarah professing her intention to marry him.

"Because," she breathed against his lips, "I finally realized that you're a very attractive man and I have no doubt that you'll be an excellent lover, but you're hardly what one would want in a husband."

"I beg your pardon?" Jarrod opened his eyes and stepped back, all thoughts of kissing her temporarily forgotten as he stared down at Sarah's upturned face.

She smiled. "There's no need to beg my pardon, Jays. I invited you to kiss me."

"You *ordered* me to kiss you," Jarrod corrected. "But that's neither here nor there at the moment." He frowned. "What makes you think that marriageable young women consider me unsuitable as a husband? Because I assure you most young ladies and their parents or guardians find me eminently suitable."

"I didn't assume *most* young women would consider you an unsuitable husband," Sarah corrected.

"I believe your exact words were—" Jarrod began.

"I know what my exact words were," she interrupted. "I wasn't speaking in general terms of what most young women want." She looked him squarely in the eye. "I was stating *my* view."

"Your view of my suitability as a husband?"

She nodded. "As opposed to your suitability as a lover, yes."

"An opinion you base, of course, on your vast experience," Jarrod reminded her.

Sarah wrinkled her nose at him. "I'm well aware that I'm lacking in experience, Jays. That's why I came to you."

"To learn how to kiss."

The husky timbre of his voice sent shivers down Sarah's spine. She slanted a look at him from beneath the cover of her eyelashes. "Among other things . . ."

She was an innocent, but the warmth in her voice and the look in her eyes were invitations as old as time. Jarrod's body tightened even further and he marveled at the strength of his trouser buttons. "You want me," he confirmed. "As your lover."

"As my *first* lover," she corrected, tracing a line through that fascinating wedge of hair on his chest with the tip of her index finger.

"Your first?" Jarrod caught hold of her hand, halting her exploration. "Have you others waiting in the wings?" He consulted a mental list of men Sarah might have chosen as prospective lovers and frowned once again. There were dozens of likely prospects. Men of all shapes and sizes and from all walks of life. Men who were older, younger, richer, poorer, more handsome, and less handsome than he was. Men whose only common trait would be their desire to take his place in Sarah Eckersley's bed and become her next lover.

"Not yet," Sarah answered. "But I'm a young woman, Jays. And your reputation precedes you."

Jarrod lifted his eyebrow in query. "How so?"

"You've a reputation for demanding absolute perfection in everything you do," Sarah explained. "I don't doubt that you'll prove to be a most excellent tutor, but I believe it would be most unrealistic to suppose that in the course of my lifetime, you will be my only lover. Or my only tutor. I am, after all, nearly nine years your junior."

Looking at her, Jarrod found it much more likely that he would be quite satisfied to become her first and only lover. He was disappointed to think that Sarah felt otherwise. "You're *eight* years my junior," he reminded her. "And you're assuming I'll be willing to accommodate your request."

"Aren't you?"

Jarrod relaxed his grip on her hand, then reached out and cradled her face in his hands. "If, as you say, my reputation precedes me, then you should know that I pride myself on being a gentleman. And no gentleman would agree to divest a young lady—any young lady—of her maidenhead. Especially a young lady he's known and"—he faltered, surprised to find the word *loved* on the tip of his tongue—"regarded fondly since she was a child. A young lady who happens to be the daughter of the rector who's always held that gentleman in high esteem." He leaned closer. "Good lord, Sarah, what were you thinking to come here at this time of night? Where are your aunt and your father? What were they thinking to let you?"·

Sarah paused, then looked at him sharply. "When I left her, Aunt Etta was sleeping soundly in our room at Ibbetson's Hotel."

Ibbetson's? A tiny prickling feeling of unease lifted the hair on the back of Jarrod's neck. He had assumed that Sarah, her father, and her aunt were renting a town house for the season. Ibbetson's wasn't as fine a hotel as the Clarendon or Grillon's or the Pulteney, but it catered to members of the clergy and to academics and was completely respectable. "And your father?"

"My father died, Jarrod," Sarah answered flatly. "Two months ago."

Jarrod was stunned by the news. He released her, then stepped back out of reach. "I'm sorry," he said, bowing his head in a gesture of respect for the reverend, staring at the toes of his boots for a moment before he met Sarah's gaze once again. "I wasn't aware—" He faltered. "I don't recall a notice. . . ."

"Why should you?" Sarah demanded, cutting him off. "You didn't bother to renew our acquaintance after our dance last season. Or pay Papa or me a call. Why should you notice his death?"

Her accusation stung. He had purposely refrained from paying Sarah Eckersley and her father a call after their dance last season because Jarrod hadn't wanted Sarah to think he meant to court her after one dance—no matter how much he enjoyed it. And Jarrod couldn't pay a call on the reverend without Sarah assuming he might be willing to offer her more than friendship. And Jarrod knew that was out of the question. He would never marry and he couldn't offer Sarah anything less.

"Rectors in villages much the size of Helford Green don't rate notice in the London papers," she continued, blinking back the hot rush of tears burning her eyes as she related the bitter facts. Her father had spent his adult life serving his fellow men, teaching God's word, and bringing goodness and hope and light into the lives of everyone around him. His death had gone all but unnoticed except to his parishioners, while a ne'er-do-well member of the ton could overturn a phaeton and be memorialized in every rag in London. "Especially when compared to an *outstanding* young peer like Lord Brinson."

Jarrod had been away from London on a mission two months ago and although he'd caught up on the news and the gossip when he returned, Jarrod had to search his memory for a connection. "Lord Brinson? Lord *Peter* Brinson? The young fool who bet that he could make three circles around the park in under five minutes? That Lord Brinson?"

Sarah nodded.

"Peter Brinson hasn't had a sober moment since he reached his majority," Jarrod told her. "What has he to do with your father?"

"He died the same day Papa died," Sarah answered in a tone of voice flavored with bitterness.

"I see." Although Sarah's father wouldn't have minded the quiet anonymity of his death, it was galling to realize that an irresponsible young peer who had never done a day's work—either good or bad—and who had died while racing his phaeton around Hyde Park in response to a dare had had his passing recognized and his brief life gloriously recounted for the entire population of London while the Reverend Eckersley's life and work had gone largely unnoticed.

"Everyone who was anyone in the ton attended Lord Brinson's funeral," Sarah replied, pinning Jarrod with an accusing look.

"I wasn't one of them." Jarrod met her gaze without flinching. "I was in Scotland when your father died. Had I known of his passing, I would have gone to Helford Green to pay my last respects."

"Would you?" she challenged.

"Of course I would have," he snapped. "And you know it. I was very fond of your father and, what's more, I respected him. He was a good man and there are far too few truly good men." Jarrod looked at Sarah. "And I don't intend to dishonor his memory by compromising his daughter. You're in mourning, Sarah. You shouldn't be in London or at Ibbetson's and you certainly shouldn't be here. It isn't proper."

It wasn't and Sarah knew it as well as he did, but Jarrod's censure stung and try as she might, Sarah couldn't hold her tongue. "You are in no position to lecture me on propriety, Jays. I'm a rector's daughter. I've always followed the rules. I've always done what was right and proper, while you've always done exactly as you pleased."

Jarrod bit his bottom lip to keep from smiling. "Your memory is faulty, Sarah. As I recall, you were a little hoyden who sneaked out of the rectory every chance you got. You couldn't have always done what was right and proper because you followed me everywhere I went whenever I was at Shepherdston Hall. You were everywhere I turned. I was amazed by your tenacity. And I distinctly remember taking to horseback whenever I wanted to escape you." He had been thirteen at the time and perpetually annoyed at having a girl of five shadowing his every move.

"You were only at Shepherdston Hall twice a year—at Easter and Christmas," she informed him. "That meant that the rest of the year, I was a proper young lady." Sarah fought the childish urge to stick her tongue out at him.

"Because you had a father and an aunt who loved you enough to set rules and to see that you followed them."

"Because there was no alternative," she corrected. "We lived a quiet country life in a quiet country village where the rector's daughter had to be above reproach. I had never been to London until my first season."

"Which was what?" Jarrod asked. "Two or three seasons ago?"

"Five," she replied, ever so sweetly. "I made my curtsy along with Adelaide and Alyssa Carrollton."

"Adelaide and Alyssa Carrollton are well married," Jarrod said. "As are their sisters, Anne and Amelia." Adelaide had married Lord Hastings. Anne had married Lord Garrison. Amelia wed Lord Brookestone. And Alyssa, the youngest Carrollton sister, had married Griffin Abernathy, founding member of the Free Fellows League and one of Jarrod's closest friends.

"Yes, I know," Sarah said.

"As a veteran of five campaigns, I would have thought that you would have snagged a rich peer by now and have an heir and a spare to show for it."

"I would have thought the same of you," Sarah parried. "Except that I happen to know that . . ."

"I'm not in the market for a marchioness," he concluded.

"That you would rather take a lover than take a wife." She contradicted, meeting his steady brown-eyed gaze.

"I have my reasons, Sarah." Jarrod turned his back to her and walked to the fireplace.

"So do I," she replied, softly.

"And you're wrong, you know." Jarrod stared into the fire, mesmerized by the blue and orange flames licking at the coal. "I've never done exactly as I pleased," he said, at last. "It may have seemed that way to you, but that was only because I was born to parents who didn't care what I did or where I went so long as I stayed out of their way. I would have given anything to have what you had. Now, forget about this harebrained scheme." Jarrod turned away from the fire and began to pace the width of carpet in front of it. "Take your aunt and go home and mourn your father."

"Would that I could," Sarah retorted, "but I no longer have a home to—" She broke off abruptly, clamping her teeth down on her wayward tongue, appalled that she'd admitted so much.

Jarrod stopped his pacing and turned to face her. "What happened to the rectory?"

"Nothing," she said. "The rectory and the living belong to the rector."

"And?" he prompted when she finished speaking.

"Aunt Etta and I do not."

# Chapter 4

*Chance reveals virtues and vices as light reveals objects.*
—*La Rochefoucauld, 1613–1680*

"Someone else has been awarded the Helford Green rectory and the living attached to it." Usually exceedingly quick on the uptake, Jarrod could only blame his temporary stupidity on his surprise at having Sarah Eckersley pay him a late-night call in order to present him with such a tempting and troubling proposition. He should have discerned the situation immediately.

"Yes," Sarah confirmed. "And that someone would be the new rector."

"Surely a man of God can find it in his heart to allow a grieving daughter to remain in the only home she's ever known," Jarrod suggested.

"As a matter of fact, Reverend Tinsley did ask that I remain in residence at the rectory—"

"See?" Jarrod interrupted with a self-satisfied smile. "I knew it."

"As governess to his children."

"As governess?" Jarrod repeated the phrases as if he'd never heard the words before. "To his children?"

"Two girls and a boy. Polly, Pippa, and Paul. Ages seven, five, and three." She studied Jarrod's expression, then crossed her fingers and hid her hand in the folds of her nightgown. "I was asked to stay on for a small stipend of twelve pounds a year plus room and board. Of course, I will have to relinquish my bedchamber to the rector's daughters and move my personal things to the little room in the attic."

Jarrod knew the room Sarah described. He had been to the rectory. Before being sent to Knightsguild for his formal secular education, Jarrod had received his religious instruction from Sarah's father at the rectory. The little attic room had been built as living quarters for a maid or a manservant, but Reverend Eckersley had declared it much too small for that purpose and had used it instead as a workshop, where he spent long hours repairing prayer books, hymnals, and on occasion, altar cloths and vestments. Jarrod remembered helping the reverend carry the books from the sanctuary to the workshop and back again. "Not bloody likely."

"Pardon?" He'd mumbled something, but Sarah couldn't understand a word of it.

"What about your aunt?" Jarrod asked instead of repeating his words. "Will she be forced to give up her room as well?"

"Young Master Tinsley will have Aunt Etta's room," Sarah told him. "He cannot share with the girls and there are only three bedchambers in the rectory."

"Why can't young Master Tinsley take the attic room?" Jarrod demanded. "While you share with your aunt?" He didn't like the idea of Sarah becoming governess to anyone's children—especially children who would displace her from her bedchamber in the only home she had ever known. And he didn't like the idea of anyone removing Sarah's aunt from the bedchamber she had occupied since Sarah was a small child. It seemed an especially callous thing to do—especially for a man of the cloth.

Sarah pretended to laugh, but her laughter sounded hollow, even to her own ears. "Because it simply isn't done, Jays. A governess cannot take a room that should belong to a member of the family. You know that."

"I know that it makes more sense to have young Master

Tinsley take the smaller of the rooms since he is smaller and to allow you and your aunt to share the larger bedchamber."

Sarah bit her bottom lip. "It makes no difference, Jays, because Reverend Tinsley hasn't offered Aunt Etta a home at the rectory."

"Why not?" Jarrod arched his eyebrow in query.

"I don't know." Sarah lifted her chin a notch higher, looked Jarrod in the eye, and dared him to challenge her decision. "But staying at the rectory or going anywhere else without her is out of the question. I won't consider it."

Jarrod expelled the breath he hadn't realized he'd been holding and met Sarah's challenging gaze. "I wouldn't expect otherwise."

"I've lost Papa," she said softly. "And I would rather lose my home than lose Aunt Etta."

"I don't own the living," Jarrod announced abruptly. The position as rector of Helford Green came with a glebe of several hundred acres of flourishing orchards, fertile farm and grazing land, rent, and tithes that provided the clergyman with a handsome income. The owner of the living had the duty of inviting a man of the cloth to accept the living and the responsibility of ministering to the souls who lived and worked in Helford Green. Although the Marquess of Shepherdston was the largest landowner in the county, he didn't own the rector's living. It belonged to the present Viscount Dunbridge—the late Lord Dunbridge's nephew and Sarah's aunt Etta's nephew by marriage. Jarrod took a deep breath. "If you've come here tonight with this outrageous proposition because you believed that . . ."

Sarah sucked in a breath. "I came to you because I've received several proposals since Papa died. But the proposal that included marriage didn't include Aunt Etta and the proposals that did include her, didn't include matrimony."

"What sort of proposals have you received?" Jarrod asked. "And from whom?"

Sarah held up her fingers and counted the offers one by one. "I've received three other offers of the position of governess, in addition to Reverend Tinsley's offer, and two offers to act as companion—one from Lady Manwaring, one from Lord Deavers, and—"

Jarrod didn't allow her to finish. "Lady Manwaring is a harridan who would make your life miserable and Lord Deavers is a lecherous old scoundrel."

"Captain Howard asked me to accompany him on his return to his regiment in India and Lieutenant Slater offered to set me up in a nice little house on Curzon Street." Sarah bit her bottom lip. "Unfortunately, he wasn't amenable to the idea of Aunt Etta living with me."

"Unless he is in possession of a fortune, a lieutenant in His Majesty's army couldn't keep a cat in a little house on Curzon Street, much less a lady and her aunt," Jarrod pronounced. "Lieutenants are notoriously strapped for blunt. And India is no place for a lady, so accompanying Captain Howard is entirely out of the question."

"That is not for you to decide, Jays," Sarah informed him, hating the fact that his argument was sound and the fact that he didn't seem bothered at all by the idea that she might want to accompany Captain Howard to India or take Lieutenant Slater up on his offer of a house on Curzon Street. "You are not my guardian."

"Who *is* your guardian?" he asked. "And better still, *where* is your guardian?"

"I don't have one," she replied in a lofty tone. "At least, not yet."

"And why is that?"

"Because I convinced the magistrate that he wouldn't have to appoint a guardian for me if he granted me the season in which to find my own," she replied.

"Why would the magistrate have to *appoint* a guardian?" Jarrod frowned. "Didn't your father name one in his will?"

Sarah shook her head. "There was no reason for Papa to make a will. The Church provided his living. He didn't have anything of value."

"He had you," Jarrod said. "And he should have made sure your future was secure."

"He expected me to marry, Jays." Bristling at the note of criticism in Jarrod's tone of voice, Sarah glared at him. "And once I married, he expected that my husband would provide a secure future for me."

"Then why the devil haven't you found someone who would?"

"I've only been in town a sennight. What would you have me do, Jays? Run about London proposing to every man I meet?"

"Of course not!" he snapped. "But a sennight appears to have been long enough for you to see Captain Howard, Lieutenant Slater, and Lord Deavers."

"Captain Howard sent a note after Papa died. Lord Deavers did the same. And I ran into Lieutenant Slater while walking Precious in the park."

"What the devil is a Precious?"

"Aunt Etta's spaniel." She looked up at him. "And Lieutenant Slater is the only young man I've spoken to except you."

"And he propositioned you over a spaniel! You've endured five seasons. Surely you must know someone in the market for a bride."

"I've only 'endured' three seasons," Sarah corrected. "Including this one. Aunt Etta was in mourning for her sister-in-law one season and Papa suffered through a bout of pleurisy during another. We didn't come to town those years."

"What about the other two?" he asked. "Didn't you meet anyone then? Or are you that hard to please?"

*"Hard to please?"* Sarah's voice rose an octave. "I'm not hard to please."

"Then why haven't you married?"

*Because I've been waiting for you to ask me.* Sarah had to bite her tongue to keep from blurting out the truth and facing another disappointment. So she settled for a half-truth. "Because I've decided to become the mistress of my own fate." She hazarded a glance at Jarrod. "And I cannot begin a career as a . . ." She hesitated.

"Courtesan?" Jarrod supplied the term.

Sarah nodded and continued, ". . . without practical experience, and I had hoped that you would *find it in your heart*"—she chose the same phrase Jarrod had used earlier—"to help me acquire the knowledge I'll need."

Frustrated by her stubbornness, irritated at her late father for dying and leaving his only child to fend for herself, and more tempted than he liked to admit by the audacious beauty standing before him, Jarrod raked his fingers through his hair, then bent down and retrieved her cloak from the floor. "I cannot do what you're asking me to do, Sarah." He draped her velvet cloak over her shoulders. It was still wet, but Jarrod tied the cords in a neat bow beneath her chin anyway.

Jarrod's dismissal hurt. Sarah bit her bottom lip to keep it from quivering and counted the chimes of the clock on the mantel as she fought to maintain her composure. Her pride was in tatters and her hopeful dreams that Jarrod Shepherdston would welcome her into his arms were shattered, but she wasn't going to let him see her cry over them. "You *can*," she accused, "but you won't."

"I can't," he said.

"Is it me?" she asked, glancing down at the cloak Jarrod had used to cover her. "Is there something wrong with me? Something I should do? Or say? Or wear?" She looked up. "I know my nightdress is . . . isn't . . . I know it probably isn't the sort of garment your lovers usually wear, but I . . ."

"Sarah, there's nothing wrong with you or your nightdress." He swallowed hard in a valiant attempt to forget the sight of the damp white cotton nightgown clinging to her curves in all the right places. "You look very . . . very . . ." *Beautiful. Seductive.* "Appealing."

She smiled at him. "You find me appealing?"

"Very," Jarrod answered honestly.

"Then why won't you help me?"

"Sarah," he soothed, "try to understand. I'm a gentleman and I was brought up to believe that there are some boundaries a gentleman must never cross." He smiled at her. "Compromising the daughter of an old friend is one of those boundaries."

"And who taught you that principle of gentlemanly etiquette?" she retorted. "Your father?"

# Chapter 5

*In every enterprise consider where you would come out.*

*—Publilius Syrus, first century B.C.*

Jarrod froze as if she'd struck him and Sarah could have bitten out her tongue when she recognized the look of shock and surprise on his face.

"I'm sorry," she whispered, instantly regretting her taunt. She stared at the toes of her slippers, too ashamed to look him in the eyes. It was one thing to challenge Jarrod into a war of words. She had always done that, but it was quite another to cause pain. Sarah had crossed the line when she resorted to using sins of the father in order to hurt the son.

It hadn't become common knowledge because the staff at Shepherdston Hall was extremely loyal and protective of Jarrod, but there were those in Helford Green who knew that the fifth Marquess of Shepherdston had been orphaned and inherited the title under secret and tragic circumstances. It had happened in London and Sarah had never learned the details, but she had heard enough of the scandalous whispers to fling a dart at Jarrod and have it strike home.

"No need to be sorry," he said. "In a roundabout way, I suppose I did learn that lesson in gentlemanly etiquette from my father. But only because your father schooled me in a different set of principles." Reaching out, Jarrod lifted

Sarah's chin so he could see her face. "He taught you those same principles. Are you willing to compromise them, Sarah?"

Sarah lifted her chin out of his reach. "Yes, I am."

"Why?" Jarrod pinched the bridge of his nose. Sarah had been stubborn as a child and Jarrod could see that she hadn't changed in that regard. She was as stubborn as ever.

"To keep a roof over Aunt Etta's head. To keep food on the table and a fire in the hearth." *To keep from being forced into marriage with Lord Dunbridge.* Sarah reached into the pocket of her cloak for the calling card she'd been carrying since its arrival shortly after her father's funeral, searching for the familiar worn edges, but her pocket was empty. She glanced down at the floor, fighting her rising sense of dismay when she realized the card to which she had clung as a last resort—the calling card guaranteeing her an audience at Miss Jones's Home for Displaced Women—was gone.

Sarah bit her bottom lip. When it arrived, that calling card had seemed like the answer to her prayers. Especially since the other answer to her prayers had failed to materialize in the days and weeks and months following her father's funeral. Sarah had prayed she wouldn't need it. She had prayed Jarrod would ride to her rescue, but neither God nor Jarrod had heard her prayers and Sarah had held on to the card because it promised her a place to live if her outrageous plan failed and Jarrod disappointed her once again. She had lost the card, but she knew the name printed on it and the address on Portman Square. She couldn't present the card to gain an audience as the accompanying note had instructed, but the card had been addressed to her and sent by post to the rectory. Sarah consoled herself with the knowledge that while the card that had served as her personal talisman all the way from Helford Green to London was gone, whoever had sent the card would certainly recognize her name if she presented herself at the front door.

"If that's your reason, I'll buy you a house." Jarrod walked to his desk, pulled out a sheet of paper and a pen, and began to write. "I'll make you a gift of it and you and your aunt can live there for the rest of your lives."

"On what?" she asked.

Her question was food for thought that gave Jarrod pause. "On an allowance," he answered. "I'll provide you with a generous allowance with which to furnish the house and run the household. You can have servants, a carriage, the whole lot. . . ."

"Thank you, Jays," Sarah replied sweetly. "And will you buy me a house on Curzon Street?"

"Yes," he agreed. "On Curzon Street or any street you want."

Sarah sighed. "Just like Lieutenant Slater."

"Not at all like Lieutenant Slater." Jarrod bristled at the suggestion and at the trap she'd set for him. A trap he'd failed to recognize.

"How is it different?"

"Your aunt Henrietta can live there with you." He squeezed his eyes shut and searched for a graceful way out of the tangle he'd stepped into.

"Thank you, your lordship. That's most generous of you, but you know I can't accept a house from you." She pursed her lips at him and feigned a pout. "I'm surprised that you would be so bold as to suggest that I might. You are, after all, a bachelor and no relation to me or to Aunt Etta and . . ."

"Stop it, Sarah," he warned. "I'm in no mood to tolerate your baiting." His head ached from a night without sleep and his body ached with the need for sexual release.

"That's unfortunate, Jays, because I'm in no mood to have your charity thrust upon me."

"By Jupiter, Sarah, I'm not offering charity!" Jarrod placed his palm against the surface of his desk and caressed the wood grain in an effort to keep from pounding his fist against it.

"What would you call it?"

"A home," he snapped. "I would call what I'm offering you and your aunt a home."

"A home we couldn't possibly afford to purchase on our own."

"There wouldn't be any need to purchase it," Jarrod told her. "It would be a gift and, unlike Lieutenant Slater, I wouldn't expect convenient sexual congress in return for that gift."

Sarah blushed at his frankness. "Whether you did or you didn't wouldn't matter. My reputation would be ruined either way," Sarah pointed out. "And if that's the case, I'd prefer an equitable exchange of convenient sexual congress as payment for the roof over our heads."

"I can't believe you would rather prostitute yourself than accept a gift." Jarrod shook his head. "It makes no sense."

"Neither does the fact that accepting such a gift and linking my name to yours without benefit of clergy would mark me as a fallen woman whether I remained chaste or not," Sarah replied. "It's a matter of pride and a matter of choice. I'm a lady with no husband, father, uncle, or brother. I can't enter the dining room of my hotel without a chaperone or ride down St. James's Street in an open carriage, or pay a call on any unmarried man for any reason without damaging my reputation." She looked at Jarrod. "I'd rather sacrifice that reputation for a purpose than lose it for no reason at all."

"Be reasonable, Sarah. . . ."

"I am being reasonable."

They faced each other over the width of Jarrod's desk. Jarrod snorted.

"All right, then," Sarah invited, "tell me your definition of reasonable."

"Accepting the house I've offered."

"Done," Sarah announced, extending her hand for him to shake. "I'll accept your offer of a house, if you'll agree to become my protector and tutor me in the art of seduction."

Jarrod groaned. "You know I can't do that."

"Then we seem to have reached an impasse."

Jarrod thought for a moment, seeking a solution to an impossible problem. "I'll help you find a husband."

Sarah took a deep breath and played devil's advocate. "What makes you think I want one?"

"All young ladies want husbands," he answered. "No one chooses the life of a courtesan."

It was Sarah's turn to snort in disbelief. "Really? Think again. Or better yet, look around you, Jays. If you were a female would you choose to become a wife? Would you choose to become some strange man's chattel when you could remain unmarried and choose your own path? A mistress has a much better life than a wife."

*"Some"*—he emphasized the word—"mistresses have better lives than *some* wives. But you're fooling yourself if you assume that is always the case. Mistresses can be as maltreated and neglected as wives."

"Thank you very much for enlightening me about the standards of our society," she retorted.

"It's the least I can do," Jarrod answered in kind. "To prepare you for the path you seem determined to pursue."

Sarah gave him a sugary sweet smile. "It's the *very* least you can do. For I'm quite certain that you could prepare me for a great many things I'll need to know in order to succeed."

"Succeed?" The idea caught him off guard.

"Of course, succeed," she said. "What is the point of sacrificing myself otherwise? If I can't do well enough to support myself and provide a home where Aunt Etta can live out the remainder of her days in the manner in which she's most comfortable, why bother?" She looked at Jarrod. "If I were on my own, I could seek another type of employment, but I am not on my own. I have Aunt Etta to consider."

"Have you?" Jarrod challenged. "You just refused the offer of a house. I don't think you've given any thought to Aunt Etta's situation."

"Of course I have," Sarah argued. "I've thought of little else since Lord Dunbridge forced us to vacate the rectory."

Jarrod arched an eyebrow. "And the best you could come up with was a harebrained scheme of sneaking out of a hotel room in the middle of the night and traipsing about town in your nightgown in order to tempt me into helping you begin a career as a part of the Cyprian corps?"

Sarah stared at him. "Were you tempted, Jays?"

"Yes, Sarah, I was tempted," he admitted. "Am tempted. But I've been tempted before by women who were experts in the art."

"Did you succumb to their temptation?"

Jarrod smiled a teasing sort of smile. "What sort of gentleman would I be if I answered that?"

"An honest one?" she suggested.

"Perhaps," he mused. "But I could also be a lying braggart, and, in any case, I refuse to answer an impudent question simply to satisfy your virginal curiosity."

"Then kiss me."

"What?"

"Give in to temptation and satisfy my virginal curiosity at the same time. I won't tell," she whispered, moving closer. "No one need know."

"I'll know, Sarah," Jarrod told her. "And so will you." He looked down at her. "I'll know I crossed the boundary no gentleman should ever cross and you'll know you tempted me into it."

"I'll know you chose not to resist," Sarah contradicted.

"And I'll know you've chosen a life for which you're entirely ill-suited."

Sarah heaved an exasperated sigh.

"There is no getting around it. You were meant to be a wife, Sarah. No matter what you believe about the inequality of marriage, you were meant to be married. You were meant to have a husband and children."

That was true. And she wanted both one day. But she wanted Jarrod to be her husband and since that wasn't likely to happen, she'd make certain the man the magistrate had in mind as her guardian and husband wouldn't want her. Marriage was permanent. If she married someone else, she wouldn't be free to marry Jarrod or become his lover and, unlike a great many ladies of the ton, Sarah would not forsake her vows. If she took the vows of matrimony, she meant to keep them. She wouldn't commit adultery for Jarrod or for anyone else. "I'd rather remain unmarried than spend the rest of my life with a man I don't love."

"Yet you profess to wanting to share your body with a multitude of men you don't love," Jarrod mused.

"Who's to say I wouldn't love one or two of them?" she asked.

"Who's to say you would?" he shot back.

*I would,* Sarah thought. Especially if Jarrod was one of them. Because she had been madly in love with Jarrod Shepherdston since she was five and that wasn't likely to change. Unfortunately, neither was the fact that Jarrod had never made any bones about his distrust of marriage. Sarah was under no illusions. Jarrod simply wasn't in the market for a marchioness and as long as he remained opposed to marriage, so would she.

"And what of your aunt's feelings? What of her dreams and aspirations for you? Have you thought about those? Or about how your decision to join the ranks of the demimonde will affect her? How she will feel when members of the ton ostracize you? How she will feel when the ladies who stood in line beside you as you made your curtsies give you the cut direct when they cannot cross the street to avoid meeting you? And if your aunt lives with you, she'll be tarred with the same brush and her reputation will be as blackened as yours. How is she going to feel when lifelong friends and acquaintances no longer acknowledge her?"

"Her true friends *will* acknowledge her," Sarah said. "Those who don't aren't worth worrying about."

"That's your opinion," Jarrod interjected. "Your aunt may feel differently."

"She won't," Sarah affirmed.

"How do you know? Did you ask her?" He pinned Sarah with a look. "Did you discuss this with her or did you decide the best course of action on your own?"

"I saw no point in worrying her with the details."

"So you waited until she fell asleep, then crept out of the hotel."

"And came to you for help." Sarah looked him in the eye, then crossed the floor and reached for the doorknob. "My mistake."

Jarrod took a step toward her. "I'll speak to Lord Dunbridge about the living. Perhaps I can persuade him to change his mind about Reverend Tinsley."

"We don't need your intercession, Jays," Sarah told him. "There are other places Aunt Etta and I can go. We'll be fine."

"Blast it, Sarah! You came to me for help—"

Sarah turned in the doorway at the sound of her name. "And you refused. Remember?"

"I refused to seduce you," he corrected. "I didn't refuse other forms of help. Now, tell me how long before the magistrate makes his decision?"

Sarah bit her bottom lip.

"How long?" he repeated, a bit more forcefully.

"Three weeks."

"Well," Jarrod pronounced, "I'm sure we can come to some arrangement. Dunbridge is a businessman. If I can't persuade him to change his mind about the reverend in three weeks' time, I'm sure I can convince him of the benefits of providing you and your aunt with a place to live."

"Thank you, Lord Shepherdston." She bowed her head and executed a formal curtsy that set Jarrod's teeth on edge. "I'll see myself out."

Jarrod was tempted to let her. But he was a gentleman and his manners and his protective instincts prevailed. He glanced at the clock. It was nearly half past five. The household would be stirring soon and his day would begin with a morning ride and breakfast with his godfather, Lord Mayhew, followed by a meeting of the Free Fellows League in their usual room at White's. "Wait!"

"Yes?" Sarah tried, but failed to conceal the hopeful note in her voice.

Jarrod rubbed his hand over the stubble on his chin. He

shouldn't venture out in the company of a lady without shaving or donning a fresh shirt, but since it was still early and the lady in question was liable to sneak out the front door if he took the time to do either, Jarrod decided against it. Most of the ton would be home in bed by now, and the few still out and about would probably look as disreputable as he did. "If all else fails, I can always purchase you a husband."

He meant it as a joke, but Sarah wasn't smiling. "If all else fails, I can always ensure that you'll have wasted your money. Good-bye, Jarrod."

"Not so fast," Jarrod cautioned. "I'm going with you to the hotel."

Sarah frowned. "That's not necessary. . . ."

But Jarrod had already shrugged out of his dressing gown and was reaching for the jacket hanging on the back of his chair. He shoved his arms into the sleeves of his jacket and pulled it on over his shirt, ignoring the linen neckcloth still draped across the chair. "We'll take your coach to Ibbetson's. I'll wait until you're safely inside the hotel, then hire a hack to bring me back here." He looked at her. "That way there will be less risk of being seen together."

"There won't be any risk if you'll just hire me a hack and let me go back on my own," Sarah told him.

"Hire a hack?" Jarrod's heart skipped several beats as he narrowed his gaze at her and dared her to lie. "Tell me you didn't come here in a hired hack. Alone and dressed like that?"

"I didn't," she said. "Mr. Birdwell dropped me off at the top of Park Lane and returned to the hotel."

"He dropped you off? You *walked* from the top of Park Lane?" Jarrod was incredulous. "In that downpour?"

"It was less than a mile," Sarah offered. "And I made it safely."

"You were soaking wet."

"I got soaked leaving the hotel. A little more rain didn't hurt. So if you'll just find me a coach, I'll be out of your way."

Jarrod raked his fingers through his hair in an obvious show of frustration. "Confound it, Sarah, have you any idea of the danger you were in?"

"I made it in under ten minutes."

"You could have had your throat slit or been raped in less time than that."

"You're joking," she said. "On Park Lane? In the heart of Mayfair?"

Jarrod shook his head. "I'm not joking. This may be the heart of Mayfair, but pickpockets and footpads still roam the streets. Just last week, Lady Gentry and her daughter were set upon and robbed at knifepoint, three doors down from here, within moments of alighting from their coach after returning from the opera." Jarrod placed his hand beneath her elbow and escorted her to the front door. "I'll see you to the hotel, Sarah, and I'll hear no more arguments about it. Wait here," he ordered. "I'll be right back." He opened the door and started down the steps, then changed his mind, and turned to look at Sarah. "I want your word that you'll stay where you are while I hail a coach."

Sarah shook her head.

Jarrod closed his eyes, gritted his teeth, and counted to ten. Twice. "All right," he said, at last, holding out his hand. "Come with me."

Sarah shook her head once again.

"Am I to assume that you won't promise to wait and you won't come with me without some sort of inducement?" Jarrod concluded.

"You are correct, Lord Shepherdston."

Jarrod arched his eyebrow. "Would you consider monetary inducement?"

"I'll consider a loan of fare for the hired hack as long as I'm the only passenger in it."

Jarrod grinned suddenly. "Sarah, Sarah, Sarah. What am I going to do with you?"

"You could tutor me," she reminded him.

"Not a chance."

"Suit yourself," she said, "but I came for lessons in seduction, Jays, and I don't intend to leave without one."

"I'm afraid you're going to have to," Jarrod said. "Because I'm not taking you to bed."

"You don't have to take me to bed to keep your promise," Sarah suggested.

"My promise?" He arched his eyebrow.

Sarah moved closer. "Your promise to kiss me."

Jarrod eyed her approach warily. "Will you give me your word of honor that you'll wait here while I secure transport for us to Ibbetson's?"

"If you give me your word of honor that you'll kiss me like a lover instead of a sister."

Jarrod didn't know how she managed, but Sarah had read his mind. He was fighting the inevitable. Jarrod knew it was simply a matter of time before he gave in to her demand and he was weary of fighting. Because the truth was that he was as eager for a taste of her as she was for her first taste of passion.

He exhaled a long breath, then took her in his arms. "All right, Sarah, I concede. But don't say I didn't warn you." He leaned down, bringing his lips within a hairsbreadth of hers. "Because you're about to receive your kissing lesson."

# Chapter 6

*Give me a kiss, and to that kiss a score,*
*Then to that twenty, add a hundred more:*
*A thousand to that hundred: so kiss on,*
*To make that thousand up a million.*
*Treble that million, and when that is done,*
*Let's kiss afresh, as when we first begun.*
*—Robert Herrick, 1591–1674*

*S*econds before his lips touched hers, Jarrod made one last desperate attempt to save himself. He tried to back away, tried to give her room to retreat, but Sarah showed no signs of retreating. Standing on tiptoe, she leaned toward him, lifted her chin, and pursed her lips. . . .

He stared down at her upturned face and the way she puckered her lips and was lost. . . .

Sarah tried to keep her eyes open as Jarrod closed the distance between his lips and hers, but her eyes closed of their own accord as Jarrod covered her mouth with his. As she exchanged breaths with him for the first time, Sarah fulfilled the romantic dream of a lifetime.

Jarrod Shepherdston was finally kissing her. And his kiss was a thousand times better than she had ever imagined. Sarah marveled at the tenderness with which he covered her mouth, then gave a startled gasp at the unexpected feel of his tongue against her lips.

Jarrod used his tongue to tease, tantalize, and seduce and although she was willing and incredibly eager, it was apparent to Jarrod that sweet, innocent, tempting Sarah had never kissed a man before.

It was equally apparent to Jarrod that he never wanted any other man to have the chance.

"Heaven help me!" he murmured, a heartbeat before he redoubled his efforts and lavished her mouth with attention, paying particular interest to her plump bottom lip, savoring the texture, flicking his tongue over it, touching the roughness of the myriad tiny abrasions she made with her teeth each time she bit her bottom lip.

Jarrod captured her breath, swallowing the soft sigh that escaped her lips as he deepened the kiss. She tasted of his whisky and the tart sweetness of untutored innocence and that combination released a storm of hidden emotions. Jarrod moved his mouth over hers, kissing her harder, then softer, then harder once more, testing her response, slipping his tongue past her teeth, exploring the sweet hot interior of her mouth with practiced finesse.

He made love to her mouth, teaching her everything he knew about the fine art of kissing in her first lesson.

And Sarah proved herself a most excellent student by following his lead. She moved her lips beneath his and kissed him back with a newfound talent and enthusiasm that inspired him as much as it surprised him.

She progressed rapidly, mirroring his actions and inventing a few of her own as she moved from student to teacher in the space of a few heartbeats. The jolt of pure pleasure he felt as she experimented with her tongue and teeth and mouth, finding additional ways to entice him, shook him down to his toes, threatening to steal his breath away along with his control.

The idea should have terrified him. It should have sent him running back to his study, should have had him barring the door to keep her out, but Jarrod welcomed her in. He traced the elegant line of her neck with the tips of his fingers, then tangled his fingers in her hair and leisurely stroked the inside of her mouth with his tongue.

Sarah was ignorant of the language of love, but her body was not. It recognized the ancient mating ritual and responded in kind. Her breasts plumped, the tips of them hardening into insistent little points, clamoring to be noticed. The surge of current that went through her body at the boldness of his kiss settled in the region between her thighs, causing an unrelenting ache for something she couldn't name—something she suspected *he* would have no trouble recognizing or supplying.

Sarah moaned softly, pressing herself against him in an effort to assuage the aching as she returned his kiss, following his lead, learning the taste of him, the thrust and parry of his tongue and the rasp of his teeth.

He heard her soft moan and somewhere in the midst of kissing her, Jarrod forgot she was an innocent. He held her close against him with one hand splayed against her bottom, while he used his other hand to blaze a path from the soft curls at the nape of her neck, over her shoulder, down her arm, and between their bodies. He slipped his hand beneath her cloak and pushed her nightgown off her shoulder, gently cupping the soft underside of her breast.

Sarah gasped at the pleasure his touch engendered and Jarrod rubbed the pad of his thumb across the hard tip of her breast, then filled his palm with the weight of it.

Jarrod answered Sarah's gasp by gathering a fistful of cotton and lifting the hem of her nightgown. She nearly yelped in astonishment as he slid his hand beneath the fabric and placed it against her bare bottom. The sudden, startling impropriety of his touch sent her senses reeling, but Sarah didn't pull away. She settled more comfortably in his arms, yielding to his naughty breach of etiquette, opening herself up to more of his alluring surprises, welcoming the erotic sensation, as he sent more shivers up and down her spine.

Jarrod didn't disappoint her. He was wedging his thigh

between hers, exposing the length of her naked leg, allowing her to feel the hard ridge at the front of his breeches, when the front door opened.

⤳

*"What the devil!" Jarrod growled as the front door* swung open and a blast of cool air and rain hit him in the face.

"Good morning, my boy. I know I'm early, but I saw your lights and—" Lord Robert Mayhew finished shaking the rain off his umbrella and looked up. "Good heavens!"

Jarrod let go of the hem of Sarah's nightgown, but not before his godfather caught sight of an extremely shapely bottom and extremely bare leg and hip.

Lord Mayhew took one glance at the scene in front of him and quickly turned his back. "I beg your pardon, Jarrod. I knew we wouldn't be riding in this downpour, but I never thought . . . I didn't realize you might—" Mayhew cleared his throat, and apologized once again. "I'm terribly sorry. We can forgo breakfast. I'll dine at the club."

"Wait! Please!" Jarrod shook his head as if to clear it. What the devil had happened to his self-control? His discipline? What the devil had happened to his good sense and his good intentions? He had just managed to do what he said he wouldn't do and had compromised her in the marble entry hall of his town house in full view of anyone coming down the main staircase from upstairs and anyone coming up the front walk and in the front door. Thank goodness he'd sent the staff to bed hours ago and thank goodness they had yet to begin their morning routine, or the footman who was normally stationed in the hallway would have gotten an eyeful. Just like Lord Rob. Because Jarrod had been so consumed by the pleasure of making love to Sarah Eckersley's mouth that he hadn't heard Lord Rob's coach drive up or the sound of his godfather's footsteps on the walkway. "I was about to take Sar—the young lady—home and we've need of private transportation. May we use your coach?"

"Yes, of course," Lord Mayhew answered, eager to make amends for his untimely interruption. "It's parked out front and my driver is entirely trustworthy."

"Thank you, sir," Jarrod answered respectfully. Bending slightly at the knees, he swung Sarah up into his arms.

Mayhew stepped aside to allow Jarrod to pass.

"I'll return shortly, sir," Jarrod called over his shoulder as he carried Sarah to Mayhew's coach. "Please, make yourself at home."

Lord Robert waved him off. "Don't bother about me. Take your time, my boy. No need to rush." He grinned at Jarrod. "I'll wait."

Blushing furiously, Sarah buried her face against Jarrod's shirtfront as the driver jumped down from his perch and opened the vehicle door. Jarrod handed her up into the coach. Sarah settled onto the forward-facing seat and waited as Jarrod climbed in and sat beside her.

"Where to, sir?" the driver called down.

"Ibbetson's," Jarrod answered. "Around the park." The shortest way to the hotel was through the park, but at this time of morning, it was also the most congested. The members of the ton who hadn't yet made it home to bed would be taking the shorter route through the park, and the early risers, like he and Lord Mayhew and his Free Fellow colleagues, who would normally be saddling up for their morning horseback rides along Rotten Row, would be making their way to their clubs for coffee and breakfast.

"Do you think he saw me?" she asked as the coach pulled away from Jarrod's front gate, merging with the early morning traffic.

Jarrod knew his godfather had seen quite a bit, but he didn't have the heart to tell her the extent of the damage. "Only your leg," Jarrod replied. "Not your face or your . . ." He stopped.

"Just my leg? Nothing else?"

"A bit of leg. That's all."

"Are you certain?"

"Fairly certain," Jarrod answered. "And there's no need to worry. Lord Rob is the soul of discretion."

*"Lord Rob?"* Sarah felt slightly ill.

"Yes." Jarrod nodded. "Lord Robert Mayhew. My uncle and my godfather."

Sarah covered her face with her hands. She had never met Lord Mayhew, but she had heard Jarrod speak of him for as long as she could remember. "Oh, dear lord . . ."

"It's all right," Jarrod consoled. "He doesn't know you."

"He knew my father," Sarah reminded him. "If not personally, then as the rector of Helford Green. Papa christened you. And your godfather was there, wasn't he?"

"I suppose he was." Jarrod traced the frown lines on Sarah's forehead with the tip of his finger. "I really don't recall the details."

Jarrod's attempt at levity was lost on her.

"Then he might remember Aunt Etta."

"It's possible," Jarrod told her. "Lord Rob knows a great many people. But I doubt he'd remember your aunt from seeing her once at my christening. It's been thirty years. If he's acquainted with your aunt, it's far more likely that he remembers her as Viscountess Dunbridge."

"What if he sees me with Aunt Etta? What if he realizes who I am?" If he learned her identity, Jarrod's godfather could pressure his godson to do the right thing. Lord Mayhew could pressure Jarrod into finding her a protector, a guardian, or a husband. Sarah shivered involuntarily at the thought. Or worse. Because his opinion mattered to Jarrod, Lord Mayhew might be the only man alive who could coerce Jarrod into marrying her. And marrying her against his will was the last thing Sarah wanted from Jarrod Shepherdston.

"Sarah, sweet." Jarrod took her face in his hands and looked her in the eyes. "I honestly don't think Lord Rob recognized you from the shape of your leg or your lovely derrière."

"My *derrière?*" she squeaked. "I thought you said he only saw a bit of my leg."

"I said I was fairly certain he only saw a bit of your leg," Jarrod corrected. "But he might have seen more."

Sarah's blush came close to matching the vibrant, shiny copper color of her hair and the freckles scattered across her nose. Knowing that Jarrod's godfather had seen her bare leg was enough to make her blush; knowing he might have seen her bare bottom was enough to give her hives.

"That will never do, you know?" Jarrod stared down at her with an unreadable expression on his face.

"What?"

"Blushing at the mere suggestion of a gentleman seeing previously unexposed parts of your anatomy. Not in the profession you intend to pursue."

"I'm not blushing at the mere suggestion of a gentleman seeing previously unexposed parts of my anatomy," Sarah informed him. "I'm blushing at the idea of your *godfather* seeing them. It's almost as bad as having *my* father walk in during my kitchen bath."

"Kitchen bath?" Jarrod raised his eyebrow in query. "What is that?"

Sarah closed her eyes for a moment, then opened them again and smiled. She had known Jarrod for so long she often forgot how very wealthy he was and how different their lives had been. "The stairs in the rectory are too narrow for anyone to carry a full-sized bathing tub into the bedchambers. Whenever I wanted to soak in a full-sized bath, I had to do so in front of the fire in the kitchen. And once, when I was three and ten, my father entered the kitchen while I was bathing. I don't know who was more surprised or who was more embarrassed." She made a face at the memory. "I thought I would die of mortification. And Papa wouldn't look me in the face for over a week."

Jarrod took a deep breath. "You do realize that if you

take a lover, he'll have the right to see you in the bath or in any other state of dress or undress."

Sarah nodded. "You aren't likely to remind me of my father or of your godfather."

"I'm not your lover," he reminded her.

"Yet," she said, leaning closer.

"You demanded a kissing lesson, Sarah, and I gave you one. That's as far as it goes."

Sarah averted her face, shrugged her shoulders to hide her disappointment and the hurt he'd carelessly inflicted, and pretended a nonchalance she didn't feel. "And I learned a great deal from it, Jays. It will just have to do until I find another young man to further my education."

"Sarah . . ." Jarrod spoke her name through clenched teeth.

"Unless you change your mind."

"I'm not going to change my mind."

"Whatever you say, Jays." She shrugged her shoulders once again. "Your loss is another gentleman's gain."

Jarrod looked at her. "I've no doubt of that," he said softly. "No doubt at all." Especially after the kiss they had shared. Jarrod's body still ached with wanting. *He* ached with wanting. Jarrod hated to admit it, even to himself, but he was beginning to hate the idea of Sarah with other young men. And he felt duty bound to discourage her. "If I were you, I wouldn't set my hopes on a young gentleman."

"Why not?"

"Younger men tend to be more interested in receiving satisfaction than they are in giving it. They are less settled, in greater demand, more easily distracted, and a great many are on allowances provided by disapproving papas."

"You are none of those things," Sarah pointed out.

"I am an exception," he admitted. "The point is that you might prefer an older lover like Lord Rob. He's wealthy and generous and he's been a widower for many years."

"And he's already seen my bare leg and derrière," Sarah added. "And I've already done my blushing, so he could continue my education with a great deal less bother than you've had to endure." She looked Jarrod in the eye. "Tell me, Jays, do you intend to return to your house and sing my praises to Lord Mayhew? Or bemoan my flaws? Will you suggest that he marry me or simply become my protector?"

"No, that's not what I intend," Jarrod said.

"What *do* you intend?" she asked.

A vivid mental image of everything they could do in the coach in the minutes left to them before they arrived at Ibbetson's Hotel popped into Jarrod's head. The upholstered seats were covered in thick, soft velvet and the windows were hung with matching curtains. It was dark and comfortable and private and he and Sarah could . . . Jarrod sighed. After he relieved Sarah Eckersley of her virtue, he could see her home to her room at Ibbetson's Hotel. He could set her on the path she claimed to have chosen with no one the wiser.

And with no strings attached.

Jarrod gritted his teeth. He could have what he wanted without answering to anyone. She had no father, brother, cousin, uncle, or guardian to demand satisfaction. He could be her tutor. He could teach her everything he knew about lovemaking—about taking pleasure and giving it. And when the affair ran its course, he could say good-bye without guilt because Sarah wasn't interested in becoming the next Marchioness of Shepherdston. She only wanted him for her first lover. Hadn't she told him that he was hardly her idea of a husband?

"I intend to see you safely to your hotel," he said at last. "And then I intend to return home and have breakfast with Lord Rob and go about my usual business."

"And pretend this morning never happened?"

"Exactly," he replied. And except for the fact that he would have to answer a few of Lord Rob's questions and add a meeting with Lord Dunbridge about the Helford Green living to the list of his usual business, Jarrod would do just that.

"Well"—Sarah tilted her head and looked at him from beneath the cover of her lashes—"you can try."

"Ibbetson's Hotel." The driver announced their arrival at their destination.

Sarah opened the door and stepped down from the carriage before Jarrod or the driver could assist her. "Thank you for the lesson, Jays," she said as she closed the door in his face.

"*Sa-rah . . .*"

"I'll look forward to the next one."

## Chapter 7

*Ask me no questions, and I'll tell you no fibs.*
—*Oliver Goldsmith, c. 1728–1774*

"Come in," Lord Mayhew called from Jarrod's study as Jarrod entered his town house a quarter of an hour after dropping Sarah off at her hotel. True to his word, Lord Mayhew had made himself at home by stoking the fire, settling onto a comfortable chair, and propping his feet upon the matching leather ottoman. "Henderson brought a tray of coffee. I'll pour you a cup. Go ahead and warm yourself by the fire."

Jarrod gratefully accepted the cup of coffee his godfather offered. He took the cup from the saucer and wrapped both hands around the delicate china cup, as he walked over to stand in front of the fireplace. "Thanks for the coffee and for the loan of your coach."

"You're welcome." Lord Mayhew gave Jarrod a rueful smile. "It's the least I could do after my untimely intrusion."

Jarrod took a sip of coffee. "No need to apologize, Lord Rob," he said. "The young lady was leaving. Your *timely* intrusion prevented me from making what would have been a terrible mistake."

Lord Mayhew lifted an eyebrow. "The young lady's mode of dress would lead one to conclude that the mistake you fear you would have made was committed earlier in the evening."

"It wasn't," Jarrod answered. "I managed to refrain from taking her upstairs to bed." Jarrod took another swallow of coffee. "Despite her mode of dress."

Lord Mayhew raised his coffee cup. "My boy, I salute you! You have the willpower of a bloody saint!"

"Don't salute me." Jarrod left the fireplace and walked over to the chair opposite Lord Rob's. Jarrod sat down on the chair and Lord Rob pushed the ottoman an inch or so closer to him, encouraging Jarrod to share it. "You arrived in the midst of our first kiss."

"Then I'm glad I could be of service," Lord Mayhew quipped. "Because you were headed for a tumble. And it's doubtful that you would have made it upstairs."

Jarrod nodded. "As I said, your arrival prevented me from making a huge mistake."

"What's a godfather for if not to prevent his godson from making a terrible mistake?" He poured himself another cup of coffee, added two lumps of sugar, and stirred it. "It's been my experience that what our hearts and heads tell us is often quite at odds with what our bodies urge us to do."

They sat in companionable silence, sipping coffee and staring at the fire for some minutes before Jarrod spoke. "I did the right thing."

Lord Mayhew didn't pretend not to understand. "I've known you all your life, my boy, and I've never known you *not* to do the right thing." He nudged Jarrod's foot with the toe of his boot. "Sometimes I think you were born knowing right from wrong and exactly what to do."

Jarrod placed his empty coffee cup on its saucer, then closed his eyes and leaned his head back against the chair leather. "It's an illusion," he said softly. "I always try to do what's right, but I don't always succeed."

"Tonight you succeeded," Lord Mayhew reminded him.

"Yes," Jarrod agreed, opening his eyes to look at the man who had been more of a father to him than his own father had ever been. "Tonight, I succeeded."

"You succeeded in doing what you thought was right

and yet I hear more regret than satisfaction in your voice."
Lord Mayhew frowned. "Enlighten me."

"I wanted to fail," Jarrod said, simply. "I wanted to do as
she asked. I wanted to forget about right and wrong. I
wanted to forget about honor and duty and respect. I
wanted . . . *her.*"

"Then why didn't you take her?" Mayhew asked.

"Because I'm a gentleman," Jarrod replied with a snort
of disgust. "Because I've spent my life living by a code of
honor and I couldn't betray it. Even for her. Especially for
her." He shook his head as if to clear it.

"You are a gentleman," Lord Mayhew confirmed.
"There's no doubt about that. What's more, you are an unmarried gentleman, and Jarrod, my boy, you must know that
there is no dishonor in taking pleasure when it's offered."

"There is when I know that by doing so, I would be set-
ting her on the Cyprian path."

"You think she's an innocent?" Lord Mayhew's eyes
widened at the suggestion that his godson had been hoodwinked by a slip of a girl professing to be a virgin.

"I know she is."

"Because she told you she was?"

Jarrod shook his head. "Because she came to me for her
first lesson in seduction."

Lord Mayhew frowned again. "She *came* to you?"

Jarrod nodded.

"You didn't send for her?"

"I couldn't have sent for her," Jarrod said, "even if I had
wanted to because I didn't know she was in town until she
showed up on my doorstep."

"When you escorted her home, where did you take
her?"

"She's staying at Ibbetson's Hotel. I took her there."

"Did you see her go in?"

Jarrod thought for a moment. He had let her out in front
of the hotel, but he hadn't seen her go inside. Jarrod narrowed his gaze at his godfather. "I've answered your questions. Now, why don't you tell me why you asked them?"

"Because I found this on the floor of your study after you and she departed." Lord Mayhew took a well-worn calling card from his jacket pocket and handed it to Jarrod.

"Miss Jones's Home for Displaced Women," Jarrod read aloud. "Number forty-seven Portman Square, London." He looked up at Mayhew. "I don't recall a home for displaced women on Portman Square."

"That's because there isn't one," Mayhew said.

"And number forty-seven Portman Square is . . ." Jarrod jumped to his feet. "Bloody hell!"

"I take it the young lady isn't a virgin after all," Mayhew guessed.

"Oh, she is," Jarrod answered, crossing the room to ring for Henderson. "But she won't be for long. Not if she intends to pay a call to number forty-seven Portman Square."

Henderson appeared almost immediately. "More coffee, sir? Or are you ready to break your fast?"

Jarrod glanced at his godfather.

Lord Mayhew shook his head.

"No," Jarrod answered, walking to his desk and hurriedly scribbling out two notes before blotting and sealing them. "Tell Fenton I need hot water for shaving and a fresh shirt and linen immediately. And see that these are delivered right away." He handed Henderson the notes. "And please order my coach readied and brought around as soon as possible."

"Very good, sir." Henderson bowed before exiting the study.

"Take my coach," Mayhew offered. "And save yourself some time. I'll stay here."

"I can't take your coach," Jarrod told him. "Because you're going to need it to take you to Portman Square."

"Why am *I* going to Portman Square?"

"Because I've a previous engagement elsewhere," Jarrod explained.

"I won't recognize the person you seek," Lord Rob replied. "All I saw was red hair, a shapely leg, and the birthmark on her round little bottom."

"She has a birthmark?"

Lord Rob nodded. "Yes, indeed. A strawberry-shaped one on her right cheek."

"Ask for the newest red-haired innocent with a strawberry birthmark." Jarrod flung the words over his shoulder as he left the study and took the stairs two at a time.

"Dyed red or natural?"

"Natural," Jarrod answered. "And pay whatever it takes to keep her innocent until I get there."

❧

*"I'm the Marquess of Shepherdston."* Jarrod introduced himself to the clerk stationed behind the registration desk at Ibbetson's Hotel. "I believe you have Lady Dunbridge and her niece, Miss Eckersley, as guests."

"You are correct, Lord Shepherdston," the clerk acknowledged. "We are delighted to have Lady Dunbridge and Miss Eckersley patronize our hotel for another season."

"Would you inform the ladies that I have come to pay a call?"

"It would give me great pleasure to do so, my lord, but the ladies have asked that they not be disturbed until breakfast."

Jarrod glanced toward the public dining room. It was crowded with clergymen and academics, easily recognizable in their somber black clothing, enjoying a hearty morning meal. "Then it appears that I've come at an opportune time. I'll order coffee and wait over there." He nodded toward a vacant table.

The clerk chuckled. "I beg your pardon, my lord, but we are currently serving *first* breakfast and ladies aren't permitted."

"What the devil is first breakfast?" Jarrod demanded, frustrated by the delay and the almost certain knowledge that his visit to Ibbetson's would be a waste of time. "And why aren't ladies permitted?"

"First breakfast is restricted to the male members of the nobility, senior clergymen, and senior academics."

"Is there a second breakfast?"

"Yes, sir, but it's restricted to junior fellows, vicars, curates, deacons, laymen, and clerks."

"Are ladies permitted at second breakfast?"

"The senior clergy and academics discourage the practice of inviting them, but ladies are permitted if they are in the company of their husbands or other male family members."

"How much longer until second breakfast?" Jarrod asked.

"I'm afraid you've missed it, sir," the clerk told him. "Second breakfast begins an hour before first breakfast; and third breakfast, for employees and servants, is a half hour before that one."

Jarrod wanted to laugh at the irony of calling the current meal first breakfast when it was, in fact, the third. "What of your female guests who aren't accompanied by husbands or other male family members?"

"Our unaccompanied female guests generally have tea or hot chocolate and toast sent to their rooms."

"What if your female guests desire something more substantial than tea or hot chocolate and toast? Is there a time when ladies are permitted in the public eating areas?"

"Yes, of course." The clerk nodded enthusiastically. "The ladies' breakfast begins promptly at one."

"In the afternoon?"

"Of course, sir. Before the ladies begin paying morning calls."

Damnation! Female guests accustomed to country hours might be hungry for half the day before they were allowed to eat in the public dining areas of the hotel in which they were paying guests. Jarrod had been born into a society of wealth and privilege and had lived within its confines all of his life, yet he despaired of ever understanding it. Sometimes it seemed as if everything was upside down. He glanced at the clock on the wall behind the desk. He had a meeting with the Free Fellows at White's in a quarter of an hour, a pair of meetings at the War Office, and he'd invited Lord Dunbridge to join him for coffee at the Cocoa Tree before luncheon.

"Will you deliver a note to Lady Dunbridge and Miss Eckersley?"

"Most assuredly, your lordship, and at no charge to our registered guests."

"Thank goodness," Jarrod muttered.

"Are you registered as a guest here, Lord Shepherdston?"

Jarrod glared at the clerk. "No, I am not."

"Then I'm afraid I must charge you sixpence."

"Fine."

"In advance, sir."

Jarrod reached inside his jacket for his change purse. He removed sixpence and placed it on the desk.

"Thank you, sir." The desk clerk gave Jarrod a bland smile. "If you will be so good as to entrust the note to my care, I will see that it is delivered promptly."

"I'll require pen, paper, and wax," Jarrod said, in a deceptively soft tone of voice. "In order to write and seal the note you are to deliver."

"Very good, sir," the clerk replied. "But because you are not a registered guest, I am afraid I must charge you another sixpence. In advance."

Jarrod placed another sixpence on the desk, grabbed the paper, pen, ink, and wax, carried them to the small vacant table, and sat down to write his note. He ordered coffee from a passing waiter and wasn't the least bit surprised to learn that a single cup of coffee for an unregistered guest cost sixpence.

He wondered how much more it would cost him before he set eyes on Sarah Eckersley once again.

# Chapter 8

*A noble person attracts noble people, and knows how to hold on to them.*

—Johann Wolfgang von Goethe, 1749–1832

"What do you mean he's late?" Colin, Viscount Grantham, demanded when Griffin, first Duke of Avon, announced that Jarrod had sent a note saying he might be delayed. "Jarrod is never late."

Griff cupped his hand around his ear, exaggerating the motion as the casement clock chimed the half hour. "There is always a first time. And today is Jarrod's. He's late."

"He's not the only one." Colin glanced around. The Free Fellows were meeting in their customary meeting room at White's. The room was set with enough coffee, spirits, and cigars for six men: the three original Free Fellows—Griffin, Colin, and Jarrod—and the three newest ones—Daniel, Duke of Sussex; Jonathan Manners, the Earl of Barclay; and Alexander Courtland, the Marquess of Courtland. Barclay had settled onto a chair near the fire and Courtland sat at one end of the massive leather sofa. But Sussex's habitual place was empty. "Where's His Grace? Hasn't he returned from the coast yet?"

Griff nodded. "He must have returned late yesterday because I saw him last night at his mother's gala. I didn't get the opportunity to speak with him in the crush of people there, but I saw him."

"So did I," Barclay added.

"Then where is he?" Colin asked.

Courtland shrugged his shoulders, then leaned forward to pour himself a cup of coffee from the silver coffee service on the low table. "I was at the duchess's ball last evening, but I arrived later. I didn't see Daniel."

"This isn't like Sussex," Colin said. "He knows we're meeting this morning. He's supposed to brief us on the progress of his mission."

"Shepherdston is late and Sussex is missing," Barclay added. "It's a most unusual morning already."

Although they'd originally begun as a secret group of schoolboys, the Free Fellows League had grown and changed as its members had grown and changed. The members had put their secret league to work against Bonaparte, working very closely with the Foreign Office and the War Office.

The secret work that Colin and Jarrod and Sussex did came under the auspices of a staff of graduates of the Royal Military College and Lieutenant Colonel Colquhoun Grant. While Grant gathered battlefield information on the Peninsula, Jarrod, Colin, and Sussex gathered information on a much larger field of battle and all of it was analyzed, enciphered, deciphered, and included in the constant flow of military dispatches overseen by Griffin's father, the Earl of Weymouth.

When Griffin became a national hero, the prince regent and prime minister had asked that he retire from active duty in his cavalry regiment and he'd agreed. But retirement from the regiment hadn't kept him from engaging the enemy. And when his role as a national hero had become public, the Free Fellows League, and each member's connection to it, nonetheless remained secret to all but a handful of close associates.

Griffin and Jarrod and Sussex's positions in society made them subject to more social obligations and more scrutiny than the other Free Fellows. They were limited, in many ways, to planning, arranging, and financing the clandestine war against Bonaparte, but they were still very much a part of it. The three continued to engage in the occasional secret smuggling holiday, but Colin, as a relatively unimportant and poor viscount, had been the primary foot soldier in the field and the Free Fellow most at risk.

But that had all changed when Colin married an heiress. With two of the original Free Fellows married, more help was needed. Jarrod and Colin had already recruited Sussex while Griffin was serving with his cavalry regiment on the Peninsula. Later, while Colin was on his honeymoon, the others had approached Barclay and Courtland.

The number of close associates had expanded slightly with the addition of Sussex and the two newest candidates for admission into the Free Fellows League—Jonathan Manners, the eleventh Earl of Barclay; and Alexander Courtland, second Marquess of Courtland—but Jarrod, Griffin, and Colin were satisfied that their secret was safe and that the associates close to the three newcomers were entirely trustworthy.

As the newest members of the League, Barclay and Courtland had gradually assumed Colin's role as primary foot soldiers in their clandestine war with their French counterparts. And Sussex and Jarrod had undertaken more smuggling missions so the married members of the League could stay close to London to fulfill social and business obligations and to spend more time with their wives.

Sussex had spent the past two days on a smuggling mission to France. He had been scheduled to return in time to attend his mother's annual gala ball and Griffin and Barclay had seen him there, but neither Sussex nor Jarrod had yet arrived at White's.

Jarrod had sent word that he would be late. But they had heard nothing from Sussex. And that was unprecedented and very troubling.

"You're certain you saw Daniel at the duchess's party last night?" Colin asked Griffin.

"I'm quite certain," Griff answered.

"But you said there was a huge crush." Colin began to pace back and forth in Jarrod's customary pattern.

"There was." Griff looked at Colin and frowned. "Which is why I didn't catch a glimpse of you and Gillian all evening."

"You didn't catch a glimpse of us all evening because Gillian and I weren't invited," Colin replied.

"What do you mean you weren't invited?" Courtland and Barclay demanded in unison.

"I'm only a viscount."

"There were a dozen viscounts and viscountesses there," Barclay protested.

"And you have one of the oldest and most revered titles in Scotland," Griffin added. "Granthams and McElreaths have held titles from the time of Macbeth."

"Aye," Colin agreed, in a thick burr. "But they were Scottish titles and, present company excluded, when have the English ever been impressed by Scottish titles?" He shrugged his shoulders. "Besides, everyone knows there's no money behind the title."

"That may have been true once," Griff reminded him, "but your hard work and your marriage to Gillian put money behind the title. Tons of money." Griff ran his fingers through his hair. Colin had married Gillian Davies, the daughter of Baron Carter Davies, a silk and linen merchant who owned a fleet of ships and dozens of lucrative trade routes all over the world. Gillian's father had become one of the richest men in England and been rewarded with the title of baron for services to the Crown, but he and his wife and daughter had yet to be fully accepted by some members of the ton. "Of course tons of money doesn't mean a thing to the Dowager Duchess of Sussex, who is, and has always been, a terrible snob. But don't let it bother you. You're in excellent company, you know. She only invited Alyssa and me because I'm the hero of Fuentes de Oñoro and because His Highness elevated me to the rank of duke." He stared at his friend, trying to read between the lines. "And you know that if Daniel had realized his mother had omitted your name from the guest list, he would have invited you himself."

"I know that." Colin laughed. "And I don't need consoling, Griff. Believe me, I'd rather spend a quiet evening at home with Gillian than fight my way through the crush of the ton at Sussex House. And you can be sure Gillian feels likewise." Once upon a time, Colin would have felt slighted by the duchess's snub, but now, he truly didn't feel the slight. His only regret was that he knew Daniel would be embarrassed to learn that his mother had slighted one of his friends. But he and Gillian were about to celebrate their first wedding anniversary and they enjoyed each other's company far too much to worry about missing the social event of the year. "If there's anything she despises, it's the snobbery of the duchess's set."

Griff raised his hands in a sign of surrender. "Daniel and I are the ones who need consoling. Count yourself fortunate that your mother-in-law isn't a part of the Duchess of Sussex's set like mine is." He smiled. "Alyssa and I would rather have stayed home like you and Gillian, and you know Daniel would rather avoid all the fuss, but . . . It's worse for him. The duchess is his mother. There was no escape for him."

Colin nodded. "I can't imagine returning from a mission and having to face that."

"It's the same for me," Jonathan said gloomily. "Because my aunt would never forgive me for missing her party either. And if my aunt is unhappy, my mother is unhappy. Unfortunately, those two sisters are as alike as peas in a pod and they're both capable of making my life miserable."

The Free Fellows had all become as close as brothers, but only Sussex and Manners were related. Their mothers were sisters. Daniel's mother had married a duke. Jonathan's mother had married the younger son of an earl. Until he'd unexpectedly inherited his paternal uncle's title, Jonathan had always been the poor cousin whose aunt limited his contact with her son. The duchess had made certain that Jonathan and Daniel had gone to different schools. Jonathan had been sent to Knightsguild with Griffin, Colin, and Jarrod, and Daniel had followed in his father's footsteps and had gone to Eton. Fortunately for Jonathan, Daniel had sought his companionship whenever possible and had generously rewarded Jonathan for information about the Free Fellows League. Jonathan had slept in the cot next to Jarrod's and had often overheard bits of information about the mysterious League and the three boys who had formed it and patterned it after King Arthur and his Knights of the Round Table. He eagerly shared his information with Daniel and Daniel had supplied him with coins and trinkets in return. The cousins had thrilled to the exploits of the Free Fellows League and both boys had aspired to join it.

It had taken years, but Sussex and Barclay had finally been granted membership and earned their secret code names. Shepherdston was Merlin. Avon was Lancelot. Grantham was Galahad. Sussex was Arthur. Barclay had become Bedivere and Courtland had become Tristram.

"I shudder to think about it," Alex added.

"I know. I've been there," Colin said. "More times than I can count and I know that even if everything went smoothly, a trip to the coast of France and back in two days is a hardship."

"Daniel had to ride like the hounds of hell were on his heels in order to make it to his mother's party on time. And it's not as if he could beg off. He's the duke. It's his house and, what's more, he actually lives there." Griff's smile grew into a broad grin. "Think about it. He probably had to fight his way through the crowd of coaches to get down the drive to the house. No doubt he overslept."

"I did no such thing."

Four Free Fellows turned at the sound of the protest to find Jarrod standing in the doorway.

"Shepherdston!" they greeted him.

"My tardiness had nothing to do with oversleeping," Jarrod continued in a sharp tone. "I am only a quarter of an hour late despite the fact that I've been up all night."

"We were talking about Sussex oversleeping," Colin said. He walked over to the silver coffeepot, poured a steaming cup of the brew, and carried it over to Jarrod. "Not your going without." He thrust the cup in Jarrod's hand. "Drink this. You look like hell."

It was true. Jarrod's brown eyes were bloodshot and there were dark circles beneath them. "Thanks," he said, gratefully accepting the coffee.

"What did you do, Shepherdston? Put in an appearance at the Duchess of Sussex's ball last night then go home and work on dispatches?" Barclay inquired.

Jarrod shook his head. "You know better than that. Unlike the rest of you, I declined my invitation." He met Colin's gaze and smiled. "How was Her Grace's party? Did you and your lovely viscountess have a good time?"

"We had a very nice time," Colin told him. "But not at Sussex House."

Jarrod frowned. "You didn't go?"

The Duchess of Sussex's annual gala was the invitation of the season. No one declined except confirmed bachelors like Jarrod who need not count on winning the duchess's approval to retain their secure social standing in the ton. If anything, Jarrod's consistent refusal to grace the Duchess of Sussex's party with his presence increased his desirability among the ton's other hostesses.

"Colin and Gillian stayed home," Griff answered to spare Colin another explanation.

"Why?" Jarrod demanded. "Was Gillian ill?"

"No," Colin assured him. "She's fine."

"Then why the devil didn't you take her to the duchess's party? Gillian would have loved it. It's the biggest ball of the season and the most exclusive."

"Too exclusive," Colin answered.

Jarrod frowned.

"Colin and Gillian didn't receive their invitations in time to attend," Griff replied, diplomatically.

"Why the devil not?" Jarrod glanced toward Sussex's customary seat.

Jonathan intercepted his glance. "You know the duchess."

"Yes." Jarrod sighed. "I know the duchess. That's why I declined. She only invites me to her celebrations because I'm unmarried and available to partner the eligible young ladies."

"She invites you because you're considered unattainable," Alex corrected. "And she would like to be the one to snag you."

"She's still a lovely, well-preserved lady." Jarrod pretended not to understand. "But she's still a bit too old and too tyrannical for my taste. She outranks me and she would never let me forget it."

Courtland choked on his coffee at the idea of the Duchess of Sussex sharing a bed with anyone—much less Shepherdston. As far as he was concerned, Daniel's conception was the second miracle birth.

Jarrod glanced at Colin and couldn't resist baiting him a bit. "Once upon a time, you and I were both considered unattainable. Apparently, she's decided to punish you for going and getting yourself leg-shackled last season without her help or approval, else you'd have received your invitation this season."

Colin chuckled. "I prefer marriage to the Duchess of Sussex's invitations."

"And I prefer to remain unmarried." Jarrod winked at Barclay and Courtland. "Unlike these two, who, no doubt, accepted her invitation and ventured into dangerous territory last evening." He took a drink of coffee, then looked at the others. "So I stayed home and spent most of the night deciphering."

"Did you get them all done?" Colin asked.

"Unfortunately, I was interrupted." Jarrod didn't offer

any explanations for the interruption and the others didn't ask for one.

"I thought the dispatches were needed at the War Office this morning," Griff ventured.

"They are." Jarrod turned to Colin. "Do you think Gillian would mind . . . ?"

Colin had accidentally discovered, shortly after his marriage, that his bride was extremely proficient at solving word puzzles and deciphering French code and Jarrod wasn't above asking Gillian for help when he needed it. Jarrod didn't doubt for a moment that Gillian could be trusted with the information.

"She would be pleased to help," Colin said with a smile.

It was true. Colin's wife didn't know the history of the Free Fellows League or all of the work it did, but she knew he and his friends were part of it and that continuing their secret work was vital to the war effort. Gillian had a gift for numbers and an uncanny ability to break code. And she would die before she would betray him or any member of the League. In a few short months, Gillian had become the Free Fellows League's secret weapon and she was delighted to have the opportunity to contribute to the fight against Bonaparte.

Jarrod reached inside his jacket and removed the key to his desk drawer. "They're locked in the top drawer of my desk." He handed the key to Colin. "I'd be obliged if you'd get them and take them to your viscountess. I'll stop by your house and pick them up on my way to my meeting with Scovell later this morning. Tell Henderson I sent you."

Colin pocketed the key with a nod.

"Now," Jarrod continued, "where's Sussex? I want to know why he didn't invite Colin and his viscountess to his mother's party and I want to hear his report on his mission."

"Our sentiments exactly," Griff told him.

Jarrod frowned.

"As you can see, Daniel isn't here yet," Courtland added. "We spent the past quarter hour waiting for both of you."

"I apologize for being late," Jarrod said. "But something unexpected came up and it couldn't be helped. And I did send word to His Grace"—he nodded toward Griff—"that I had been unavoidably detained. I take it that Sussex didn't send word."

Griff shook his head. He and Sussex were the highest-ranking Free Fellows, but Jarrod was the leader of the group and the two dukes deferred to his leadership. "Not yet."

"You haven't seen him?"

"Not since last night," Griff explained. "And I only saw him briefly from across the room last night. By the time I made it through the crush to where I'd seen him standing, he was gone." He turned to Jonathan. "Barclay saw him, too."

"So he made it back safely." Jarrod heaved a sigh of relief. He hated sending the sitting Duke of Sussex on secret missions because there would be hell to pay and a million questions to answer if anything happened to him.

Griff nodded. "You can rest easily on that account. His Grace made it back to town safe and sound."

"Then where is he?" Jarrod asked, pinning each of them with a look.

"Unless he escorted a lady home from the party and decided to stay overnight or simply overslept, we've no idea," Barclay answered.

"We need to get an idea," Jarrod told them. "I've a very full schedule this morning, with personal matters that demand my immediate attention and meetings at the War Office in a few hours with men who require the most accurate and current information we can give them on the French movements along the coast." He finished his coffee and set the empty cup on its saucer on the silver tray. "As there's no point in meeting without him, let's see if we can find our errant King Arthur before eleven of the clock this morning."

"Where shall we begin?" Courtland asked.

"Anywhere but Madam Theodora's," Jarrod replied.

Puzzled, Barclay asked, "Why not?" Everyone knew Madam Theodora's was the Free Fellows' preferred house of pleasure.

"Because that's where I'm going to look," Jarrod answered. "I'll see you all here at the usual time this evening."

"Well," Colin drawled as Jarrod left the room, "our Merlin must have a personal matter that demands immediate attention."

# Chapter 9

*Skill'd to retire, and in retiring draw*
*Hearts after them tangled in amorous nets.*

—John Milton, 1608–1674

"What's the meaning of this?" Jarrod tossed the worn calling card on the top of Madam Theodora's elegant gilt writing desk.

"Lord Shepherdston!" Madam Theodora looked up from her ledger book and smiled a warm, welcoming smile. "What a wonderful surprise! But I must warn you that if you've come looking for Lord Mayhew, you will find him in the Green Salon auditioning a roomful of girls." She leaned forward. "It seems he's developed a taste for red-haired innocents half his age."

"Actually," Jarrod drawled, "I came looking for Miss Jones's Home for Displaced Women." He tapped the edge of the calling card against the gilt surface of her desk. "According to this, it's located at number forty-seven Portman Square. I believe that's the number on this door."

Theodora blanched, then reached for the card with a trembling hand. "Where did you get this?"

"Someone left it on the floor of my study," Jarrod replied.

"That's impossible!" Theodora exclaimed. "Those cards are only sent to—" She broke off when she recognized the implacable look on Jarrod's face.

"Displaced women?" Jarrod suggested in his deceptively silky drawl.

"Yes!" Theodora seized the opportunity to confirm his suggestion. "They are sent to women in need. Women who have no place to go."

"And you welcome these women into your home with open arms out of the goodness of your heart."

"I feed and clothe and shelter them," Theodora told him. "Even educate them if necessary. I provide them with a home and family and companionship."

"And I take it the companionship is almost exclusively male."

Theodora's pale blue eyes flashed fire. "How dare you pass judgment on me, Lord Shepherdston? When you have been one of my best and most frequent visitors?"

*"Customers,"* Jarrod corrected. "Let's be frank and put the proper name on it. I have been one of your best and most frequent *customers* and I have paid very well for the companionship you provided to me."

"And I have supplied you with the most excellent companionship your coin can buy," she retorted.

"To my very great pleasure," Jarrod allowed. "But to my very great shame, I never questioned how my companions came to be my companions."

Theodora shrugged. "Then you're typical of your class, my lord."

Jarrod raised his eyebrows in query.

"You're a gentleman," Theodora told him. "And very few gentlemen accustomed to pleasure ever question how the pleasure is supplied."

Jarrod shook his head. "And now I know that you supply it by luring displaced women into a life of prostitution."

"Economics," she retorted. "Supply and demand. You pay me and I supply women to meet the demand of wealthy gentlemen like you." She stared up at him. "How did you think they came to be here?"

"I suppose I was naïve enough to assume the women were here because they wanted to be here. I didn't expect that you would recruit daughters of recently deceased country clergymen."

"Why shouldn't I *recruit* daughters of clergymen?" She pushed back her gilt chair and stood up. "*I* am the daughter of a country clergyman. My father was a vicar."

"You?" Jarrod was clearly taken aback.

Madam Theodora was a lovely, elegant, and sophisticated woman with silver blonde hair and pale blue eyes. Jarrod knew that she was older than he by a half dozen or so years, but she had the complexion and the slim, willowy figure of a young girl. She wasn't tall, but her figure gave the illusion of height, and her manner of dress and exquisite taste in clothes heightened the illusion.

She spoke flawless French and several other languages, priding herself on greeting her foreign guests in their native tongues. She was also an accomplished musician, often entertaining her guests with her pianoforte or harp. Always graceful and gracious, Theodora had a talent for making her guests feel as if they were the most important men in the world. In bed and out of it. And she made certain that the women in her employ possessed the same ability.

Her home on Portman Square wasn't simply a house of pleasure, it was a refuge from the pressures of everyday life, a place where men were stimulated physically and mentally.

Having shared Theodora's bed on numerous occasions, Jarrod knew just how talented she was, but it came as something of a shock to discover that he knew next to nothing about her. "I would have guessed that you were French or the daughter of French émigrés."

"Not at all." Theodora smoothed the front of her silk dress as she considered his comment. "I'm as much a part of England as the Thames."

"But a vicar's daughter . . ."

"You would be surprised at the number of vicars' daughters employed here. And at the number who chose a life of sin to escape a life of hypocrisy. Vicars' daughters are taught to worship, please, and obey from the cradle.

Those who embrace this life make excellent Cyprians."
Theodora moved close enough to touch him on the arm.
"What don't you understand, your lordship?" she asked.
"That we've fallen from grace? Or that some of us have
done so willingly?"

"Did you?" he asked.

She ignored his question and posed one of her own.
"Come, your lordship, what did you think happened to
those of us who were gently brought up and educated, then
left without dowries or means of support?"

"If I thought about it at all," Jarrod admitted, "I suppose
I thought you eventually married someone who didn't require a dowry."

Theodora gave an inelegant snort. "Well, I suppose you
were right, Lord Shepherdston; eventually some of us do
marry. But a great many of us do not. And when we don't
marry, we often end up as governesses or companions or
housekeepers and lose our virtue when the masters of the
house decide to use us for their pleasure. Afterward, we acquire protectors who set us up in convenient little houses.
But those affairs are generally of short duration. Gentlemen suffer financial reversals every day and many are very
fickle in their affections. A fortunate few of us are lucky
enough to keep the house when we lose our benefactors
and go into business for ourselves."

"You didn't choose this life," he said. "You're speaking
from firsthand experience."

"Perhaps." Theodora gave him a brief salute. "Perhaps
my virtue was taken from me while I was employed as a
governess in the household of a man who will never be
granted license to darken this door." She smiled at Jarrod.
"Perhaps I didn't choose this sort of life in the beginning,
but I chose it at last."

"You accepted it," Jarrod corrected. "You didn't
choose it."

"I chose to make the best of it," Theodora retorted. "I
chose to create a place of beauty and brilliance and pleasure. An exclusive place where gentlemen would willingly

part with exorbitant amounts of money in order to share my bed or the beds of the women I employ. I chose to become the mistress of my fate, and the beauty of maintaining an exclusive establishment with a select clientele is that I can keep out the riffraff."

"What about the women you employ? Did you give them a choice when you lured them to your front door with the promise of safe haven? Did you offer them employment as Cyprians? Did you abuse their trust?"

"I took them in."

"And made them earn their keep by prostituting themselves."

"That's the way of the world," Theodora reminded him. "Don't throw stones at me for profiting from it. I offer women an alternative, and believe me, Lord Shepherdston, it's a much better alternative than working as governesses, companions, or housekeepers, where they're paid twelve pounds or less a year and subject to having attentions forced on them several times a week by the gentleman of the house or his sons or his friends. And subject to being immediately dismissed without references when they begin breeding. My girls make ten times that amount because I allow them to keep the gifts and pocket money the gentlemen give them. As long as they follow the rules, they have a home here for as long as they want one and they're free to leave whenever they choose. They receive medical attention when they require it, and when accidents occur, I arrange homes for their children."

"If life here is so good and everyone has chosen this way of life, why do you need to solicit new women?"

"Because girls find protectors. Because they leave to set up competing establishments and take time off to deliver accidents." She met Jarrod's stern gaze. "And because there are always gentlemen like your friend, Lord Mayhew, who demand red-haired virgins."

Jarrod ignored the madam's snide remark about Lord Mayhew and got to the heart of the matter. "How do you recruit them?"

"You know how," she retorted. "I send the cards."

"How do you know where to send your little calling cards?"

"That's none of your business, Lord Shepherdston."

"It became my business when someone left your calling card on the floor of my study."

"Who left the card on your floor?" she demanded.

"That's none of *your* business, Madam Theodora." He threw her words back at her. "But you will tell me how it arrived in that someone's possession."

She shrugged her shoulders in a blasé gesture, designed to capture a man's attention. "It's no great secret," she said. "I read the obituaries, Lord Shepherdston."

"The *obituaries?*" He said the word as if he'd never heard it before.

"Yes," she confirmed. "I subscribe to a number of newspapers and journals and take special note of the death notices—especially the notices of clergymen with daughters. And I listen to the gossip around me. When I hear of young women who have no place to go, I send a note and a calling card. I don't try to persuade them to come, I simply provide an option."

"And you tell them what's expected of them when they knock on your front door and present the calling card you sent them." Jarrod's drawl was razor sharp.

"Of course not," she protested. "I give them time to settle into the routine of the house before I introduce the subject of what's expected of them."

"How long?" Jarrod demanded.

"Long enough," she evaded.

"How long?"

"A fortnight."

"A fortnight?" Jarrod was aghast. "You give them a fortnight to adjust to losing their virginity?" He looked at Theodora with new eyes, then turned and reached for the doorknob. "May God forgive you," he said softly.

"I don't need God's forgiveness," Theodora snapped. "He needs mine."

Jarrod turned in the doorway. "Then I pray you both get what you need."

"What about you, Lord Shepherdston?" she demanded. "What do you need?"

"A breath of fresh air," he retorted. "And I've been told that the best place to find that in Miss Jones's Home for Displaced Women is the Green Salon."

"You won't find anything in the Green Salon that you can't have right here," she promised.

"I'll find my friend, Lord Mayhew. You see, he didn't come here to recruit innocent bed partners. He came here because I asked him to prevent other men from doing so."

"Why?"

"Because it seems I've suddenly developed a taste for saving red-haired innocents."

*"You took long enough,"* Lord Rob complained when Jarrod entered the Green Salon. "These young ladies are better card sharps than I counted on. Luck has deserted me and Theodora is charging me by the bloody hour for each girl."

Jarrod took one look at the scene before him and burst out laughing. Lord Rob was playing whist with three redhaired young women, none of whom bore any resemblance to Sarah Eckersley. Jarrod exhaled in relief.

"Meet Mina, Phyllis, and Joan." The girls nodded at Jarrod as Lord Mayhew introduced them. "Ladies, my godson, Lord—"

Jarrod gave a quick shake of his head.

"X." Mayhew grinned. "X, my boy, I've been playing whist with these ladies for the better part of an hour now and losing badly."

"Losing?"

Lord Rob chuckled. "Who can pay attention to cards when surrounded by all this beauty?"

"Nothing less than a bloody saint," Jarrod retorted.

"Touché, my boy," Mayhew acknowledged. "My point is that these young ladies refuse to take my chits and I'm running out of blunt."

Jarrod took out his leather purse.

"Quick!" Lord Rob exclaimed. "Save yourself! Hide your purse before these lovely ladies discover a way to part you from it."

"No need." Jarrod removed several pound notes and handed them to Lord Rob, then showed his godfather the empty interior of his wallet. "You already have." He turned to the young women. "Ladies, he has all my cash."

The girls giggled.

Lord Rob laid his cards facedown on the table and looked up at Jarrod. "Did you find your little visitor?"

"No," Jarrod answered.

"So"—Lord Rob rubbed his palms together—"what's next?"

"Are these the only . . ."

Lord Mayhew nodded. "Mina, Phyllis, and Joan are the most recent red-haired residents. As to whether or not they're true . . ." He shrugged. "I've no way of determining without . . ."

Jarrod turned to look at the young women. "Are you here of your own free will?"

The women nodded in unison.

"And do you understand what sort of establishment this is?" Jarrod asked.

"We didn't at first," Phyllis answered. "But we do now."

"Oh?" Jarrod lifted his eyebrow.

"We thought it was a home for displaced women," Joan told him, "but it's really a house of pleasure for men."

"Do any of you want to stay?"

"I do," Mina announced. "I like it here. It's better than where I was before and I don't mind giving some gentleman my virtue." She shrugged. "If the truth be told, my uncle took it years ago. When I was little."

She was still little and didn't look to be a day over three

and ten, but she was adamant about what she wanted. The other two girls weren't so sure.

"If you want to come home with me," Lord Rob offered, "I'm more than willing to pay your debt to Madam Theodora and help you find suitable employment."

"In return for what?" they asked.

"Another rubber of whist," Lord Rob answered. "And a chance to recoup my fortune."

# Chapter 10

*Even God lends a hand to honest boldness.*
—*Menander, c. 342–292 B.C.*

"Sarah, what is going on?" Lady Dunbridge asked.

"Blister it!" Sarah jabbed the embroidery needle into her tender flesh and dropped the sampler she was pretending to embroider. She sucked the drop of blood from her puncture wound and looked up as her aunt spoke. "Nothing, Aunt Etta."

"Language, dear," Lady Dunbridge admonished.

"Sorry." Sarah mumbled an apology.

"Your mumbled apology is acceptable." Henrietta Dunbridge frowned at her niece. "Your answer is not." At the sound of Lady Dunbridge's voice, Precious woke up from her nap in her basket on the floor beside Sarah's feet and eyed her mistress warily.

"Pardon?"

"I may be getting old, but I'm far from my dotage and far from blind." Aunt Etta took immediate exception to Sarah's attempt to evade her question. "I've known you all your life and you've never had much patience for needlework. Today appears to be no exception." Lady Dunbridge pursed her lips. "You've barely spared a moment for Precious and none for Budgie, whose cage you forgot to uncover this morning." She walked over to the window and removed the cloth from the budgie's cage. "You're making a mess of your sampler and you've been as fidgety as a cat in a room full of rocking chairs. Do you want to tell me what this is all about or shall I open the note from Lord Shepherdston and read it for myself?" She waved a folded piece of paper at Sarah.

"Jays sent a note?" Sarah reached for the piece of paper.

"Indeed, he did," Aunt Henrietta confirmed, holding it just out of Sarah's reach. "It's addressed to Lady Dunbridge and Miss Eckersley and it was delivered with our chocolate and toast."

Sarah frowned. "I don't recall seeing it."

"That's because it was on the tray and I got to it first." Lady Dunbridge smiled. "I found it rather queer that I should receive a note from a young man I haven't seen in ages and one who could not have known that I was in town."

"What does it say?" Sarah asked.

"I haven't read it yet," Lady Dunbridge replied. "And I don't intend to read it until I get an explanation from you."

Sarah took a deep breath. "I don't know where to begin," she hedged.

"Start where you slipped out of the hotel last night," Lady Dunbridge suggested dryly.

Sarah was wide-eyed with surprise.

"I woke up and your side of the bed was empty," Lady Dunbridge offered. "At first, I thought you'd made a trip to the privy, but when you failed to return within a reasonable amount of time, I supposed you slipped out to meet a gentleman."

Sarah gasped. "Aunt Etta!"

Her aunt shrugged. "Perhaps I *hoped* you'd slipped out to meet a gentleman when I looked out the window and saw Mr. Birdwell returning from somewhere with our coach."

"You're incorrigible," Sarah accused.

"You can't blame an old lady for wanting to see her only niece happily wedded and bedded." Lady Dunbridge winked.

"There is nothing old about you, Aunt Etta," Sarah told her. "You'll always be young."

"Thank you, darling, but don't change the subject. Tell me what happened after I fell asleep and you sneaked out of the hotel."

"I paid a call on Lord Shepherdston."

"Thank goodness!" Lady Dunbridge breathed a sigh of relief. "I hoped you'd slipped out to meet a gentleman, but I was afraid you had taken it into your head to pay a call on my nephew by marriage to try to change his mind about tossing us out of the rectory."

"I would never willingly pay a call on Lord Dunbridge," Sarah assured her aunt. "And never at night."

"I'm thrilled to hear it," Lady Dunbridge replied. "Especially if you intend to continue paying late-night calls alone and in nothing more than your nightgown."

"I didn't take the time to dress because I didn't want to wake you."

"Try again," Lady Dunbridge said.

Sarah frowned. Aunt Etta had always had the ability to see through her. She had always known when Sarah attempted to tell anything except the entire truth. "I didn't take the time to dress because I didn't want to wake you and because I wanted to be able to slip back into the hotel and into bed without anyone knowing—including you." Sarah met her aunt's gaze. "And because I thought I might have a better chance of persuading Lord Shepherdston to help me if I had something to offer."

"What were you offering?" Lady Dunbridge narrowed her gaze at her niece. "And what did you want Lord Shepherdston to help you do?"

"I was offering myself," Sarah whispered. "Because I wanted Lord Shepherdston to help me become a courtesan."

Lady Dunbridge coughed. "I had no idea your ambitions ran in that direction." She stared at her niece. "I would have sworn that you were the wife and mother sort."

"That's what he said," Sarah admitted.

"Who?"

"Ja—I mean, Lord Shepherdston," Sarah continued, "said there was no getting around it, I was meant to be a wife. He said I was meant to be married and meant to have a husband and children."

"So," Lady Dunbridge sighed, "you haven't outgrown it." Sarah had been chasing after Jarrod Shepherdston since she was five.

"Outgrow it?" Sarah was stunned by the concept.

Lady Dunbridge shrugged her shoulders. "It happens, my dear. People grow out of love every day."

"Did you outgrow what you felt for Uncle Cal?"

"Yes, I did." Lady Dunbridge surprised Sarah with her frankness. "And it only took me four years."

Sarah could hardly believe her ears. "What happened?"

"I couldn't continue to love him once I realized the rumors were true."

"What rumors?" Sarah had always believed Aunt Etta had been madly in love with her handsome lord.

"The rumors that he'd only married me to secure an heir. His first wife was barren, you know. I couldn't believe my good fortune when he began paying court to me. He was older and incredibly handsome and a viscount and I was the daughter of a baronet. I fell madly, passionately in love with him and believed he felt the same way about me. He was a tender, ardent lover and I thought I was the most fortunate of wives. But I failed to produce an heir or any child after two years of marriage and Calvin blamed me. He grew increasingly distant. When he began spending less time with me and more time in London, I began to pay attention to the whispers that Calvin had a mistress. It was true and, what's more, he had loved her for years."

Sarah stared at her aunt. "What did you do?"

"What could I do?" Lady Dunbridge replied. "We were married. I had to make the best of it. So I told myself that being a viscountess was enough. But it wasn't. It might have been foolish, but I had romantic dreams. I knew the way of the world, but I wanted to be loved and I wanted my husband to be the person who loved me. Since that wasn't likely to happen, I told myself that I would not love a man who didn't love me. I told myself that I would learn not to love him and, after two years of being rejected and neglected, I succeeded." She met Sarah's gaze. "I was married for ten years and for six of those years, I pretended to be happy. I pretended not to mind staying alone in London or spending longer periods of time on my own in the country. Until one day, I no longer had to pretend. I was living in Helford Green when I received word that Calvin had died in his mistress's arms in London."

"Weren't you angry?" Sarah asked.

"I was furious at him for not returning my love and for making me feel inadequate. But most of all, I was furious at myself for wasting all those years turning myself inside out loving someone who didn't want the love I offered and who blamed me for his own failings. When your mother became ill, I was glad to be able to move into the rectory and help your father take care of you. You are my sister's child, but you're the daughter I dreamed of having." She smiled at Sarah. "My anger died with Calvin. If I have any regrets, it's that I was completely faithful to Calvin from the day I met him until the day he died. I wish I had had the courage to approach the man I wanted and ask him to be my lover."

"It's not as simple as it sounds," Sarah warned. "It's embarrassing to ask and even worse when they refuse." She looked at her aunt. "And Lord Shepherdston flatly refused to do as I asked."

"Of course he did," Lady Dunbridge said. "You're an innocent and he is a man of honor."

"You haven't seen him in ages," Sarah reminded her aunt. "How do you know he's a man of honor?"

"That's simple," Lady Dunbridge replied. "If he weren't a man of honor, you would no longer be innocent."

"I went to him because I no longer wanted to be innocent," Sarah protested.

"You went hoping that if you offered yourself to him, he would fall to his knees, declare his love, and beg you to marry him—and you would have your heart's desire."

Sarah's mouth fell open. "How did you know?"

"I've lived with you long enough to know that you're a hopeless romantic. I never told you the entire truth about my marriage because I wanted you to hold on to the dream of a great romantic love for as long as possible. I wanted you to have what you wanted. I hoped a young man would come along and sweep you off your feet and that you would be loved and cherished and protected, but that won't happen until you get Lord Shepherdston out of your heart."

"I don't want him out of my heart," Sarah protested.

"What if he doesn't want to be there?" Lady Dunbridge asked quietly. "Love can be a curse as well as a blessing. Believe me, I know. Loving someone who doesn't love you in return is miserable. And being loved by someone you don't love in return is equally wretched. You have loved Lord Shepherdston with the purity and passion and honesty of an innocent child for most of your life. But you're a grown woman now and adult carnal love is rarely as pure and honest as the love of a child. It's passionate and messy and until you experience it, entirely beyond your ken."

"I don't intend to go to my grave without ever having spent a night in Jarrod Shepherdston's arms," Sarah insisted.

"Can you settle for one night?" Lady Dunbridge questioned.

"It wouldn't be just one night."

Lady Dunbridge pursed her lips in thought. "Suppose it was. Suppose you had your night of passion and he still didn't love you? Can you spend the rest of your life watching him live his life without you?"

"No." Sarah got up from her chair and dropped her forgotten sampler on the cushion. "Because I know he loves me. I know that we're meant to spend our lives together. All I have to do is prove it to Jays."

"How are you going to manage that?"

"I have no idea."

Lady Dunbridge smiled. Sarah had always been loyal and stubborn to a fault. Once she had her heart set on something, she didn't let go until she achieved her goal. And Sarah had her heart set on marrying Jarrod Shepherdston. Unfortunately, he appeared to be as stubborn as she was. "Let's see what he wants." She broke the seal on the note and read it aloud. "Lady Dunbridge: I request permission to call upon your niece—"

Sarah's heart began to race. Was it possible Jarrod had changed his mind?

"—to discuss her present plight," Lady Dunbridge continued. "As we require a chaperone, I ask that you join us promptly at one o'clock this afternoon at the ladies' breakfast at your hotel. Shepherdston." Lady Dunbridge finished reading the note, then handed it to Sarah so her niece could read it for herself. "I certainly hope that's not Lord Shepherdston's idea of a love note."

Sarah read the note, then folded it in a small square and tucked it in the bodice of her dress above her heart. "Me, too." She giggled in spite of herself. "But I'm keeping it. Just in case."

"Well"—Lady Dunbridge rubbed her palms together in anticipation—"now that we have a time and a place to start, we must decide how best to proceed."

"You're willing to help me?"

"I'm willing to help you," Lady Dunbridge assured her, "so long as helping you consists of making Lord Shepherdston *believe* you've chosen to become a courtesan. Because I refuse to help you become one."

"I don't want to become anyone else's mistress," Sarah said. "I only want Jays to believe I would."

"All right," Lady Dunbridge said. "If that's what you feel you must do in order to gain his undivided attention, I suppose I might have an old friend or two in London willing to help you give a good imitation of it."

# Chapter 11

*Believe one who has proved it. Believe an expert.*
—*Virgil, 70–19 B.C.*

*Jarrod arrived at Colin and Gillian's town house at 21*
Park Lane at a quarter past nine that morning.

Britton, the butler, greeted him at the front door. "Good
morning, Lord Shepherdston. May I say that it's a pleasure
to see you again?"

Jarrod took off his hat and coat and handed them to
Britton. "Thank you, Britton. It's a pleasure to see you
again."

"Lord and Lady Grantham are expecting you, sir.
They're waiting in the breakfast room." He stepped back to
allow Jarrod to enter, then closed the front door and led the
way to the breakfast room.

"Jarrod, come in." Colin stood up and motioned Jarrod
to the table. "Pour yourself a cup of coffee." Colin nodded
toward the sideboard. "Have you had breakfast?"

"I'm fine," Jarrod replied, even as his rumbling stomach
betrayed him.

"Won't you please take a few minutes to eat something,
Lord Shepherdston?" Gillian asked as Colin walked over
to the sideboard and began to fill a plate from the variety of
breakfast foods warming in the chafing dishes. "Colin and
I have spent most of the morning going over the documents he brought home. We were just about to sit down to

breakfast ourselves." She smiled at Jarrod. "We'd be pleased to have you join us."

Jarrod glanced around the room, looking for a clock, and found one on the marble mantel at the far end of the room. "I've appointments at the War Office at ten."

Gillian looked down at the elegant jeweled timepiece pinned to the bodice of her dress. "Please accept our invitation to breakfast and trust that we won't allow you to be late for your appointment."

"You might as well give in gracefully," Colin advised Jarrod as he carried his wife's plate to the table and set it down in front of her, then went back to the sideboard and picked up another plate. "It's a matter of courtesy. You're a marquess. She's a viscountess. She won't sit down to breakfast unless you join us," Colin continued. "Gillian's hungry. I'm hungry, and judging from the rumbling in your stomach, I'd say you're hungry. So stop being an arse and sit down. We can talk while we eat. I'll serve your plate. What will you have? Eggs? Sausage? Kidneys? Kippers?"

Jarrod sat down. "I'll have whatever you're having."

Colin nodded and began piling the plate full of food.

"Coffee or tea?" Gillian asked, reaching for another cup and saucer.

"Coffee," Jarrod answered. "No cream or sugar."

Gillian filled his cup from the silver coffeepot and handed it to him, then poured more tea for herself.

Colin delivered Jarrod's breakfast and went back to the sideboard, where he filled a plate for himself. He carried his plate back to the table, sat down beside his wife, and began to eat.

Jarrod placed his napkin in his lap, picked up his fork, and attacked the food on his plate, spearing a forkful of eggs. "Excellent." He looked at Gillian. "Thank you for breakfast and for your hard work."

"It isn't difficult work," she told him. "Just tedious."

Jarrod begged to differ. He'd seen any number of men fail at code breaking. But Colin's wife succeeded time and again with seeming ease. "Were you able to accomplish much in the short amount of time I gave you?"

"Quite a bit," Colin answered, "considering."

Jarrod quirked an eyebrow in query.

"We enciphered the dummy letters for the couriers to carry back to France using a mix of old codes and newly created ones." Colin smiled at Gillian.

"Oh?" Jarrod asked.

"They're quite convincing," Colin told him. "They'll fool everyone except the most dedicated code breakers."

"We composed them as a mix of all clear and code," Gillian said, "and made it possible to decipher bits and pieces in order to whet their appetites." She smiled, clearly relishing her role in helping defeat the French. "Then we entered meaningless codes after the closing."

It was British policy to enclose false messages along with the real ones in the military dispatches the couriers carried back to their commanders in the hopes that if the couriers were captured, the information they carried would confuse, rather than help the enemy. Commanding officers in possession of key codes were the only people able to differentiate between the false and the real documents and only because Scovell, Colquhoun, and their most trusted network of spies and messengers—including the Free Fellows—delivered the key codes and cipher tables separately. They knew the French had a similar policy. Original cipher charts rarely fell into enemy hands and most of the information they obtained from captured couriers proved useless when deciphered.

"But they should keep them busy for a while," Colin said.

"What about the dispatches I was deciphering?" Jarrod asked.

"We completed the deciphering on all but the one written entirely in code," Colin reported.

Jarrod knew the letter he meant. Because ciphering took time and a certain level of skill, most letters contained a combination of French and code, where only the most sensitive information was written in cipher. Since they'd begun work deciphering, the Free Fellows had discovered almost all battlefield missives contained more French than code. Political dispatches, letters outlining battle strategy and specific plans, and any messages detailing Bonaparte's movements were more code. And the French *Grand Chiffre*, or Grand Code, had proven extremely adaptable and difficult to break. Of the half dozen letters in the dispatch, only one had been written entirely in code. Jarrod spent a good deal of time on that letter and had been working on it when Sarah had arrived. He'd locked it in his desk drawer where it had stayed until Colin had retrieved it after the Free Fellows meeting. "Any luck at all?"

Colin ate a bite of sausage before answering. "We know it's from King Joseph of Spain to one of his subordinates. But we don't know which subordinate."

"Unfortunately," Gillian added, "a king is surrounded by nothing but subordinates. We've been forced to go down the list of those whose names we know and that takes time."

"You've uncovered more information than I was able to discover," Jarrod told them, pleased with the progress they'd made.

"Because your cipher table is incorrect," Gillian told him. "The code has changed since our last batch of intercepted mail. I took the liberty of correcting several deciphering errors in the letters you deciphered."

Jarrod arched an eyebrow in query.

Colin grinned. Because he was the leader of the League, Jarrod liked to think that he was better at deciphering French code than the other Free Fellows, but the truth was that although Jarrod was good, Colin had a more complete grasp of the French language and Sussex was better at deciphering, and Gillian was faster and more accurate than any of them and much better at discerning changes in numerical code. "The changes are subtle, but there are definite changes since we deciphered the last batch of dispatches." Colin reached for a leather pouch on the seat of the chair beside him, pulled out several sheets of paper, and handed them across the table to Jarrod. "See for yourself. Gilly made a list of the changes and copied new cipher tables for the men who will need them."

"It looks as if it's a code within a code," Gillian pointed out. "A complicated numerical code hidden within a simpler one."

Jarrod frowned. "From Joseph to one of his subordinates? Were you able to break it?"

She shook her head. "I've deciphered some of the words, but not enough to understand the content."

Jarrod studied Gillian's corrected cipher sheet. "The complex code must mean something. But what?"

"The code is more complicated. There are strange gaps in it of varying lengths with numerals inserted in a seemingly random manner. But there's nothing random about them. Look." Gillian pointed to a numeral in one section of code, then a second numeral in another section. "When we combine the numerals in the different sections, we get a very large number." She jotted down the numbers. "But that's only part of the pattern. All of the different elements mean something. Otherwise, why change the code? There's a pattern, but I haven't learned what it is yet."

Jarrod took another bite of his breakfast, then pushed his plate aside and spread the deciphered messages out in front of him. "Five thousand here." He pointed to one notation. "Eleven thousand here." He looked at Colin. "Have we intercepted treasury information? Are we looking at francs or pounds? There are no references to any military commanders or military encampments." Jarrod slapped the sheet of paper with his hand. "For all we know, *King Joseph*"—he sneered at the title Bonaparte had bestowed upon Joseph when he'd overthrown the rightful king of Spain and installed his older brother as His Catholic Majesty—"could be ordering supplies for a dinner party. Five thousand casks of wine. Eleven thousand pearl buttons. Fifteen hundred crystal goblets."

Colin nodded. "I agree. So far, the only thing I know for sure is that we aren't talking about ships or cargo." He winked at Gillian. "I've learned quite a bit about the shipping business in the past year, and there are no references to any seaports currently held by the French or their allies or any references to any of the trade routes we know the French use."

"Or to any known port of call," Gillian added, "French or otherwise."

Jarrod pointed to the cipher chart. "What are these?"

Gillian grimaced. "Abbreviations."

"Yours or theirs?" Jarrod asked.

"Theirs," she replied, taking a sip of her tea.

"Any idea what they represent?"

"I think the abbreviations are parts of words inserted at random intervals to confuse would-be interceptors." Gillian wrinkled her brow as she looked at the messages once again. "I'll figure it out." She looked at her husband and then at Jarrod. "All I need is a bit more time."

Jarrod smiled at Gillian. "Don't frown so, Lady Grantham, you've done the job of half a dozen men in less than four hours."

"I despise not knowing the answers," she admitted. "The puzzles nag at me until I can't think of anything except solving them."

"You mustn't let that happen," Jarrod teased. "You must think of yourself and of your husband, else he'll force me to seek help in other quarters."

"He wouldn't dream of being so selfish," Colin contradicted his friend. "Her talent is much too valuable to our cause."

"Indeed." Glancing at the clock on the mantel, Jarrod drained his cup, removed his napkin from his lap, and placed it beside his plate. He pushed his chair back from the table, then gathered the deciphered letters and the new ciphering charts, folded them in half, and tucked them inside a secret pocket sewn into his jacket. He looked at

Colin. "Will you see that the leather pouch and the dummy letters are returned to Lord Weymouth?"

Uniformed couriers carried military dispatches from London to the front, but spies secreted messages written on scraps of paper everywhere. At home in London, Jarrod settled for secret pockets sewn into his clothing. Leaning forward, he brushed Gillian's cheek with his. "Thank you once again, Lady Grantham, for breakfast and for sharing your extraordinary talent. The gentlemen in the War Office will be pleased."

"I'll see you to the door," Colin told him.

Gillian understood. There were secrets Colin could and did share with her, such as the deciphering, but there were secrets he couldn't share with anyone except his colleagues. She looked up at Jarrod. "We serve breakfast at the same time every day. You are welcome to join us anytime, my lord."

Jarrod straightened to his full height and gave Gillian a crooked smile. "You and Colin are newlyweds," he reminded her. "And I don't want to wear out my welcome."

"You needn't worry about that possibility." Gillian returned his smile. "For it will never happen."

Jarrod frowned.

"I'll always make time for my husband." Her cheeks turned a becoming shade of pink. "And I shall always welcome his friends into our home whatever the hour or circumstance." She looked Jarrod in the eye. "Especially you, Lord Shepherdston, for you and His Grace, the Duke of Avon, are my husband's dearest friends. You sheltered Colin and provided him with a means of providing for his family when his father would not. You have been the most loyal of friends and are as beloved to me and to Colin as any brother. . . ."

Jarrod stared down at the floor as the color rose in his face.

He was blushing. Jarrod, who never reacted with anything except wit, cynicism, or anger, was blushing. Realizing that he'd just witnessed a unique occurrence, Colin moved to assist his wife as Gillian pushed her chair away from the table and stood up. "And now that I have unwittingly embarrassed you with my gratitude and my profession of affection, I shall leave you and Colin to speak in private." She turned her face up to receive Colin's brief kiss, then patted Jarrod's sleeve as she walked by.

Colin watched as his wife left the room, then turned to Jarrod. "Any word as to Sussex's whereabouts?"

Jarrod blinked in surprise.

Colin wouldn't mention it while Gillian was in the room, but he was worried about Sussex and eager to learn if Jarrod had any news. "You did say you were going to forty-seven Portman Square this morning to look for him," Colin reminded him.

Jarrod had gone to Portman Square, but he'd forgotten all about looking for Sussex. "I went," he told Colin, "but I saw no sign of him."

"It's no wonder." Colin grinned. "Who would think to look for our missing King Arthur when you had other more pressing needs?" Although he no longer had the desire or the need to visit the house on Portman Square, Colin was familiar with its residents and well aware of the delights to be found behind its red doors.

Jarrod ignored Colin's good-natured teasing. "Have you heard anything?"

Colin shook his head. "I left White's and went to your house to collect the dispatches, then I brought them directly home to Gillian." He frowned at Jarrod. "As ordered. Remember?"

"Yes, of course." Jarrod cleared his throat. "What about Griff or Barclay or Courtland? Have you any word from them?"

"I haven't heard from anyone except you since this morning." Colin studied his friend. "Jarrod, are you all right?"

"Of course," Jarrod answered. "Why do you ask?"

"Because you've been acting oddly since Gillian . . ."

Jarrod gave Colin a rather pensive smile. "You're a lucky fellow," he said. "She is quite the lady."

Colin didn't pretend not to understand. "Yes, I am. And yes, she is."

"What's the secret?" Jarrod asked.

"To what?" Colin asked.

"You and your viscountess and Griff and his duchess. The four of you seem blissfully happy and at peace."

"We are," Colin said.

"But you're leg-shackled," Jarrod reminded him. "For life."

Colin smiled. "We're married, Jarrod, and marriage isn't the horror we believed it would be when we were boys."

"It is in my experience."

"Not when you love the person you marry," Colin said simply. "Not when they love you in return."

To his credit, Jarrod refrained from scoffing at Colin's words, but he had yet to come to terms with the idea. "I don't believe love exists for people like"—he almost said *people like us,* but he amended his statement at the last minute—"me."

Colin clapped him on the back as they walked to the front door. "Because you've yet to experience it. But believe me, Jarrod: love exists for all of us. Whether we believe in it or not. Whether we believe we deserve it or not."

Jarrod turned to Colin and held out his hand. "Then pity the poor woman who loves me, for I've been told that I'm hardly husband material." He hadn't realized quite how much Sarah's words stung until he repeated them to Colin.

Jarrod expected Colin to defend him, but to his surprise, Colin laughed. "You will be surprised how quickly that will change when you meet the right woman."

"I'm thirty," Jarrod replied. "I'm too old to change for any woman." He listened as the massive casement clock chimed the hour. "And I'm late for my meeting."

Colin's laughter followed him out the front door.

"You're changing already, my friend," he warned. "Or the world is coming to an end—because the always punctual Marquess of Shepherdston has been late twice in one morning."

# *Chapter 12*

*We are not all capable of everything.*
—*Virgil, 70–19 B.C.*

*The gentlemen at the War Office gratefully accepted* the deciphered information Jarrod delivered. And the special group of gentlemen in the cramped offices in the building off Abchurch Lane, who were skilled in the arts of secret writings and whose job it was to encipher the bulk of the messages headed for the French coast, were pleasantly surprised to find their duties lightened by the exceptional work of Jarrod's code breakers, especially the correction of the ciphering tables and the enciphering of the dummy dispatches.

Even their disappointment at the code breakers' failure to decipher the one letter written entirely in *Grand Chiffre* was tempered by their elation at the information contained in the portion that had been deciphered. King Joseph of Spain had written the letter. British spies had intercepted it. That meant the English government now had King Joseph of Spain's code. All they needed was the time to decipher it. And Lord Shepherdston's code breakers had already done the lion's share of the work.

"Good work, my boy." The Earl of Weymouth congratulated Jarrod as they left the Abchurch Lane offices.

"Thank you, sir." Jarrod was inordinately pleased to receive a compliment from Griffin's father. Both Jarrod and

Colin had begun their work at the War Office under Weymouth's tutelage three years earlier, shortly before Griffin left his job at the War Office and purchased a commission as a major in the Eleventh Blues cavalry regiment commanded by Sir Raleigh Jeffcoat.

But Colquhoun Grant had needed young volunteers to help him organize a network of spies and smugglers to ferret out information on enemy movements and to intercept enemy dispatches and letters from the front. The job of intercepting enemy dispatches and mail had grown to include the deciphering of it, and Jarrod and Colin followed Griff's example and left their administrative posts under Lord Weymouth for the more dangerous duty of becoming master spies and code breakers.

The secret Free Fellows League had discovered its purpose.

The Earl of Weymouth had regretted losing two of his ablest assistants, but he understood Jarrod's and Colin's desire to go where they were most needed. When Grant left London to join Wellington on the Peninsula, Weymouth had assumed the portion of his duties that included collecting the captured enemy mail and delivering it to code breakers for deciphering. The Marquess of Shepherdston and a black-robed gentleman in the offices in the little building off Abchurch Lane were two of the people to whom Weymouth sent military dispatches on a regular basis. Both were entirely trustworthy and Weymouth knew it.

"My superiors were very pleased with the information you presented."

"I'm gratified to hear it," Jarrod told him.

"They were pleased with everything except your tardiness." Weymouth met Jarrod's gaze. "And since I have never known you to be late for anything at any time, I was astonished by it."

"I apologize for keeping you waiting, Lord Weymouth," Jarrod told him. "But it couldn't be helped. I was delayed while collecting the ciphers."

"Then I suppose it was for the best," Weymouth said.

"Just don't let it happen again. Especially when both our reputations are on the line."

"It won't, sir."

"Good." Weymouth rubbed his palms together. "I won't ask how you did it because I know you're duty bound not to divulge the identities of your network of spies, smugglers, and code breakers even to me, but I hope that you will commend them for me."

Jarrod nodded. "I'll do so, sir."

They had reached Weymouth's carriage. "Can I offer you a lift?"

"No, sir," Jarrod replied. "My carriage is just down the way."

"Very good then." The earl climbed into the coach, then turned and issued an invitation. "Griffin and I are having luncheon at the club," he said. "Why don't you join us there?"

"I would love to, sir," Jarrod answered truthfully, "but I'm meeting Viscount Dunbridge for coffee shortly."

Weymouth grimaced. "Dunbridge? Don't tell me he's one of your—" He held up his hand. "Don't tell me."

Jarrod shook his head. "My meeting with Dunbridge has no bearing on the work I do for the government. Our meeting is purely personal. It concerns the environs surrounding Shepherdston Hall, particularly the benefice and the glebe Dunbridge owns."

Weymouth drew his eyebrows together. "Having trouble with your neighbor?"

"Something like that." Jarrod didn't volunteer any more information and the earl didn't press.

"Watch your back," Weymouth cautioned, waving goodbye. "Neighbors can be a damnable nuisance and I've heard Dunbridge is as obstinate as the day is long and he doesn't like to lose."

Jarrod had heard that as well. On several occasions. From several different people. "I trust that we'll be able to reach an equitable arrangement."

"Pay whatever you have to," Weymouth advised. "Es-

tates as large as Shepherdston Hall can be difficult enough
to manage when there aren't any quarrels with the neighbors and nearly impossible to manage when there are."

"I'll do my best," Jarrod promised as Weymouth's coach
merged into traffic.

❧

Less than an hour later, Jarrod sat at an inconspic-
uous table in the Cocoa Tree, a coffeehouse within comfortable walking distance from White's, and awaited the
arrival of Reginald Blanchard, fourth Viscount Dunbridge.
He'd never been introduced to the viscount, but he'd seen
him on several occasions and was acquainted with a few of
the men with whom the viscount associated. And he hadn't
wasted the time he'd spent since leaving Lord Weymouth
at the corner of Abchurch Lane and Lombard Street. Jarrod
had used it to make discreet inquiries at Brooks's and Boo-
dle's and White's.

As he watched the viscount approach, Jarrod wondered
how much of what he'd been told and what he'd surmised
about Dunbridge was true.

"I am pleased to accept your invitation to coffee, Lord
Shepherdston," Dunbridge said, moments after he joined
Jarrod at his table in the Cocoa Tree.

Jarrod didn't normally frequent the Cocoa Tree, but
he'd chosen it because he knew it was a favorite meeting
place for Dunbridge and his friends. "Thank you for coming, Lord Dunbridge." Jarrod shook hands with the viscount, then gestured toward the empty seat, inviting
Dunbridge to sit down. "I was told the Cocoa Tree was a
great favorite of yours," Jarrod said. "So I took the liberty
of ordering your customary refreshments."

Jarrod studied the other man as a waiter brought a fresh
pot of coffee and filled two cups with the strong, aromatic
brew. The coffeehouse was beginning to fill up and the
waiter set a plate of biscuits and crumpets and a crock of

butter in the center of the table, then quickly turned his attention to his other customers.

A decade older than Jarrod, Reginald Blanchard, fourth Viscount Dunbridge, was a trim, fastidious man with regular features; dark, almost obsidian eyes; a receding hairline; soft, carefully manicured hands and a penchant for tightly fitted clothes, bold satin waistcoats, and lace cuffs. He was a devoted follower of Brummell and he spent most mornings styling his hair and fashioning his neckcloths and most afternoons at the Cocoa Tree drinking pot after pot of cognac-laced coffee while discussing the various methods of styling his hair and fashioning his neckcloths.

He had attended Eton and matriculated from Trinity College at Oxford with little fanfare. He'd been ordained into the clergy and had promptly turned his back on it by settling in London and pursuing a career as a dandy. Unfortunately, Blanchard hadn't been able to truly indulge his passion for clothes or his rakish lifestyle until his uncle, the third Viscount Dunbridge, had died without issue.

His inheritance of the title and the lands and income attached to it had enabled the fourth Lord Dunbridge to finally fulfill his ambition and become a member, albeit a minor member, of the prince regent's circle of friends.

Wealthy, indolent, and self-indulgent, Dunbridge had had every advantage and squandered most of them. As far as Jarrod was concerned, Dunbridge was the sort of gentleman who gave other gentlemen a bad name. He embodied the worst traits of the members of his class and Jarrod disliked him on sight.

"I must admit to some curiosity as to why you requested this meeting," Lord Dunbridge said as he settled onto his chair. He reached for a crumpet, then picked up his knife and carefully sliced it in half before slathering the top section in butter. "We've never seemed to have much in common and rarely move in the same circles."

Jarrod allowed himself a slight smile at the viscount's

opening gambit. "It's true that I rarely move in your exalted circle, but we do have something in common."

"Oh?" Dunbridge took a bite of his crumpet and washed it down with coffee.

"We are both considerable property owners," Jarrod told him.

Dunbridge set his coffee cup down on his saucer and looked at Jarrod. "That's true of a great many gentlemen," he pointed out.

"I agree," Jarrod answered. "But not all gentlemen own adjoining properties in Bedfordshire."

"Have we a property or tenant dispute in Bedfordshire, Lord Shepherdston? Are we quarreling?"

"That depends."

"Upon what?" Dunbridge asked. "Because I must confess that I find real estate discussions rather tedious."

"Upon whether you intend to keep the living and the glebe attached to the rectory in the village of Helford Green."

"I see." Dunbridge narrowed his gaze at Jarrod. "Tell me, Lord Shepherdston, what business is it of yours?"

Jarrod clenched his teeth and a muscle began to tick in his jaw. "I wish to purchase it or secure a long-term lease for it if purchasing it is out of the question."

"Why would you wish to purchase the Helford Green benefice?"

"I have need of it," Jarrod answered succinctly. "And according to my sources, your primary holdings are in Somerset and here in London. The Helford Green benefice, which connects to my holdings, is your only Bedfordshire property."

"So you wish to own *all* of Bedfordshire instead of only the major portion of it," Dunbridge concluded.

"I don't own *all* of Bedfordshire," Jarrod drawled.

"You own all of Helford Green," Lord Dunbridge said. "Except the rectory, glebe, and village."

"Helford Green is a very small piece of Bedfordshire,"

Jarrod replied. "And I only wish to purchase the living, along with the rectory and the glebe."

Lord Dunbridge leaned his elbows on the table, steepled his fingertips, and pressed his mouth against them. "For what purpose?"

"To adjoin it to my existing property."

"Which would give you ownership of everything in Helford Green." Lord Dunbridge took another drink of coffee. "I'm afraid the Helford Green benefice is not for sale."

Jarrod drew his brows together. He hadn't touched his coffee or the plate of refreshments except to trace the silver rim of his cup with the pad of his index finger in a clockwise direction. "I'm offering top price."

Dunbridge took a deep breath. "It isn't for sale to you at any price, Lord Shepherdston."

"May I ask why not?"

"It's been in my family for years," Dunbridge answered, "and I've no wish to part with it. I took my first at Trinity College, you know. And was ordained into the clergy."

"Yes, I know," Jarrod answered.

Dunbridge smiled. "I'd heard you were a thorough man, Lord Shepherdston, and I see that you've done your research."

Jarrod acknowledged the other man's compliment. "I like to know with whom I'm dealing."

"Then you must know that while I've nothing against you, I rather enjoy knowing there's a portion of Bedfordshire that belongs to someone other than the mighty Marquess of Shepherdston."

"Fair enough," Jarrod allowed.

"And that I rather enjoy knowing the Helford Green church and glebe are mine to award to whomever I like," Dunbridge continued. "Whenever and however I like."

"Which brings us to the topic of selecting a new rector to fill the position left by Reverend Eckersley's untimely death."

"Are you offering to purchase the glebe because you've someone in mind for the position?"

"I might," Jarrod replied. "Either way, the Marquesses of Shepherdston are traditionally consulted before a selection is made. We have been the principal landowners in Bedfordshire for generations and the principal patrons of the church in Helford Green despite the fact that we've never possessed the living." Jarrod shrugged his shoulders and pretended a nonchalance he didn't feel. "I had hoped, in coming here today, that I might remedy that situation and relieve you of the chore of overseeing property in a distant county by adding the rectory and the glebe to my already substantial holdings."

"I never took you or the previous marquess to be particularly religious men," Dunbridge said rather pointedly.

Jarrod eyed the viscount's ridiculously high collar and elaborately tied cravat, tight trousers and bright waistcoat, and the dark curls he brushed forward to minimize his receding hairline, and answered in kind. "Were I to judge you by your appearance, I might make the same assumption about you, Dunbridge." He stared at the older man. "The fact is that I was christened and received my religious training in that church. It holds a special place in my memories and since you have only rarely set foot inside it, I didn't realize the attachment it held for you. You see, Lord Dunbridge, while your family owned the land and the crumbling remains of a sixteenth-century abbey, your predecessors were unable to finance the construction of a church."

"Yet the church stands upon the abbey's remains." Dunbridge didn't bother to conceal his smirk.

"Only because my ancestor financed the construction of it in order that the villagers might worship there. *My* tithes continue to fund the church, as do the tithes of the people employed in my household, who make up the vast majority of the parishioners. And I had hoped the owner of the living would take those facts into consideration before choosing the next rector."

"I'm afraid you're too late in presenting your concerns, Lord Shepherdston," Dunbridge said in an obsequious tone of voice Jarrod was certain bore no resemblance to the man's true feelings. "We've already awarded the living."

"We?" Jarrod queried.

"Bishop Fulton and I."

"Then the rumors are true," Jarrod pronounced in a regretful tone of voice that bore no resemblance to his true feelings either. He met the viscount's unblinking gaze and found it entirely too reptilian.

"I wasn't aware there were rumors circulating London over anything as inconsequential as the selection of a new rector for a village the size of Helford Green," Dunbridge retorted.

"There are rumors about everything in London," Jarrod reminded him. "No matter how inconsequential." He reversed direction and began to trace the silver rim of his coffee cup counterclockwise. "The only thing in question is the veracity of the rumors and I suppose I've no choice but to put that to the test by asking you for confirmation."

Dunbridge laughed and reached for another crumpet. "You can't expect that I should know all the rumors going about town. Or be able to verify them."

"You'll be able to verify the answer to this one," Jarrod told him, well aware that the game of cat and mouse was about to begin in earnest. "I heard the name of the man you've chosen as the new rector is a Reverend Phillip Tinsley."

"That's correct," Dunbridge confirmed.

"What do you know about him?" Jarrod asked.

"What do you mean what do I know about him?" Dunbridge answered Jarrod's question with a question.

"I mean, what do you know about him? You chose him for some reason. What do you know about him? What sort of man is he?" Jarrod demanded.

"He's a devoted man of the cloth."

Jarrod gave an exaggerated sigh. "That's a relief."

"How so?" Dunbridge demanded.

Jarrod smiled. "I heard he was looking for a governess."

Dunbridge shrugged his shoulders. "That's to be expected. After all, Reverend Tinsley is a family man with a wife and three children. Two boys and a girl, I believe."

"Two girls and a boy," Jarrod corrected. "Polly, Pippa, and Paul. Ages seven, five, and three."

"You've already made their acquaintance." Dunbridge widened his eyes in surprise. "Have you a candidate I may present as governess to Reverend Tinsley's family?"

"No, I have not," Jarrod answered. "I simply wanted to know the manner of the man before I inquired about available governesses on his behalf."

"Then you're extremely well informed," Dunbridge remarked, "for Reverend Tinsley and his family only just arrived."

"Oh?" Jarrod lifted his eyebrow. "I was given to understand that the reverend and his family have already settled into the rectory and that he had already been inducted to the living."

Lord Dunbridge inclined his head. "Once again, I commend your sources, Lord Shepherdston, on the accuracy of their information." He smiled thinly at Jarrod. "There doesn't appear to be a thing that I can tell you that you don't already know."

"You might try telling me what's become of the former residents of the rectory," Jarrod suggested. "Reverend Eckersley was a dear friend and teacher and I would like to know what's become of his daughter and his sister-in-law."

Lord Dunbridge smirked. "Didn't your sources tell you? Congratulations are in order. Miss Eckersley is engaged to be married."

"To whom?" Jarrod fought to veil his hostility.

"To me, of course!" Dunbridge exclaimed.

Jarrod half-expected Dunbridge to thump his chest like a male gorilla displaying dominance or hop onto the table and crow like a bantam rooster or flaunt his magnificent plumage like a male peacock.

"She and Lady Dunbridge—my aunt by marriage—are

making their home with me at my town house." Dunbridge leaned closer to Jarrod and giggled like a schoolgirl as he confided, "I'll wager your sources didn't mention a word about that."

"No," Jarrod agreed, "they didn't." Nor did they mention Dunbridge's fantastic imagination or his ability to switch from hostile adversary to girlish confidant in the space of a heartbeat.

"Oh, it's all quite proper," the viscount confided. "After all, she is my betrothed and Lady Dunbridge is there to chaperone—at least until we're wed."

"And then?"

"I'll pension Aunt Henrietta off and into a home of her own. Can't have the relations butting in on the honeymoon or telling us how to live our lives."

"Quite right," Jarrod said. "So, when's the happy day?"

"At the end of the season."

"The end of the season?" Jarrod gritted his teeth. "Why not the beginning? What's the delay?"

"She's in mourning for her father," Dunbridge replied. "And Brummell declared that a society wedding of the magnitude of my wedding to Miss Eckersley simply couldn't take place before six months had passed."

"You consulted with Brummell about the wedding?" Jarrod was stunned by the extent of the viscount's fantasy.

"Of course," Dunbridge told him. "Brummell is the one who suggested it. He said I should marry and get myself an heir before I got too set in my ways. He remarked upon it again just last week."

"Again?"

"Yes," Lord Dunbridge confided. "He first remarked upon my need for a bucolic bride several months ago. He declared it should be a nice little nobody who would look up to me and be a satisfactory ornament upon my arm when we were out among the ton, but who would be most happy rusticating alone in the country."

"Did he, now?" Jarrod had never understood the fascination Brummell held for the prince regent and most of the other members of the ton. As far as Jarrod was concerned, George—nicknamed Beau—Brummell was a fastidious manipulator who used his wit and elegant taste to dupe those in the ton who had neither.

"But when I approached Reverend Eckersley with the matter, he informed me that he didn't feel his daughter and I would suit because Miss Eckersley had her heart set upon marrying someone else." Lord Dunbridge shrugged his shoulders. "I, of course, determined to set my cap for someone else until I realized that I would be doing Miss Eckersley a favor by sparing her the embarrassment of wearing her heart on her sleeve for someone who did not return her affections." Lord Dunbridge studied Jarrod, gauging his reaction. "And when Reverend Eckersley died suddenly, shortly after our conversation, I considered it a good omen and a sign that mine was the best course of action. I determined to press my suit with Miss Eckersley and, to my great delight, she accepted."

Jarrod fought to maintain his friendly façade a bit longer. "Have you consulted Brummell since Miss Eckersley accepted your proposal?"

"Of course," Dunbridge affirmed. "Brummell knows all there is to know about good taste and fashion and he is the regent's dearest friend. It's our hope that His Grace, the archbishop of Canterbury, will perform the ceremony and that the prince regent will stand in for Miss Eckersley's father and give the bride away."

"That would be quite an honor," Jarrod said.

"If it can be arranged," Dunbridge continued spinning his Banbury tale, "for we wish to be married in London and have our hearts set on Westminster and as you know, Prinny does so love to spend the end of the season at Brighton."

"Will you go to Brighton?"

"Oh, no." Dunbridge shook his head. "If Prinny and the archbishop cannot do the honors, then Bishop Fulton has agreed to perform the ceremony and Squire Perkins, the magistrate, has agreed to act in Reverend Eckersley's stead and give the bride away." He gave Jarrod a speculative look. "I don't suppose you'd care to attend. . . ."

"Miss Eckersley's wedding?" Jarrod grinned broadly. "I wouldn't miss it for the world! Just name the day and time. I'll be there with bells on."

"Then I shall see you there, Lord Shepherdston," Dunbridge said. "Just as soon as Brummell settles on the date. Provided, of course, that he decides you should be invited."

"Why shouldn't I be invited?" Jarrod asked.

"It's my understanding that Brummell doesn't particularly care for you, Lord Shepherdston. It seems you've made a point of slighting him."

Slighting him? Jarrod frowned. He barely paid attention to the man. But, of course, Brummell demanded attention whenever he entered a room and would surely consider Jarrod's lack of interest in his comings and goings a slight.

"Of course an apology just might be the thing," Dunbridge suggested. "After all, Beau Brummell is the arbiter of everything fashionable in London," he reminded Jarrod. "It doesn't do to get on his bad side."

"No, of course not," Jarrod answered in as conciliatory a tone as he could manage. "You're exactly right, Lord Dunbridge. And since I would truly like to be present when Miss Eckersley weds, I'll do my utmost to make it happen."

"That's very smart of you, Lord Shepherdston, because the Beau will do his utmost to ensure that hers is a most spectacular wedding. He's very good to those in his set. And I'm quite certain that once you've made your apology, he'll be delighted to have you as a guest." Dunbridge talked as if he'd rather marry George Brummell than Sarah Eckersley. "Once everything between the two of you is resolved, I'll see that you're made aware of the day." He smiled at Jarrod. "I'll wager Brummell already has an idea which day will prove to be the best day for a wedding."

"Let's hope he has an idea for a better groom," Jarrod replied. "Because I'll wager that if Miss Eckersley decides to accompany any man down the aisle at the end of the season, it won't be you."

Dunbridge glared at Jarrod. "I'll take that wager, Lord Shepherdston. Because I've no doubt that Miss Sarah Eckersley will marry me at the end of the season. She has no choice. She's in mourning. The doors of the ton are closed to her for another four months. And I've already let it be known that she belongs to me. Who would dare challenge my right to her—especially when she comes with no dowry and an aging aunt in tow? I'll send you notice to mark your calendar when the time comes. And as you know so much about me, you ought to know that I never leave anything to chance." He pushed back his chair and stood up. "What would make a suitable wedding present, I wonder?" He tapped his finger against his cheek, pretending to give the matter serious thought. "Shall we make it official and say five hundred pounds?"

Jarrod shrugged his shoulders. "Why not make it official and say a thousand pounds?"

"Done," Dunbridge replied. "Thank you for the coffee and refreshments, Lord Shepherdston, and forgive me for taking such delight in the moment, but it's not every day that one gets the best of the Marquess of Shepherdston. Brummell was right in advising me that I should refuse to do business with you. It has been a pleasure."

"One hasn't gotten the better of the Marquess of Shepherdston," Jarrod retaliated. "And I don't care a twopenny damn about Brummell's advice."

"I still own the Helford Green living," Dunbridge crowed. "And whoever owns the living at Helford Green owns Miss Eckersley. I own both."

"Do you?" Jarrod asked. "For I was told that you had ceded the living back to the Church."

"That arrangement is temporary."

"Indeed it is," Jarrod informed him. "As temporary as your alleged betrothal to Miss Eckersley. Because my representatives are negotiating the sale of the Helford Green living with His Grace, the archbishop of Canterbury, even as we speak."

"Bishop Fulton . . ." Dunbridge began.

"Bishop Fulton desperately desires a new addition to the cathedral in Bath. I was delighted to be able to fund it in exchange for his recommendation that the Church sell the Helford Green benefice and glebe to me." Jarrod was bluffing, but Lord Dunbridge didn't know that.

"He wouldn't. . . ."

"He is," Jarrod countered.

"I'll lodge a protest with the ecclesiastical courts," Dunbridge promised.

"Be my guest." Jarrod smiled.

"And I'll hold you to our wager. It will be duly recorded in the betting books at White's for everyone to see. And when Miss Eckersley and I are wed, I'll expect to collect my thousand pounds."

"You are welcome to expect whatever you like," Jarrod said. "So write legibly and spell my name correctly. Shepherdston. No *a*. Two *e*'s. You may have been ordained, but according to my sources, you *failed* to take a first at Trinity College because you couldn't spell 'cat' without assistance."

"You can have the Helford Green living and the glebe." Dunbridge rose from his chair. "And be damned. It served its purpose. I've got what I wanted. I've got Miss Eckersley."

Jarrod narrowed his gaze at the viscount. "You've got a vivid imagination, a packet of lies, and a vulgar waistcoat," he said. "Nothing more."

# Chapter 13

*I'll be with you in the squeezing of a lemon.*
—*Oliver Goldsmith, 1728–1744*

"That's the fourth dress you've discarded," Lady Dunbridge commented dryly. "It's not like you to be so indecisive, Sarah."

"Then you decide." Standing arms akimbo in a long chemise, black short corset, and black stockings, Sarah replied, "Which one should I wear?"

Lady Dunbridge stared at the discarded dresses. All four were black. Two were black muslin. One was black silk and the other a lightweight black merino.

Dear Simon had only been dead two months and it wasn't at all proper for them to be in London for the season at all. But then, they had had little choice in the matter. It was London or Helford Green and they couldn't remain in Helford Green after the scene at the rectory. So, London it was. It should have been the ideal place for Sarah to find a husband other than horrid Reggie Blanchard, who had his mind set on having her for a wife. And someone other than Jarrod Shepherdston, the perennial bachelor, on whom Sarah had long ago set her heart. But they were in deep mourning and none of their friends or acquaintances were likely to invite them to take part in the "at homes," teas, soirees, musicales, or balls to which they would normally have been invited. Nor would they receive vouchers to Almack's.

Lady Dunbridge sighed. Simon Eckersley had been one of the most accommodating men ever born. It was most unfortunate that a man so accommodating in life had taken ill and died just before the early season commenced. His death and their state of mourning made their present predicament so much more difficult.

"There was nothing wrong with the one you had on before, my dear," Lady Dunbridge said at last.

"I couldn't wear that one to breakfast," Sarah told her. "It's so . . . so . . . plain. And black."

"All your day dresses and all your afternoon dresses are black." Lady Dunbridge looked down at her own black dress.

They'd dyed everything black upon Simon's passing, except one day dress and one afternoon dress apiece, two nightgowns, two sets of underthings, and their ball gowns. And the only reason those garments had escaped the dye vat was because Henrietta couldn't bear the thought of ruining Sarah's entire wardrobe. She wouldn't stay in mourning forever and she'd need something to look forward to when she despaired of ever wearing color again.

Sarah glanced at the clock, then pulled another black dress out of the wardrobe and looked over at her aunt. "I know they're all black, but they are all cut differently and made up in different fabrics. I want to look my best when we go downstairs to meet Jays."

Lady Dunbridge took a deep breath and slowly exhaled it. "*We* aren't meeting Jays downstairs."

"Why not?" Sarah dropped the dress on the bed as she whirled around to face her aunt.

"*I'm* meeting him," Lady Dunbridge clarified. "Alone."

"Oh, but Aunt Etta . . ." Sarah began. She had dreamed of Jarrod's kisses, dreamed of seeing him again and receiving another of his kissing lessons. She hadn't expected him to give her another kissing lesson at breakfast, but she had expected to be able to see him.

"I've already acknowledged his invitation and sent word of my acceptance." She took pity on her niece. "Sarah, my dear, I know you want to see your young man. I know you're disappointed that you won't be able to share a table with him and bask in his company, but I've given this matter a great deal of thought since we received young Shepherdston's note and I think it's time for a change in strategy. And it's best that I initiate the change."

Sara frowned. "I don't understand."

"You've been chasing him since you were a little girl," Lady Dunbridge explained. "And that was fine when you were a child. But you're a grown woman now and it's time you spurred him into doing the chasing."

"I tried that last night," Sarah admitted as she began tidying the mess she'd made. "But it didn't work. Jays has never chased anyone."

"Because he's never had to chase anyone," Lady Dunbridge answered. "He's a young, handsome, rich, unmarried marquess who has always attracted attention and women who flock around him."

"That's not likely to change."

Lady Dunbridge smiled a knowing smile. "You'd be surprised how much a man is willing to change when he's motivated to do so."

"He wasn't motivated to change when I approached him," Sarah reminded her.

"Because you approached him," Lady Dunbridge said. "Because he didn't want to be the instrument of your downfall. He didn't want to be the man to dishonor you or betray your father's trust. But I'll wager our marquess is more possessive than he knows."

"Jays isn't possessive at all," Sarah argued. "He offered to help me find a husband and if that failed, he offered to purchase one for me."

Aunt Etta lifted one elegantly arched eyebrow. "Did he now? How interesting."

"How humiliating." Sarah sighed. "As if I couldn't find one on my own if I wanted to."

"Beginning today, you do want to," Aunt Etta told her, putting the finishing touches on her hair before smoothing invisible creases from her skirts.

"But . . ."

"Don't you see, my dear? You've made it too easy for him. Just like nearly everything else in his life. Lord Shepherdston has never really had to work for anything he wanted. It's all been handed to him. He didn't take your threat seriously because he knows you've adored him since childhood. He knows you will never follow through with your plan to become a courtesan because that would make him unhappy and your adoration of him has never wavered. He knows he can count on it whenever he needs it."

"He's never needed it," Sarah answered.

Lady Dunbridge smiled another of her mysterious smiles. "He's taken it for granted, but he's always counted on having your unwavering adoration. The problem is that he's never done anything to earn it except breathe the same air you breathe. It's time we changed that. It's time we made him earn your affection—or at the very least, worry about losing it to someone else."

"Like Lord Mayhew," Sarah muttered.

"Like whom?" Lady Dunbridge's ears seemed to prick up at the mention of Lord Mayhew's name.

"Lord Mayhew," Sarah repeated.

"Lord Robert Mayhew?"

Sarah nodded.

"What about him?" Lady Dunbridge glanced in the mirror once again.

"He's Lord Shepherdston's godfather," Sarah explained. "And Jays suggested that a man like Lord Mayhew might be a better protector for me than a younger man."

"I'm sure Lord Mayhew would make an excellent protector for any woman. Young or old."

The dreamy expression on Aunt Etta's face caught Sarah by surprise. "You know him?"

"I did once." Lady Dunbridge nodded. "We met years ago when we were both rather unhappily married." She bit her bottom lip. "I heard his wife died a year or so before Calvin died."

"What happened?" Sarah asked.

"I believe she died the way your mother died," Lady Dunbridge said.

Sarah met her aunt's gaze and asked the question she'd wondered about most of her life. "How *did* my mother die?"

"Bathsheba never recovered her strength after losing the baby. She simply wasted away."

Sarah inhaled sharply. "What baby?"

Was it possible? Lady Dunbridge drew her brows together. Could Sarah have lived all these years without knowing how her mother died? Had she and Simon neglected to explain it to her while it was happening? "Your younger brother or sister," Henrietta said gently. "I'm sorry, my dear, I thought you knew. Your mother lost a child shortly before your fifth natal day." She swallowed hard and blinked away a rush of tears for her sister, who had died far too young and who hadn't lived to see her beautiful little girl grow up. "She grew weaker and weaker until one morning, she failed to wake up."

"I don't remember her." Sarah had always been ashamed to admit it, but it was true. She couldn't remember her mother's face. "I only remember you."

"That's probably because your mother and I looked a great deal alike. When she became ill, Calvin was living in London with his mistress so I left Somerset and journeyed to Helford Green to take care of you and your father and mother. My husband didn't need me, but my sister and her family did. As Bathsheba lay on her deathbed, I promised her I'd take care of you. And when she died, I kept my promise by staying in Helford Green." She glanced out the hotel window. "I never returned to Somerset."

"I always hoped that you and Papa would marry," Sarah admitted.

Lady Dunbridge nodded. "I know you did, but we couldn't have married even if we'd been inclined to do so."

The Church of England forbade marriage between a man and the sister of his late wife. Although it was forbidden, Lady Dunbridge knew that other men had gotten around the prohibition, but Simon Eckersley had been a man of principles. He would never have tried to get around it. Even if he'd wanted to. "And neither of us was inclined," she continued. "I was fond of your father the way a sister is fond of her brother and he felt the same about me. Goodness!" She produced the handkerchief she kept tucked in her sleeve and blotted her eyes before looking up at Sarah. "But I've become a veritable watering pot." She sniffed. "It's been years since I dwelt on these things." She shrugged her shoulders, then looked at Sarah and grimaced. "Your mention of Lord Mayhew's name was a bit of a shock. Of course, my flirtation with him was quite brief. It can't begin to compare with the grand passion you have for his godson in strength or duration."

"Only in satisfaction," Sarah replied, stepping into the last black dress she'd pulled out of the wardrobe. "Or lack thereof." She turned around and presented her back to her aunt.

Lady Dunbridge chuckled as she began buttoning the row of onyx buttons at the back of Sarah's dress. "We're about to change that."

"If you say so," Sarah answered.

"O ye of little faith," Henrietta declared, quoting scripture.

"I have plenty of faith in the fact that one day Jays will realize he loves me. As for him pursuing me . . ." Sarah shrugged. "I'll believe it when I see it."

"Believe it," Aunt Etta said. "Because the chase is about to begin."

❧

*Jarrod walked through the door of his London town* house at half past twelve calling for his valet. He had half an hour to change his shirt, neckcloth, waistcoat, and breeches and make it to Ibbetson's Hotel in time for his appointment with Sarah and Lady Dunbridge.

"Sir!" Henderson hurried to catch up with him. "You're home early."

"I shouldn't be home at all," Jarrod told him. "I have an appointment at Ibbetson's Hotel at one."

"Yes, sir, I know," Henderson told him. "Lady Dunbridge sent an affirmative reply to your invitation to join you for breakfast." He gave Jarrod a strange look.

"It's the ladies' breakfast at her hotel," Jarrod explained. "It begins at one in the afternoon."

"Indeed, sir."

"Have I received any more messages?" Jarrod asked, making his way across the marble entry hall toward the stairs.

"No, sir."

Jarrod stopped in his tracks and looked at his butler. "None at all?"

"No, sir."

"Nothing from His Grace, the Duke of Sussex?"

"Nothing, sir," Henderson told him. "Are we hoping to hear from His Grace?"

"Yes, we are," Jarrod answered. "Because His Grace failed to appear at White's this morning."

And that, Henderson knew, was unprecedented.

"No one has seen him since his mother's ball last evening," Jarrod continued. "And that was only a brief glimpse. And no one has seen or heard from him this morning. I'd believe he was delayed in France if Avon and Barclay hadn't sworn they'd caught a glimpse of him at Sussex House last night. And if he hadn't brought the dispatches here last night."

"He didn't bring them, sir," Henderson informed him. "He sent someone in his stead."

"Travers?" Jarrod mentioned the name of the Duke of Sussex's secretary.

"No." Henderson shook his head. "I'd never seen the fellow before. He told me that King Arthur commanded that he bring his offerings to Merlin. He handed me the pouch and a round of cheese and returned to his coach."

"The duke's coach?"

"No, sir, an unmarked one."

Jarrod frowned. "The dispatches were sealed. They showed no signs of tampering and the information they contained appears to be genuine."

"The messenger repeated the correct phrase: 'What is bread without cheese? Or cheese without French wine?' And delivered a round of French cheese," Henderson added.

The Free Fellow entrusted with the dispatches usually delivered them to Jarrod or to Henderson, but there were times when that wasn't possible; so the Free Fellows had devised a code for each mission whereby anyone sent in their stead was required to relay a specific message and deliver a specific item. The messages and the items were decided upon at the planning of each mission and given to Henderson, who accepted pouches in Jarrod's absence.

The butler looked stricken. "Perhaps I was mistaken in the message and the cheese, sir."

Jarrod shook his head. "There's no need to blame yourself, Henderson. You were not mistaken in the message or the cheese. That was the message we settled upon before the mission and His Grace chose a round of cheese as the item. Avon and Barclay both saw him at his mother's party last night. But he didn't appear at White's this morning."

"His Grace would never miss a meeting unless something was wrong."

"I agree," Jarrod answered as Henderson confirmed his worst fears. "And we're all concerned." He glanced back over his shoulder at his butler. "Where's Fenton?"

"He's out, sir," Henderson replied. "It's Thursday. Fenton's half day. He has the afternoon and evening off."

"Then come with me." Jarrod took the stairs two at a time, shrugging out of his jacket and unbuttoning his waistcoat as he went. "I'll require your assistance because the sooner I conclude breakfast with Lady Dunbridge, the sooner I can concentrate on finding Sussex."

Henderson hurried to keep up with him, accepting the clothing Jarrod was discarding as he climbed the stairs.

"If you don't mind my inquiring, sir, what happened to your garments? Was there an accident?"

"No accident," he said. "It was deliberate."

"Deliberate?"

Jarrod nodded. "I took the liberty of pointing out Lord Dunbridge's deplorable taste in waistcoats after we concluded our business at the Cocoa Tree Coffeehouse." He managed a slight smile at the memory. "And he took the liberty of dousing me with his beverage." He wrinkled his nose. "A rather strong brew, liberally laced with cognac."

Henderson gasped. "Will we be demanding satisfaction, sir?"

Jarrod shook his head. "I insulted him first. And the ruination of a set of clothing is not reason enough for me to call a man out. No matter how much I despise him."

"But, sir, Lord Dunbridge is only a viscount. You're a marquess and he assaulted your person."

Jarrod recognized the disapproval in Henderson's tone of voice. While hierarchy was important to members of the peerage, it was doubly so for the men and women who worked belowstairs.

"That's true," Jarrod agreed. "But assaulting my person with a cup of coffee is hardly a gibbeting offense. And it wouldn't be at all sporting or gentlemanly of me to call Lord Dunbridge out when I deliberately provoked him." He finished untying his neckcloth and pulled it from around his neck. "There was no real harm done. My honor is intact. And my reputation is not so fragile that it can't sustain an angry man's insult. Frankly, I would have been more surprised if he hadn't retaliated. He may have been ordained into the clergy, but I knew better than to expect him to turn the other cheek." He reached the landing and headed down the passageway toward his bedchamber. "Unfortunately, I didn't anticipate the manner in which he would retaliate or the time it would take me to return home and exchange my stained garments for clean ones."

Jarrod entered his bedchamber and went directly to his wardrobe. He opened the doors and removed another jacket, waistcoat, and pair of breeches, then crossed to his dressing room in search of a clean, starched shirt and neck-cloth. He located his tissue-wrapped shirts and carried them back to his bedchamber and placed them on his bed.

Henderson applied himself to the job at hand, lending assistance where he could, unwrapping the tissue from the starched shirt and unrolling a clean neckcloth as Jarrod stripped off his soiled shirt and pulled the clean one over his head.

Jarrod settled the shirt into place, then sat down on a wing chair and tugged off his boots. He peeled off his tight coffee-splattered breeches, then stepped into a fresh pair, skimming them over his legs and hips before buttoning them at the waist. He glanced at the ormolu clock on the mantel and urged his butler on as Henderson turned up the ends of his collar and draped a new cravat around Jarrod's neck. "Hurry, Henderson."

"I am attempting to, sir."

"Then add some speed, man," Jarrod ordered.

"That will only be possible if you stop fidgeting, sir." Henderson had originally trained as a gentleman's gentle-man, but it had been fifteen years since he'd served as a valet and fashioning flawless four-in-hands was damnably exacting and frustrating work.

"I can't," Jarrod snapped. He was dead on his feet and running almost entirely on nervous energy. If he stopped now, he'd be no good to anyone until he managed to get some sleep.

"No doubt a result of too much coffee."

Jarrod cracked a smile at Henderson's dry wit. "I do seem to have had more than my share this morning." He nodded toward his stained clothing.

"You've been without sleep for over twenty-four hours," Henderson reminded him.

"And getting an early start hasn't helped at all," Jarrod joked. "I've been running late all morning and I've no wish to perpetuate that state of affairs."

Henderson was astonished by Lord Shepherdston's admission. His lordship had grown up with the notion that punctuality was the politeness of kings. It had been instilled upon him almost from the cradle that gentlemen never kept other gentlemen waiting and, as a consequence, Lord Shepherdston was never late. "I beg your pardon, sir," Henderson apologized as he deftly executed the final loop on Lord Shepherdston's four-in-hand. "For I've no wish for that state of affairs to continue either. After all . . ."

"*L'exactitude est la politesse des rois,*" Jarrod quoted. "Punctuality is the politeness of kings." He buttoned his waistcoat, then splashed a small amount of his favorite wood spice scent on to eliminate the lingering aroma of Dunbridge's coffee. Jarrod wished he had time for a full bath, but that was out of the question. He'd barely make it as it was and could only hope that Sarah and her aunt, like most women of his acquaintance, were perpetually tardy. He gave the clock a final glance. "You can reach me at the main dining salon in Ibbetson's Hotel," Jarrod told him. "Send word immediately if you hear anything about our King Arthur."

"Of course, sir."

"Thank you for your assistance, Henderson. I was afraid I'd be late again. But I'm ready with eight minutes to spare."

# Chapter 14

*Punctuality is the politeness of kings.*
—*Louis XVIII, 1755–1824*

*H*e was late.

Lady Dunbridge smoothed her palms down the front of her dress and shifted her weight from side to side on the massively uncomfortable chair. And the chair constituted a mere fraction of the discomfort she felt at being on the receiving end of so many pointed looks as she'd crossed the sitting area and entered the dining room unescorted.

The dining salon might welcome unescorted ladies during the two hours designated as the ladies' breakfast, but the same could not be said of the gentlemen occupying the sitting area she'd had to cross. They appeared to frown upon having unescorted ladies anywhere on the premises.

Lady Dunbridge tapped her foot against the floor in an impatient staccato, then glanced at the clock on the opposite wall. It was ten minutes past the hour of one. Exactly two minutes since she'd last looked at it.

In his invitation, the Marquess of Shepherdston had requested that she and Sarah be prompt and she'd complied.

*He* had kept her waiting ten minutes.

Lady Dunbridge lifted her hand, signaled the waiter, and asked for pen and paper.

"I hope you weren't requesting that for me."

Lady Dunbridge looked up and met the Marquess of Shepherdston's brown-eyed gaze.

"As a matter of fact, I was," she replied coolly. "I was about to leave you a note and retire to the comfort of my room. You may not have noticed, Lord Shepherdston, but I am the only unescorted woman in this room and it's a very uncomfortable situation."

Jarrod bowed over her hand. "I'm very sorry my tardiness put you in an uncomfortable situation, Lady Dunbridge, but circumstances prevented me from arriving promptly." The circumstance that had caused his tardiness had been an overturned fruit wagon that had snarled traffic at the top of Park Lane. Jarrod had been forced to go the long way around the park in order to get around it. "I hope I didn't keep you waiting long."

"Ten minutes," Lady Dunbridge replied. "I arrived promptly as requested. You are late."

There was no denying the truth. He was late. Again. And Lady Dunbridge deserved his apologies. "Again, I offer my most sincere apologies." He placed his hand on the back of the chair opposite hers. "May I?"

She hesitated for a moment, then inclined her head in a regal nod. "Please."

Jarrod sat down and signaled the waiter. "Would you care for breakfast?" he asked.

She shook her head. "No, but a pot of tea and a plate of biscuits would be nice."

"Please bring the lady a pot of tea and a plate of biscuits," Jarrod instructed the waiter.

"Anything for you, sir?"

"I've had breakfast," he told the waiter. "But you may bring another cup for the young lady who will be joining us momentarily."

"Sarah won't be joining us momentarily," Lady Dunbridge informed him. "She won't be joining us at all."

"Oh?" Jarrod arched his eyebrow but he couldn't conceal his disappointment in learning that Sarah wouldn't be making an appearance at the ladies' breakfast. "Why not?"

Lady Dunbridge smiled. "She's resting."

"Resting?" he repeated, sitting up straighter. "Is she ill?"

"Just tired." Lady Dunbridge met his gaze. "She was out late last evening." She smiled at Jarrod. "Didn't return until dawn."

"I heard the Duchess of Sussex's party lasted well into the wee hours of the morning," he bluffed. "Most of London was in attendance. I hope Miss Eckersley enjoyed herself."

Lady Dunbridge gave him credit for trying to protect her niece. "I believe you know better than that," she replied. "Since she spent a good part of her evening with you."

"I didn't attend Her Grace's gala," he said.

"Neither did my niece," Lady Dunbridge told him. "As you well know since she was at your house quite early this morning."

"You knew your niece sneaked out of this hotel and came to my house last night?" Jarrod was surprised.

"I knew," Lady Dunbridge told her.

"You knew what she intended and you didn't try to stop her?" Jarrod was shocked.

"I didn't stop her because she didn't tell me about her visit to Park Lane until this morning." Lady Dunbridge paused while the waiter delivered her tea and biscuits, then calmly poured herself a cup as soon as he departed. "And I must admit that I had to commend her for her courage if not her choice."

"You commended her on her courage?"

"Of course." Lady Dunbridge took a sip of her tea, then reached for a biscuit and nibbled on the edge of it. "You can't think it was easy for her to travel from this hotel to your house alone after dark." She gave a delicate shudder, then stared at the young marquess. "Why shouldn't I commend her on her courage? I believe that traveling alone in London at night took a great deal of courage."

"Especially in the rain and wearing what she was wearing," Jarrod added dryly.

Lady Dunbridge leaned forward. "Sarah assured me she wore her black velvet evening cloak for warmth."

"She did," Jarrod rushed to reassure her. "And she kept it on after she arrived even though I had a nice fire burning in the study." He saw no point in telling Lady Dunbridge that Sarah had kept her traveling cloak on right up until the moment she'd tried to tempt him into seducing her by dropping it on the floor of his study to reveal the nightgown she wore beneath it.

"I'm so glad!" Lady Dunbridge heaved a sigh of relief. "It was bad enough for her to pay a call on her own so late at night—even if it was to an old friend who has been like an older brother to her all these years. She is in mourning for her papa, God rest his soul. And I would so hate for her reputation to suffer. It would be so upsetting and such an inconvenience. You see, Lord Shepherdston, we've come to town to find Sarah a husband." She looked at Jarrod. "The magistrate said a guardian would do, but what do magistrates know? What girl wants a guardian instead of a husband?"

"I was under the impression that your niece does," Jarrod said.

"She may say that, but Sarah was meant to be married," Lady Dunbridge confided.

"I agree," Jarrod replied. "But apparently Sarah does not."

"She says she prefers to do her own choosing and would rather pursue a career as a courtesan than marry, but look where that's gotten her. She's had no practical experience with men other than her father. And her judgment is flawed. Sarah chooses with her heart instead of her head. Why else would she choose you? I know that she's known you for years and that she feels safe and comfortable with you. But that's no way to judge a prospective husband."

"She didn't want me for a husband," Jarrod said. "Only as a lover."

Lady Dunbridge threw up her hands and shook her head. "All the more reason for her not to do the choosing.

Lovers take what you have to offer and promise you the moon and the stars in return. But they rarely deliver the goods. And when the love affair is over, they fob you off with a few jewels and move on to the next conquest. Answer me this, Lord Shepherdston, what good would having you as a lover be for a girl in Sarah's position?"

"I happen to be a very generous lover." Her criticism stung and Jarrod was eager to prove Lady Dunbridge wrong.

Lady Dunbridge made a clucking sound with her tongue. "I beg your pardon, Lord Shepherdston, but that's exactly my point. You are no doubt a very generous lover. And I'm sure my niece would be very happy with the fabulous pieces of jewelry you would give her to mark special occasions, but would you care enough for her to provide for her future when the affair was over?"

"I am very fond of Sarah," he protested.

"Of course you are," Lady Dunbridge said. "But you're fond of her in the way a child is fond of a puppy or a kitten."

"I offered to buy her a house."

"And I'm sure she was most appreciative of your grand gesture, but what good is a house when she has no one to share it?" Lady Dunbridge countered.

"She would have you to share it," Jarrod said. "I proposed buying a house for the two of you. Sarah refused it."

"Of course she did." Lady Dunbridge nodded. "She's unmarried. She can't accept a gift like that from you. And she wouldn't even if she could."

"Why not?" he demanded. "It would be a roof over her head."

"It would also be the worst kind of charity," Lady Dunbridge pronounced. "And you know it. She offered you the gift of herself. You refused her."

Jarrod frowned. "You know I couldn't take what she offered."

"Other men would have."

Jarrod nodded. "Yes, I know, but I couldn't." He looked up and met Lady Dunbridge's steady brown-eyed gaze.

"Other women would have accepted the house," she said simply. "But Sarah couldn't. She wants you. But since you have an aversion to marrying her . . ."

"I don't have an aversion to marrying Sarah," he corrected. "My aversion, as you put it, is for marriage in general."

"I'm sure my niece will be delighted to learn that your rejection of her wasn't personal," Lady Dunbridge retorted dryly.

"It *wasn't* personal," he insisted. "Except to her."

"It doesn't matter," she said. "The fact is that you've no wish to wed her for whatever reason and you've proven yourself too honorable to take her outside the bonds of marriage. Sarah will have to readjust her thinking and learn to accept someone else as her husband or as her lover."

Jarrod focused his gaze on the tablecloth, glaring at it as if he wished to burn a hole in it with his eyes. "What if Sarah doesn't want to rearrange her thinking?"

Lady Dunbridge arched a brow and eyed Jarrod in a speculative manner. So, Lord Shepherdston didn't like the idea of Sarah readjusting her thinking in order to accept someone else as her husband. "She won't, of course, but we don't always get what we want in life. Life is made up of compromises, disappointments, and changes in one's outlook. Sarah says she'd rather pursue a career as a courtesan than settle for less. But I think she protests too much and I intend to see that she becomes the wife of someone who won't think of her as a sort of bothersome younger sister." She looked up at Shepherdston from beneath the cover of her lashes to gauge his expression.

"I don't think of her as a sort of bothersome younger sister," Shepherdston corrected. "I don't think of her in any way at all except as a young lady of my acquaintance." As soon as the words left his mouth, Jarrod knew he'd lied to Lady Dunbridge. He'd thought of Sarah quite a bit in the past few hours and most definitely not as a younger sister.

"Then it's a good thing you've an aversion to marriage

in general, because thinking of her as a young lady of your acquaintance is much worse than thinking fondly of her." Lady Dunbridge drew her brows together. Poor Sarah! The marquess hadn't a drop of romance in his soul and didn't know the first thing about courting a woman.

He started to protest, but Lady Dunbridge held up her hand to halt his flow of words. "You needn't worry about explaining," she sympathized. "You cannot help your feelings any more than Sarah can help hers. And that makes everything worse for us because Sarah risked her reputation to pay her call on you. And would-be suitors take a dim view of things like that. If word of it ever reached the ears of the ton . . ."

"I assure you that no one will ever hear a word of Sarah's visit from me."

"I'll hold you to that," Lady Dunbridge promised. "Because you know we aren't going to breathe a word of it. Gentlemen—especially would-be suitors—tend to become very annoyed when their intended's virtue comes into question." She paused long enough to moisten her mouth with a sip of tea. "I suppose it would be different if Sarah were a great beauty or a great heiress. Suitors are generally willing to overlook tiny flaws in a girl's virtue if she's beautiful and rich, just as most people in the ton overlook the flaws in your virtue because you're a handsome, rich marquess. But Sarah is none of those things."

"I think your niece is quite beautiful," Jarrod said.

"I know you do." Lady Dunbridge pretended not to understand his compliment. "I do, too. But that's because we know her *inner* beauty. Most people never see past her red hair and freckled complexion. But there's no mistaking the fact that she will never be a great beauty. And unless she marries a fortune, Sarah will never be rich."

"Madam, believe me when I tell you your niece is already a great beauty. Her red hair is her crowning glory and the few freckles she has across the bridge of her nose are quite endearing." He frowned at Lady Dunbridge. How could the woman look at Sarah and not see how beautiful she was? "And as for marrying wealth, I was given to understand that she's betrothed to your nephew by marriage, Lord Dunbridge."

"You heard the gossip." It was a statement, not a question.

"I did."

"Is that why you refused her offer?" Lady Dunbridge demanded.

"No."

"Good." She nodded. "Now, if you would be so kind as to tell me where you heard about Sarah's alleged betrothal."

"I heard it from the horse's mouth, so to speak. I had coffee and conversation with Lord Dunbridge this morning."

"Sharing coffee and conversation with Reggie must have been a trial," Lady Dunbridge sympathized. "You poor man."

Jarrod gave a graceful shrug of his shoulder. "Actually, *he* had coffee. I spent the majority of my time trying to persuade him to relinquish the Helford Green living."

"Were you successful?"

Jarrod shook his head. "He wouldn't hear of parting with it. In fact, your nephew by marriage appears to hear only what he chooses to hear."

Lady Dunbridge widened her eyes in a show of surprise. "Then you understand our dilemma. Sarah is not Reggie's betrothed. She flatly refused his suit, as did I." She rolled her eyes. "Not that he asked me. But . . ."

"He's a reasonably attractive, wealthy viscount," Jarrod commented, "with a country house in Somerset and a fashionable address in London. I'm sure there are ladies who would be thrilled to become the next Lady Dunbridge."

"I'm sure you're correct, Lord Shepherdston, but Sarah isn't one of them." She pinned him with a look. "You met Reggie. Would you want him as husband for my niece?"

Jarrod grimaced. "I can't recommend him for his fashion sense or his veracity, but I suppose she could do worse."

"You didn't answer the question," Lady Dunbridge pointed out.

Jarrod gave her a mysterious half-smile. "No, I didn't."

"Why not?" She took a sip from her teacup and nibbled on another biscuit.

"I think you know the answer to that," he replied.

"Suppose I want to hear you say it aloud."

"No, Lady Dunbridge, I have no wish to see your niece marry a liar who prides himself on his nightmare of a wardrobe and the fact that he's forced her hand by evicting her from her home."

"If you understand that about Reggie Blanchard, then you understand that he's the sort of man who pulls the wings off butterflies for amusement. He would be the death of a girl like Sarah."

"I did what I could, ma'am," Jarrod said. "I spoke to him about the Helford Green living. He refuses to sell it, lease it, or rent it to me for any price. He confessed to enjoying owning the rectory because it kept me from owning everything in the village. I did everything in my power to persuade him to change his mind, including telling him that I was in the process of purchasing it from the Church." He stared at the tablecloth once again.

"Are you?"

"Not yet. But I'll be requesting an audience at Lambeth Palace first thing in the morning."

Lady Dunbridge nodded. "Thank you for trying, Lord Shepherdston. I don't know that seeking an audience with the archbishop of Canterbury will do any good, but I appreciate your attempt at persuading him."

"You don't have to thank me, Lady Dunbridge," he told her. "I promised Sarah I would speak to Dunbridge about the living and I've kept my word. Unless the archbishop grants my request, I've done all I can do."

"No, you haven't. . . ."

Jarrod knew what she was going to say and held up his hands as if to ward her off. "I'm not interested in marrying any woman or in making her my marchioness."

"I'm not asking you to marry her," Lady Dunbridge protested, playing her trump card, "or make her your marchioness. I'm asking you to smooth the way so that some-one else might marry her."

"Why do you need me for that?"

Lady Dunbridge sighed heavily once again, as if she de-spaired of Jarrod's understanding of the unwritten rules of society and the ton. "I need you to do something about Reggie's lies. No one is going to pay court to Sarah if they believe she's already betrothed to Reggie."

Jarrod frowned. "You do realize that if I go around Lon-don contradicting Lord Dunbridge it's tantamount to call-ing him a liar."

"He *is* a liar," she insisted.

"Yes, he is," Jarrod agreed, "but my pointing that out in public may result in his calling me out in order to save his honor."

Lady Dunbridge pursed her lips. "Can you best him?"

"Yes."

"Then there's no reason to worry," she said.

"Perhaps not," he replied, "but I'd prefer not to engage in a duel in order to save my honor or protect your niece's."

"That's understandable," Lady Dunbridge agreed, "and we wouldn't want that either. Especially if there's the slightest chance that he could best you, because we're al-ready in mourning."

"And . . . ?" Jarrod was curious to see where Lady Dun-bridge was leading him.

"How many calling cards and invitations do you think we'll receive while we're here?"

"Very few."

"Unless the powerful, well-connected, and well-respected Marquess of Shepherdston lets it be known that the late Reverend Simon Eckersley's last request was that his daughter find a suitable husband from among the mem-bers of the ton."

"Was that his last request?"

"In a manner of speaking," Lady Dunbridge hedged.

Jarrod leveled his gaze at her. "In what manner of speaking?"

"Simon professed a desire to see her happily wed."

"Close enough."

"Then you'll make it known that we're doing what Simon wanted?"

"I'll let it be known." He hesitated a moment, then reached across the table and covered her gloved hand with his own. "Rest assured, Lady Dunbridge, that I am a man of my word. I will use what influence I have to see that you and Sarah are invited wherever there are young men seeking wives."

"Thank you, Lord Shepherdston." Lady Dunbridge stood up. "I knew we could count on you to do the right thing."

"I am glad I can be of service," he murmured, standing up and bowing low over her hand.

"There is one other small matter," Lady Dunbridge drawled.

"Oh?"

"Sarah and I will require an invitation to Lady Garrison's gala tonight. . . ."

"Ma'am . . ." He clenched his teeth.

"And an escort." Lady Dunbridge smiled at him. "To go about town alone will only add fuel to Reggie's lies and provide him with an excuse to stand at our side and legitimize his fiction," she said. "Having you as our escort would do just the opposite."

"Lady Dunbridge, I—"

"Oh, thank you, Lord Shepherdston, I knew you would understand."

# Chapter 15

*These widows, sir, are the most perverse creatures in the world.*

—Joseph Addison, 1672–1719

*Jarrod wasn't quite certain how or why it had happened,* but he knew without a doubt that it *had* happened. Lady Dunbridge had bested him. He had been expertly outmaneuvered by a woman he'd never imagined might be capable of doing it.

Jarrod exhaled. He had to admire the way Lady Dunbridge had handled him, turning every situation from disadvantage to advantage, patiently maneuvering him into agreeing to do her bidding. It was brilliant strategy. And it had worked because he'd never seen it coming. Jarrod squeezed his eyes shut and shook his head. She was to be commended for doing the near impossible.

In the space of an hour he had gone from being his own man to becoming little more than an entrée into the rarefied world of the ton, an escort assigned to garner invitations, protect Sarah and her aunt from rogues like Reggie Blanchard, and open the ton's doors—and keep them open—despite the fact that the ladies from Helford Green were in mourning.

"I don't know how she managed it." Jarrod looked into his shaving mirror and met his butler's gaze as he detailed the results of his meeting with Lady Dunbridge. "One minute I was adamantly informing her that I had done everything in my power to help her and in the next moment, I found myself hoodwinked into escorting her and her niece to a ball this evening."

"Females have a way of doing that, sir," Henderson commiserated. "I'm not sure how they accomplish it either, but I suspect they do it with their tongues. . . ."

Jarrod groaned at Henderson's description, for the mention of tongues brought back a vivid memory of kissing Sarah, of plundering the depths of her mouth, of tasting her thoroughly.

"They talk us to death," Henderson continued, explaining his theory. "They use so many words in so many different ways that we get tired of listening. And the minute we stop listening to every word, they turn the tables on us and take control of everything."

Jarrod eyed his butler with newfound respect. Henderson had spent a lifetime in service and his insight into the nature of men and women was uncanny. "I believe that's exactly how it happened," Jarrod admitted. "Although I thought I was listening to every word, it's now quite apparent to me that I missed a few vital ones."

"You could always beg off," Henderson suggested. "Plead a previous engagement or an emergency of some sort."

"I could," Jarrod agreed. "But I won't." He looked at Henderson. "I gave Lady Dunbridge my word and I intend to keep it."

"Then send a note 'round to the members of the ton who covet your presence at their gatherings and ask that as a personal favor to you, they include the ladies in all your invitations just as they would if the ladies were your relatives or your houseguests."

Jarrod nodded. "That's an excellent way to ensure the ladies receive invitations to all the coveted events of the season, Henderson, but they'll still require an escort to keep Lord Dunbridge at bay."

Henderson frowned. He'd seen the invitations to tonight's events. He knew which society ladies were hosting balls. "May I inquire to which ball you intend to escort the ladies?"

"Lady Garrison's."

"Lady Garrison's, sir?" Henderson's frown grew fiercer. "Are you certain you wish to attend that ball?"

"I don't wish to attend any ball," Jarrod answered. "But the ladies would like to attend Lady Garrison's."

"Do *you* have to take them, sir?" Henderson asked, handing Jarrod a towel as the marquess finished shaving. "You're still dead on—" Henderson caught himself. "You look exhausted."

"I'll be fine." Jarrod took the towel and wiped the remnants of shaving soap from his face before swiping a trickle of water from his chest and tossing the towel aside. "I slept."

After leaving Lady Dunbridge at Ibbetson's Hotel, Jarrod had returned home and spent an hour catching up on his correspondence. He'd written a note to Bishop Fulton offering a generous donation to fund a new addition to the cathedral in Bath in exchange for the bishop's recommendation that the Church sell him the Helford Green benefice and glebe. Then he'd written to the archbishop of Canterbury requesting an audience at Lambeth Palace following morning services. He had sent a note to Lady Garrison informing her that he would be escorting Lady Dunbridge and her niece to Lady Garrison's ball that evening. He'd read a stack of correspondence from Pomfrey at Shepherdston Hall, then sent a coded message to Daniel at Sussex House, telling him of the Free Fellows League meeting that evening. After completing those tasks, Jarrod had retired to his bedchamber and slept for a couple of hours. He'd ordered a hot bath upon awakening, then bathed, shaved, and begun dressing for the evening ahead.

The Free Fellows were meeting at White's in half an hour to summarize the days' events. Praying that the Duke of Sussex's absence from this morning's meeting was an anomaly, Jarrod hoped he was worrying for naught and that Sussex would be at White's to brief them on his mission.

"Not nearly long enough," Henderson told him. "Sir,

isn't there anyone else we could engage to escort the ladies? If His Grace doesn't appear for this evening's meeting, one must suppose something untoward has happened and plan accordingly. And if that is the case, you are the logical choice to assume the next mission."

"Who do you suggest we engage to escort the ladies?"

"I suggest we ask Lord Mayhew to substitute for you."

Jarrod recognized the wisdom in that. "Lord Rob *is* completely trustworthy."

"And, if I may point out, sir, Lord Mayhew adores ladies and is quite at home in the ton," Henderson added.

"That's true," Jarrod agreed. He could count on Lord Rob to squire the ladies about London and to enjoy doing it. And Jarrod would be free to attend to his Free Fellow duties without worrying about Sarah and her aunt. Lord Rob would be able to discourage any attention Lord Dunbridge might pay to them. Yes, Jarrod decided, Henderson was correct. Lord Rob was the perfect choice. "Good idea, Henderson," Jarrod said. "I'll ask him about it tonight at Lady Garrison's."

Henderson frowned at him. "Sir, the point in asking Lord Mayhew to escort the ladies is to have him accompany them to Lady Garrison's this evening so that you might avoid it."

Jarrod smiled. "I'm aware of the point, Henderson. But Lady Dunbridge is expecting me tonight and I don't intend to go back upon my word at this late hour." He knew Henderson was right. He knew that it would be a relatively simple matter to ask Lord Rob to stand in his stead this evening, but Jarrod wouldn't consider the possibility because deep inside, he knew he wanted to see Sarah again. He'd been sorely disappointed when she hadn't joined him and her aunt for breakfast. In fact, Jarrod hadn't realized just how much he'd looked forward to seeing Sarah until she'd failed to appear. Jarrod met Henderson's gaze in the mirror. "It's time I accepted one of Lady Garrison's invitations. Past time, I think."

Henderson shook his head. "I don't like the idea of you going there alone."

"I know you don't," Jarrod said. "And I appreciate your concern, but it was bound to happen sooner or later. I couldn't avoid it forever. Besides, I won't be alone. I'll be escorting Lady Dunbridge and her niece." He smiled at his butler. "I left a stack of outgoing correspondence, including my acceptance of Lady Garrison's invitation, on the tray on my desk in the study. Please see that they're delivered right away and send a note around to Lord Rob and ask that he meet me at Lady Garrison's tonight." Naked from the waist up, Jarrod stepped away from the shaving stand and pulled a clean dress shirt over his head.

"Very good, sir." Henderson collected a length of linen from the bureau drawer and draped it around Jarrod's collar. He fashioned the neckcloth into a small bow tie and handed Jarrod an embroidered black waistcoat.

"Have we received a reply from Lambeth Palace?" Jarrod asked, slipping his arms into the waistcoat and buttoning the onyx buttons.

Henderson nodded. "His Grace sent a messenger to tell us that he's granting your request for an audience at nine tomorrow morning. And His Grace said to tell you that he expects to see you *at* morning services."

Jarrod groaned.

"It's a small price to pay for his granting an audience on such short notice," Henderson reminded him.

Jarrod sat down on a wing chair to put on his shoes, then stood up and allowed Henderson to assist him with his coat before grabbing his hat and gloves off the dressing table. "Yes, it is," Jarrod agreed. "But it's a price I'd rather avoid."

"One must always pay the piper, sir," Henderson said. "Everything comes at a price."

Jarrod nodded. "Any other words of wisdom?"

"Lady Garrison's party begins promptly at nine. In order to get to Richmond, you'll need to pick up the ladies you're escorting no later than a quarter 'til eight to avoid arriving late," Henderson said. "Your coach and coachmen are waiting outside."

"Thank you, Fairy Godmother," Jarrod teased.

Henderson didn't bat an eye or miss a beat. "You're welcome, Cinderella. Now, remember to return home before the last stroke of midnight or you risk turning into a turnip."

"I believe you mean a pumpkin." Jarrod laughed. "And I'll have to risk it because the party won't be over until well beyond midnight."

"Pumpkins. Turnips." Henderson shrugged. "What's the difference? They're both vegetables and the result is the same. A fat-headed marquess."

"Is that your way of telling me not to overimbibe?" Jarrod asked.

Henderson shook his head. "Not at all, sir," he replied. "I am a man who enjoys spirits and I would never presume to tell you to limit your consumption of them."

"I haven't got all night," Jarrod said. "Get to the point, Henderson."

"I thought I had, sir."

Jarrod raised his eyebrow in query. "Enlighten me."

"Since you insist on going to the Garrisons', I'm simply reminding you to come home and get some sleep so you'll have all your wits about you when you face the archbishop tomorrow morning."

Jarrod gave Henderson a slight bow as he exited his room. "Message understood, sir."

# Chapter 16

*We are the boys*
*That fear no noise*
*Where the thundering cannons roar.*
—Oliver Goldsmith, 1728–1774

"Has anyone seen or heard from Daniel?" Jarrod asked without preamble as soon as Griff, Colin, Jonathan, and Alex settled into their customary places in the private room at White's.

"Not a word," Griff answered.

"I made discreet inquiries all day," Alex, Marquess of Courtland, the youngest and newest member of the League, reported, "and no one has seen him since last night."

Jonathan nodded. "He seems to have vanished."

"He couldn't have vanished without someone seeing him." Jarrod drained his coffee cup, set it on a side table, and began to pace. "Someone saw something."

Colin hooked the leg of a leather ottoman with the toe of his boot and pulled it out of Jarrod's path. He pushed the ottoman closer to Griff, allowing more room so Jarrod might wear out the carpet unimpeded. "True," Colin agreed, "but so far, we've been unable to locate anyone who has."

"I even paid a call upon the dowager duchess at Sussex House this afternoon," Jonathan added. "She hasn't seen him since last evening either, but that's not unusual since her apartments are in the opposite wing."

"Did she sound concerned?" Griff shifted his weight on the sofa, then propped his right leg on the ottoman Colin had removed from Jarrod's path. Leaning forward, he reached down to massage his thigh in an effort to relieve the ache from the saber cut he'd taken across his hip and thigh during the battle of Fuentes de Oñoro. It had been two years since his injury, but the wound still pained him when he stood for long periods of time or when he danced, and he'd spent a good portion of the previous evening dancing with his wife at the Duchess of Sussex's ball.

"Not at all," Jonathan told them. "If anything, Aunt Lavinia was quite annoyed with him for including Lady St. Germaine on the guest list without informing her."

"Why wasn't Lady St. Germaine's name on the duchess's guest list in the first place?" Jarrod demanded, pacing harder and faster, equally annoyed that Daniel had managed to include the Marchioness of St. Germaine on his mother's guest list, yet neglected to add Colin and Gillian to the list. "When did Sussex add the marchioness's name to the list? And for that matter, why weren't Viscount Grantham and his viscountess's names added?"

Griff made a circling motion in the air with his finger and Jarrod automatically turned and began pacing in the opposite direction. It was Griff's way of attempting to save Jarrod a few pounds, for Shepherdston's notorious tendency to pace the width and breadth of their favorite private meeting room at White's wore out carpets at an alarming rate and the gentlemen's club billed the marquess every time they replaced the carpet.

"She didn't mention Grantham or his viscountess," Jonathan said. "But Aunt Lavinia was in quite a lather about Lady St. Germaine. Apparently she dislikes the Marchioness of St. Germaine enough to deliberately omit her name from the annual guest list."

Griff ran his fingers through his hair in a show of frustration. "That doesn't bode well for the future," he muttered. Miranda, Lady St. Germaine, was his wife's closest friend and had served as Alyssa's maid of honor at their wedding. Miranda was a frequent guest at Griff and Alyssa's Park Lane house and Abernathy Manor, their country house in Northamptonshire, and Griff was privy to Miranda's aspirations regarding the Duke of Sussex.

"Maybe not." Jonathan grinned. "Because apparently Daniel sends the marchioness an invitation every year and adds her name to the final guest list. I understand that this battle of wills between Aunt Lavinia and Daniel has become so heated that my aunt refuses to tell Daniel when the invitations go out or allow him to see the final guest list. Last night she gave the staff strict orders that Miranda was not to be allowed entrance to Sussex House unless she was accompanied by the prince regent. Aunt Lavinia was furious because Miranda got past the footmen and Weldon, the butler."

"That's outrageous!" Courtland exclaimed. "Lady St. Germaine has never done anything to warrant having the duchess bar her from the house."

"Except threaten her," Griff said softly.

"Miranda threatened Aunt Lavinia?" Jonathan couldn't contain a small satisfied smile. "I would have paid money to see that."

"Then open your eyes, Barclay," Colin said. "Because as long as Miranda St. Germaine remains unattached she's a threat to the duchess."

Jonathan widened his eyes and his smile as understanding dawned. "I assumed Daniel's infatuation with Miranda was over and done with years ago."

"So does everyone else," Jarrod said. "Except Her Grace, the Duchess of Sussex . . ."

"Who is afraid of losing her influence over society and over her son if she's consigned to the lesser role of dowager duchess," Colin added.

"But Her Grace is already the dowager duchess," Courtland pointed out.

"Her position as mistress of Sussex House and everything else Sussex owns is only secure because her son is unmarried," Griff said softly.

"But Aunt Lavinia's been pushing young ladies in Daniel's direction for years," Jonathan pointed out.

"She's been pushing young ladies in Sussex's direction," Colin agreed, "but Sussex hasn't paid an iota of attention to any of them. . . ."

"Except Alyssa," Griff added, reminding them all that he had almost lost his wife to Sussex when Sussex's mother and Alyssa's mother, who were fast friends, had planned to unite their families with a marriage between their offspring. But Griff and Alyssa had ruined the plan when they chose each other. "Not that I can fault the man's taste in the least."

"Be fair," Jarrod reminded him. "You know there were extenuating circumstances to Sussex's pursuit of Alyssa."

"I know that *now*," Griff agreed. "But I didn't know it or appreciate it at the time." It had taken him a while to get over his jealousy of Sussex and to forgive the man for seeing Alyssa's potential as a duchess, but Griff had finally managed. He genuinely liked Sussex as a man and as a friend and fellow Free Fellow and Griff truly admired the way he carried the burden of his position in society—a position to which Daniel had been born and one that had been thrust upon Griff and to which he was still learning to adjust.

"Barclay, you're his cousin. You've known Daniel longer than any of us. So tell us, how many ladies, other than Griff's duchess, have captured and held Sussex's attention for longer than a night or two?" Jarrod asked.

"One," Jonathan answered.

"And the lady's name is . . ." Colin prompted.

"Miranda, Marchioness St. Germaine."

Jarrod turned to Griffin. "Have you seen Miranda since the party last night?"

Griff frowned. "No. Alyssa asked Miranda and her mother to accompany us, but Miranda suggested we meet at Sussex House so that Lord and Lady Tressingham and my parents could ride with us."

"Did you see Miranda or her mother there?" Colin asked.

Griff shook his head. "No."

"She was there," Jonathan said. "Because Aunt Lavinia was furious with Daniel for inviting her and furious with Miranda for not having the good manners to stay away from where she wasn't invited."

Jarrod stopped pacing. He met Colin's gaze and they both looked at Griff. "Did Alyssa say anything about Miranda leaving town?"

"No."

"They're together." Jarrod grinned. "For whatever reason, Sussex and Miranda are together."

Colin hesitated. "Maybe."

Jarrod glared at Colin.

But Colin wasn't deterred. "Sussex and Miranda may be together, but it's just as likely that they aren't."

"Nobody has seen either one of them," Jarrod insisted.

"Nobody we've talked to has seen either one of them," Colin clarified. "But that doesn't mean they've headed to Scotland or that they're sharing an address."

"Grantham's right," Courtland said. "We can't assume anything. We're just going to have to keep looking until we hear from Sussex."

Griff glanced at Jarrod. "They're right."

"I know," Jarrod agreed. "But I'd like to think Sussex and Miranda are otherwise engaged."

"Because the alternative is that Daniel may be in trouble." Colin gave voice to their fears. "We may not want to think about it, but we'll be remiss in our duty if we don't. We're engaged in a desperate and dangerous business and we all know there are French agents here in London. . . ."

". . . And if any of them suspected Daniel might be involved in a little clandestine smuggling . . ." Jonathan picked up the direction of Colin's thoughts.

". . . The crush at the Duchess of Sussex's party would have been the perfect place to set a trap for him. No one would have noticed anything unusual in all that crowd,"

Courtland said. He shuddered, remembering how close one French agent had come to penetrating the League not so very long ago.

"I was hoping Sussex would be here tonight with a ready explanation for his absence this morning," Jarrod admitted.

"As were we all," Jonathan said grimly.

"Then I suppose we're all in agreement that his continued absence and the information we've gathered today means we'll need to do a bit of reconnoitering among the ton tonight," Jarrod said.

"Agreed," all the Free Fellows replied in unison.

"Luckily we all dressed the part." Jarrod spread his hands wide to indicate his own formal evening dress, then nodded at each of the other Free Fellows, who were all wearing evening clothes.

Courtland grimaced. "I'm escorting my mother to the opera. Where are the rest of you going?"

"Lady Cleveland's," Jonathan replied.

"Colin and Gillian and Alyssa and I are going to my sister-in-law's ball," Griff said.

"I'm also going to Lady Garrison's ball," Jarrod offered.

Griff was clearly surprised. "You are?"

Jarrod nodded.

"I'm sure my sister-in-law will be delighted," Griff said. "But are you sure you want to go there?"

"Quite sure," Jarrod said. "She did invite me. I think it's time I accept her invitation."

"Every hostess in London invites you to her parties," Griff reminded him. "And unless our League business requires it or it's one of Alyssa's gatherings, you rarely attend any of them."

"I'm making an exception for Lady Garrison," Jarrod replied.

"A major exception," Griff said. "And what I want to know is why?"

Jarrod smiled. "Let's just say that it's time I stayed on your duchess's good side by accepting her sister's invitation."

Colin glanced skyward and shook his head at Jarrod's

patently transparent prevarication. "Let's just say that it probably has something to do with the wager entered into the betting books this afternoon." Although Colin rarely wagered except with his closest friends, his father was an inveterate gambler and Colin had made it a matter of habit to check the betting books at White's in the morning and in the afternoon almost every day to see if his father had wagered on anything recorded on the pages.

"Damnation!" Jarrod swore. "He certainly didn't waste any time recording it. I only had coffee with him this morning."

"It was on the books by early afternoon," Colin told him.

"Has anyone else taken the wager?"

"Of course," Colin answered. "A wager that large is bound to attract attention."

"Your father's?" Jarrod asked.

"Thankfully no," Colin replied, refilling his coffee cup and taking a sip of the brew. "But there are several others who can't afford to lose that amount."

"Who?" Jarrod demanded.

"Carville, Jackson, Munford, and several others."

"For or against?"

"Those I mentioned are betting on you," Colin told him. "The others are wagering against it."

"I haven't looked at the books lately," Jonathan said. "So tell us, who wagered what?"

"Yes." Courtland was fairly chomping at the bit for details. "Who did what?"

"Lord Dunbridge recorded a wager he made with Jarrod," Colin answered.

Griff scowled. Dunbridge wasn't one of their contemporaries. And as far as he knew, Jarrod was barely acquainted with the man. "What sort of wager would you have with a dandy like Lord Dunbridge?"

"A thousand-pound wager," Colin answered.

"Jupiter!" Barclay exclaimed.

"Must be a sure thing," Courtland added.

"Far from it, I'd say," Colin replied. "Lord Dunbridge

wagered a thousand pounds that he would marry a certain young lady at the end of the season."

"At least he had the good manners not to mention her by name," Jarrod said.

"Oh, but he did," Colin told him. "*I* had the good manners not to mention her by name, but Dunbridge wrote it out for all to see."

"I don't believe it!" Jarrod was outraged at that breach of etiquette. One might mention a mistress or a widow or a woman of dubious character in wagers of this nature, but never an unmarried young lady of good family.

"Believe it," Colin said. "It's there in plain English." He stood up, then walked to the bell and summoned a footman to bring the current betting book.

The footman returned moments later with the book in hand. Colin handed it to Jarrod.

The entry page was dated with the day's date, time, and year. Several gentlemen had scrawled their names beneath the wager, recording wagers of their own on the outcome, including the three gentlemen Colin mentioned, all of whom were betting on Jarrod.

Jarrod read the recorded wager aloud. "I, Reginald Blanchard, fourth Viscount Dunbridge, do record this wager of one thousand pounds with Jarrod, fifth Marquess of Shepherdston: I wager that Miss Sarah Eckersley and I shall be married by His Grace, the archbishop of Canterbury, at Westminster Abbey at season's end. Lord Shepherdston wagers that I shan't marry Miss Eckersley at season's end or at any other time. The cash to be paid at the outcome." Jarrod finished reading the entry and raked his fingers through his hair. "Bloody hell!"

"What on earth possessed you to wager a thousand pounds on Lord Dunbridge's proposed nuptials?" Griff was astonished by the amount and by Jarrod's uncharacteristic behavior.

"I'm acquainted with the young lady he hopes to marry."

"And?" Griff prompted.

"Eckersley." Colin snapped his fingers. "Wasn't that the name of the young woman you danced with at Esme Harralson's ball last season? The night I met Gillian?"

Jarrod didn't answer.

Colin frowned. "Jarrod?"

"Yes," Jarrod ground out. "And I can guarantee Dunbridge won't win his wager, because I won't allow it."

"Is the young lady a relative or ward?" Courtland asked.

"No," Jarrod answered, "but she may as well be, for her aunt has asked me to keep Dunbridge at bay."

"How do you intend to do that?" Jonathan inquired.

"I'm escorting her and her aunt to Lady Garrison's tonight," Jarrod said.

# Chapter 17

*His conduct still right, with his argument wrong.*
—*Oliver Goldsmith, 1728–1774*

"*He's here.*" *Sarah stepped back from the window over-* looking the front door entrance and breathed a prayer of thanks that their bedchamber faced the street. She bent to gather her tiny reticule, fan, invitation, and dance card from where she'd left them on the bed.

The engraved invitations and the dance card had been delivered to their room shortly after lunch. Sarah and Lady Dunbridge had been thrilled to receive them and the personal note from their hostess commending them for their courage and determination to fulfill Reverend Eckersley's dying request.

Sarah hadn't understood the significance of the note until Aunt Etta had calmly explained that by informing Lady Garrison that Sarah's participation in the season was at the behest of her dying father, Lord Shepherdston had opened the doors of the ton that had been previously closed to them because they were in mourning. They had only had a few hours in which to prepare for the ball, but that had been proven to be a mixed blessing because there had been no time to worry about what to wear or how they would be received.

"Hurry, Aunt Etta," Sarah urged. "Jays is a great believer in punctuality."

"Is that so?" Lady Dunbridge arched an eyebrow.

Sarah thrust her aunt's fan and invitation into Lady Dunbridge's hands and nodded.

"Couldn't prove it by me," Lady Dunbridge declared. "He kept me waiting ten minutes at breakfast and I believe it's only fair that I return the favor."

"Aunt Etta . . ."

"Let him wait, Sarah," Lady Dunbridge said. "It does a man good. They're always rushing about. Hurrying here and there. Chomping at the bit." She waved her arms. "I've never known a man who knew how and when to take his time."

"But—"

"Let him wait. It will remind him that he isn't quite the master of all he surveys and it will give him something to which to look forward." Lady Dunbridge reached out and smoothed a stray lock of Sarah's hair into place. "And it will keep *you* from seeming overly eager for his company."

Sarah frowned. "We'll be late to Lady Garrison's."

Lady Dunbridge shook her head. "We aren't going to be late. But it wouldn't matter if we were, as long as you are worth waiting for." She smiled at her niece, then turned Sarah around so that she could see her reflection in the mirror. "And we've made certain that you are worth waiting for."

Jarrod arrived at Ibbetson's Hotel at half past seven o'clock of the evening. When they appeared in the hotel lobby, the ladies from Helford Green had kept him waiting a full ten minutes.

"Good evening, Lord Shepherdston."

Jarrod halted his impatient pacing and turned to greet them. "Good evening, Miss Eckersley, Lady Dunbridge."

He noticed Sarah's hair first. Her thick, curly red hair was piled into a loose bun on the top of her head and held into place by a black velvet-covered clasp. A dozen or so long tendrils had been allowed to escape the bun and curled artfully around her face and neck. Her hairstyle was simple and elegant and it suited her completely.

Jarrod's brown eyes darkened. He would have liked to have seen more of her, but she was enveloped from shoulders to shoes in black. Black gloves. Black stockings. Black shoes. Black velvet evening cape. The same black velvet cape she'd worn to his house the night before.

"We'd better hurry if we want to avoid arriving late," Sarah reminded him, lifting her skirts in her hand and moving toward the doorway.

"You're beautiful." Jarrod said the first thing that came to mind and realized it was the absolute truth.

"How can you tell?" Sarah asked. "When you haven't seen my gown yet?"

Jarrod suddenly found himself hard-pressed to keep from imagining what she was or was not wearing beneath her cloak.

"I don't have to see your gown to know that it's a most becoming garment and that you look beautiful in it," he replied in a husky tone of voice that bore little resemblance to his usual speaking voice.

Jarrod's voice sent shivers up and down Sarah's spine. "You're too kind, Lord Shepherdston." She looked up at him from beneath the cover of her lashes, then gave him another brilliant smile.

"I'm not the least bit kind," Jarrod said. "I'm speaking the truth."

"Then I appreciate your honesty," Sarah said. "And you needn't worry, for I'm wearing a very proper evening gown beneath my cloak."

She had read his mind. "I'm relieved to hear it," he answered.

"I thought you might be." Sarah chuckled. "And may I say that you look very handsome in your evening clothes?"

There was no denying that a powerful attraction was suddenly at work, for the very air they breathed was charged with electricity.

"You may indeed." He leaned close enough to catch a tantalizing whiff of the fragrance Sarah had used to rinse her hair. Lemons and roses, with a hint of vanilla.

"I prefer what you were wearing last night," Sarah said in a lowered voice. "But you're almost as handsome fully dressed."

Jarrod swallowed hard. "The clothes I wore last night are only appropriate for quiet evenings at home, but I thank you for the compliment just the same."

"You're welcome, Jays," Sarah said. "What a coincidence! Because the clothes I wore last night are only appropriate for quiet evenings at home, so I hope I shall have the opportunity to spend another quiet evening at home with you. And that I shall have the pleasure of seeing you dressed that way again soon."

Damned if she wasn't trying to seduce him again with her husky voice and that expression in her eyes. Jarrod's body tightened in response and his imagination ran rampant as he began to speculate on Sarah's definition of a very proper evening gown.

Lady Dunbridge cleared her throat. "I apologize for interrupting, my dears, but you did arrange for us to receive invitations to Lady Garrison's ball, Lord Shepherdston, and I would be remiss in my duty as a chaperone if I didn't suggest that we at least make an appearance." She patted Jarrod's arm. "Richmond is a distance and I, for one, would like to avoid the worst of the traffic."

Jarrod blinked in bemusement, then flinched as if she'd scalded him. "Lady Dunbridge."

"Very good, Lord Shepherdston," Lady Dunbridge drawled in a patronizing tone. "You remembered my name. Did you also remember that I am supposed to accompany you to Lady Garrison's?"

"Yes, ma'am." Jarrod nodded.

"Then I suggest we exit the hotel and climb into your handsome coach in order that we may begin the journey," Lady Dunbridge replied, taking up her evening shawl and fan and leading the way through the front entrance of the hotel and down the gravel walkway to Shepherdston's coach.

"Shall we?" Jarrod asked, offering Sarah his arm.

Sarah tucked her gloved hand into the crook of Jarrod's elbow as they followed her aunt out the door.

Jarrod handed the ladies into the comfortable coach, then climbed in and sat down. Etiquette demanded that when riding with ladies, a gentleman should ride with his back to the driver on the seat facing the back of the coach. That seating arrangement was meant to keep ladies, especially unmarried ladies, from being pressed against a gentleman's body and prevent their suffering *mal de mer* from the swaying of the coach, but it did nothing to prevent a gentleman from looking his fill at the ladies seated across from him or prevent him from enjoying the view.

Jarrod focused his gaze on a spot above Sarah's head and pretended he was unaffected by her closeness. But his sole concern was keeping his body under control while the enticing scent of lemon and roses conjured up erotic visions of bathtubs and soft, wet, slippery skin.

"We neglected to thank you for securing our invitation this evening," Lady Dunbridge spoke at last, hoping to diffuse some of the tension in the coach.

"Lady Garrison was happy to extend the invitation," Jarrod said. "She'd only excluded you because she knows you're in mourning for Reverend Eckersley. Once I explained that Reverend Eckersley's dying request was that Sarah attend the season, Lady Garrison was delighted to have you as her guests."

"Thank you for making it possible all the same," Lady Dunbridge said. "For we want Sarah to have as many opportunities as possible in order to catch the eye of a young suitor."

Jarrod looked at Sarah. "I don't see how she could fail to catch the eye of a young suitor."

"I agree completely," Lady Dunbridge told him. "The trick isn't so much in catching the eyes of potential suitors as it is in winnowing out the unsuitable ones." She smiled at Jarrod. "I don't come to town as often as I once did and I haven't kept current on the list of fortune hunters, gamblers, imbibers, womanizers, and general ne'er-do-wells we wish to avoid. I do hope that we may depend on you to help us in that regard and to keep Reggie Blanchard at bay."

"You may depend upon it," he replied. "I won't let you down."

"Thank heavens," Lady Dunbridge breathed. "For I must admit I was dreading the heavy responsibility of choosing a suitable husband for my niece. Try as I might, I cannot seem to judge character on a moment's acquaintance. . . ."

Sarah looked up and met Jarrod's gaze. "I suppose it's a result of years of listening to Papa's sermons on Matthew 7:1." She paused, waiting for Jarrod to repeat the verse, and when he didn't, she added, "Come now, Lord Shepherdston, I know Papa taught you scripture."

"For God's sake, Sarah, it's been over twenty years. I don't remember every line of scripture."

"For God's sake, you should, Jays." She gave him a smug smile at her play on words. "I do."

"Matthew 7:1." Jarrod fumbled for a Bible verse that fit the topic. " 'By their fruits ye shall know them.' "

"That's Matthew 7:20," she said. "Matthew 7:1 is 'Judge not, that ye be not judged.' " She spread her hands, palms up. "Like Aunt Etta, I appear to be no judge of character at all."

Jarrod waited for Sarah to congratulate him on dredging one bit of scripture from the depths of his childhood memories and was strangely disappointed when she didn't. "I wouldn't say that you're no judge of character," he said, resuming the threads of their conversation. "You know enough not to want Reggie Blanchard, despite his wealth and breeding."

"That's true," Sarah answered. "But only because I've had occasion to be around Lord Dunbridge enough to discern his character." She looked at him from beneath the cover of her lashes. "Matthew 7:20."

He puffed up with pride like a peacock, but his pride was short-lived.

"I've no experience with any other men. Except you."

Jarrod squirmed on his seat. "That's as it should be, Miss Eckersley," he said. "You are an unmarried lady. You're supposed to be inexperienced."

"Yes," Sarah said, rather morosely, "unless the magistrate and Lord Dunbridge have their way, then my lack of experience is going to ensure that I find myself the unwilling participant in Lord Dunbridge's wedding."

"No one is going to force you to marry Dunbridge," Jarrod told her.

"Really?" Sarah leaned forward.

Jarrod nodded. "*I'll* see to it."

"How?" Sarah held her breath.

"By finding someone else to marry you."

Sarah released the breath she'd been holding and did her best to hide her disappointment as she looked over at Jarrod. "I suppose that's as it should be, Lord Shepherdston," she said softly, tossing his phrase back at him. "I've done everything I know to do. . . ."

Jarrod frowned.

"The rest is up to you."

"Sarah . . ." Why had he been so eager to promise something over which he had no real control? He wasn't her legal guardian. He wasn't a relative. He couldn't force her to marry the man of his choosing or keep her from marrying one not of his choosing. The only thing Jarrod could legally do was marry her himself and he wasn't prepared to do that. Jarrod clamped his lips together and focused on the small window at the rear of the coach.

Sarah bit her bottom lip and quickly turned to look out the side window, fighting the sting of tears, and her growing frustration with Jarrod for being so eager to give her away.

*It was only a few miles as the crow flies from Ibbet-*son's Hotel to the Garrisons' magnificent estate in Richmond, but the crush of vehicles heading out of Mayfair for Lady Garrison's ball and the crush of vehicles heading into

Mayfair and into town for the opera or to Vauxhall Gardens made for slow going.

The atmosphere in the coach had turned decidedly chilly and Jarrod concluded that it would have been much faster, and a great deal less torturous, to walk. He was just about to call a halt to the driver in order to get out and do just that when the journey came to a merciful end. Jarrod breathed a sigh of relief as he alighted from the coach before it rolled to a stop. He wasn't sure he could have managed an additional block in such close quarters. Jarrod had thought Sarah's attempts at seduction were torture, but he soon learned that her silence was worse. He preferred the daringly outrageous Sarah to the one who bit her bottom lip and blinked back tears. He didn't like seeing her suffer, especially when he realized that he'd been the one to cause it.

Jarrod waited as the coachman pulled down the steps, then watched as he extended a hand to assist Sarah from the coach to the pavement, then did the same for Lady Dunbridge.

"Shall we?" Jarrod offered Lady Dunbridge his arm.

She shook her head. "See to Sarah. I'll follow."

Jarrod did as she asked, reluctantly offering Sarah his arm.

She placed her gloved hand on his arm and allowed him to lead her up the steps and into the house. Lady Dunbridge followed.

The Garrisons' butler met them at the door.

Jarrod placed his engraved invitation in the butler's hand, then leaned close enough to give the butler their names.

Lord Shepherdston, Lady Dunbridge, and Miss Eckersley," the man announced.

They stepped forward.

Sarah turned her back to Jarrod and untied the cords on her cape. She shrugged the garment off her shoulders and handed it to the waiting maid while Jarrod deposited his hat and coat with a footman.

He turned back to Sarah and froze when she turned to face him.

Her very proper evening gown was made of a bronze silk and bordered in black velvet. It shimmered when she moved and fit her like a second skin, molding itself to the curves of her body and thrusting her breasts into prominence. The design of the dress was elegant and simple. And as Jarrod attempted to focus his gaze on something other than her velvet-edged décolletage, he realized that the design suited the purpose. It was designed as a simple and elegant means of torturing the human male.

The wide neckline was modest compared to some of the others he'd seen. It covered the essentials, but it wasn't nearly modest enough for Jarrod's peace of mind. The black velvet ribbon bordering it screamed to be noticed, framing Sarah's décolletage for all to admire. And the fact that she wore no jewelry other than a pair of tiny square black onyx earrings meant there was nothing to distract from the creamy expanse of flesh.

It was almost impossible for Jarrod to look down at her and not feast on the enticing display of cleavage. Any man his height or taller would profit from a unique vantage point where it was possible to see everything except the very tips of her breasts. Fortunately, there were only a handful of men in the ton who could equal or better the Marquess of Shepherdston's stature. Jarrod stared at the offering and sucked in a breath as he remembered the way her breasts had felt in the palm of his hand, the weight and softness of them, and the way the tips had hardened beneath his thumb.

"Do you like it?" Sarah asked.

He scowled at her. "I thought you said you were wearing a very proper evening gown." Blister it! But he hated feeling this way! What had happened to him? And what had happened to her? And when had it happened?

This was Sarah. Sarah of the knobby knees, bright orange hair, freckles, and flat chest. Sweet, innocent Sarah who had never tempted him before. Or presented him with such a moral dilemma.

"It *is* proper," she protested.

He gave a derisive snort. "It might be proper if it came with a shawl or scarf or a fichu attached." He looked down at her again, marveling at the way her bodice clung to the tips of her breasts and continued to keep her covered, despite the rise and fall of her chest as she breathed. "But it isn't proper like that."

"Fichus are hopelessly old-fashioned." Sarah glanced around. "None of the other ladies are wearing them and my neckline isn't nearly as revealing as hers." She nodded toward a young lady wearing pale green, then to a young lady in blue and another in silver. "Or hers. Or hers."

"It is from my vantage point," he growled.

Frowning, Sarah glanced down and realized he was right. She'd never considered that a man as tall as Jays might be able to see more of her figure than she had intended. She shrugged her shoulders. "I didn't realize . . ."

"Don't!" Jarrod hissed through clenched teeth, fighting an almost primal urge to tug at the bodice of her dress. But he couldn't say which he wanted most. To tug it up? Or tug it down?

"Don't what?"

"Don't do that." He hissed a bit louder.

"What?"

"Don't shrug your shoulders," he ordered, staring down at her bodice, studying its construction the way an engineer studied a bridge. "Or bend at the waist. Or lift your arms. Or sit beside any gentleman taller than you. Or dance . . ."

"Don't be ridiculous, Jays."

"Ridiculous? Me?" Jarrod glared at her. "You're the one wearing a scrap of silk that's within a hairsbreadth of revealing your bosom in all its lovely glory. I can't imagine how it stays in place as it is," he told her. But that was a lie. He knew exactly what kept her bodice in place and he also knew that if the room got any warmer, Sarah was in danger of exposing herself to the entire assembly. Heaven only knew what had kept it in place this long. "Blast it, Sarah! The nightgown you wore last evening was less revealing! And it was damp."

Sarah gasped. "Jays, there are people about! Someone might hear you!"

"Someone already has," Lady Dunbridge remarked dryly. "Fortunately, *I* am that someone." She pinned Jarrod with a look. "And you, sir, assured me at breakfast that Sarah had kept her traveling cloak *on* during her visit."

"She did," Jarrod hastily replied. "For all but a moment."

Lady Dunbridge arched an eyebrow. "A moment long enough for you to notice that her nightgown was damp . . ."

It had been impossible for him *not* to notice her nightgown was damp when he'd grabbed handfuls of it, shoving it out of the way so he could pull her against him and caress her bare bottom. But Lady Dunbridge didn't need to know that, so Jarrod kept that bit of information to himself. "It was raining quite heavily when she arrived and steam rose from her garments when she warmed herself by the fire. As velvet is not impervious to the weather, I assumed whatever she wore beneath her cape had to be nearly as damp as the outer garment."

"Nice recovery," Lady Dunbridge said. "It's all stuff and nonsense, but I commend you for being able to engage your brain and think on your feet." She smiled up at Jarrod. "Most men only think with that other part of their anatomy."

Jarrod's jaw dropped open at Lady Dunbridge's impudent reply.

"But you've just proven that you are not most men. Come now, Lord Shepherdston, don't look so surprised. You're a man of the world and far from innocent and I am a woman of three and forty who was married for ten years to a man who only thought with that part of his anatomy. We understand the nature of the beast and what is at stake here. Now," she said, taking advantage of Jarrod's continued silence, "say hello to our host and hostess and ask Sarah to dance."

Jarrod shook his head. "I don't think she ought to dance in that dress."

Lady Dunbridge bit the inside of her cheek to keep from laughing at the obstinate expression on his face. "Lord Shepherdston, the purpose of our being here is to show Sarah off to prospective suitors. Her dress is entirely suited to that purpose."

He drew his brows together in a mighty frown. "It is too well suited for that purpose."

"In your opinion," Sarah retorted.

"Yes," he answered. "In my opinion. And as I am a man, and might be considered a prospective suitor by some, my opinion is valid."

"Of course it is," Lady Dunbridge soothed.

"I came here to dance," Sarah told him. "And I intend to do just that."

Jarrod looked down at her nicely displayed bounty and made a command decision. "The only dancing you're going to be doing in that dress this evening is with me."

"Thank you for asking, Lord Shepherdston," Sarah replied, turning the tables on him by placing her hand in his and leading him toward the dance floor. "I'd be delighted."

# Chapter 18

*I feel again a spark of that ancient flame.*
—*Virgil, 70–19 B.C.*

"*That was nicely done.*"

"I thought so," Lady Dunbridge replied softly to the man who spoke from behind her right shoulder. "She handles herself well and I'm very proud of her."

"I was talking about you."

"Oh." It was all she could think to say, for his presence and the sound of his voice sent shivers up and down her spine.

He placed his hands on her shoulders. "I got your note, Henrietta."

She closed her eyes and savored the feel of his hands on her person. "I didn't know if you would come."

"Why wouldn't I come?" he asked. "When I've been waiting for you to send for me for years. Why didn't you?"

Lady Dunbridge turned around and looked at the man with whom she had once fallen deeply in love. She hadn't seen him except at a distance for years, yet he hadn't changed. Oh, there were a few wrinkles at the corners of his mouth, a network of fine lines surrounding his blue eyes, and a sprinkling of gray at his temples, but he was every bit as handsome as he had been twenty years earlier. He was still the man she loved. "I wanted to," she answered. "So many times. I struggled to keep from begging you to come to me in every letter I wrote you."

"You wrote to me?" That came as a surprise to him, for the only note he'd ever received from her was the one she'd written that morning asking for his help. "After your husband died?"

"And before," she admitted in a whisper. "I knew it was wrong. We were both still married, but I wrote to you anyway. I poured out my heart and soul to you. But you never answered my letters, and eventually I stopped sending them." She hadn't quit writing letters to him, but she had stopped posting them. "I thought you'd forgotten about me or that you'd reconciled with your wife. Before I knew it, one year faded into the next and twenty years had gone by."

"There was no possibility of reconciliation, Henrietta," he replied. "My wife didn't want it." Lord Mayhew ran his hands over her bare shoulders and down her arms.

Lady Dunbridge shivered at his touch as her nerve endings suddenly remembered the gentle caress of a lover's hand. "I'm sorry," she said. "I had hoped that you could persuade her to reconsider. . . ."

Lord Mayhew managed a smile. "I didn't want her to reconsider," he admitted. "Not after I met you."

Lady Dunbridge looked up at him. "But . . ." She had spent years trying to forget him, years praying for forgiveness for loving a married man—especially during the years that she remained married, but estranged, from her husband. In the nineteen years she'd lived with her niece and brother-in-law at the rectory in Helford Green, Henrietta Dunbridge had remembered Robert Mayhew in every prayer. And her prayer for him had never varied. "I prayed for you," she confided. "I prayed for us both."

"For what did you pray, Henrietta?"

"I prayed that we would both know love once again."

Lord Mayhew stared down at her. "Your prayers were answered, Henrietta," he whispered. "When I look in your eyes I know that I am loved. That I have been loved for a very long time."

"Oh, Robert . . ." Lady Dunbridge trembled on the brink of tears.

"Look into my eyes," he instructed, "and you'll see the love I have for you. It's been there from the start." He pressed his finger against her lips when she would have spoken, then tenderly traced the contour of her bottom lip. "I looked at you twenty years ago and suddenly, I knew love."

"What happened?" she asked. "If we love each other so much, why haven't we been together? Why didn't you answer my letters?"

"I never received your letters," he said simply. "And I'm quite certain you never received mine."

Lady Dunbridge frowned. "You wrote me?" she asked, in an echo of his earlier question.

"Nearly every day after you left London and returned to Somerset," Lord Mayhew told her. "But my letters were returned unopened."

Henrietta's eyes widened as suspicion dawned. "Calvin?" The house in Somerset was the Dunbridge county seat. It had been in the family for generations and staffed entirely by loyal family retainers who collected and sorted the mail.

Lord Mayhew shook his head. "His butler or secretary, most likely." He sighed. "I should have used my wife's name on the outside of the first letters instead of my own so there would have been less chance of them being returned to me. But I never dreamed your husband would object. . . ." He shrugged his shoulders. "Still, I should have known better. A gentleman doesn't correspond with another gentleman's wife without permission and, apparently, Lord Dunbridge withheld his permission."

"Why?" she asked. "He didn't want me. He was living in London with his mistress."

"But you were Caesar's wife," Lord Mayhew said softly.

"And Caesar's wife must be above suspicion," Lady Dunbridge quoted bitterly.

"I didn't give up," Lord Mayhew continued. "I tried

again when I learned that you were living in Helford Green taking care of your sister's family." He smiled down at her. "You inspire great loyalty in the men who care about you, Henrietta."

Lady Dunbridge closed her eyes and pictured her brother-in-law's face. "He didn't."

"He did," Lord Mayhew answered. "The letters I wrote you at the rectory in Helford Green were returned opened, along with a note advising me of the wages of sin—particularly the sin of adultery."

"We never . . ." she began.

"Literary adultery," he clarified. "For want of a better term. Although we had never physically consummated our 'adulterous' union, we had committed adultery in our hearts because our letters spoke of our passionate feelings for one another. And Reverend Eckersley warned me that by writing you and encouraging you to write me, I was putting your immortal soul at risk. For it was simply a matter of time before we sinned in the flesh." He stared down at her. "He knew my feelings, since he'd read my letters, and I think we can safely assume that he knew your feelings as well."

"I inspire something in the men who care about me," Lady Dunbridge remarked. "But I'm not certain I would call it loyalty."

"What would you call it?"

Lady Dunbridge thought for a moment before she replied. "Fear. My husband feared I would besmirch his name. My brother-in-law feared I would leave him to care for himself and his daughter alone." Lady Dunbridge glared up at the ceiling and stamped her foot. "Simon Eckersley, how could you?"

"Don't be too angry with him. In his own way, he was looking out for you."

"He was looking out for my soul," Lady Dunbridge snapped. "And there was no need for that once Calvin died. There was no danger of adultery. Calvin was dead and so was your wife. We were free."

"Yes, we were," Lord Mayhew agreed. "But losing you was what Reverend Eckersley feared most. And he was right to fear it because I intended to come for you after your husband died. Unfortunately, Serena's death had horrible unexpected and inexplicable repercussions. Within months of Serena's passing, my wife's sister and her husband were dead. I was left as guardian of their son, and Jarrod needed me. My life and responsibilities changed overnight. And although I desperately wanted to marry you, I knew in my heart that Jarrod wasn't able to absorb another upheaval in his life. He needed stability. He needed security. He needed my love. And he needed to know that I was constant. I owed him that. And I was determined to be available whenever he needed me. I was determined to give him my undivided attention."

"Perhaps it's just as well," Lady Dunbridge said at last. "Because Simon and Sarah needed me just as much as Lord Shepherdston needed you."

Lord Mayhew reached over and lifted her chin with the tip of his index finger. "Am I mistaken, Henrietta, or are you under the impression that I've given up?"

Lady Dunbridge held her breath. "Have you?"

"Not at all," he vowed. "The good reverend was right. It was simply a matter of time before we sinned in the flesh. I wanted you then, Henrietta, and I want you now. Body and soul."

"Robert, it's been twenty years," she murmured, suddenly shy and uncertain.

"Impossible," he said softly, "because you don't look a day older than twenty."

She smiled. "You said the same thing twenty years ago."

"It was true then," Lord Mayhew said. "And it's true now." He began to massage her shoulders in a slow, relaxing motion. "You're every bit as beautiful today as you were twenty years ago." He took a step forward, then leaned close enough to whisper, "So, my dear Henrietta, tell me how I can be of service."

"I want you to help me arrange a marriage."

Lord Mayhew lifted an eyebrow. Her answer wasn't quite what he'd expected, but he was willing. "Dare I hope that it might be ours?"

"After all these years?"

Lord Mayhew saw the hope in her eyes, remembered the girl she had been, and smiled. "I loved you twenty years ago. I wanted to marry you twenty years ago, but we were both married to other people. Now we're free and I find myself still hopelessly in love with you." He looked at her. "And if we wait much longer, we'll be too old to enjoy the honeymoon, so Henrietta, I'm asking if you will do me the honor of becoming my wife?"

Lady Dunbridge's eyes sparkled with unshed tears. "Oh, Robert . . ."

He looked down at her. "Shall I take that to mean yes?"

"Yes!"

Lord Mayhew thought his heart might burst from the joy. He hadn't realized how much he'd loved Henrietta Dunbridge, how much he'd missed her, and how much he'd longed to make her his until he'd walked into the Garrisons' ballroom and seen her again. And she hadn't changed. She was still the beautiful young woman with reddish blonde hair and light brown eyes with whom he'd fallen in love all those years ago. "Shall we make it a small and intimate wedding? Or would you like a huge society affair?"

"I should like to make it a small, intimate, double wedding," she clarified. "And soon."

Lord Mayhew frowned. "With whom would you like to share our nuptials?"

"Sarah." She smiled up at him. "I've waited twenty years to taste your lips and to feel your arms about me and I don't want to wait a moment longer than necessary, but I have to see Sarah settled first."

"I can secure a special license in the morning," he replied. "And we can make arrangements with your niece and her intended." He leaned down to whisper, "Tell me, Henrietta, where would you like to honeymoon?"

Henrietta blushed. "In whatever bed you call home."

"That's my darling girl." Lord Mayhew was fairly crowing with pride.

"I'm three and forty," she reminded him. "I haven't shared a bed with a man in two and twenty years or felt passion for much longer than that." She blushed again.

"Oh, my precious girl." Lord Mayhew reached out and smoothed a stray lock of hair from her face. The fact that they were at a public ball was the only thing that kept him from kissing her senseless. "I knew Dunbridge kept a mistress in a house on Portman Square, but I didn't realize that he had neglected his wife so entirely."

"I was barren," she answered succinctly. "Once he discovered that, there was no need for him to pay attention to me."

Lord Mayhew frowned. "Are you certain you were barren? Because I had heard it said that Dunbridge had been rendered barren by some childhood illness or injury and that his first wife's family threatened to sue when they learned of it. He'd married her in order to secure his fortune and her family felt that he had married her falsely by promising to make her not only his viscountess, but the mother of his heir."

"I had no idea," Lady Dunbridge breathed.

"None, Henrietta?" He gave her a crooked smile. "I think you're smarter than that."

"I had no idea when I married him," she said. "And he blamed me, but I always thought he was at fault. After all, he had a previous wife and a mistress who had never conceived." She shrugged. "Of course, I couldn't prove it unless I produced a child and, well, that was impossible without breaking my vows and . . ." She looked up at Lord Mayhew.

"Breaking your vows was something you simply could not do," he replied gently. "Even for me."

"I wanted to," she admitted. "And I've regretted not doing so for more years than I care to count, but we met at the wrong time in our lives. Had we met a few years earlier or a few years later, things would have been different."

"Very different," he agreed.

"So, tell me, Robert, how do you feel about children?"

He lit up with pleasure. "Is that a possibility?"

She nodded. "I still have my monthly courses."

He frowned. "A minor nuisance well worth the bother if it means we might have children."

"I can't promise to give you a son," she answered, her brown eyes sparkling, "but I promise to try." She took out her handkerchief and dabbed at her eyes.

"A son. A daughter. Either. Both." His words tumbled out, one atop the other. "I'd be thrilled. And so would my current heir. He's always told me I should have been a father."

Lady Dunbridge paused. "Your current heir?"

Lord Mayhew nodded. "My nephew, Jarrod. The Marquess of Shepherdston."

"Shepherdston?" Lady Dunbridge pursed her lips and frowned. "Oh, dear . . ."

He leaned close. "Henrietta, darling, what is it?"

"I knew Shepherdston was your nephew and your godson, but I didn't realize he was also your heir. . . ."

"My darling, Jarrod will be delighted at the news that we're getting married."

"Of course he will," she said. "It will solve his problem."

"What problem?"

"The problem of what to do about Sarah." Lady Dunbridge began twisting her handkerchief into knots and nodded toward the dance floor, where Lord Shepherdston and Sarah were squared off in the quadrille. "My niece."

Lord Mayhew followed her gaze to where Jarrod stood facing a slender red-haired girl in a bronze-colored evening gown and grinned. "Is that the marriage you wanted me to help you arrange?"

"Yes. I had hoped that you might be willing to do a favor for an old friend and playact."

"Playact?"

Lady Dunbridge nodded. "I wanted you to pretend to pay court to Sarah in order to make Lord Shepherdston reconsider what he'd told her about you being a much more suitable lover for her than a younger man." She paused to catch her breath. "I had no idea that the sight of you and the sound of your voice would remind me of how much I loved you—how much I still love you."

"Say it again," he commanded.

"I love you, Robert. I shall love you until I die and beyond."

"God, Henrietta, I've waited close to half my life to hear you say that."

"I don't really want a double wedding," Lady Dunbridge confided. "I don't want to compete with another bride on my wedding day—even if Sarah is the other bride. But if you and I get married right away, there will be no reason for Lord Shepherdston to marry Sarah. He'll know that she'll have a home with us. And he'll know that you will always take care of her."

"Which is why you suggested a double wedding . . ."

Lady Dunbridge nodded. "Shepherdston isn't in any hurry to wed and Sarah's young enough that she can afford to wait for him to make up his mind—now that he's sworn not to let Reggie Blanchard force her hand. Whereas, I've waited *years* to marry you."

Lord Mayhew stared at the two dancers. "Tell me, my love, does your niece happen to have a strawberry birthmark?"

"Yes," Lady Dunbridge answered. "She does. On her . . ." She blushed again.

"Derrière?"

Lady Dunbridge nodded. "How did you know?"

"I caught a glimpse of it early this morning when I arrived at Jarrod's town house for breakfast." He reached down and removed Henrietta's mangled handkerchief from her hands. "Jarrod and I ride together on the Row in the park two days a week and breakfast afterwards. But it was raining this morning and I knew we wouldn't be riding so I arrived for breakfast earlier than expected and inadvertently interrupted a most ardent kiss between Jarrod and a red-haired young lady with nice legs and a strawberry birthmark on her posterior."

"Oh, my . . . Sarah!"

"You knew she was at Jarrod's house alone at five-thirty in the morning?"

Lady Dunbridge shook her head. "I found out afterwards." She looked up at Robert Mayhew and suddenly the words came tumbling out as she explained everything that had happened since they'd been put out of the rectory. "Sarah loves him. She's loved him since she was a little girl. But Lord Shepherdston wants nothing to do with marriage."

Lord Mayhew nodded. "He has reasons for not wanting to marry that reach deep into his childhood. A childhood that was lonely most of the time and exceedingly difficult the rest of the time." He sighed. "I don't pretend to understand all of what he feels, but I know that he feels unlovable, unworthy of being loved."

"I think Sarah understands that," Lady Dunbridge confided. "Or at least, senses it. She's determined not to marry anyone else. As long as he remains unmarried, she's going to do the same—even if that means pursuing the life of a courtesan."

Lord Mayhew didn't like the sound of that. "Do you know anything about Miss Jones's Home for Displaced Women?"

Lady Dunbridge shook her head. "I've never heard of it."

"Your niece was carrying a card with that name and a Portman Square address printed on it. She dropped it on the floor of Jarrod's study."

"Did you say a Portman Square address?"

"Yes, my dear, you heard me correctly."

"Would that address happen to be number forty-seven Portman Square?" she asked.

"It would," he told her. "Do you know it?"

"That house belonged to my husband," Lady Dunbridge said. "He purchased it for his mistress."

"You knew?" he asked gently.

"Of course I knew," she said with a sigh.

"I always wondered," Lord Mayhew told her. "Despite what you may think, his association with her wasn't common knowledge."

"It was to me," Lady Dunbridge answered. "I knew he had a mistress in a house in London. But I didn't know where it was or who owned it until I accidentally came across the deed to it after he died. It was tucked into a packet of correspondence he'd addressed to me. I didn't want the house, but I saw no reason why the new viscount should have it, so I sent the deed to her." She was quiet for a moment. "I'm glad to know she's put it to good use."

Lord Mayhew quirked an eyebrow and bit the inside of his cheek to keep from laughing. "Oh, she's put it to good use, but not to the altruistic good you suppose."

"Running a home for displaced women seems very altruistic," Lady Dunbridge said.

"But things aren't always what they seem," Lord Mayhew reminded her. "That home for displaced women is one of London's most exclusive houses of pleasure."

Lady Dunbridge widened her eyes.

"I know because I've been there many times and was there again this morning."

Lady Dunbridge bit her bottom lip and looked down at the floor in an effort to hide her dismay.

Lord Mayhew reached out and lifted her chin with the tip of his index finger, raising her face so he could look her in the eyes. "I tell you this not to hurt you, Henrietta, but to be completely truthful. I'm a man of normal appetites and have patronized Portman Square many times in the past and enjoyed it."

"But she was my husband's . . ."

"Sssh, my love." He placed his finger against her lips. *"I* knew who she was. I've patronized her house of pleasure because it is convenient and entirely discreet, but I've never sought pleasure from her. I never shared her bed. And this morning I was there for an entirely different reason."

"What reason?" Lady Dunbridge fought to keep the jealousy out of her voice.

"Jarrod sent me to make sure your niece wasn't one of the residents there."

"He knows Sarah isn't . . ."

Lord Mayhew shook his head. "He did, but I did not. He went to great pains not to reveal her identity or even hint that she was a young lady of good family. When I found her card on the floor of his study, I assumed Jarrod had sent for one of Madam—" He caught himself before he said the name he was sure would distress Henrietta. "I assumed she was one of the girls who reside at Portman Square. But Jarrod knew better. He was terrified that your niece meant to make good on her threat. He ordered me to go to Portman Square to interview any red-haired innocents in residence and to make certain they stayed that way until he arrived."

"Did you?"

"I did," he confirmed. "I spent the morning playing whist with three innocent red-haired young women. And I'm happy to report that your niece wasn't among them."

"Thank heavens."

"I paid for the time I spent with the three girls so no one else could purchase them. We spent a couple of hours or so playing half a dozen rubbers of whist. For cash," he said. "It cost me one hundred and eighty-seven pounds of my own money and another one hundred and sixty-three pounds of Jarrod's money to pay my gaming debt to the girls and to purchase the freedom of two of them."

"Only two, Robert?" Lady Dunbridge was surprised. "What about the third one?"

"She chose to stay," he replied. "I tried to dissuade her, but she chose to remain. It was her decision. The point is that Jarrod sent me to protect Sarah's virtue. He isn't immune to her. Believe me, the kiss I witnessed this morning was a prelude to lovemaking. There was no doubt about that. Jarrod wanted her, but he stopped short of taking her."

"He swore nothing happened," Lady Dunbridge muttered indignantly. "He swore she kept her cloak on."

Lord Mayhew smiled. "She had it on. *He* had it hiked almost to her waist, but she was wearing her cloak."

"But he wants a lover and she wants a husband." She looked up at Lord Mayhew. "And I won't allow him to make her his mistress. I can't. Even if that's what she says she wants, because I know that is no life for her."

"You may not be able to prevent his taking her to bed if that's what she wants," he told her. "But we can ensure that he makes it legal."

"How?"

"By reminding him that he compromised a young lady and that I was witness to it."

"Forcing his hand?" She made a clucking sound with her tongue. "Oh, Robert, he isn't going to like that at all and neither is she. Sarah wants him to come to her of his own volition. And I'd rather it happen that way, too."

"I don't know if he'll ever decide to marry her," Lord Mayhew conceded. "But I know he'd agree to it if we forced him. He's too honorable not to. But he's having a very hard time keeping his hands off her, so we'll give nature a chance to take its course."

"How long?" she asked.

"When do you want to get married?"

"Tonight," she answered.

Lord Mayhew laughed. "Tonight is impossible, I'm afraid. I can't purchase a special license until I make a trip to Lambeth Palace tomorrow morning."

"I suppose I can wait until morning."

"Tomorrow it is," he assured her. "At nine?"

Lady Dunbridge nodded. "Do you mind very much if we keep it a secret for a bit?"

Lord Mayhew frowned. "For how long?"

"I'd like to give Sarah a bit more time to do things her way. Maybe he'll fall in love with her. Maybe he'll decide he can't do without her. . . ." Lady Dunbridge paused. "I wish she could stand up for me tomorrow, but given a choice, I'd rather have you. . . ."

"Then that's the way it will be," he promised. "Make some excuse to Sarah tomorrow morning. Shopping or errands to run. I'll meet you outside Ackermann's at eight-thirty," he said. "We can throw a huge celebration later after we've had some time to ourselves. I've waited twenty years, Henrietta. Forgive me if I'm a bit selfish."

"Oh, Robert, I knew you'd understand. And it won't be for long. I promise. If she can't make him fall in love with her, then we'll force his hand."

"In the meantime, we'll leave them alone together as much as possible and hope that they'll be doing what we're going to be doing every chance we get." He leered at her and waggled his eyebrows.

Lady Dunbridge laughed.

"I hope you've had enough of your dry spell, Henrietta," he continued, "because I have lots of ideas to inspire passion and I mean to try them all out on you."

"Just be prepared, Lord Mayhew," she teased, "for I have a few ideas of my own. . . ."

# Chapter 19

*A great flame follows a little spark.*
—*Dante Alighieri, 1265–1321*

"Lord Rob and your aunt seem to be getting along quite famously," Jarrod said, nodding at Lord Mayhew and Lady Dunbridge standing by the dance floor as he and Sarah waited to negotiate the dance steps of the quadrille. "For a couple recently met."

"They're not recently met," Sarah told him, straining to get a good look at Lord Mayhew. "They're renewing an old friendship. Like us."

"Heaven help Lord Rob if that's what they're doing," Jarrod murmured.

"What did you think we were doing?" she asked. "Besides dancing, of course?"

"I'm not certain," he admitted, eyeing her warily. "It looks as if we're only dancing. And it feels as if we're only dancing but I know there's something more. I know I'll be called upon to pay the piper."

"You may relax, Jarrod," Sarah said pertly. "We're only dancing. And it isn't costing you a penny."

"That's what you say, but I keep waiting for you to do something outrageous."

"Such as?"

"Demand another lesson."

"In what?" Sarah opened her eyes wide in a show of innocence.

"Kissing. Seduction. The art of slipping out of a hot, overcrowded ballroom and into the cool night air . . ." He grimaced. "I don't know. Something outrageous."

"Perhaps I've decided to spare you the agony," Sarah told him. "Perhaps I've decided to let someone else further my education." She crossed her fingers as she stretched the truth, then hid her hand in the folds of her skirt so he couldn't see it.

"You certainly dressed for the occasion." He glared down at her bosom. "Tell me, have you the modesty to wear a petticoat beneath it?"

Sarah frowned. So they were back to that again. "How gentlemanly of you to ask!"

He wasn't quite without manners. The tips of his ears turned red as Jarrod had the grace to blush at his own audacity. That was not the sort of question a gentleman generally asked a lady—especially a virginal young lady—in the midst of a ball.

"Tell me, Jays, what is it about my gown you don't like?"

"Nothing," he answered honestly. "Everything."

"That certainly clarifies things," she commented dryly.

He stiffened. "I fail to see the humor in the situation."

"You would if you could see the expression on your face, Jays." She smiled up at him. "You wanted me off your hands. And you're supposed to be helping me find another suitor, yet you scowl at every man who dares look my way."

"My scowl is the only thing keeping you safe," he said.

"Don't be silly," she admonished. "I'm perfectly safe."

He laughed. "Spoken with the true conviction of an innocent who doesn't know how much danger she's in."

"How much danger can there be with you here to protect me?" she demanded.

"More than you know," he said softly.

"You're scowling again."

He glanced at a crowd of young rakes waiting for the present dancers to relinquish their partners. "At the moment, my scowls are the only thing standing between you and certain ruin."

"Cheer up, Jays." Sarah's brown eyes sparkled as she teased him. "We're dancing, yet you look like a man about to meet Madame Guillotine."

"Why shouldn't I?" he countered. "When meeting Madame Guillotine might be easier? And I'm in danger of losing my head either way?"

Sarah's smile grew broader. "Thank you, Jays. I believe that's the nicest thing you've ever said to me."

"I've paid you compliments," he said. "I believe I told you you were beautiful in the coach earlier this evening."

"Yes, you did," Sarah agreed. "And you said my bosom was quite lovely. And I know you mean it because you keep staring down at it as if it were a window full of French pastries you can't wait to sample."

"Blister it, Sarah," he muttered through clenched teeth. "I keep staring at your bosom because I keep waiting for your bodice to relinquish its grip and obey the laws of gravity."

"And what will you do if it does?" she baited, turning her back to him as the steps of the dance took her away, then brought her back to face him. "Sample my pastries?"

Jarrod all but broke out in a sweat. "Stop it, Sarah."

"Stop what, Jays?"

"Stop flirting with me," he warned. "And stop putting images in my head, lest you find yourself with more than you can handle."

"Is it possible, Jays? Are you really in danger of losing your head over me?" There was a hopeful note in her voice that Jarrod couldn't fail to recognize. "Because in all the years I've known you, you never once hinted that you might lose your head for me."

"I'm in danger of losing my patience," he snapped. "And my sense of humor."

"You've already lost your sense of humor," Sarah pointed out.

"Then don't force me to lose my patience," Jarrod cautioned once again. "It's all I have left." He closed his eyes in an attempt to blot out the image Sarah had put there. Images of him sinking to his knees on the Garrisons' marble dance floor in order to kiss and caress and taste the lovely bosom she had arranged just for him. And it was just for him—because Jarrod had no intention of letting any other man get close enough to view the bounty. His body responded to the mental images and Jarrod groaned as dancing became an effort of will.

He stopped suddenly, at the end of a square, and the gentleman dancing beside them careened into him, knocking Jarrod sideways. Sarah missed a step and fell heavily against him. The twin points of her breasts pressed into his chest and her body molded itself against his for a brief second. Jarrod placed his hand at her back to steady her.

Sarah looked up at him, a worried expression on her face. "Did I inadvertently tread on your toes?"

"No."

"You groaned," Sarah informed him. "As if you were in pain. I wondered if I'd trod on your toes."

He couldn't help but smile at her innocence. "My toes are fine."

"Then perhaps you should release me."

Jarrod squeezed his eyes shut. He hadn't realized he was still holding her against his chest until she'd reminded him. Bloody hell, but he was making a cake of himself in front of a hundred or so witnesses. And there didn't seem to be a blasted thing he could do about it. He exhaled, then slid his hand down the line of her spine and over the curve of her bottom, savoring the feel of silk and heat as he did so. He groaned again. Louder.

She frowned. "Are you in pain elsewhere?"

"Most definitely," he answered.

"Is there anything I can do?" she asked.

There were a great many things she could do to alleviate his suffering, Jarrod thought. And all of them involved the sort of things no innocent should know. Damnation, but he ached with need. And all because Sarah tempted him with every breath she took. Bloody hell, but her dress was the most incredible garment he'd ever seen any woman wear. And he fervently hoped, for the sake of his peace of mind and her virtue, that Sarah never wore it again. "I think you've done enough already."

"Have I?"

"You know you have." He looked down at her, fixing his gaze on her soft pink lips instead of her soft breasts and realized they both had the same effect on him. Everything receded except the sight and scent and feel of her in his arms. He wanted very much to kiss her and his arms trembled with restraint as he fought to keep from pressing her closer and covering her lips with his own. It was all Jarrod could do to keep from ushering Sarah from the ballroom, up the stairs to the nearest bedroom, so he could satisfy his curiosity and slake his hunger by finding out what the devil was keeping her dress up.

Sarah looked up at him and Jarrod's body tightened in response as she moistened her lips with the tip of her tongue in a self-conscious gesture that sent his blood rushing southward to the part of his anatomy throbbing against the front of his trousers.

He ached with the need for release and suddenly realized that he couldn't remember ever wanting a woman as much as he wanted Sarah. *Sarah.* He licked his lips, tasted the thin sheen of perspiration dotting his upper lip, and realized he was literally burning with the need to kiss her.

Sarah sighed. "I couldn't help it," she admitted. "It's our anniversary of sorts."

"Oh?" Jarrod quirked an eyebrow at her. "What anniversary is that?"

"The anniversary of our first dance." She stared up at him, willing him to remember. "Last year at—"

"Lady Harralson's gala," he said. "I haven't forgotten."

She nodded. "You spent most of the evening staring at Gillian Davies. And *I* spent most of the evening staring at you."

"You accused me of being afraid to ask Gillian to dance," he said.

"I was jealous," Sarah admitted, "because I thought you were interested in her."

"You thought I wanted to make her my marchioness," he corrected.

"Yes."

"She's happily married to one of my closest friends," Jarrod said.

"Lord Grantham," Sarah said. "Yes, I know. I read about their marriage in the paper shortly afterward."

"I was there that evening to get a look at her before Colin approached her father. I heard there was rumor going round about her and I wanted to see for myself what sort of young lady she was." That wasn't the complete truth, but it was all that Jarrod could reveal without betraying Gillian's secret and the trust of his Free Fellows League comrades.

"You told me then that you weren't in the market for a wife."

"And you asked why I was there if I hadn't come to find a wife," he remembered.

"Would you believe I came to dance?" Sarah repeated the question he'd asked her.

"You don't appear to be dancing." Jarrod answered with the same answer Sarah had given him.

They weren't. They'd stopped in the middle of the square and the other dancers had continued around them.

"Only because you haven't asked me," Sarah said.

Jarrod offered her his arm. "Shall we rejoin the dancers?"

Sarah shook her head.

"No?" He took her arm just the same and steered her out of the square, off the dance floor to the sidelines.

"I prefer to wait for a waltz," she admitted. "Do you think Lady Garrison allows the waltz? Lady Harralson did. We waltzed the last time we danced."

It had been the only time they'd ever danced, but Jarrod

didn't see the point of reminding her of that. "Shall we stay on the sidelines and watch or would you rather we withdraw to the refreshment tables?" he asked politely.

Sarah glanced down at her feet, then took a deep breath and looked up to meet his gaze. "I'd prefer that we withdraw to the Garrisons' garden. I've heard it's quite lovely this time of evening."

Jarrod's breath caught in his throat. He coughed. "Sarah, did it ever occur to you that you might be a little too bold for your own good?"

"It occurred to me," she admitted, "but I'm only bold with you because you aren't very good at reading between the lines. I decided it was best to tell you what I want."

"I excel at reading between the lines." Jarrod took exception to the fact that she considered him too dull-witted to see through her game of seduction. "When it's a book I'm eager to read. But this . . ." He raked his fingers through his hair. "Sarah, I'm only human and you're driving me to distraction."

"It's time someone did," she told him. "You've been alone too long."

"I'm alone because I prefer it," he said. Because it was less dangerous. As long as he was alone, his heart was safe. He couldn't be hurt. He couldn't have his heart trampled or fall prey to the madness that was love. "And because I've no room in my life for distractions."

"No room?" She pretended not to understand. "You've an awfully big house," she said. "And Aunt Etta and I don't take up much room."

"You know what I mean."

"That you would rather be alone than share your empty life with a woman?"

"Yes," he said firmly.

Sarah bit her bottom lip. "Any woman or am I the exception?"

"Any woman," he said.

Sarah exhaled. "I'm relieved to hear it."

"And while we're on the subject, you would do well to learn that when it comes to women, I, like most gentlemen, prefer to do the chasing."

Sarah stuck her tongue out at him as she'd done when she was a child and knew he was saying things he didn't mean in order to drive her away. "Liar."

Jarrod blinked. It had been years since anyone, male or female, had had the audacity to call him a liar to his face. "What did you call me?" he asked in a haughty tone designed to make her cower in fright before turning to run.

But Sarah was made of sterner stuff. "I called you a liar, Jays."

"If you were a man, I'd call you out for such an insult."

"If I were a man, we wouldn't be having this conversation," Sarah reminded him. "And you wouldn't feel the need to lie."

"I am not lying," he ground out.

"Yes, you are," she said, waving off his sputtered denials. "I could always tell when you were lying."

"How?" he demanded.

"You don't look me in the eye when you're trying to lie and your actions always betray you," she explained. "You say one thing, but do another."

Jarrod frowned at her logic.

"When was the last time you chased a woman?"

He couldn't answer.

"There are plenty of women in London who are a lot bolder and prettier than I am," she continued. "If you enjoyed the chase, as you call it, as much as you want me to believe, you'd be out doing it. Instead of staying home at night."

"I'd be a fool to chase women during the London season," Jarrod countered. "When I've no interest in marrying and when every single young woman in town is looking to find a husband. Preferably a rich, titled one."

"Then chase the married ones." Sarah glanced around. "I'm quite sure there are any number of married ladies who would be glad for you to chase them."

Jarrod looked affronted. "I don't dally with other men's wives."

"So, you don't chase unmarried ladies and you don't dally with other men's wives. . . ." Sarah pursed her lips. "So, what does that leave? Widows? Servants? Women of dubious character? Actresses? Dancers? Opera singers?"

"Widows are often just as eager to marry a marquess as virginal young ladies," he informed her. "And a gentleman doesn't slake his desires on the women in his household who feel they cannot refuse his attention."

"So," she drawled, tapping her index finger against her cheek, "you don't chase widows or slake your desires on your female servants. So that means you must chase women of dubious character." She looked him in the eye. "Except that you don't. Because you're rich and titled, and actresses, dancers, opera singers, and women of dubious character don't require chasing. They require gifts of jewelry and cash. And you've plenty of cash to buy jewelry, don't you, Jays? You can pay for companionship and pay to be rid of it."

Jarrod met her gaze. "Did it ever occur to you that I might have a special lady friend with whom I share a pillow?"

It had. And Sarah fervently prayed that was not the case. She selfishly hoped Jarrod paid for his companionship instead of sharing a pillow with a special lady friend. "Do you?"

"Yes."

"Thank goodness." Sarah breathed a sigh of relief.

"You don't mind?" he asked.

"Of course not," Sarah said. "I'd prefer you pay for your companionship. That makes it business. And when it's business, there's less chance of romantic entanglements."

"Didn't you understand what I said, Sarah?" Jarrod was bewildered by her reaction. "I said I have a special lady friend with whom I share a pillow."

"You lied," she replied.

"I looked you in the eye and said yes."

"And you lied," Sarah told him. "And for that you must pay a penance."

"How did you arrive at that conclusion?"

"You're a man of honor, Jays, and no man of honor would ever admit such a thing to an innocent young lady like me."

Jarrod snorted. Her logic was convoluted at best, but she'd arrived at the truth just the same.

"And now, it's time."

He gave her a wary look. "For what?"

"To pay the piper and do your penance."

"Sarah . . ." He said her name in a tone of voice that was part warning and part seduction.

"I want more lessons, Jays, and I believe you mentioned kissing, seduction, the art of slipping out of a hot, over-crowded ballroom and into the cool night air, or something equally outrageous." She gave him what she hoped was a come-hither look. She was playing with fire and knew it. "Besides, aren't you the least bit curious to find out if I do have the modesty to wear a petticoat beneath this dress?"

"Ladies who play with fire often get burned," he cautioned.

"I hope so," she breathed fervently. "For I'm on fire for the taste of another one of your kisses."

# Chapter 20

❧

*When the blood burns, how prodigal the soul*
*Lends the tongue vows.*
—William Shakespeare, 1564–1616

They disappeared from the crowd of dancers, quickly working their way around the refreshment tables at the far end of the ballroom toward the opened terrace doors. Jarrod caught sight of Griffin and Alyssa standing near the terrace doors, but he didn't let the possibility of Griffin and Alyssa seeing them deter him. Placing his hand on the small of Sarah's back, Jarrod guided her around the punch table and through the last set of doors, where they slipped into the cool dark of the evening.

Jarrod led her down the terrace steps along a lantern-lit stone path to the garden. He didn't stop until he reached the entrance to a thick hedgerow maze.

"Ja—"

Jarrod swallowed the soft sigh that escaped her lips along with his name as he took her in his arms and covered her mouth with his. He teased the seam of her lips, encouraging her to open her mouth and allow him further liberties.

Sarah obliged, parting her lips in silent invitation as he swept his tongue past her teeth and into the deep recesses of her mouth, exploring, searching, satisfying . . . tasting her with his mouth while his hands roamed at will. Sarah shivered with delight and anticipation as her knees grew weak and she melted against him.

Jarrod felt her legs give way and quickly scooped her up in his arms and stepped into the maze.

Sarah protested when he broke the kiss.

"I'm sorry to interrupt your second kissing lesson, my sweet," he murmured, nibbling at the corner of her mouth, "but we were far too exposed at the entrance of the maze where anyone might look out and see us."

She glanced around. "No one can see us now."

"It's still early yet," he said. "When the ballroom gets a bit warmer, couples will empty onto the terrace and move out into the garden. That's why the path is lit." He leaned forward and kissed her again. "And the maze is a favorite trysting place. Fortunately, most couples never make it past all the benches and the belvedere to where we're going."

"Where *are* we going?" Sarah whispered, looping her arms around his neck and holding on as he carried her deep into the maze, past several stone benches and a small grotto with a round belvedere made of marble and surrounded by columns in the Classical style.

"Somewhere where we'll have privacy," he answered, flawlessly negotiating the twists and turns of the maze.

Sarah narrowed her gaze at him, squinting in the dark. "You do this too well." The green-eyed monster of jealousy added a suspicious tone to her voice. "You've been here before."

He grinned.

Sarah saw the flash of his white teeth. "With whom?" she demanded.

"That, my dear Miss Nosey Nell," he said, using the name he'd called her when they were children, and punctuating each word with a kiss on the tip of her nose, "is none of your business." Jarrod stopped suddenly and set her on her feet.

The folly sitting in the center of the maze had been built shortly after the house had been constructed. The exterior of the folly was an exact replica of the exterior of the mansion, built on a much smaller scale and with one difference.

The mansion had a solid roof. The roof of the folly was

constructed around a series of skylights to allow sunlight in the daytime and moonlight at night. In the folly, one might sleep beneath the stars. The interior was one large room, big enough for four adults to move around in quite comfortably and was an ideal playhouse for children.

It had once served that purpose, before the Garrisons' day, but when Jarrod had last been inside the folly, the child-sized furniture had been removed and replaced with a comfortable chaise longue and a dozen or so pillows and throws. As the Garrison children were both too young to require a playhouse, Jarrod hoped the folly was still furnished as a pleasure house for adults.

Reaching up beside the front door of the folly, Jarrod removed his gloves, then felt for the key secreted in a compartment behind the right front lamp. It was still there. He took the key and fitted it into the front door slot and turned the lock.

The door swung open on well-oiled hinges. Jarrod quickly ushered Sarah inside, then closed and locked the door, pocketing the key.

Sarah gasped.

The folly was one large room and the only furnishings in it were a large bed, a bedside table, a rocking chair, and a large mirror.

"I see the Garrisons have improved upon the furnishings since I was here last." Jarrod walked over to the bed and patted the coverlet. It was freshly laundered. He turned to Sarah and smiled.

"And when was that?"

"Sarah, Sarah . . ." He clucked his tongue. "Jealousy does not become you."

"I'm not jealous," she protested. "Just curious."

Jarrod laughed. "Now who's lying?"

"Maybe I am a little jealous," she admitted. "But only because I thought you'd remain . . . that you'd stay . . . you know . . ." She fumbled for the right words.

"Celibate?" He sat down on the bed and arched an eyebrow. "Virginal?"

She nodded. "Until I grew up." She pinned him with an accusing stare. "But you didn't."

"Of course I didn't," he said. "I'm a normal, healthy man with natural urges and desires. I satisfied them every chance I got." He winked at her and surprised himself by paraphrasing item number six of the Official Free Fellows League Charter. "Of course, I took no pleasure in the task. I looked upon it in the same manner as medicine that must be swallowed. I sacrificed myself on the altar of learning time and again in order that I might become a better teacher for *you*."

Sarah laughed. "Last night . . ." she began.

"This morning . . ." he corrected.

"This morning you flatly refused to consider teaching me."

Jarrod nodded. "You took me by surprise this morning. I wasn't prepared for your proposition." He reached out and took hold of her hand, tugging it gently until Sarah stepped forward. He opened his legs and pulled her between them. "But I've had all day to think about it and all evening to stare at your bosom and . . ." He shrugged his shoulders. "Perhaps I was too hasty in my decision. I believe you're right. I am the perfect man to teach you what you need to know—especially if you don't intend to marry. I mean, no young lady should be completely innocent when she begins her career. . . ."

"Or when she marries," Sarah quickly added. "If she marries."

"Exactly," Jarrod agreed. "Every young lady should have some idea of what's to be expected of her. . . ."

"How true," she breathed, mere inches from his lips.

"And every teacher ought to receive some sort of compensation for his dedication to imparting the lesson at hand. . . ." He paused.

"I agree completely." Sarah leaned closer, shivering with anticipation as Jarrod released her hand in order to tug at the neckline of her gown.

"Mind if I satisfy my curiosity?" he asked politely.

"Be my guest," she invited.

Jarrod hooked his index finger in the center of the square of her neckline at the valley separating her breasts. Feeling for the fabric of her bodice and corset, Jarrod ran his finger from side to side.

Sarah moaned as his knuckle brushed the tips of her breasts. She moved forward without realizing it until her thigh was pressed against the hard ridge at the apex of his opened legs.

Jarrod applied constant gentle pressure until her dress gave up the ghost and her breasts popped free from their restraint. "What have we here?" he mused. "A French pastry with a pink frosted rosebud just for me." He looked at her to gauge her reaction, then leaned close and slowly licked the underside of her breast, tasting the tiny beads of perspiration there before he moved upward and covered the sensitive tip with his mouth.

Good heavens! Sarah's knees buckled, but Jarrod was prepared. Catching her around the waist, he settled her weight on his thigh, holding her still with the arm about her waist while he began a second assault on her senses by slipping his other hand beneath her skirts.

Fire, like the fire of a glass of sherry on an empty stomach, shot through her, only this fire was a thousand times better than anything alcohol induced. Sarah gasped. The tip of her breast swelled into a hard little nub as he ministered to it with his tongue and teeth and his hot, wet kisses. He kissed and nipped and sucked until her nipple grew harder and she ached in the secret places of her body—all the secret places proper ladies never admitted to having.

Sarah arched her back, filling the folly with the little incoherent sounds she made deep in her throat. She wiggled in his arms, moving steadily closer until she finally reached up, clamped her fingers into his thick black hair, and held him pressed against her. She whimpered hoarsely as Jarrod continued to tease her with his wicked tongue, delighting in igniting spontaneous currents of hot desire that flared throughout her body.

Jarrod chuckled deep in his throat, thrilled with Sarah's exuberant response to his touch and heady with the powerful sensations swirling around them and with the incredible realization that the rector's daughter from Helford Green enjoyed his touch as much as he enjoyed touching her.

Turning his head so that he might breathe once again, Jarrod shifted her weight off his thigh and onto the bed, then slowly worked his way over to her other breast. He wanted to unbutton her dress and shove it down over her hips, but he fought to control that urge as he nuzzled her other breast, lavishing it with a rush of hot, moist air.

God, but he wanted to touch her, all of her. He wanted to suckle at her breast and taste the sweet hot essence of her. He wanted to bury his length inside her warmth and to feel the heat of her surrounding him as he throbbed and pulsed within. He wanted to capture her lips and swallow her cries as he made hot sweet love to her. He wanted to wrap her legs around his hips and take her on the journey of her life where they were joined in pleasure.

And he wanted to feel her touch him. To taste and caress him as he tasted and caressed her.

Jarrod worked his way from her breasts back to her lips. He plundered her mouth with his warm, rough tongue, tasting, devouring, wanting, as he worked his way beneath her single petticoat to her stockinged thighs and beyond, past her garters to the bare skin. He ran his hand over the top of her thigh and down into the valley between her legs.

Sarah sucked in a ragged breath as he found the opening in her brief drawers and touched the triangle of soft hair hidden there. Placing her hands against his chest, Sarah broke the kiss. "Jays?"

"Sssh, sweetheart," he whispered against her mouth, "I'm not going to hurt you."

"Jarrod . . ."

Jarrod took a deep breath. He knew he was taking advantage of her inexperience, knew he was venturing into uncharted territory, praying that he could explore all she'd allow him to explore, then find his way back with her virtue and his sanity intact. He knew he should stop what he was doing and send her straight back to her aunt, but for the first time in his life, Jarrod couldn't force himself to do what he knew to be right. For the first time in his life, he wanted to throw caution to the wind and feel.

And Sarah was what he wanted most to feel. Jarrod sighed. Who would have thought that little Sarah Eckersley could make him burn? Who would have thought that she would be so eager to join him in the conflagration? "Do you want me to stop?"

"No," she sighed.

"Then, what is it?" He kissed her chin, then the corner of her mouth, then the tip of her nose, and finally, her eyelids, before working his way down again.

"I ache," she whispered shyly. "I ache in places I've never ached before."

Jarrod chuckled. "What do you think that means, my sweet?"

"I'm not sure," Sarah admitted. "But what you're doing isn't quite enough. It seems as if I'm striving for something. Something to soothe the ache."

"Oh?" He arched his eyebrow and gave her a wanton look. God, but she was incredible! How could he ask for more?

"I don't mean to criticize," she added quickly, as he leisurely stroked her soft curls with his finger. "Because what you're doing is quite the most wonderful thing I've ever felt other than what you did to my . . ." She blushed bright red.

"Breasts?" he offered.

"Yes," she whispered. "I loved the way you took me in your mouth as a baby would do."

"Like this?" He followed his suggestion with action, covering the point of her luscious ivory globe with his hot mouth, sucking deeply, drawing her nipple as far into his mouth as possible.

Sarah closed her eyes and gifted him with a low, keening moan.

Jarrod held his breath, struggling to maintain control as the sound and sight and scent of her passion threatened to send him over the edge.

"How about the other?" He treated her other breast to the same tender ministrations and Sarah nearly came off the bed as a rush of intense pleasure surged through her.

"Good heavens!"

He flicked his tongue over her nipple, then reluctantly released it and leaned over her. "You were saying?"

"I can't remember," she gasped. "I can't think. All I can do is feel."

"That's as it should be, my sweet," Jarrod murmured against her ear, moments before he thrust his tongue in it and sent new shivers of pleasure coursing through her. "Now, feel this. . . ." He traced the contours of her mound, then slid his fingers inside its slick warmth and teased the tight little bud hidden within the folds.

"Oh, yes . . ."

There were no words to describe the shock she felt at the multitude of delicious and forbidden sensations as Jarrod's wicked and wonderfully skilled fingers slipped inside her petal-soft folds. She moaned his name and thrust her hips against his incredibly talented fingers, feeling the impact of those sensations deep inside her as yearnings she never knew she had shot to the surface and begged to be assuaged.

"How about this?" He slid a finger inside her.

Sarah quivered uncontrollably.

"If that's how you feel about one, let's try another, shall we?" He withdrew his hand, then slid two fingers inside her, massaging, stretching, readying her for more. . . .

"Oh, God, Jays, it's so . . ." Sarah grabbed at his shoulders. Missed. Then grabbed again and held on as Jarrod began a steady rhythm. Caressing her, stroking in and out with his fingers as she arched her back, flexing and squirming in an effort to get closer to him. Or have him get closer to her.

Sarah knew she should be scandalized by Jarrod's fa-

miliarity with the forbidden places on her body; knew she
should be alarmed at the way he knew exactly what to do to
increase the pleasure and the ache and at the way she allowed him to do whatever he wanted to do. Sarah had always known she was putty in Jarrod's hands, but she hadn't
realized he had known exactly how to mold it. She had
sensed it, but she hadn't known how much she wanted Jarrod to love her until now. He knew her much better than
she knew herself and he'd been right to refuse her offer to
become her first lover, for having felt this, how could she
ever let him go? And staying free was the thing Jarrod
wanted most.

Sarah knew they shouldn't be doing what they were doing. But she didn't care. She knew she should be shocked
or embarrassed by the liberties he was taking. By the liberties she was allowing. Even encouraging. But how could
she be shocked or embarrassed when it was her beloved
Jays? And when all he gave was incredible pleasure?

This was what she wanted. What she needed. And she
needed it from Jarrod. It didn't matter that he didn't love
her or that he didn't want to marry her. She loved him. She
had always loved him and that was enough. Because he felt
something for her. He couldn't stroke her with such infinite
tenderness and probe her secret places with such care if he
didn't.

"Please," she murmured in such a heartfelt tone of voice
that Jarrod couldn't tell if she was inviting him to continue
or begging him to stop. He deepened his caress, wiggling
his fingers against her slippery warmth. Sarah squeezed
her legs together in reaction, before opening them again to
give him access. And Jarrod had his answer.

Sarah squirmed as pleasure—hot and thick and
dangerous—surged through her body, filling her with urgent longings she couldn't name and a buffet of vibrant
emotions—all of them emanating from the place Jarrod
graced with his glorious attention. She thrust her hips upward as she moaned her pleasure and gasped out his name
in short frantic little breaths.

Jarrod kissed her again, gently at first, then harder, consciously matching the action of his fingers to that of his tongue as he feverishly worked his magic on her. He knew she was desperately close to finding release, even if she didn't quite know what to expect or what was happening to her.

Chafing beneath his self-imposed restraint, Jarrod ached to join her in blissful release, but he took his time. Laving her folds with the honey she lavished on his fingers, Jarrod pressed his thumb against her aching core.

Sarah sighed against his lips, then shuddered deeply as her tenuous control shattered, the tension she felt dissolved, and she came apart in his arms. She opened her eyes and looked up at him with such an expression of sheer awe and joy that Jarrod's breath caught in his throat. He was humbled by the look in her eyes and rewarded tenfold for his remarkable restraint.

"Better?" he asked.

Sarah blushed. "Much better." She stretched like a cat, delighting in the feeling, then suddenly she reached up, and framed Jarrod's face between her palms. "Thank you," she said simply, before pulling his face down to meet her lips.

"Glad I could be of service," he whispered seconds before he captured her mouth with his own.

Jarrod kissed her again—this time with all the pent-up passion and frustration and longing he'd been holding in check so long. He kissed her until her breasts heaved with exertion, until her bones seemed to turn to jelly, until all she could do was cling to him while she fervently returned his kisses measure for measure.

Shaking with need and reeling from the flood of sensations surrounding him as Sarah matched him stroke for stroke with her tongue, Jarrod pulled his mouth away from hers.

"What's wrong?" she asked.

"Nothing's wrong," he answered.

"Then why did you stop kissing me?"

"Because I want you." Jarrod leaned his forehead against hers and drew a shaky breath. "Because I want more."

Sarah suddenly realized that while she felt much better after the release of the tension he'd built inside her, Jarrod seemed to feel much worse. "Tell me what to do."

Jarrod gave a shaky laugh. "It isn't something one usually asks of an innocent young lady after their first dance."

"What you just did to me isn't something one usually does to an innocent young lady after their first or *second* dance," Sarah reminded him.

"Even the third or fourth," Jarrod added in that same shaky laugh.

"Then why don't we skip the third and fourth dances while you teach me everything I should know about giving you the same kind of pleasure you gave me?"

"Oh, Sarah, my sweet," he murmured. "It will take a lot longer than that." Jarrod was beginning to think that it might take him a lifetime to teach her everything he wanted her to know about pleasuring him.

"Start with what you want most." The smile Sarah gave him was beatific. "I've got all night. And you're the only man who's signed my dance card."

"Jesus!" Jarrod swore. "I forgot about the dance. We've been out here entirely too long." He pulled Sarah's bodice back over her breasts, hiding them from view, and groaned as he stood up to help her to her feet.

Sarah looked up at him. "What is it?"

"I can't go back inside like this."

He looked perfectly presentable. Sarah stared at him in the glow of the moonlight. His cravat was a bit askew, but other than that, not a hair was out of place. She wasn't sure she could say the same. "Like what?"

"This." He took her hand and guided it to the front of his trousers.

The hard ridge she'd felt earlier seemed to have grown so large it was pushing against his trouser front. "Oh." She applied a little pressure, then began massaging him in a slow circular motion, before tracing the length of it through the fabric. "Can you walk like this?"

"Barely," Jarrod choked out. "And dancing is out of the question."

"Does it hurt?"

Jarrod leaned down and kissed her on the nose. "It aches like the bloody devil."

Sarah frowned. "Does this happen often?"

"Only when I'm with you." He surprised himself by speaking the truth. He had always prided himself on his control and Jarrod couldn't remember the last time he had been unable to control an erection. Unfortunately, he didn't seem to be able to control this one or the reason for it. "Suffice it to say that I can't make an appearance in the ballroom until this subsides."

"Is there anything I can do to help?"

Was it possible? Had he died and gone to heaven? Or had the rector's daughter from Helford Green just offered to help him alleviate the ache in the place he needed it most? And the fact that she didn't truly understand what she was offering didn't seem to matter at all.

God, how he wished she could help, but he hadn't quite lost all his manners or his good sense and Jarrod knew that was something he couldn't ask. He closed his eyes instead, and mentally counted to twenty in an effort to erase the images of Sarah doing everything he wanted her to do. Kneeling before him. Or leaning over him while he reclined on the bed. Even taking him in hand and bringing him to satisfaction. Or lying beneath him, her legs tightly wrapped around his waist, as he buried himself inside her.

He'd just counted twenty-four when Jarrod felt Sarah fumbling for the buttons on his trousers. "Sarah, don't . . ."

Too late.

She released the buttons and stared at the hard ridge straining against his stockinette drawers in the vee of his trousers.

"Mind if I satisfy my curiosity?" she asked politely, in an echo of his earlier words.

"Be my guest," he invited.

Sarah hooked a finger in the waistband of his drawers and tugged.

The hard length of him sprang free.

Jarrod inhaled sharply.

"What have we here?" she mused, tracing it with the tip of her gloved finger. "A French éclair without the frosting?"

Jarrod closed his eyes and bit his bottom lip as Sarah ran her finger up and down his shaft. "This éclair's all English," he managed through gritted teeth, "and loaded with cream. Mind your glove, my lady, so you don't get any on it."

Sarah looked closely and saw that he was right. A drop of pearly white liquid glistened at the top. She quickly unbuttoned and removed her glove so she could touch him with her bare hand. The feel of him took her by surprise. She expected hardness, but the top of him wasn't hard. It was soft. Incredibly, velvety soft. And that intrigued her. She traced the length of him with her bare finger, stopping to touch the liquid. She rubbed the pearly drop into the velvety soft flesh, then watched, fascinated, as another drop immediately took its place. "You *are* loaded with cream," she said, reaching out to grasp him.

"Easy," he cautioned, shuddering with a mixture of exquisite pain and pleasure as she gripped him. "You can't squeeze it out. You have to coax it out." He took her hand and showed her the motion. "Although, I doubt it will take much coaxing."

He was right. Sarah proved to be a most adept and enthusiastic pupil. Jarrod quivered with pleasure and came very close to spilling himself in her hand as Sarah pumped him just the way he'd showed her. Just the way he liked. Until he reached the limit of his control.

"Stop," he ordered, leaning his forehead against the top of her head in order to catch his breath and gain control of his racing heart.

Sarah eased her grip on him and gently moved her hand up and down. "Better?"

"No," he answered.

"Don't you like it?"

"I love it." His chest was heaving with effort and he ground out the words between each breath. "But you must stop. I only have so much control," he said. "And I'm at the limit." Jarrod reached down and caught hold of her wrist, forcing her to end the magnificent torture.

Sarah stopped the motion, but she didn't let go. "What happens if I continue and you lose control?"

"I spill my seed," he said. "And you'll have cream all over your talented little hand."

"It's a sin to spill your seed anywhere but inside a woman," Sarah told him.

"Where did you hear that?"

"From the Bible." She added, "Papa had whole sermons devoted to the sin of needlessly spilling one's seed and how it leads straight to hell."

"Believe me, my sweet," Jarrod groaned, "it isn't needless. Quite the contrary. And if it's a sin, then every man you're ever likely to meet is going to hell because it's done quite regularly."

"Will you be able to return to the ballroom afterward?"

He managed a nod.

"And dance?"

"Yes."

"Then may I continue?"

Jarrod conceded. How could he refuse so polite a request? How could he refuse to do what his body urged him to do? How could he not want to take her in his arms and make love to her forever?

"So long as you can locate my handkerchief."

# Chapter 21

*The gods have their own rules.*

—Ovid, 43 B.C.–A.D. 18

*It was over in less than a minute.*
Sarah caught the cream on his handkerchief as he spilled it, then carefully patted his flaccid member dry and tucked it back into his stockinette drawers and buttoned his trousers. She folded the handkerchief into a neat little square, then turned her back to him and busied herself in smoothing out the coverlet on the bed and fluffing the pillows, erasing all signs of use, giving Jarrod time to compose himself.

"You may turn around now," he told her. "I'm presentable."

Sarah handed Jarrod his handkerchief. "And if I prefer you in disarray?"

"Then you must keep that preference and how you came to have it to yourself," he told her. His knees still felt like jelly and he blushed like a schoolboy as he took the square of soiled linen from her and shoved it into the inside pocket of his jacket.

Sarah found that boyish reaction more endearing than anything he could have done. "Can't I share it?" she asked sweetly. "If only with you."

"*Only* with me."

"There's no one else with whom I want to share it," she

said softly. "And there's no need for you to be embarrassed," she told him. "I wasn't embarrassed for you to make me lose control. And you shouldn't be embarrassed because I did the same for you." She walked up to him and straightened his cravat. "I'm honored that you trusted me enough to allow me to ease the ache I caused."

"I'm not . . ." Still reeling from his own audacity at allowing Sarah to perform such an intimate act for him, Jarrod found it hard to give voice to his feelings. "Christ, Sarah! I've never done anything like that in my life."

"You seemed quite good at it for a novice," she teased.

He made a face at her. "*That* I've done more times than I care to remember." Jarrod reached out and smoothed a stray lock of red hair back into place, then handed her her black glove. "And if your father was right, I'm well on my way to hell, because I've never allowed a lady to witness that particular act before, much less participate, and tonight I encouraged an innocent young lady to do both."

"Papa must have misinterpreted the scripture," Sarah decided. "For nothing that extraordinary can be sinful. And you needn't worry about shocking me," she continued, even though she allowed that she'd been more than a little shocked at the powerful feelings surging through her at the sight of so potent a man as Jays made vulnerable by the motion of a woman's hand. She wanted to hold him and protect him and love him forever. "I'm not so innocent anymore," she told him proudly, "thanks to my most excellent tutor."

"Still more innocent than you know," he replied.

"We did what we set out to do," she reminded him. "We made it possible for you to return to the ballroom and we found the perfect way to do it." She stood on tiptoe and planted a kiss at the corner of his mouth. "A most pleasurable way, I might add."

"Very pleasurable," Jarrod agreed. "For me."

"For me as well," she admitted.

Jarrod smiled at her. "Imagine Little Miss Nosey Nell so full of surprises."

"Imagine Know-It-All Jays able to appreciate it at last."
His kiss took *her* by surprise.

Without warning, Jarrod leaned over, pulled her close, and kissed her, hard.

Sarah looped her arms around his neck, closed her eyes, and kissed him back. She used her tongue to tempt and tease him as they played a game of advance and retreat, of give and take, of mutual surrender. She followed his lead until he relinquished control and followed hers. They played the game over and over again, leading each other on a merry chase with every stroke of their tongues as they teased and tormented each other with kisses that were so hungry and hot and wet and deep that Jarrod was finally forced to end them. "I believe that's enough kissing for tonight," he said softly, tenderly. "Any more and I won't be able to stand it."

"We can't have that, now can we?" she teased.

"Careful," he issued another warning, "ladies who play with fire often get burned—twice in one night."

"Luckily, I know how to handle it now," she said.

Jarrod burst out laughing. "Oh, Sarah . . ." He broke off before he made a complete fool of himself. He wanted to tell her how much he'd missed having her to spar with, how much he'd missed having someone follow him around, how much he'd missed showing her the things that interested him, the things he knew. Once he'd gone to great lengths to pretend disgust at her ignorance as he'd patiently taught her the names of the trees and birds, flowers and rocks surrounding Helford Green and Shepherdston Hall. But he'd been secretly pleased to have someone with whom to share his knowledge and now, suddenly, he delighted in giving her pleasure and showing her how to please him. But that was as far as it could go. He'd already compromised her beyond the bounds of decency. He couldn't allow himself to ruin her completely. She deserved better. She deserved the best.

"Yes?" Sarah leaned closer, waiting for him to say what was in his heart, waiting for him to trust her with his heart as he had just trusted her with his body.

"We'd better get back to the party," he said. "We've been gone much too long. Your aunt will be looking for us."

Sarah did her best to hide her disappointment as he placed his arm around her and ushered her to the front door of the folly. She waited while he locked the door and returned the key to its hiding place, then took his hand and let him lead her out of the maze.

"How do you do it?" she asked as they turned the first corner of the maze in the dark.

"Do what?"

"Find your way through this labyrinth of passages," she said. "You never did tell me how you knew your way around the maze. Or the first girl you brought here for your nefarious purposes." She did her best to imitate him by arching an eyebrow, but she failed miserably.

"No." He grinned. "I never did."

"Jays!" she protested. "It's only fair. You discovered the truth about my petticoat and my modesty."

"Yes, I did." He grinned again. "And by the by, I like the 'modest' way you look in your black gloves, with your black, lace-edged, lawn petticoat pushed up above your knees, with your black stockings and lacy drawers exposed, and with your lacy black corset displaying your French pastries so beautifully."

She couldn't see his smoldering look in the shadows cast by the maze, but she could feel it; and every tantalizing squeeze of his hand, every moment spent walking politely side by side instead of in each other's arms, was pure torture and Sarah's body ached with the need for more kissing and touching.

She couldn't get the sight of him out of her mind. She couldn't forget the expression on his face as she'd brought him to satisfaction with her hand, couldn't forget the way his strong male body strained for release, the way that same powerful body had trembled uncontrollably as he found it, and the flush of embarrassment he'd suffered when he'd opened his eyes and remembered where he was and what he'd just allowed her to do.

She had wondered if he'd felt the same way when he'd brought her to satisfaction with his fingers. Now she knew. "I'm wearing black because I'm in mourning, otherwise you'd have seen the modest way I look in my white gloves, with my white, lace-edged, lawn petticoat pushed up above my knees, and my white stockings and white lacy drawers exposed, and with my lacy white corset displaying my French pastries so beautifully."

"And if I prefer you in black?" He echoed her earlier sentiment.

"That can be arranged," she said simply. "So long as you tell me how you know your way around this maze so well."

"I may take you up on that," he warned. "I may show up at your door in the wee hours of the morning offering more lessons in exchange for a chance to catch you in your black undergarments."

"I'll look forward to it," Sarah answered honestly. "So long as you keep your end of the bargain and tell me who you've brought to the maze."

"You are stubborn, aren't you?"

"As stubborn as you are," she retorted.

"All right, Miss Jealous Nosey Nell, I'll tell you." He relented. "The first girl I brought to the folly was my nursemaid."

"Your nursemaid?"

He nodded.

"You brought your nursemaid to the Garrisons' garden?"

"Actually, she brought me to the maze and not the other way around. I was three or four, I believe, and the garden didn't belong to the Garrisons then," he said. "It belonged to the Shepherdstons. It was my family home. I was born here." He squeezed Sarah's fingers. "I know the maze like the back of my hand because I used to play in it." Jarrod took a deep breath, then slowly exhaled it. "My great-grandmother spent a small fortune constructing the folly. She had it built in the garden shortly after she and my great-grandfather built the house. My great-grandfather called it Eleanor's Folly after her. When I was small, it was my playhouse. And later . . ." He paused, struggling for words. "Later, it was used for other purposes."

"For trysting?" she asked.

"In a manner of speaking," he said. "But I haven't been inside the folly or on the property at all since I was six and ten years old. And tonight is the first time *I've* ever used it for anything other than a place where I could be alone."

Eleanor's Folly had been his favorite hideaway from the time he'd been old enough to find his way to it until he'd sold the house and grounds. It had been his escape from the unbearable situation inside the main house. When he was home from school, Jarrod had spent most of his waking hours in it because Eleanor's Folly was the place he loved most.

But when Jarrod inherited the title of Marquess of Shepherdston, he'd sold the Richmond house and Eleanor's Folly to the present Lord Garrison's father to escape the memories.

The present Lord Garrison had inherited it, along with his father's title, when his father died.

Jarrod had sworn never to set foot inside the house or on the property again. And he'd kept that promise for fifteen years.

He'd broken it tonight because Sarah Eckersley and her aunt had asked him to escort them to Lady Garrison's ball.

"Then I'm doubly honored you made an exception for me," Sarah told him. "Thank you, Jarrod."

"You're welcome, Sarah."

They entered another turn in the maze. Jarrod leaned toward her and was about to give her another kiss in the moonlight when a man and woman came around the corner.

"There you are." Lady Dunbridge hurried toward Sarah. "You disappeared in the crowd of dancers and I lost sight of you."

"Jarrod asked to show me the garden," Sarah told her. "But I should have let you know where we were going before I left the ballroom."

"I was hoping that might be the case," Lady Dunbridge said. "But I became worried when you were gone for so long. I was afraid someone else might have waylaid you or that you had become lost in the maze. Thank goodness Lord Mayhew offered to help me look for you."

"It's my fault," Jarrod apologized. "I shouldn't have brought her out here without informing you."

"I should think you would have had the good manners to ask me." Lady Dunbridge gave him a serious look. "Instead of *informing* me."

Jarrod nodded his head. "You're quite right, Lady Dunbridge," he replied in a conciliatory tone. "I should have *asked* permission to escort Miss Eckersley into the garden. Please accept my apologies."

"Well." Lord Mayhew stepped from behind Lady Dunbridge.

Sarah blanched at the sight of him. She closed her eyes and waited for him to remark upon their earlier encounter, but it never came. He didn't recognize her. But then, how could he? When all he'd seen was her bare leg and her posterior?

"I'm sure my godson meant no harm or disrespect," Lord Mayhew was saying; "it's been a long time since he's had to answer to anyone and he's accustomed to doing things his own way. But Miss Eckersley is here now and I'm sure she's none the worse for wear for having seen the garden by moonlight." He looked at Jarrod.

"I'm sure you're right," Lady Dunbridge said. "And I had no objection to Lord Shepherdston showing Sarah the garden or anything else; it's just that there are people inside who are bound to notice that they were gone an extraordinarily long amount of time."

"If any untoward gossip should result from our absence from the ballroom, I assure you that I will take care of it," Jarrod told her. "In the meantime, I shall assure you, Lady Dunbridge, that I've returned Sarah to you with her virtue intact."

Lady Dunbridge glanced at her niece.

Sarah nodded. "Lord Shepherdston showed me the folly and was a perfect gentleman the whole time." She pursed her lips and added, "Much to my dismay."

"Sarah!"

"It's true." Sarah couldn't quite meet her aunt's gaze. "I should have liked to have gotten a few wildly passionate kisses from my excursion into a beautiful moonlit garden and the mysterious depths of a maze with a man, but Lord Shepherdston's behavior was beyond reproach."

She gave a dramatic sigh and Jarrod bit the inside of his cheek to keep from smiling at her overacting.

Lady Dunbridge looked from Sarah to Jarrod and back again. Sarah was lying through her teeth and Henrietta knew it. "If you say so."

"I do, Aunt Etta," Sarah assured her. "And I will say it to anyone who dares say otherwise."

"Very well, my dear," Lady Dunbridge replied. "But you would both do well to remember your father's teachings." Lady Dunbridge firmed her lips and thought for a minute. "I suggest you begin with two scriptures. Colossians 2:21 and First Corinthians 7:9."

"Yes, ma'am," Sarah replied in an uncharacteristically meek voice that fooled no one.

"By the by." Lord Robert walked over to Sarah and bowed. "We haven't been formally introduced, but I am Robert Mayhew, Lord Shepherdston's godfather and maternal uncle by marriage, and you must be Lady Dunbridge's niece. . . ."

Remembering his manners, Jarrod turned to Sarah and continued the introductions. "Miss Sarah Eckersley, may I introduce Lord Mayhew, seventh Earl of Mayhew?" He turned to Lord Rob. "Lord Mayhew, Miss Sarah Eckersley."

Lord Mayhew rubbed his palms together in anticipation. "And now that we've all toured the gardens together and seen part of the maze, why don't we return to the ballroom and see if any damage has been done?" Lord Mayhew offered an immediate solution and explanation for Sarah and Jarrod's absence, as well as his and Lady Dunbridge's, and he gave credence to the fiction by escorting Sarah back into the ballroom while Jarrod escorted Lady Dunbridge. "Shall we, my dear?"

"I'd be delighted, Lord Mayhew," Sarah answered. "And thank you."

Jarrod arched an eyebrow in query as he offered Lady Dunbridge his arm. "Colossians 2:21, ma'am?"

"Touch not; taste not; handle not, Lord Shepherdston."

Jarrod couldn't help but grin. "Very apropos."

"I thought so." She smiled up at him.

"Dare I ask for a translation of First Corinthians 7:9?"

"It is better to marry than to burn."

"You may have a point there, Lady Dunbridge," Jarrod conceded.

"You gave me your word, Lord Shepherdston," she reminded him. "And depending upon what we face when we enter that ballroom once more, you may have no choice."

# Chapter 22

*Never say more than is necessary.*
—*Richard Brinsley Sheridan, 1751–1816*

*The ballroom was abuzz with whispers when they reen-* tered it, but the whispering was more about Jarrod's extraordinary appearance at the Garrisons. No one seemed to care that he'd left the ballroom in the middle of a quadrille then suddenly reappeared in the company of Lady Dunbridge, Lord Mayhew, and Lady Dunbridge's niece.

The fact that Lord Garrison's house had once belonged to the Marquess of Shepherdston was no secret, nor was the fact that Lord Shepherdston hadn't set foot upon the property for any reason in over fifteen years.

The fact that he had done so tonight in order to escort a young lady and her aunt was the primary topic of speculation. Even for his host and hostess.

"I hope his coming here tonight hasn't set the tongues wagging again about the old tragedy," Lady Garrison commented as she and her sister, Alyssa, the Duchess of Avon, stood with their husbands near the terrace doors and the refreshment tables set up at the far end of the ballroom.

"Oh, Anne," Alyssa sighed. "Don't start worrying about that. You were thrilled when he accepted your invitation."

"I know," Anne admitted, "but I've been inviting him to every gathering we've had since Richard and I married and he's always refused. I suppose I've grown more accustomed to his refusal. And when he asked that I include Lady Dunbridge and Miss Eckersley in the invitation even though they are in deep mourning, I wasn't at all sure I was doing the right thing in agreeing."

"You did exactly the right thing," her husband said. "Lord Shepherdston must have a reason for his request and I, for one, think that we should respect it."

"I agree," Anne said. "It's just that I'm not quite sure what to say to people now that he's here. And everyone is speculating about it."

"Just tell them the truth," Griff advised. "That the Marquess of Shepherdston accepted your invitation and escorted Lady Dunbridge and her niece to your party. Let folks draw their own conclusions."

Alyssa nodded. "They will anyway. You can't stop people from talking."

"I don't mind people talking," Anne said. "So long as they talk about how magnificent the house is or how splendid the party was, or how beautiful the garden looks, and what an excellent hostess I am." She frowned. "I just don't want them to start talking about the fact that it's the first time in years that Lord Shepherdston has set foot in the house." She appealed to Alyssa and Griff for understanding. "It isn't as if we've never asked him to attend our gatherings. And it isn't as if the marquess still owns the place. Richard's father bought it and spent a fortune gutting the east wing, rebuilding, and remodeling, and turning the house into the showplace it is so that everyone would forget about the rest of it. I don't want all his hard work to go for naught."

Griffin frowned at his sister-in-law. "Richard's father was able to gut, rebuild, remodel, and turn this house into a showplace because Jarrod Shepherdston practically gave it to him."

Anne was clearly surprised.

"He's right, my dear," Richard agreed. "Jarrod sold us the place for a mere fraction of what it was worth. My father could never have afforded to purchase a house the size of this one—with its extensive gardens and the view—otherwise. And Jarrod's only stipulations were that it not be torn down and that its exterior and the exterior of the folly remain unchanged because they were both designed and constructed by Wren. He said destroying the house and the folly would only add to the crimes already committed here. And he was right." Richard gave his wife a tender look. "Be glad Shepherdston was willing to part with so large a part of his heritage, because it's made your reputation as a premier hostess possible."

"And if anyone is ill-mannered enough to mention the tragedy that took place here, kindly inform them that you are delighted to welcome Lord Shepherdston as your guest whenever he chooses to come and equally delighted to welcome whomever he chooses to bring," Alyssa told her older sister. "And then, I suggest you strike the name of that ill-mannered person permanently off your guest list."

"Easy for you to say," Anne retorted. "You're a duchess."

Griffin laughed. "Yes, she is, but she'd have done it as a viscountess, too."

"Speaking of which," Alyssa drawled, "this viscountess turned duchess would like to know if you intend to allow waltzing this evening, because I would like to waltz with my husband and I'm sure many of your guests would like to do the same."

"I don't care how many of her guests would like to do the same," Griffin said. "I'm not waltzing with anyone but you."

Alyssa laughed. "I didn't mean to imply all Anne's guests wanted to waltz with *you,* my darling," she clarified. "Only that they all wanted to waltz."

"If the duchess commands that we allow the waltz . . ."

"She does," Alyssa interjected.

"Then, how can we refuse?" Anne replied with a smile.

*Jarrod stood before Sarah in the ballroom. "Would* you care to dance?" he asked.

"I would love to," she said, "but Aunt Etta warned me that it would be unwise for us to dance two dances in a row after disappearing into the garden together." She looked up at him. "Unless I wish to see you become my unwilling bridegroom . . ."

Jarrod knew she was teasing, but there was a hopeful note in her voice that he couldn't ignore. "Sarah, it's not that I don't want to marry you . . ."

"I know," she said sadly. "It's just that you don't want to marry. It's not me you find abhorrent, just the idea of being tied to me for life."

When she put it that way, his reasons for not wanting to marry seemed inconsequential, but Jarrod knew better. Nothing was ever inconsequential once vows were spoken. There were always consequences. And he was involved in a dangerous enterprise. So dangerous that he dare not risk Sarah's life. And yet . . . Jarrod thought of Griffin and Alyssa and Colin and Gillian. His colleagues were involved in the same enterprise yet they had wives they cherished and who cherished them in return. Wives who shared their burdens and kept their secrets. Wives who were completely dependable and trustworthy. Wives who gave them a home to return to instead of an empty house. Wives who gave them a reason to return home.

But Griff and Colin had been born to parents who loved each other. His friends understood the language and the rules of love. His friends believed in the ideal and had been fortunate enough to find wives who shared their beliefs and spoke the same language.

Sarah's words had been truer than she knew when she accused him of hardly being husband material. Jarrod didn't know where to begin. He was ignorant of the rules and the language and more than a little leery of the ideal. He'd grown up with parents who shared a name, a title, and a son and very little else—outside the bedchamber. His parents hadn't liked or respected each other, but they were both passionate about pleasure. He was too old to blame his parents for his bachelor state—that was his own doing. But his profound distrust of the institution of marriage, and of the world in which he lived, had been deeply rooted in his childhood. "Sarah . . ."

She glanced toward the chairs on the sideline beside the dance floor, where the older ladies and gentlemen, the ladies who were increasing, and the ladies who were in mourning sat, and managed a smile. "Just escort me to the chairs on the sidelines beside Aunt Etta and Lord Mayhew. Don't worry about me, I'll be fine."

"I'll sit with you," he offered.

"And do what?" she asked. "Twiddle your thumbs? You'd be bored to tears inside five minutes." She sighed. "I know I will. Besides, you've better things to do." She nodded at someone across the room. "The Duke of Avon is trying to get your attention."

Jarrod turned and saw Griffin beckoning to him, then turned back to Sarah. "We've business together."

"I've known you since we were children, Jays," she said. "I know about your business together. I'm aware that Griffin Abernathy and Colin McElreath are your closest friends."

Free Fellows League business. Important business. But Jarrod was torn between staying with Sarah and fulfilling his obligations to his colleagues. "Sarah . . ."

"Go on," she urged, shooing him away with her hands. "You mustn't keep the duke waiting."

"I'll be back to claim my waltz," he promised. "With or without Aunt Etta's approval."

*"You certainly know how to stir up the ton and set* tongues a-wagging in speculation," Griffin said when Jarrod joined him and Alyssa after dutifully escorting Sarah

Eckersley to a chair near her aunt and fetching her a glass of punch.

Jarrod nodded. "It's a gift I was born to. We Shepherd-stons seem to possess it in abundance. And this house seems to bring out the worst of it. Fortunately my appearance *inside* the house has caused more speculation and whispers than my disappearance *outside* it."

"Oh, there have been whispers about that as well," Griff told him. "And we've done what we could to minimize the damage."

"I wondered if you saw us," Jarrod said.

"Going out and coming in," Alyssa said. "And I must say your entrance was very nicely orchestrated. Who is going to suspect you went to the garden for any reason except to view it? Or question the length of time it took you and Miss Eckersley to negotiate the maze when you and Miss Eckersley and Lady Dunbridge and Lord Mayhew made such a congenial entrance when you returned?"

"You," Jarrod replied.

Alyssa's eyes sparkled. "Well, except me, of course," she told him. "Because I suspect everyone of behaving as Griff and I would have behaved if we had had the chance to slip out of a ballroom and find a private place away from the noise and the crowd before we were married. Especially if there was a terrace and a beautiful moonlit garden just outside the door." She smiled up at her husband, recalling the night they had slipped away from the noise and the crowd and nearly made love on the fainting couch in the ladies' retiring room at Almack's.

"As if that ended when we were married," Griff replied, remembering all the other times he and Alyssa had managed to slip away since he'd returned home from the war to a duchy and a hero's welcome and invitations to every fete and party in England.

Jarrod looked serious, but he didn't confirm or deny. "You're my dear friends. If you suspect, you can bet there will be others here who aren't my friends who will think the same. Especially since we're *here*. It will bring back some of the old gossip. Like father, like son."

"I believe you mean the gods visit the sins of the fathers upon the children," Griffin said.

"Or I am a man more sinned against than sinning," Alyssa offered.

Jarrod managed a smile for Alyssa's benefit. "You've heard the gossip going around tonight. Will she suffer for agreeing to accompany me on a tour of the garden?"

"I haven't heard any unfavorable comments about her." Alyssa chewed on her bottom lip. "But now that I'm a duchess no one ever confides the juicy gossip to me. Miranda's the one . . ."

"Speaking of which," Jarrod said, "I thought she'd be here tonight."

"So did I," Alyssa told him. "I know she was invited and I know she planned to come, but I haven't seen or heard from her since last night."

"No one has," Griff added. "Or from Sussex either."

Jarrod looked at Alyssa. "Is there any chance that Lady St. Germaine and His Grace are together?"

"One can always hope," Alyssa said.

"My sentiments exactly," Griff added. "In the meantime, no one I've talked to today knows where they are or what's happened to them." He fixed his gaze on Jarrod. "I'm beginning to get alarmed. Have you spoken with Colin yet?"

Jarrod shook his head. "Not yet. Why?"

"He told me to tell you that you should ask Gillian to dance," Griff said.

Alyssa gave her husband a funny look.

"It's code, Puss," Griffin told her.

Jarrod frowned. "Yes, it's code. And what the devil is the good of having one if you tell your wife about it?"

"She'll find out eventually," Griff said with a shrug. "Telling her is quicker."

"But not nearly as fun," Alyssa reproached. She rapped Jarrod on the forearm with her fan. "Besides, you know that I'm completely trustworthy."

"That's not the point," Jarrod said.

"It never is," Alyssa retorted, rapping him again with her fan. "But the results are the same."

"Now, Lys." Griffin closed his fist around her fan. "No need to beat him into submission, because he's absolutely right. You are completely trustworthy, but there are others within hearing distance who aren't."

Alyssa sighed. "Shall I make our excuses?"

"I don't know yet." Griff looked at Jarrod. "What do you think?"

"Let's hear what he has to say and decide afterward," Jarrod reasoned.

Griff leaned down and kissed his wife. "I'll try not to be too long."

Alyssa nodded, knowing her husband would tell her what he could when he could despite Jarrod's objections. "Lord Shepherdston?"

She addressed him formally, so he answered in kind. "Yes, Your Grace?"

"Once you've danced with Lady Grantham, perhaps you should ask me to dance," she suggested much to Griffin's surprise.

Griff gave his wife a disapproving glance. "Lys."

Alyssa ignored him and smiled up at Jarrod. "That's code for 'He doesn't want me to know it, because he knows how much I like to dance, but my husband's leg is paining him tonight. He's trying his best to ignore the pain and partner me, but I'm afraid the waltz is beyond him.'"

"I understand and obey, Your Grace," Jarrod told her. "And will be honored to waltz with you."

# Chapter 23

What is not clear is not French.
—Antoine de Rivarol, 1753–1801

"*You sent for us?*" Jarrod asked when he and Griffin joined Colin and Gillian.

Colin nodded. "Are you done with dancing?"

"For now," Jarrod answered. "I promised Her Grace a dance and Sarah a waltz, but we are sitting these dances out on orders from Lady Dunbridge and Lord Rob."

Colin glanced down the way to a row of chairs set along the sidelines where those who chose not to dance could watch. Sarah and her aunt were sipping glasses of punch alongside Lord Rob and the Duchess of Avon. "I noticed that Lady Dunbridge and Lord Rob appear quite cozy together and that Miss Eckersley hasn't danced with anyone except you all evening," Colin said. "Are they protecting her reputation or yours?"

Jarrod's face and the tips of his ears reddened. "Probably both. And she hasn't danced with anyone except me because I don't dare let anyone else near her," he confided. "Unless it's someone I trust implicitly like you or Griff or Lord Mayhew."

"Why not?" Colin asked.

"Have you seen the dress she's wearing?"

"It's lovely," Gillian said with a smile.

"I beg your pardon, Lady Grantham," Jarrod said. "But it's

damn—*almost*—indecent. I can't look down without . . ."

Gillian chuckled. "That's funny, Lord Shepherdston, because Colin says the same thing about mine."

Jarrod glanced at Gillian's evening gown and saw that except for the color and fancy embroidery on the skirts, it was an identical style as Sarah's. Right down to the low cut of the squared neckline. But he'd barely noticed it on Gillian. And it wasn't because Gillian's bosom was any less gorgeous than Sarah's or any less visible; it was because Gillian was Colin's wife.

"You're in trouble, my friend," Colin told him.

Jarrod shook his head. "It's just that it's *Sarah*. I've known her since she was five. We grew up together." He looked at Colin and Gillian. "Red-haired, knobby-kneed, freckle-faced, hoydenish Sarah, who hadn't a prayer of growing up to be a beauty or of having a real figure, and look at her." He nodded toward her and Sarah looked over and smiled. "Look at the way she's turned out."

"It's a good thing you aren't her guardian," Colin said. "Or you'd be fighting the fellows off with a stick."

"That's just it," Jarrod said. "She doesn't have a guardian to fight the fellows off with a stick. She doesn't have anyone to look out for her."

"Except you," Gillian said softly. "And the way that you're scowling, it's going to take someone very brave or very foolhardy to approach her." She smiled at Jarrod. "I'd say Miss Eckersley has quite a champion in you, Lord Shepherdston."

"That may be, but I'm not supposed to be her champion," Jarrod protested. "I'm supposed to help her find one."

"It looks as if you've accomplished your mission," Gillian told him.

"Killed two birds with one stone, so to speak." Griffin grinned.

"Speaking of which," Colin said. "Gillian needs a few moments of your time, Jarrod."

"Oh?" Jarrod turned to Colin's wife.

"I apologize for taking you away from your amusements,

but I believe I may have the solution to the puzzle you presented to me," she said. "Unfortunately, it only came to me
a short time ago when Colin and I were dancing."

"Can you tell us about it here?" Griffin asked. "Or will
we need to see the puzzle?"

"You'll need to see it in order to confirm it, my lords,
but I can tell you what I think and why I think it," Gillian
said.

"She's already explained it to me," Colin said. "And I
thought that you should hear it as soon as possible."

Griffin glanced around. "This is my sister-in-law's gathering and it should be fairly secure, but I'll wager there are
a good many curious ears about. So much so that I suggest
we separate."

"I agree," Colin said, as two couples he didn't know and
who had appeared to be making their way to the dance
floor stopped to chat with one another directly behind
Shepherdston.

"I could drop by after the ball," Jarrod suggested. "If
you don't mind."

Gillian bit her bottom lip then looked to Colin for help.

"We may need to act before then," Colin said. "That's
why we wanted to speak to you and Griffin as soon as possible. Gillian can explain what she's discovered while you
two dance."

Jarrod lifted an eyebrow at Colin.

Gillian smiled. "It was my idea, Lord Shepherdston.
You're the center of attention here tonight. If you dance
every dance with Miss Eckersley, everyone will remember
it and talk. If you dance one or two dances with other
ladies, no one will think anything of your dances with Miss
Eckersley. So, I'll tell you what we've discovered and
Colin will explain it to His Grace."

Jarrod nodded. "Lady Grantham, will you do me the
honor of a dance?" he asked, reaching for her hand.

"I'd be delighted." She placed her hand in his.

"With your permission, of course." Jarrod grinned at
Colin.

"Of course," Colin replied. "So long as you allow me a dance with Miss Eckersley."

Jarrod scowled.

Colin smiled at Jarrod's reaction. "That's my wife you're holding," he said.

"I'm aware of that."

"And we're trying to prevent you from doing further damage to Miss Eckersley's reputation," Colin said, looking Jarrod in the eye. "So, why don't we agree to be the gentlemen we profess to be and refrain from looking down when we dance. Agreed?"

Griff watched the standoff with some amusement. Neither Jarrod nor Colin had ever been possessive, but then, neither had he until he'd met and married Alyssa.

"Agreed," Jarrod replied.

"Good," Griff said. "And since I'm unable to do my share of the dancing tonight, that goes double for me."

And as Lord Shepherdston led her onto the dance floor and guided her into the first steps of the waltz, Gillian, Lady Grantham, struggled to hide her knowing smile.

"What have you learned?" Jarrod wasted no time in getting to the point, for the waltz would only last a few minutes.

"I believe the large numbers refer to the numbers of troops Kin"—she'd almost said King Joseph, but quickly corrected her error—"*the author of the message* intends to move in or to have ready to meet ours." She gave Jarrod a moment to digest the information before continuing. "It's the only thing, other than large denominations of cash, that fits." She bit her bottom lip. "And there were no references to pounds or francs that I could find."

"He might still be ordering supplies," Jarrod reminded her.

"That's true," she agreed, "but if that is the case, there would be no need to encode the entire missive when most of it could be written *en clair.*"

Jarrod nodded. "You're right. We've already intercepted numerous letters of complaints he's written to his brother about the lack of supplies for the court. Although they contained a sentence or two of code, none of them were written wholly in code."

"Exactly," Gillian said. "And if there's no need for him to complain about the lack of supplies for the court in code, there would be no reason for him to order them in code. He's made no secret of the fact that there isn't enough cash to keep his court in the style to which they've grown accustomed. Or that he's terribly upset with his brother for not doing more to help him fill the lack."

"Five thousand. Eleven thousand. Fifteen hundred. *Troops.*" He smiled at Gillian. "It makes perfect sense. I believe your supposition is correct, Lady Grantham."

"There's more," she said. "The abbreviations I thought were random weren't."

He frowned.

"I *thought* the placement of the abbreviations were random. I thought they had been inserted to confuse us. But I believe I was wrong in that assumption," she elaborated. "After giving it a great deal of thought, I've decided that the abbreviations are there to help the recipient of the message—whom I've concluded is a marshal named Jourdan."

"Jourdan?" Jarrod had read the message Gillian had deciphered and he couldn't recall seeing Jourdan's name or an abbreviation of it anywhere. "Are you sure it was Jourdan?"

"Yes."

"Completely sure?"

"Almost."

"If I'm to present this information to the gentlemen in the War Office, I need to be confident that it's correct," Jarrod told her.

Gillian took a deep breath. "I can't prove it," she said. "The information will have to do that. But I believe that I'm correct." She looked up at Jarrod. "I *feel* it."

"All right," he said. "Now, tell me why."

"Because the only other similar name is Junot, and Colin said that Junot was recalled to Paris in January and retired from active duty. It has to be Jourdan. I went down the list of all the names of all the known officers with whom the author might correspond on a regular basis."

"How do you know they correspond regularly?" Jarrod asked the questions he knew the gentlemen in the War Office would ask.

"The greeting was informal, even friendly," she answered before resuming her theory. "I compared the names on the list to the abbreviated words. But none of the letters were right, of course, until Colin said something tonight that made me think that I might not be looking at them in the right way."

"What way?"

"Backwards. That's the answer," Gillian said. "The abbreviations are backwards. I'll stake my life on it. The author of this message sent it to Marshal Jourdan. The other abbreviations coincide with other officers' names—and not merely subordinates, but generals and colonels. When I discovered that, I realized the large numbers had to be troops." Although she struggled to keep a neutral countenance as she waltzed with Jarrod, she was practically vibrating with energy.

Jarrod grinned. It was the opportunity for which the Free Fellows League had been looking. It was a chance to make a real difference in the war and help further the work that Scovell did in the field and the argument Lord Weymouth had put before the prime minister that the government needed a department devoted to the recruiting and training of ciphers in time of war *and* in time of peace. Lord Bathurst's current group of decipherers in London was ragtag at best, and far too slow to be of any real use.

"My dear Gillian, I am so pleased I could kiss you!"

Gillian looked so surprised by Jarrod's comment that he couldn't help teasing her a bit more. "Unfortunately, I'll have to ask Colin to do it for me."

"Thank you," Gillian breathed.

"How did you do it? Here? Without any of the tables or messages?"

"I memorized the message and the list of officers' names and I've been working on the puzzle in my mind all day," she said. "But it didn't fall into place until Colin and I were dancing and he made a comment about someone being turned inside out and backwards. I thought about it for a moment and realized that might be the answer. The letters in the abbreviation that occurred most frequently were *n, a,* and *d.* At first I was looking for officers whose names started with *N.*" She smiled at Jarrod, for Colin's comment had actually been that Jarrod was so besotted by Sarah Eckersley that he was in danger of being turned inside out and backwards. The mention of Jarrod had made her think of Jourdan.

"How do you know it isn't Marshal Ney?"

"Ney backwards is y-e-n. Using the cipher tables, we've already identified the numerals corresponding to *y* and *e.* Ney didn't fit. And according to the newspapers, he's campaigning in Germany, not the Peninsula. And Ney doesn't serve under the author's command." She paused to consider her words. "None of the abbreviations matched the deciphering table until I began spelling backwards. The only officer under the author's command whose name contained those letters in that order was Marshal Jourdan. Since the abbreviation of this name was in the greeting of the message, I knew it was meant for him. We'll have to look at the original again to confirm it, but I feel certain my theory is correct."

"I've no doubt about it," Jarrod complimented her. "I marvel at your ability to solve puzzles."

The music reached its crescendo and the dance was ending.

"I suppose it's a gift," she said. "And one for which I can't take credit, since I appear to have been born with it."

"I am sincerely grateful for it," Jarrod assured her.

"There is something more," she said. "Something of which I'm less certain, but which I'm afraid requires immediate action." She glanced around. "Unfortunately, I don't dare tell you here, where we may be overheard, for fear of starting a panic."

He bowed politely and moved to escort her off the dance floor. "Will it wait until morning?"

"I don't think so," she said.

"Then may I call upon you and Colin after the ball this evening?"

"Yes," Gillian told him. "We aren't staying for the midnight supper, so we'll be waiting when you arrive."

"I thank you for the dance, Lady Grantham, and for your hard work."

"You're welcome, Lord Shepherdston."

"I'll take you back to your husband now." Jarrod escorted Gillian back to Colin.

"She told you?" Colin asked.

Jarrod nodded. "Griff?"

"He'll meet us at our house after the ball," Colin said. "Come the back way through the mews."

"What about the others?" Jarrod asked.

"I don't know," Colin said. "But I think this last bit might be better left to the three of us."

Colin was cautious, but he'd never been an alarmist. Clearly, then, this last bit of information Gillian had discovered was serious. Perhaps dangerous. And Jarrod respected Colin's decision. "All right," Jarrod assured him, "I'll be there."

But first, he had to speak to Lord Rob and arrange for his godfather to escort Lady Dunbridge and Sarah home from the ball—and to continue to escort them until further notice.

# Chapter 24

*Secure, whate'er he gives, he gives the best.*
*—Samuel Johnson, 1709–1784*

"*Will you do it?*" *Jarrod asked, after waylaying Lord* Rob in the doorway between the ballroom and the sitting room where the card tables had been set up and pulling him into Lord Garrison's study for a few minutes of private conversation.

"Of course I'll do it," Lord Rob answered. "I'll be happy to see the ladies safely home, but I'll not be happy to see you break Sarah's heart."

"Sarah?" Jarrod eyed his uncle warily. "When did she become 'Sarah' to you?"

"When I realized she was Henrietta Dunbridge's niece," Lord Rob retorted. "And don't change the subject. She's wearing her heart on her sleeve for you and you're in danger of trampling it."

"I've no intention of trampling Sarah's heart," Jarrod said. "I'm doing my damnedest to preserve it."

"By seducing her in the folly?"

"What?" He turned white.

"Henrietta and I arrived at the folly after you took Sarah inside," Lord Rob told him. "I saw you putting your clothes to rights."

"Did she?"

"No, thank heavens. I led her away from the folly and back into the maze."

"What were you doing at the folly?" Jarrod asked.

"Looking for you and Miss Eckersley." Lord Rob saw no reason to confess that he'd decided to take Henrietta to the folly for the same reason that Jarrod had taken her niece. Unfortunately, he and Henrietta had gotten a later start than Jarrod and Sarah and had taken a few wrong turns in the maze, then made use of the errors by kissing until they were aching and senseless. By the time they reached the folly, it was occupied. And although Henrietta hadn't seen Jarrod and Sarah, Lord Rob had. "Why didn't you tell me she was a lady?" he asked.

"You *knew* she was a lady," Jarrod told him. "Her aunt was standing right beside you when I introduced her."

"I meant the girl this morning," Lord Rob reminded his godson. "You introduced her as Miss Sarah Eckersley this evening. You did not introduce her as Sarah of the long red hair, lovely legs, and strawberry birthmark. But they're one and the same."

"Are they?"

"Don't make the mistake of thinking I'm a fool," Lord Rob snapped. "I saw the way you kissed the girl early this morning and I've seen the way you look at her tonight. If Sarah Eckersley and Sarah of the strawberry birthmark aren't one and the same, I'll eat my hat." He glared at his godson, truly disappointed in Jarrod for the first time in his life. "And if she is the same girl, you know bloody well that she's been compromised and that you were the man who did it."

"I kissed her, Lord Rob," Jarrod said. "I didn't dishonor her."

"This morning," Lord Rob said. "What about this evening?"

Jarrod didn't answer.

"For heaven's sake, Jarrod, she's the daughter of a recently deceased rector and she's Henrietta Dunbridge's niece."

Jarrod glared back. "What difference does it make whose daughter she is? It doesn't change anything. Her father's still dead. Her aunt is still a widow and Sarah is still without a home."

"It makes a great deal of difference to me," Lord Rob said. "And to most decent members of the ton. You are a gentleman. She was an innocent. You should never have allowed her into your home at that time of morning."

"What was I supposed to do? Have Henderson turn her back out onto the street?"

"You should have put her back in her coach and sent her back to her hotel," Lord Mayhew said.

"She didn't have a coach," Jarrod reminded him. "That's why we borrowed yours this morning."

"If she didn't have a coach, how the devil did she get from Ibbetson's Hotel to Park Lane? Which, by the by, is no place for her or her aunt to be staying without an escort." Lord Rob frowned. He'd have to remember to speak to Henrietta about that. "It's respectable, but not nearly as respectable as the Clarendon or Grillon's."

"She dismissed her coach and walked from the top of the lane to my house alone and in the rain," Jarrod interrupted, "so no one would see her coach parked outside my house."

Lord Rob raked his fingers through his hair. "Good lord! It's a miracle she wasn't accosted by anyone but you."

"I didn't accost her," Jarrod said. "I kissed her. There's a difference. And if you remember correctly, I told you why she came to my house this morning."

"What are you going to do about this?"

Jarrod sighed. "Nothing."

Lord Rob was outraged. "Nothing?"

"Sarah understands that I've no wish to marry."

"Good for Sarah," Lord Rob said sarcastically. "She's to be commended for being so understanding. I wish I could say the same and I'm certain her aunt will wish it, because tomorrow morning that girl's name and reputation are going to be offered up as fodder for the rumor mill. Every rake and rogue in town with an itch in his trousers will be knocking upon her hotel door once they hear the news that Miss Eckersley is easily persuaded to part with her virtue. And people at the party tonight will be counting the months to see if she's going to deliver the Shepherdston heir."

"She isn't," Jarrod said. "I can assure them of that."

"How? By taking out advertisements in the papers? Announcing it from the speaker's box in the House?"

"Of course not!" Jarrod began to pace the study.

"Then how, Jarrod? Because you know what will happen. All the regulars—the young bucks and the old lechers—at White's will congratulate you on your new conquest. No one will think badly of you for taking what she gave freely, but she'll be ruined. And what will you do then? Make her your mistress? Or purchase her a husband?"

"Whichever she wants," Jarrod said. "I'll do whatever she wants so long as it doesn't include marrying me."

"I don't understand." Lord Rob shook his head. "I don't understand why you find the idea of marrying her so repellent. You want her. You told me so yourself. And she wants you." He thought for a moment. "No, it's more than that. She loves you. Her heart is in her eyes every time she looks at you. You have to know it. You have to have seen it."

"I have and I do," Jarrod answered. "It hasn't changed. She's looked at me that way since I was three and ten and she was five."

"Then you should fall to your knees and thank your lucky stars for the gift of her love."

"Why?" Jarrod asked. "I never wanted it. I never asked for it. And I never encouraged it. Just the opposite." He blew out a breath. "I've done everything I know to do in order to discourage it. But she won't listen."

Jarrod sounded so much like a petulant child that Lord Rob couldn't help but smile. "Her love is a gift. You didn't have to want it. Or ask for it. Or encourage it. It is simply there for the taking."

"But why?"

Lord Rob shrugged his shoulders. "Who can say why we love the people we love?" He smiled at the man he loved as a son. "She loves you for reasons you may not understand. For reasons she may not understand. But for whatever reason, you are the man she loves. And nothing is going to change that."

"I don't want her to love me."

"Why? What's wrong with her?"

"Nothing is wrong with *her*," Jarrod said. "If I were in the market for a wife, Sarah is the first woman I'd ask. But I'm not in the market for a wife."

"You are the Marquess of Shepherdston," Lord Rob persisted. "A man with land, wealth, and hereditary titles. You have to marry someday in order to ensure succession of your line. It's your duty to your country and to your family."

"I do my duty to my country in other ways," Jarrod said. "And you are my only family. As for marrying to ensure the succession of my line, I don't intend that my line *shall* continue when I am gone."

"For God's sake, why not?" Lord Rob demanded.

Pushed to the limit, Jarrod whirled around and faced his uncle. "Because I don't want to end up like my parents!"

Lord Rob's knees gave out and he sat down hard on the top of Lord Garrison's mahogany desk. "Oh, Jarrod," he breathed. "Oh, my dear, dear boy . . ."

"I was here, Lord Rob," Jarrod reminded him. "I found them. I saw what marriage did to them. And I want no part of that!"

Lord Rob stared at the man before him. Jarrod would be one and thirty on his next natal day. Nearly sixteen years had passed since he'd inherited the title, since he'd taken possession of the Marquess of Shepherdston's signet after it had been removed from his father's lifeless hand. Sixteen years since he had become a man and the master of his own fate.

But when he looked at him, Lord Rob saw the bewildered little boy Jarrod had been. The little boy unwanted, unloved, and ignored by his father and his mother.

The need for an heir had been the only reason the previous marquess had married. He had been a rakehell who lived for the next conquest. He'd chosen his bride for her looks, her dowry, and her family name and had given little or no consideration to her nature.

And that was a mistake in judgment that he had lived to regret. The marriage between the fourth Marquess of Shepherdston and Lady Honora Blackheath was a match made in hell. It was miserable from the start and it became worse with Jarrod's birth.

The marquess had never been faithful. He cheated on his wife, on his mistress, and on whoever happened to be in his bed or in his life when someone else caught his eye. And that never changed.

But the birth of the heir gave Lady Shepherdston license to ignore her wedding vows as well—she had done her duty and provided her husband with an heir. Soon the house became crowded with past lovers, present lovers, and future lovers of both the marquess and the marchioness. And neither one had been particularly choosy about the people who shared their beds.

Jarrod was still haunted by what he'd seen, still haunted by what they had done. By the time he was five years old, he had seen almost everything, including his nursemaid and his father in bed together. At eight, he'd narrowly escaped being buggered by one of his mother's lovers by running away and locking himself in Eleanor's Folly. By the time he was ten, he'd sworn off love and lovemaking altogether, and by the time he was two and ten, Jarrod spent as much of his time as possible at Shepherdston Hall to avoid the attentions of his father's lovers who regularly propositioned him by inviting him to share their beds.

Jarrod had done his best to keep the most sordid details of his life from Griff and Colin, but he couldn't stop the whispers and gossip of the other boys at school. There was

nothing the members of the ton liked more than to gossip
about other members of the ton, and Lord and Lady Shepherdston provided their peers with deliciously juicy *on-dits*
on a daily basis. The Marquess and Marchioness of Shepherdston despised and resented each other and the marriage that kept them bound together. Bent on destruction,
they devised a vicious game where besting each other at
scandal was the prize. Neither of his parents spared a
thought for Jarrod's well-being. Their sense of their responsibilities extended only as far as seeing that he was
fed, clothed, housed, and educated.

As far as Jarrod was concerned, other than giving him
life, the greatest favor either of his parents had ever done
him was deciding to send him to the Knightsguild School
for Gentlemen shortly after his ninth birthday because it
was farther from London than Eton.

When they remembered he was alive, it was because
one of their lovers reminded them.

His childhood had been one long ongoing orgy of pain
and pleasure and deceit, from which the only escape had
been his friends at Knightsguild and their secret Free Fellows League.

And despite everything they were and everything they
had done, Jarrod had loved his parents. And on the day of
their funerals, he had sworn he would never love anyone
like that again. He would never allow anyone to hurt him
again.

"Oh, but my boy," Lord Rob said softly, "you're wrong.
Marriage wasn't responsible for your mother and father's
actions. They were."

Jarrod shook his head. "They wouldn't have been the
way they were if they hadn't gotten married."

"They would have been exactly the same whether
they'd gotten married or not. No one forced them. Your father chose your mother and she accepted. Marriage didn't
change who or what they were," Lord Rob replied. "Your
father never grew up. He fell into love with someone new
every week, but he was incapable of sustaining it. He never

took responsibility for anything in his life except his own pleasure." There was a note of bitterness in Lord Rob's voice that Jarrod had never heard before. "And even that, he often left to his bedmates. He was headstrong and childish and wildly irresponsible, and at times, terribly cruel."

Jarrod stared at his uncle, surprised by Lord Rob's assessment of the fourth Marquess of Shepherdston's character. "I thought you liked him. I thought you were his friend."

"I *did* like him," Lord Rob agreed. "That was what was damnably hard to take. He was as selfish as a child most of the time, but he was also incredibly generous at times. So much so that you couldn't help but like him. Even when you despised how he behaved and how he treated the people who loved him."

"Did *she* ever love him?"

Lord Rob shook his head. "No."

"Then why the jealous rage?"

"It wasn't jealousy," Lord Rob said slowly. "It was fury. Your mother was almost exactly like your father. And your father liked that about her. It's what attracted him to her in the first place. She was as much like one of the fellows as it was possible for a woman to be. She understood who and what he was and didn't expect him to be anything more. And Honora was every bit as selfish and irresponsible and cruel as he was. She was beautiful and she used that beauty to get her way. She used men to get her way. She had affairs and took lovers, but hers was a game of conquest just like your father's. She used men and she despised them. Just as your father used women and dismissed them. Their union was never about love. It was about power and control and the ultimate pursuit of pleasure. Their union was disastrous in most ways, but it was remarkable in another."

"In what way?" Jarrod snorted. He'd never seen anything to admire in either one of his parents and nothing to admire in their marriage.

"It produced you," Lord Rob said simply.

"And provided them with a constant, unwanted reminder of why they were together in the first place."

"That may well have been true," his uncle agreed, "but the result of their first coming together was you and if they did nothing good for the rest of their lives, they had still created an extraordinary human being. One who loved them in spite of the fact that they had never done anything to deserve it."

"What good did it do? Neither of them ever loved anything or anyone else," Jarrod said bitterly.

"Honora did," Lord Rob said. "She loved someone very much."

"Why the devil didn't she marry that person?"

"Because I was married to her," Lord Rob answered.

"Her sister?" Jarrod shuddered. He knew his mother had had nearly as many female lovers as male ones and the same was true of his father. They hadn't appeared to care about gender so long as the man or woman, or both, in their beds knew how to please them. But this . . . Please, God, Jarrod prayed. Believing their deaths had been caused by a jealous rage was bad enough, but incest . . . He took a deep breath. "She was in love with her sister?"

"No," Lord Rob explained. "Not in that way. But she loved Serena. I think Serena was the only person Honora ever loved. And Serena loved her, but she loved your father more."

"Not you?"

Lord Rob shook his head. "I wanted her to, but by the time I met and married her, Serena was already in love with her sister's husband."

Jarrod's head was reeling. "I had no idea. . . ."

"Unfortunately, neither did I at the time." Lord Rob sighed. "Serena was older than Honora by a year and should have married first. She was madly in love with your father, and everyone expected him to offer for her, but Wesley, recognizing a kindred spirit in Honora, offered for her instead."

"Did he know Serena was in love with him?"

"He knew, but Serena was high-strung and emotional and your father couldn't cope with that. He didn't care that she was in love with him. But Honora did. She married Wesley knowing that Serena wanted him, and Honora promised Serena that once she conceived the Shepherdston heir, Serena was welcome to Wesley. But I came along and unknowingly offered for Serena. Her father accepted my offer and Serena and I were wed. I didn't learn about her love for your father until much later, much too late to change the way things turned out. And you were just a boy away at school."

"What did he do?" Jarrod asked, somehow knowing that his father had been the catalyst in the tragedy.

Lord Rob took a deep breath. "They had an affair. I suppose I should be grateful that Serena and Wesley managed to delay the inevitable for as long as they did, but . . ." He paused. "She never stopped wanting him. I knew nothing about it, but at some point she crossed the line from wanting to doing. He must have been between women or finally decided to take pity on Serena or hurt your mother, but Wesley and Serena had an affair. And imagine my great pleasure when after years of failing to conceive, I learned that my wife was increasing . . ."

"With my father's child."

"I don't know," Lord Rob told him. "But whether it was his or mine made no difference to me. He or she would have been my child. My heir. But when Serena told your father about it, he broke off the affair and immediately took up with the housekeeper here at Richmond."

"And Serena died from complications of the pregnancy." Jarrod knew his aunt, Lord Rob's wife, had died with child. He hadn't known it was his father's child.

Lord Rob took another deep breath and debated on telling Jarrod the whole truth, then decided it was time the boy knew, time he understood that he was the only innocent in the entire scandalous mess.

"Serena didn't die in childbirth. She took her own life and the life of her child." He paused a moment, then continued:

"Your mother was away at the time. In Italy. I did my best to keep the news quiet." Lord Rob shuddered at the memory. He'd never seen so much blood in his life. The bathing tub had been filled with it. His wife had simply slit her wrists and bled out. By the time he found her, there was nothing anyone could have done to save her. "As a suicide, Serena couldn't be buried in consecrated ground, but the child she carried was innocent. I convinced the physician who attended her not to punish the innocent for the sins of its mother and I paid him to record her death as death by complications of pregnancy. Honora returned from Italy grief-stricken, but she seemed to be recovering, until she received the letter that had been mailed to her in Italy and had eventually found its way back to London. It was from Serena and in it, Serena had poured out her heart to your mother about her unbearable pain at Wesley's infidelity." Lord Rob raked his fingers through his hair. "Honora came to me with the letter on the pretense that she needed me to confirm that Serena had written it, but she knew Serena's handwriting as well as I did." He blew out a breath. "I think Honora simply wanted me to hurt as badly as she hurt. The letter was quite sad and quite melodramatic. Serena confessed her love for your father and said that having lain with him, and having held him in her arms, made losing him again so much more intolerable. I think Honora went a little mad at that. But I didn't see it then, didn't recognize it then. Only afterward. She seemed perfectly sane when she invited me to the house. I never suspected a thing. But I should have. I'd had Serena as an example. I should have realized that while Honora hadn't minded Wesley's infidelity to her, the fact that his infidelity to her sister caused Serena's death was unforgivable." He looked at Jarrod. "You know the rest."

Jarrod nodded. He remembered the day all too vividly. It was a Wednesday, five months to the day following his aunt Serena's death. Jarrod had arrived at the Richmond house in a hired hack, home from school for the end of term. Because it was Wednesday and the household staff's half day off, there had been no one to greet him at the front door and Jarrod had no way of knowing that less than a quarter hour earlier, Honora Shepherdston had removed a loaded pistol and ammunition from her husband's display cabinet and carried it upstairs to the master suite. She'd entered her husband's bedchamber while he was quimming the housekeeper, walked up to the bed, placed the muzzle of the pistol against the housekeeper's head, and pulled the trigger. After calmly reloading, Honora pointed the pistol at her husband.

Wesley tried to get away, but the soft feather mattresses and the weight of the housekeeper's body sprawled atop him had trapped him. Jarrod had entered the front door in time to hear his father begging for his life. But the fourth Marquess of Shepherdston's pleas had fallen on deaf ears. The pistol shot that killed him reverberated through the house as Jarrod raced up the stairs.

Jarrod had thrown open the doors to his parents' suite and rushed to his father's bedchamber. His mother, covered with blood and gore, stood beside the bed, tugging at his father's lifeless right hand.

Half of the housekeeper's face was missing and his father had no face at all. Jarrod clutched the doorframe for support, then choked, swallowed bile, and managed one word. "Mother?"

Lady Honora finished reloading and turned at the sound of her son's voice, and Jarrod found himself facing the muzzle end of the weapon. "I planned this little celebration for your homecoming, Jarrod," she said quite calmly. "My own private little celebration of your inheritance of the title. Complete with fireworks." She smiled at her son. "I invited Robert and I waited as long as I could, but he's obviously been detained. So I decided to start the party without him." She moved a few steps closer, and Jarrod had seen the look in his mother's eyes and believed he was going to die. She'd surprised him by tossing the Marquess of Shepherdston's signet ring at him. Jarrod had reacted instinctively, catching the heavy gold ring against his chest, where it left a smear of crimson against his white shirt-front. Lady Honora glanced at her husband's body, then back at her son. "Congratulations, Jarrod. You've just become the fifth Marquess of Shepherdston. The fourth one was a selfish bastard. But you'll do better. You're nothing like the spoiled and selfish Shepherdstons. You take after *my* side of the family. You're all Blackheath. . . ."

"Mother!" He saw it in her eyes, seconds before she turned the muzzle of the gun to her chest, pressed it against her heart, and pulled the trigger.

Jarrod squeezed his eyes shut. He didn't remember leaving the bedchamber, or opening the front door, but he must have, for suddenly Lord Rob was standing in the entrance hall. His uncle had taken one look at Jarrod's face and blood-splattered clothes and grasped the situation.

"Where?" Lord Rob had asked.

His uncle had expected Jarrod to point the way, but Jarrod had turned and retraced his steps up the stairs. Lord Mayhew had followed, hurrying to overtake Jarrod in an effort to prevent him from revisiting the horror, but Jarrod was already there. He stood frozen in the doorway, watching as a puddle of blood spread across the Turkey rug and flowed over the threshold, onto the floor of the sitting room.

Lord Mayhew thought he'd experienced the worst when he'd found his wife lying in a bathing tub filled with her blood, but that horror didn't begin to compare with the horror of the scene that greeted him as he entered Wesley Shepherdston's bedchamber.

The scene had haunted Jarrod for nearly sixteen years, waking him so often from his slumber that Jarrod did his utmost not to sleep. That nightmare of a memory had a way of taking him unawares, sneaking up on him when he least expected it, reminding him that he'd witnessed murder and madness and that the madness that had seized his mother flowed in his veins. She had proclaimed him all Blackheath, but she was wrong. He was Shepherdston and Blackheath and that had proved to be an extremely volatile and deadly mix. Jarrod lived in fear that the seeds of madness he carried within him could be propagated. He couldn't marry because marrying meant perpetuating his line and perpetuating his line carried the specter of madness. Jarrod broke out in a cold sweat at the thought of cursing an innocent child with those bloodlines.

"You are the only innocent person in the whole mess," Lord Rob said sadly. "You and poor Serena's unborn child."

"Poor Serena?" Jarrod asked. "You loved her in spite of everything?"

"I loved her once," Lord Rob answered. "But by the time she died, all I felt was anger and pity."

Jarrod understood. He had been angry and hurt and disgusted and grief-stricken at the time his parents died and bewildered by their complete self-destruction. And to his everlasting shame, Jarrod had loved them anyway. "I didn't . . ."

"Yes, you did," Lord Rob contradicted. "I was there, too, remember? I saw the look on your face and the pain in your eyes when you saw them like that."

But Lord Rob didn't know the whole of it. Jarrod had never revealed his mother's last words or the fact that he had seen the look in her eyes the instant before she'd decided not to kill her son and had turned the weapon on herself. It was a burden he bore alone. Something he couldn't share. For how could he describe the feeling of relief and guilt and pain and fear he'd felt when his mother had decided to spare him? "If I felt anything at all, it was relief that they couldn't hurt each other or anyone else ever again."

"Especially you." Lord Rob reached out and put his hand on Jarrod's shoulder.

"They didn't want or need my love," Jarrod said fiercely.

"No," Lord Rob agreed. "They simply took it for granted." He looked Jarrod in the eye. "As you have done with Sarah Eckersley's."

Jarrod opened his mouth to protest and realized there wasn't anything he could say to refute Lord Rob's words.

"I hear you have an appointment at Lambeth Palace tomorrow morning," Lord Rob said.

"I do," Jarrod said. "I'm to speak with His Grace about the benefice at Helford Green."

"Forget about the benefice at Helford Green," Lord Rob advised. "And purchase a special license to marry."

Jarrod closed his eyes and gritted his teeth.

"You gave Lady Dunbridge your word," Lord Rob reminded his nephew. "You promised that you would do the right thing by her niece if any untoward gossip results from tonight's visit to the folly."

Jarrod arched his eyebrow. "Are you about to start untoward gossip, Lord Rob?"

"I hadn't planned upon it," Lord Rob said. "But I will if that's what it takes to make you do the right thing," he promised. Recognizing the obstinate look on Jarrod's face, Lord Rob softened his tone. One thing his parents had given the boy was a double dose of stubbornness. "Unfortunately, I don't think it's going to be necessary for me to start the untoward gossip."

Jarrod raked his fingers through his hair. "Have you heard anything?"

"Other than the fact that you allowed Lord Dunbridge to record a wager between the two of you over Miss Eckersley's season-ending nuptials?"

Jarrod groaned. He'd forgotten about the wager.

"How long do you think that's going to remain a secret among gentlemen?" Lord Rob asked. "And how do you think Sarah is going to feel when she hears about it? Because someone is bound to tell her."

He hadn't thought about that when he'd allowed that dandified fool Dunbridge to record their wager. "Bloody hell!"

"Ask the girl to marry you, Jarrod. Give yourself a chance to love and be loved in return. Stop living in fear of being hurt again. Life is messy, my boy, but it's a hell of a lot better than the alternative. Do yourself a favor and try living it. Take a gigantic leap of faith and allow yourself to reach your full potential by putting all this sordidness behind you and becoming happy and whole and free."

"Free?" Jarrod scoffed.

"Yes, free," Lord Rob said. "Because loving the right person and being loved by the right person doesn't hold you back. It sets you free."

"Shepherdstons have traditionally never been very good at monogamy and marriage, Lord Rob," Jarrod persisted.

"Then break tradition, my boy, and excel at it." He clamped Jarrod on the shoulder. "And do it now while you're young enough to truly appreciate it."

# Chapter 25

*What dire offense from amorous causes springs,*
*What mighty contests rise from trivial things!*
—Alexander Pope, 1688–1744

"May I have the honor of a dance, Miss Eckersley?" Sarah looked up to find Reginald Blanchard, Lord Dunbridge, standing before her.

"No, Lord Dunbridge." She shook her head. "I think not."

"You cannot use your mourning as an excuse," Lord Dunbridge said. "You danced earlier. I saw you."

"I don't intend to make any excuses," she said. "I danced with my escort, who sought permission from my aunt and our hostess in order that I might do so." She stared at the man who had turned her out of the rectory. "I haven't danced with anyone else all evening."

"You will, of course, make an exception for me." He adjusted his gaudy red and purple waistcoat, preening like a peacock before her. "Your betrothed. Just as you made an exception for your escort, Lord Shepherdston."

Sarah frowned. "You, Lord Dunbridge, are laboring under a misconception if you suppose that I am your betrothed or that you are mine."

"Of course we're betrothed," Lord Dunbridge told her. "When Brummell suggested I take a wife who would suit me perfectly, I chose you. I approached your father before he died and asked for your hand in marriage."

Sarah shuddered at the idea. "My father refused to take your suit seriously and so did I."

"Why not?" Lord Dunbridge asked. "For I am serious about marrying you. And you may trust that everything is in order. Come, my dear, don't be shy. I'll not have it said that I neglected my betrothed." He reached for her hand to pull her out of her chair.

Sarah snatched her hand back, then jumped to her feet. She turned to escape and ran right into Jarrod's chest.

"Good evening, Lord Dunbridge," Jarrod said as he slipped his arm around Sarah's waist to steady her. He reached down to her wrist and opened her dance card. "I beg your pardon for interrupting, but I believe Miss Eckersley promised me this waltz."

"You cannot dance with her twice in one evening," Lord Dunbridge said. "People will talk."

"People in the ton will talk whether we dance one dance or a hundred," Lord Shepherdston told him. "That is the nature of the beast and the curse with which we live."

"I'll not have you make me a laughingstock, Lord Shepherdston, by dancing two dances with my betrothed."

"You don't need me to make you a laughingstock, Lord Dunbridge," Jarrod told him, eyeing his loud purple and red waistcoat. "You do that quite well on your own. Now, if you will excuse us, Dunbridge, Miss Eckersley and I have an appointment."

Jarrod was moving to usher Sarah past Lord Dunbridge, when the older man suddenly removed his glove and slapped Jarrod across the face with it.

The crowd of people surrounding them gasped en masse.

"Bloody hell!" Griffin saw the commotion from his vantage point across the room near the terrace doors, where he and Alyssa and Colin and Gillian and the Garrisons were conversing. "Who let him in?"

"Who?" Alyssa asked.

"Christ! It's Dunbridge." Colin followed Griffin's line of sight and answered for him.

Alyssa turned to her sister. "Was he invited?"

"His name was on the guest list," Anne replied.

"Lord Shepherdston didn't suggest that you remove it?" Colin asked.

"No," Lady Garrison answered. "Lord Shepherdston would never do that."

"No, he wouldn't," Colin said. "Because that would have been too easy."

"Damn," Griffin swore again, "Jarrod had hoped Dunbridge would give the ladies wide berth."

"Why?" Lady Garrison was curious.

"Because they asked Lord Shepherdston to keep Lord Dunbridge away from them." Griffin shook his head. "But it seems even Dunbridge is determined to make something of his visit here tonight—if only more bad memories."

"Why? How?" Lord Garrison demanded.

But Griffin had already left the group and was striding across the ballroom, ignoring the ache in his injured thigh. Colin followed close behind him. Lord Garrison was slower off the mark, but he soon followed as well.

❧

*Alyssa clucked her tongue as the three women stood* and watched their husbands cross the ballroom. The crowd had parted like the Red Sea before Moses when Griffin began crossing the floor and now Alyssa, Anne, and Gillian had a clear view of the edge of the dance floor where Lord Shepherdston and Lord Dunbridge stood facing each other like two dogs squabbling over a bone and with Sarah Eckersley caught in the middle. "This doesn't bode well for Miss Eckersley."

Anne agreed. "A disappearance into the garden with Lord Shepherdston, two dances, and now two gentlemen fighting over her."

"They haven't actually danced one entire dance," Gillian corrected, "but now the gossips will have them dancing every dance together."

"And she's been sitting on the sidelines with her aunt

and Lord Mayhew ever since they returned from their tour of the garden," Alyssa said.

❧

*Lord Garrison caught up with Griff and Colin as* they made their way across the room. "What's the matter?" he asked.

"Dunbridge just slapped Jarrod across the face with his glove," Colin answered in a low voice, mindful of the guests who were ignorant of the drama taking place.

"And we need to see that those two guests behave themselves," Griff added. "We don't want Anne's party ruined by another scandal or the floors ruined with spilled blood."

Griff, Richard Garrison, and Colin arrived just as Dunbridge spat out the challenge, "Now, you'll have an appointment with me at the dueling oak at dawn on the morrow."

Jarrod grabbed hold of Lord Dunbridge's glove and snatched it out of his hand. "I have a full schedule tomorrow," he warned. "I would prefer not to have to fit killing you into it."

"This is no jesting matter, Lord Shepherdston," Dunbridge cautioned.

"I'm not jesting."

"I've issued a challenge," Dunbridge reminded him. "An honorable gentleman would respond."

"I have responded by telling you that I've neither the time nor the inclination to meet you at the dueling oak at dawn." Jarrod narrowed his gaze at Dunbridge and spoke in his coldest tone of voice, hoping the fool would take the hint and save his own life. "Dueling is frowned upon. And you haven't enough blood in reserve or internal organs to spare to survive an encounter with me."

"Pick your seconds," Dunbridge ordered. "For I will be at the oak with mine at dawn on the morrow." He turned on his heel and blanched when he recognized Griffin and Lord Garrison, but managed to recover enough to bow to Sarah and say his farewells. "Until the morrow, my dear. Good night, my lords. Your Grace."

"Your glove, Lord Dunbridge." Jarrod waved the article beneath the other man's nose. "I doubt Brummell would approve of your leaving one of an expensive matched set behind."

"Jarrod," Griffin said when Dunbridge made his exit, "we do not need this type of notoriety."

"I'm aware of that, Your Grace."

"But we will be honored to stand beside you whatever your intentions."

Jarrod understood. "Thank you, Your Grace, but I prefer not to discuss dancing and duels in the same breath or to provide this assemblage with more fodder for gossip." A muscle began to tick in Jarrod's clenched jaw as he struggled to keep a rein on his temper. "But I assure you my intentions are honorable, for I intend to dance this dance with Miss Eckersley. And since Her Grace asked me to stand in your stead for the last waltz, I'm going to dance that one with her and then I'm going to be about my business for the evening and let tomorrow resolve itself."

"Very well," Griffin said. "We'll leave you to it."

❧

*The crowd was buzzing by the time Jarrod led Sarah* onto the dance floor once again. And the buzz of the gossip had an ominous ring to it. The scene that had taken place had been embellished to the point of legend in a matter of minutes. Fanciful new versions of confrontation between Lord Shepherdston and Lord Dunbridge were occurring at an alarming rate and the only constant was the names of the participants. By morning, Sarah's good name and reputation would be reduced to tatters.

"Oh, Jays, I'm so sorry," Sarah apologized. "This is all my fault."

"It's Dunbridge's fault," Jarrod told her. "Because he won't take no for an answer."

"Are you going to accept his challenge?" Sarah asked. "Are you going to meet him at the dueling oak at Wimbledon Downs at dawn?"

"Unless he withdraws his challenge." He nodded. "And I did everything I could to give that dandified fool a dignified way out. I sincerely hope he takes it because I would like to be in bed by dawn."

The music began and Jarrod placed his hand on Sarah's waist, took her other hand in his, and stepped into the measure of the dance.

"I didn't plan to keep you at the party quite that late, Jays."

Jarrod laughed. "Plans do have a way of changing. Consider mine. I've thought about you all evening," he whispered, leaning close.

She blushed. "Why, thank you, Lord Shepherdston, I've thought about you all evening, too."

The electricity between them was palpable.

"I was afraid my behavior earlier this evening had frightened you away."

"Were you?" Sarah asked. "Or were you simply hoping that was the case? Because you no doubt know that your behavior earlier this evening has whetted my appetite for more."

Her admission surprised him. "Has it?"

"You know it has." She met his gaze. "What about you?"

"What about me?"

"You've been quite busy tonight. I saw you dancing with Gillian. Has this evening whetted your appetite for me?"

"You know it has," he said huskily.

"Then take me home with you," Sarah suggested.

"I can't," he said. "That's where the change of plans comes in. You see, *I* had planned to take you and your aunt home at the conclusion of tonight's entertainment. But I've a meeting that requires my urgent attention, so I've asked Lord Rob to do it."

"And I was hoping that you . . ." She looked down at their feet.

"That I . . ." he encouraged softly.

"Might continue my lessons when you took me home."

"Oh?" He arched an eyebrow in the gesture that Sarah loved. "And what did you intend that we do with Aunt Etta while we were at lessons?"

"I had hoped that you would ask Lord Rob to see her home in his vehicle and that we could follow in yours."

"You've given this a great deal of thought, haven't you?"

"What else have I had to think about?" she asked. "I've been sitting here on the sidelines all evening watching you dance with other women."

Jarrod frowned. "I danced with Gillian McElreath so that Colin and Griffin could talk business in private." It wasn't a lie. He had done that. But he'd also danced with Gillian so that she could brief him on the business he needed to know.

"You danced with Gillian so she wouldn't overhear what Lord Grantham and His Grace were discussing."

"Sarah! You wound me with your accusations," he teased.

"I know you, Jarrod," she said. "When we were growing up you and your friends were always whispering and keeping secrets amongst yourselves."

He didn't recall Sarah ever being around when his friends were visiting him at Shepherdston Hall. "How do you know what we did?" he asked. "You were never around when Grantham and Abernathy visited me at Shepherdston Hall." Because he hadn't allowed her to tag along when his male friends were around.

"You didn't invite me to keep you company when they were around, so I spied on you every chance I got."

Her confession stunned him. "You spied on us?"

Sarah smiled a knowing smile. "Of course."

"How long?"

"Whenever I could slip away from the rectory," she answered. "And I would stay as long as I could. Usually until Aunt Etta called me to supper."

"No." Jarrod shook his head. "I mean, how long? How many years?"

"For always."

"Recently?" Jarrod asked. "Or just when we were children?"

"You haven't been to Shepherdston Hall recently," she reminded him. "You've stayed in London. There used to be a flurry of activity around it, with riders going in and out, but that was only when you, or Lord Grantham, were in residence," she said. "There hasn't been as much activity lately, but I suppose that's because there hasn't been anyone in residence at the hall since Lord and Lady Grantham honeymooned there."

"You didn't!"

"Of course not," she protested. "I would never spy on a honeymooning couple." *Unless it was Jarrod and a bride other than me!* "I heard someone was staying at the hall and I asked Papa who it was. He told me it was your friend Lord Grantham and his bride." She smiled up at him. "It was nice of you to lend Grantham your house for a honeymoon. I always imagined it would be a nice place for one." Smiling, Sarah closed her eyes and allowed herself to dream once again as Jarrod whirled her around the ballroom.

"Really?" He arched his eyebrow once again.

"Yes."

"I suppose you could ask Lady Grantham if that is the case," Jarrod ventured.

"I suppose I could ask her," she said, opening her eyes to look at him. "But that won't be nearly as fun as marrying you and finding out for myself."

# Chapter 26

*As true as I live.*
—Thomas Middleton, 1580–1627

*He looked stunned. Trapped like a fox in a hole. Terri-*fied that his life was about to come to an end.

"I thought you didn't want to marry. I thought you had your heart set on being a courtesan." Jarrod pinned her with a look.

"Why?" she asked, finally understanding what Aunt Etta had been trying to tell her about the anguish of loving someone who didn't love you in return. "Are you about to take me up on the offer?"

"I distinctly remember you telling me that I would make a good lover, but that I was hardly husband material."

"I lied," Sarah said simply.

"Why?"

"Because I love you, Jarrod."

He froze. "You say you love me, yet you admit to lying to me?"

"Yes," she said. "And I would do it again if I had to in order to give you what you want."

He frowned. "I don't understand."

"No, you don't," she answered. "And the sad part of it is that you may never understand. Loving isn't all taking, Jarrod. Sometimes it's giving."

"I gave," he protested. "In Eleanor's Folly, I didn't just take, I gave."

"Yes," she agreed, smiling at the memory. "You gave me incredible pleasure and you allowed me to give you pleasure. And I will always be grateful to you for teaching me about desire. But you did that with your body, Jarrod. Not with your heart."

"I don't know how to do anything with my heart," Jarrod told her. "Except protect it."

"Then you should understand that that's what I tried to do," she told him. "Whenever I dreamed of you, I always dreamed that when you saw me all grown up, you'd look at me and fall on your knees and ask me to marry you. But you made no secret of the fact that you don't want a wife, so I tried to become your lover. When that didn't work, I tried to convince you that I would rather be someone else's lover."

"Why?"

"To make you jealous," she admitted. "To make you admit that you love me a little. But you weren't jealous. And you don't love me—even a little—and I can't pretend anymore."

"Sarah . . ."

"I look at you and I see the man I love and you look at me and see a nuisance. I love you, but my love causes you aggravation and frustration. And love isn't supposed to cause aggravation and frustration." She looked up at him and there were tears in her eyes when she spoke. "It isn't supposed to be a thorn in your side. Or an itch you can't be rid of. It's supposed to be something you cherish. Something you are glad to have. You're a proud man, Lord Shepherdston. A fine, honorable man. A man any woman would be proud to call her own. But I have pride, too. I've loved you since I was a little girl. I've tried to be a part of your life and to prove to you that I could be trusted with your heart by keeping your secret. I knew about your league and I never breathed a word of it because I knew that keeping it secret was important to you. And keeping each other's secrets and overlooking each other's faults is what love and friendship is all about. But you haven't learned that yet." She stopped to draw a shaky breath. "I've loved you nearly all my life and I just realized that I was wrong."

"What do you mean you were wrong?" he asked.

"When I said you were a very attractive man and that I had no doubt you'd be an excellent lover, but you were hardly what one would want in a husband, I thought I was lying because I only said it to prick your pride and make you think. I said it to make you look at me with new eyes and see that you were exactly the right husband material for me because I loved you. Because I believed we were made for each other. But I was wrong. We weren't made for each other." She gave a sad little laugh. "I've been fighting what you've been trying to tell me all along."

The last strains of the waltz died away and Sarah stopped dancing.

"And what was that?" he asked, suddenly, terribly afraid that she had finally seen the real man, instead of the man she wanted him to be. Terribly afraid that she had finally seen the truth.

"That I shouldn't want a man who thinks my love is an aggravation, a nuisance, and a bother. Because the truth is that you *are* hardly husband material. I thought I was lying, but I was speaking the truth. I grew up knowing I wasn't beautiful and that I hadn't a title or a great fortune, and I've spent my life striving to be good enough for you. But the truth, Lord Shepherdston, is that you aren't nearly good enough for me."

❧

*Sarah cried the whole way home. She didn't make a* sound as she rode in the coach beside Aunt Etta and opposite Lord Mayhew, but she couldn't stop crying.

Once again, she'd made a cake of herself over Jarrod Shepherdston. And everything had been going so well until she'd slipped and told him how much she wanted to marry him. Everything had been going so well until she'd seen the look on his face.

She had come so close to having her dream and she had ruined it with the truth.

"Sarah," Aunt Etta said gently, "don't cry, my dear, he'll come around."

"No, he won't." She cried harder. "Not after tonight, not after what I said."

"What did you say, my dear, that was so terrible?" Lord Mayhew asked.

"I told him I loved him."

"That's good," Lord Mayhew said. "Everything is going to be all right. I promise. The boy will come around. He's stubborn, but he's not stupid."

Sarah looked up and gave Lord Mayhew a tremulous smile. "He may come around," she whispered. "But will I still want him when he does?" That was the question that frightened her so. She had loved him all her life, and now, she was afraid it had all been for naught.

"I don't think you have to worry," Lord Mayhew soothed. "For I don't think there's an inconstant bone in your body."

*Jarrod was in a rare high fit of temper by the time* he arrived at Colin and Gillian's home at 21 Park Lane. How dare Sarah do this to him? How dare she fill his head with all this nonsense about him never growing up? He'd become the marquess at six and ten. He'd shouldered the weight and the responsibility of running a large estate and managing several households and dozens of employees. Who did she think she was to tell him he wasn't good enough for her? He was the fifth Marquess of Shepherdston.

If she expected him to chase her, she was in for a surprise. He'd had women chasing him since he was two and ten years old, for God's sake! He didn't need to chase anyone.

But every time he closed his eyes he saw Sarah. Sarah laughing. Sarah smiling. Sarah confessing her love for him. Sarah crying. Sarah walking away.

His temper suddenly dissolved and disbelief set in. After all the years of following him around like a puppy wherever he went, after spying on him and trying her damnedest to seduce him, Sarah had walked away without a backward glance.

And although he'd had every opportunity, Jarrod hadn't been able to find the words to ask her to stay.

And although he'd given that arrogant damned dandy that started this mess a way out of it, Dunbridge had given no sign of withdrawing and that meant that in a few short hours, Jarrod would have to meet him at the dueling oak in order to save his honor and Sarah's reputation. The reputation he'd put at risk with his own carelessness. Jarrod didn't know if he ought to shoot Lord Dunbridge or allow the fool to shoot him.

How could he have been so foolish? How could he have allowed his life to become so chaotic in one day? When all he'd had to do to prevent it was offer to marry her when she'd showed up on his door.

So, why hadn't he?

Because he'd been afraid. Afraid that once she really knew him, once she married him, she wouldn't love him anymore.

Jarrod took off his hat and raked his fingers through his hair before ringing the bell. Blister it! But he'd never dreamed he would turn out to be such a coward. He'd never been afraid to risk anything before; but then, he had never risked his heart.

Now he was haunted by the possibility that he had killed her love. Jarrod didn't think he could endure another round of Sarah's rejection. But how could he endure losing *her?*

For the first time in his adult life, Jarrod couldn't think what to do. Jarrod Shepherdston, the man they'd called

Merlin because he could conjure up a solution to anything, was lost. And all because Sarah had walked away.

All because he had been too afraid to take what she offered.

All because he had thrown her love back in her face.

"Good evening, Lord Shepherdston," Britton, Colin and Gillian's butler, greeted as he opened the front door wide for Jarrod to enter. "Won't you come in?"

"Is it still evening, Britton?" Jarrod asked.

"No, sir, I believe you're correct," Britton replied. "It is after midnight. Allow me to take your hat and gloves, sir." The butler practically had to pry Jarrod's fingers from around the crushed silk brim of his top hat, but he managed to finally take it. "Lord and Lady Grantham are awaiting you in the study. His Grace has yet to arrive."

Jarrod wasn't surprised. After Sarah left him, Jarrod had stood in for Griffin and danced the last waltz with Alyssa, then gone in search of Lord Rob only to find that his uncle had left the party and was escorting the ladies back to their hotel. Griffin and Alyssa had still been saying their good-byes when Jarrod had left.

As he followed Britton from the front door to the study, Jarrod noticed, for the first time, that Colin's house was filled with vases of artistically arranged fresh flowers and bowls of dried flower petals and leaves that gave the rooms a nice fragrance. He never had fresh flowers in his house, or bowls of dried ones, and his shirts and linen never smelled as nice as Griff's or Colin's. And whenever Henderson or Pomfrey brought coffee or tea, they never brought along little sandwiches or biscuits or cakes, the way Britton—and Keswick and Mason, Griffin's butlers—always did.

Little sandwiches and biscuits and cakes were always available at Jarrod's houses, but he'd always had to ask for them. No one in his male-dominated households ever thought to provide the tiny comforts that Colin and Griffin now took for granted.

Jarrod entered the study and stood staring at the tray of coffee and sandwiches on the butler's table beside Gillian.

"Hello, Lord Shepherdston." Gillian looked up from the cipher table she was adjusting and saw Jarrod looking forlorn and out of place.

Colin looked up as well. "Come in, Jarrod, and get warm." It had begun to rain and the evening air was damp and chilly. "Gilly had Britton bring in some coffee."

"Yes, please, Lord Shepherdston, won't you come in and make yourself comfortable?" She motioned him toward a leather chair near the fire. A pretty embroidered pillow in a Scottish thistle design rested in the seat. "I'm working on a series of Scottish-themed designs," she explained when she noticed him eyeing the pillow. "And Colin likes to show off my needlework, but if pillows bother you, just push it aside or set it on the floor."

"Leave it where it is and sit down," Colin instructed. "Try it. I never noticed how uncomfortable those chairs were until Gilly started putting pillows in them to lean against. Makes all the difference in the world. Especially if you prop your feet on the ottoman."

Jarrod sat down and put his feet on the ottoman. Those pillows did make the chair more comfortable.

"Are you hungry?" Gillian asked. Lord Shepherdston hadn't said a word since he'd entered the study.

Suddenly realizing he hadn't eaten anything since early afternoon, Jarrod put his feet down and leaned forward.

"No." Gillian waved him back into his seat. "Stay where you are. I'll make you a plate. Would you like roast beef or chicken or cucumber?" When he didn't sit back or answer her polite query, she lifted a small plate from the table and filled it with two of each, then added a small scone and a wedge of gingerbread. "Would you like coffee or something stronger?" She looked from Jarrod to her husband and back again. "Colin," she said softly, "something's wrong with Lord Shepherdston."

Colin came around the table in two strides. "Jarrod, are you all right?"

Jarrod looked up at him. "Why didn't we ever have

vases of flowers and bowls filled with the dried pieces all over the house?" he demanded.

Colin blinked. He and Griffin had rented a London town house together until Griff married. Then Colin had moved into Jarrod's London town house. He'd kept a suite of rooms in Jarrod's London house and at Shepherdston Hall until he'd married Gillian. "I don't know," he replied. "I never noticed the lack or thought about them until I married Gillian."

Jarrod glanced at Gillian. "They're nice."

"Thank you, Lord Shepherdston." Gillian handed him the plate of food and was gratified to see him wolf the sandwiches down.

"And the pillows you made and the sandwiches that always come with the coffee and whatever it is you do to make Colin's shirts smell good . . ."

"I tuck clove and sandalwood sachets in his linen drawer," Gillian answered.

"That's nice, too."

"Thank you, again." Gillian smiled.

Jarrod nodded toward the pillow. "Sewing a design like that probably takes a long time, doesn't it?"

"Yes," Gillian answered. "When you're first learning it takes quite a bit of time to do it right, but once you master the stitches, the degree of difficulty depends on the detail of the design."

"Why do you do it?" Jarrod asked. "When it isn't necessary?"

"It's a way of showing I care," she said. "My mother calls them 'loving touches'—all these little extra things we do to make our houses and the people we care about more comfortable."

*Her mother.* Jarrod often forgot that his friends had mothers who cared about them. He had been without one so long. And had never had one who cared about him. It seemed impossible that a good many people still did.

Gillian smiled at Colin as she continued her explanation. "When Colin puts on his shirts and smells the sachets, it's a reminder that I love him and care about his comfort. When guests enter our home and see vases of flowers, they know I love my husband and home enough to welcome our friends."

Jarrod closed his eyes and groaned. "Christ!" He thought back to all the times Sarah had followed him around the grounds at Shepherdston Hall, all the times she'd tagged after him between the village and Shepherdston Hall, when she'd bring him a lunch or share hers with him. How she'd always offer him a biscuit or a piece of gingerbread and how she gifted him with sticks of peppermint and carefully embroidered handkerchiefs bearing his initials or family motto or tiny stitched replicas of his family crest every Boxing Day.

He had taken the tokens for granted, considering them the gifts of a girl trying to curry favor. When all the time, she was trying to show him how much she cared in the only way she could.

And in all the time he'd known her, Jarrod had never once given her anything in return.

"What is it, Jarrod?" Colin asked.

"She *did* love me," he replied in wonder.

"Your mother?"

"No." Jarrod shook his head. "Sarah."

"Of course she loves you," Gillian said. "One has only to look at her when you're in the room to see it."

"She *did* love me," Jarrod repeated, "but I'm afraid I killed it."

"How?" Colin demanded.

"By always taking," Jarrod said. "And never trusting her enough to give her my heart." He leaned forward, propped his elbows on his knees, and cradled his head in his hands. "I've never given her a thing."

"Then it's time you began," Griffin said from the doorway. "And you'll be getting a very early start on a very busy day, Lord Shepherdston, unless Dunbridge has withdrawn his challenge and gifted you with a couple of hours of additional sleep. . . ."

"He hasn't," Colin replied.

Griff shook his head. "Then you have a duel at dawn." He turned to Jarrod. "Since we haven't heard from Dunbridge's seconds, I'll supply the dueling pieces. I know you dislike firearms, but the choice is ours and you're an excellent shot. Dunbridge isn't." He held up his hand when Jarrod would have interrupted. "Take it from me, sword cuts hurt like the very devil and take forever to heal. You have a better chance of surviving unharmed with a pistol, and it goes without saying that we want you unharmed for myriad reasons, including the fact that you've a breakfast at White's, a meeting at Whitehall at eight, a meeting with the archbishop of Canterbury at nine, and a great deal of shopping to do."

"Shopping?"

Griffin nodded. "You love the girl, don't you?"

Jarrod looked bewildered.

"Is the world a better place when you're with her?" Griffin asked.

"Do you find yourself laughing and smiling and thinking of things you'd like to tell her at the oddest moments?" Colin added.

"Does she make you feel there's nothing in the world you can't accomplish if you put your mind to it?" Griffin asked. "Even when you're trembling in your boots at the idea of attempting it?"

Colin reached for Gillian's hand and squeezed it. "Do you find yourself looking forward to evenings at home alone with her? Or thinking about the sexes and names of your unborn children? Can you envision your life without her?"

"Do you want to give her the moon and stars?" Gillian asked.

"My heart," Jarrod burst out. "I want to give her my heart."

"Give her your heart *after* you give her a cartload of gifts," Griffin advised. "After what happened tonight and what's likely to happen when the morning newspapers hit the stands, her reputation is ruined. You're going to do a great deal of groveling before you can expect to marry the girl; otherwise, she may try to cut your heart out with a spoon. . . ."

"In other words," Colin said, "shopping. And if I were you, I'd start with a ring."

"And now that that's settled," Griffin drawled, "let's let Gillian tell us what she's discovered. . . ."

# Chapter 27

*Without hope, we live in desire.*
—*Dante Alighieri, 1265–1321*

"She's asleep at last." Lady Dunbridge tiptoed out of the bedchamber she shared with Sarah and into the tiny sitting room where Lord Mayhew waited.

Lord Mayhew shouldn't have been there at all. But the fact that he had carried Sarah up the stairs, into the room, and placed her on the bed had allowed him entrance, and now he was loath to leave. "A good night's sleep will do her a world of good," he said. "She'll see things in a better light in the morning."

"I hope so," Lady Dunbridge said. "I thought my heart would break. I've never seen anyone look so hurt and lost as Sarah did when all her lovely dreams came crashing down around her, and I could have cheerfully strangled Shepherdston with my bare hands for hurting her." She turned to Lord Mayhew. "I don't know if I dare leave her alone long enough to meet you at Ackermann's in the morning."

Lord Mayhew smiled at her. "This morning, my love. And there's no need to meet me at Ackermann's. I'll simply wait for you to complete your morning ablutions and escort you to Lambeth Palace. I can purchase a special license and we can be married there or in any church that takes your fancy along the way back."

"I had planned to ask Sarah to walk Precious for me in the park while I slipped out to meet you." She nodded toward her King Charles spaniel sleeping peacefully on Lord Mayhew's foot. "But now, I don't know that I should. . . ." She bit her bottom lip and frowned.

"We could postpone it another day or two," Lord Mayhew said. "But I've already waited twenty years to marry you and I hate the thought of adding to it."

"What about Lord Shepherdston?" Lady Dunbridge asked. "Will he really face Reggie in a duel?"

Lord Mayhew snorted. "Jarrod will be there. He was publicly challenged. He has to show up or risk losing his honor. Especially since Dunbridge also recorded that ridiculous wager and Sarah's name in the betting books at White's. . . ."

Lady Dunbridge looked at him in sudden dread. "What ridiculous wager?"

"Dunbridge wagered a thousand pounds that he would marry Miss Sarah Eckersley at season's end. Jarrod wagered that wouldn't be the case."

"Good heavens!" Lady Dunbridge exclaimed. "But Reggie has turned out to be worse than I thought. Imagine evicting a girl from her home and dragging her reputation through the mud in order to force her to marry him. How could he believe it would work?"

"How could it not work?" Lord Mayhew posed the question for the sake of argument. "When you look at it from Dunbridge's point of view? Sarah was the daughter of the late rector. Why wouldn't she want to marry a wealthy viscount?"

"Because he's Reggie Blanchard and she's in love with Jarrod Shepherdston."

"But Shepherdston has made his aversion to marriage quite clear. Dunbridge knows that all he has to do is force the issue. Once he has Sarah at his mercy, who is going to stand in his way? Especially since he's a wealthy viscount and an excellent catch for a rector's daughter? Most other girls would have crawled to Dunbridge on their knees and begged him to save them." Lord Mayhew smiled. "But our rector's daughter took a different approach. She refused to settle for Dunbridge so long as there was a chance she might have the man she loves. It was really quite extraordinary." He looked at Henrietta. "When you think about it, Dunbridge has done us a favor. He's forced Jarrod's hand, so you and I don't have to. The question at hand is whether Dunbridge has the courage to make an appearance at Wimbledon Downs."

"*He* issued the challenge."

"Yes, he did," Lord Mayhew agreed. "In the heat of the moment in order to avoid further embarrassment. Still, Jarrod gave him a dozen excuses to withdraw. Let's hope he's smart enough to make use of them."

"I don't know," Lady Dunbridge said. "When I think of the hell he's put us through these last few days and the fact that he's responsible for shredding Sarah's good name, having Lord Shepherdston skewer him might prove very satisfactory."

"I believe swords are passé," Lord Mayhew said. "Dueling pistols are the thing nowadays."

"A shot through the heart would be equally satisfying," Lady Dunbridge said with relish.

"To you, perhaps, my darling, but not for Jarrod. He's been involved in far too many scandals and seen too much destruction."

"I'd forgotten about that," Lady Dunbridge said. "I was living in Helford Green by then, and although there were a few whispers when the bodies were brought back for burial in the family plot, most everyone in the village simply let the dead stay dead for Lord Shepherdston's sake."

"Would that it was so simple for the rest of us," Lord Mayhew breathed.

"Oh, Robert, I'm so sorry," Lady Dunbridge whispered. "It was such a tragedy for Lord Shepherdston and for you. They were part of your family and you had only recently lost your wife."

Lord Mayhew sighed. "My wife's death caused it."

Lady Dunbridge covered his hand with hers. "I didn't know."

"No one did," he told her. "Not even Jarrod. Until I told him tonight."

"Oh, no."

He nodded. "I feel responsible for what happened between him and Sarah. If I hadn't just told him the truth about his parents' deaths, he might have been better able to handle hearing Sarah's declaration of love."

"If wishes were horses, beggars would ride," Lady Dunbridge quoted wistfully. "Sarah's love for him has never been a secret to Lord Shepherdston; he simply didn't realize the depths of it. He's frightened by the responsibility of loving her in return. Marriage is the least of it."

"No," Lord Mayhew disagreed. "Marriage is the heart of it. And it may seem silly to us, but we didn't grow up the way he did. I saw the destruction wrought in the name of marriage, but I was an adult. I can't imagine how he must have felt as a child. . . ."

"Living at Helford Green, with Shepherdston Hall right down the way, we heard the rumors of wild parties and other antics, but I never dreamed it could be as bad as they made it out to be." Lady Dunbridge moved closer to Lord Mayhew.

"Oh, Henrietta," he said, "it was every bit as bad as the rumors and worse." Taking a deep breath, Lord Mayhew told the story of what happened to Jarrod's parents for the second time in one night, promising himself that once he was done, he'd never breathe a word of it again for as long as he lived. "Jarrod found his parents. His mother murdered his father and the housekeeper before killing herself. And the scene has fueled Jarrod's nightmares and mine ever since. It was a scene no human being should ever have to witness, least of all a boy of sixteen who should have been left with some illusions about his parents, a boy who should have been allowed some innocence. . . ."

In the next room, Sarah, who had pretended to sleep so that Aunt Etta wouldn't worry, now lay awake listening as

Lord Mayhew revealed the whole horrible story. And when he finished telling Aunt Etta about the tragedy Jarrod had endured, Sarah discovered she loved Jarrod all the more for having become the man he was.

For if ever there was a little boy who had reason to distrust, it was the boy she'd known as Jays. And if ever a man had reason to prefer the veracity of physical desire and to question the abstract of love, it was the fifth Marquess of Shepherdston, for he had known too much of one and not enough of the other.

It didn't excuse his behavior. It only explained it. Everyone Jarrod had ever loved had let him down except Lord Mayhew and the Free Fellows. And he'd clung to them because they were the only people he trusted, the only people he knew who accepted him as he was.

Because the mighty Marquess of Shepherdston was terrified of loving and being hurt. Terrified of being alone and abandoned.

Sarah understood.

She'd loved and lost. She knew the fear of being alone. She knew the pain of feeling abandoned, first when her mother died and later, when she'd lost her father. But she had never really been alone or abandoned. She had always had Aunt Etta and Jarrod.

Aunt Etta was about to marry Lord Mayhew. And Sarah was happy for her aunt, thrilled that Aunt Etta had found love with the man she'd dreamed about after all these years.

Now, it was time for Sarah to do the same.

⟋⟍

*Jarrod waited in his coach at the dueling oak as the* sun began its ascent into the eastern sky. He stamped his feet to ward off the chill and sipped at the flask of whisky-laced coffee Colin had brought along.

Griff had brought along a pair of beautifully balanced dueling pistols and Jarrod fervently hoped he didn't have to

use them. Unlike Griff or Colin, Jarrod had never killed another human being and hoped he never would. He'd been
fortunate that his part in the war had primarily been spent in
financially supporting the numerous clandestine activities
in which the Free Fellows engaged. Oh, he'd been on smuggling runs and had been fired upon a time or two, but he'd
never shot anyone with the intent to wound or kill and he'd
never had to dispatch a man with a sword or knife as Colin
and Griff had been forced to do.

Jarrod didn't doubt that he could kill if he was forced to
do so, but an imagined slight like the one Dunbridge had
accused him of seemed a silly reason to contemplate
killing a man. Dunbridge wasn't protecting Sarah's honor
any more than he was. They were quarreling like children
over a favorite toy and the fact that he had allowed Dunbridge to maneuver him into this position infuriated him.

"Do you think he's coming?" Colin asked, shifting into
a more comfortable position.

"I haven't heard otherwise," Jarrod replied, stamping
his feet again.

"Did you stop by your house and check for messages?"
Griff asked. "I've heard that dueling participants often
back out at the last moment and when that happens, it's up
to the other participant to decide if they wish to continue
the matter or let it go."

"I roused Henderson from his bed," Jarrod said. "Dunbridge hasn't sent a message."

"He's probably sleeping in until noon," Colin grumbled.
"Or still getting dressed. It can take one of Brummell's dis-
ciples all morning just to tie a cravat."

"If he is," Jarrod warned, "and I find out about it, I *will*
kill him." He stifled a yawn. "I haven't slept more than
three hours in nearly two days."

Griff nodded. "It reminds me of my cavalry days. When
we slept with our fingers around our horse's bridles." He
reached for the flask. "And to think I left a warm and willing wife for this." He winked at Jarrod. "I may kill him
myself."

Jarrod smiled. "If it takes him all morning to tie a cravat, think how long it takes him to select one of those godawful waistcoats."

Colin laughed. "And those tight breeches! I swear he must be sewn into them. And I have to ask myself why. It isn't as if he appears to have much of which to be proud." He rubbed his hands together, then reached for the flask and took a swig of the potent coffee.

"I've heard the dandies who are a bit light in the front of their breeches supplement their length, so to speak, with sausages wrapped in a stocking," Griff said.

Jarrod threw back his head and roared with laughter. "I'll never look at another hound sniffing someone's crotch without wondering."

"Be thankful you don't have a father-in-law who's mad for the hunt. Or the fact that you go along once in a while just to please him. Those bloody hounds sniff so many crotches in the space of hunt that your ribs would be aching from silent laughter all day."

"If he doesn't hurry up, I'm going to freeze to death." Jarrod waited for Colin to pass him the flask again, but Colin reached over him and handed it to Griff.

"No more for you, my lord." Griff shook his head. "Until we find out if Dunbridge is going to make an appearance or an apology. How long has it been since you've held a dueling pistol?"

Jarrod glanced at Colin. "Almost a year. Why?"

"Because these are perfectly balanced"—Griff patted the mahogany case—"but they're ornate and heavy. His Grace, the Duke of York, presented them to me when I returned from the Peninsula."

"His Grace gave you a pair of dueling pistols?" Colin thought that was incongruous, considering Griff's horrendous experience on the battlefield.

"What else do you give a man returning from war?" Griff asked with a sardonic look on his face. "And the worst part is that I received several other gifts of firearms and these are the best of the lot. Unfortunately, they're so heavy your arm will drop a bit when you extend it. Your aim will be low. If you want to hit him in the arm, aim above and slightly to the side of your target. Try not to hit his shoulder or chest unless you want to seriously wound him."

"I don't." Jarrod looked at Griff. "That's why I would have chosen swords."

"Firearms are quicker." Griff took a swig from the flask and handed it back to Colin. "Dueling with swords is hot, sweaty work and we might be here all damned day if we have to wait for Dunbridge to change linen every time he breaks a sweat."

Jarrod laughed again, then quickly turned somber. "Thank you," he said. "For leaving your warm beds and your lovely wives to come out in the cold and act as my seconds."

"Wouldn't miss it for anything," Colin said. "That's what friends are for," he teased. "To provide a bit of excitement and adventure to those of us who prefer to stay in bed with our wives." He raised the flask. "Here's to the League and the original Free Fellows!"

"*Tri juncta in uno!*" Griffin said.

"Three joined in one!" Jarrod repeated.

◠

*The note arrived at Ibbetson's Hotel shortly after* dawn.

After dressing and then spending the better part of a half hour pacing the width and breadth of the bedchamber, Sarah finally left the room. She exited the bedchamber at the sound of a knock on the outer door and discovered Aunt Etta and Lord Mayhew locked in an embrace. "Pardon me." She blushed.

"No need, my dear." Aunt Etta spoke from her place within the circle of Lord Mayhew's arms. "This isn't a passionate embrace, it's one of relief. And it includes you."

"Jays is all right?" Sarah asked, her heart in her throat. "He survived?"

"He's fine," Aunt Etta breathed. "We just got the news."

"Thank heavens!"

"The duel didn't take place," Lord Mayhew said. "Dunbridge failed to appear. Look!" Reaching up behind his neck, Lord Mayhew removed a sheet of paper from Aunt Etta's fingers and offered it to Sarah. "Read it for yourself."

" 'Lady Dunbridge,' " Sarah read, " 'in the days to come, you will no doubt hear rumors about the small part I played in aborting the duel between your nephew-by-marriage and the Marquess of Shepherdston in regards to your niece Miss Eckersley's honor. Whatever you hear, know that I did what I could to prevent the late Lord Dunbridge's heir from certain injury at the hands of Lord Shepherdston, but more importantly, I wished to repay you in some small way for the kindness you showed me in allowing Calvin to spend his last years with me and for presenting me with the deed to this house when he died. I cannot thank you enough or express my sincere regret for the pain I caused you in loving your husband. I care not a whit what happens to the present Lord Dunbridge (as he has always been irksome to us both), but gentlemen have been bringing news and gossip from Lady Garrison's ball all evening and I am given to understand that your niece and Lord Shepherdston are an item and that you and Lord Mayhew spent a great deal of time together. Although I have never had the pleasure of meeting you or your niece, I know that you both deserve the very best life has to offer. You are a true lady and your niece cannot fail to be likewise and Lord Shepherdston and Lord Mayhew will find themselves the most fortunate of gentlemen to have a place in your lives. Please, know that I wish you only the best and that you need never fear I've designs on Lord Mayhew or Lord Shepherdston. My door is closed to them as they no longer have need of my services. I cannot ask your forgiveness, but I shall always hold you in the highest regard and shall be happy to render assistance to you again should you ever require it. Sincerest regards, Theodora Morton-Jones, number forty-seven Portman Square, London.' " Sarah finished reading the note, then carefully folded it and gave it back to her aunt, then furrowed her brow. "Forty-seven Portman Square? But that's Miss Jones's Home for Displaced Women. She sent a card after Papa died and I intended to call upon her if my plan to win Jarrod failed. . . ." Sarah's mouth dropped open as she looked up at her aunt. "Oh, my . . ."

Lady Dunbridge nodded. "Your threat of becoming a courtesan was more real than you knew. Paying a call at that particular address would have all but guaranteed it. The house belonged to my late husband. She was his mistress. And now, it seems she's become your champion and our ally."

Scooping Precious from her basket beside Lord Mayhew's feet, Sarah cradled the little dog close to her heart and allowed the tears she'd held in check to flow. Moments later, she bent and fastened the leash to the spaniel's collar.

"Where are you going?" Aunt Etta asked.

"I thought I'd take Precious for a walk so you could dress for your appointment at Lambeth Palace."

"You heard?" Aunt Etta asked with some trepidation.

"I heard," Sarah told her. "And I'm very happy for you." She glanced at Lord Mayhew. "For the both of you."

"Sarah," her aunt said, "we weren't trying to exclude you. We simply didn't want to wait any longer and we didn't feel we should announce our intentions to marry on the heels of your misunderstanding with Lord Shepherdston. And that's all it is, my dear, a misunderstanding." She patted Sarah's cheek. "You'll see."

"I know." Sarah blinked away her tears, refusing to be sad on Aunt Etta's wedding day. "I also understand that if you and Lord Mayhew desire a private ceremony, that's what you should have." She smiled up at her aunt. "I'll take Precious and—"

"Oh, no, my dear," Lord Mayhew pronounced. "This is a family celebration and you're going with us."

# Chapter 28

*At every word a reputation dies.*
—*Alexander Pope, 1688–1744*

*Jarrod took out his timepiece and looked at it. Lord* Dunbridge was a half hour late. "He isn't coming."

"Doesn't look that way," Colin agreed. "Of course, I seriously doubt he's seen a sunrise in years."

Griff nodded. "At least not since he's become a follower of the Beau."

"Well . . ." Jarrod paused. "What's the etiquette here? Do we stay or go?"

"That's up to you," Colin said. "He challenged you. Now, he's failed to keep the appointment. You can do whatever you like."

Jarrod nodded. "I believe I'd like breakfast at White's."

"With the usual companions?" Griff asked.

Jarrod nodded. "We've got business to which to attend. Sussex is still missing and now we've got the greater worry of relaying the information Gillian gave us regarding the troop movements to Wellington and informing him of the assassination plot against him, because Gillian's deciphering has proven to be entirely accurate." And alarming. In breaking the code, she had uncovered not only the troop movements, but a plot to assassinate Wellington and a great many other prominent members of British society—including the Free Fellows.

"We need to discover how *our* names got on the list of targets," Colin reminded them.

"I don't think there's any mystery as to why our names are on the list," Griff said. "I'm a national hero and you and Jarrod are attached to the War Office. What we need to discover is whether whoever is behind the leak of this information knows about the League or has targeted us for other reasons. There were other names on the list that have nothing to do with the League. Lord Bathhurst, for instance. Lord Cheltenham and Lord Naughton."

"That's true," Colin said. "We don't know if there is a solid connection to the League, but we know there *is* a connection to the War Office."

"So there is a good chance the source of the information is someone connected to the government," Griff replied.

"A much better chance than it being one of us." Jarrod grinned.

"Now all we have to do is convince Wellington that the threat is real and convince the men at Whitehall that the deciphered messages are correct," Colin said. "They're going to want to know who deciphered the messages and we all know that the men at Whitehall will never believe the information contained in the messages if we tell them Gillian deciphered them."

Jarrod nodded. Convincing the men at Whitehall that the threat was real might prove to be most challenging— especially if he couldn't offer credible evidence to prove it. But Wellington was regarded as England's best hope for defeating Bonaparte and a threat against him had to be taken seriously—especially in light of Gillian's uncanny ability to decipher so accurately. The Free Fellows all knew that she had yet to be wrong. And Wellington's wasn't the only life at stake. There were others to consider.

"Let's find out what Barclay and Courtland discovered, and then *I'll* brief the men at Whitehall," Griff said.

Jarrod started to protest that that was his job, but Griff stopped him. "I know that's your forte, Jarrod, but I can use

Knightsguild as an excuse. They know I've purchased it and plan to use it as a training college for the military. I'll tell them I intend to devote a section of it to the art of ciphering and deciphering. The government won't want to fund the education and training of cipherers once the war is won, but I intend to fund it privately so we will have a ready supply of cipherers when and if we ever need them. Let me make that argument to them at Whitehall today while you're at Lambeth Palace."

"As a national hero, your job is to remain neutral, Griff," Jarrod told him. "You shouldn't be arguing this issue. Not when they already know my political leanings and that I excel in securing financial backing for government ventures."

"Ordinarily, I would agree." Griff laughed. "But today . . ."

"But today, I have to get to Lambeth Palace and purchase a special license to marry. Christ!" Jarrod swore, feeling for his watch. "Hang Dunbridge! What time is it? I've got to be at the palace by nine."

"And after Lambeth Palace comes shopping," Colin reminded him.

❦

*White's was crowded when Griff, Colin, and Jarrod* arrived. The jeers and the catcalls began as they made their way to their customary meeting room.

"You don't seem to have any holes in you, Shepherdston," someone called out. "I guess that means Dunbridge got the worst of it."

"Congratulations in order yet? Or shall we say commiserations?"

"Shepherdston, have you seen the morning papers yet?"

"Why?" Jarrod shot back. "Is your obituary in it?"

"No, but yours will be soon." Someone laughed. "Just as soon as they print the announcement of your nuptials."

"Ignore it," Colin advised, walking beside him, his

Scottish burr thick with anger. "Remember that they're a bunch of ignorant Sassenach lords." Colin reached out and snagged a newspaper from the stack on a nearby table."

"Page three," came the helpful comment.

Colin opened the paper and quickly flipped it to the third page, in the gossip section of the paper, to a column called "Ton Tidbits," and began reading. " 'What's to become of Miss Sarah Eckersley, who was seen at Lady Garrison's elegant gala last evening in the company of the elusive Marquess of Shepherdston? Has she been taken off the market? No one can say for sure, but Miss Eckersley proved to be the bone of contention last evening when Lord Dunbridge, a devoted follower of the prince regent's close friend Mr. George Brummell, challenged Lord Shepherdston to a duel. Are wedding bells in the Marquess of Shepherdston's future? Has the perennial bachelor marquess finally succumbed to the lure of orange blossoms? Can a rustic rector's daughter take him off the market? No one seems to know for sure. . . . But we will surely find out soon. . . .' "

"Imagine the mighty Shepherdston being brought low by a rather homely rustic!"

"One Dunbridge claimed!"

There was a burst of laughter all around.

"One the Beau talked Dunbridge into pursuing for the Beau's own amusement."

There was another round of hearty laughter.

"Egads! But I heard she has red hair and freckles!"

"I'll wager Shepherdston will be increasing the size of his family by two. But will the brat look like Dunbridge or Shepherdston?"

"Won't matter," a voice answered. "It'll have Shepherdston's name and he'll have to claim him."

"Better hope it's a female, 'cause I heard that the next Marchioness of Shepherdston has the same inclinations as the last one."

Jarrod took a step toward the gentleman who'd made the

last comment, but Griff took hold of his arm. "Easy, Jarrod," he said. "Keep the larger goal in mind."

"And her a rector's daughter! Why, the old man must be spinning in his grave!"

"Still waters run deep. Look at Shepherdston. There hasn't been a hint of scandal attached to his name in years. Not since that thing with his parents . . . And all of a sudden, he's ruined a girl and fought a duel within hours of one another."

"Couldn't have done much ruining," someone else called. "Not when she's already spread her legs for Dunbridge."

"Was that you, Mannington?" Griff spun on his heel as he recognized the voice. "Look to your own glass house before you cast stones in someone else's direction. Your father was a bishop. And everyone can see what a gentleman you've turned out to be. How many governesses have you ruined now? Four? Five?"

Jarrod whirled around. "What the devil is wrong with you? You call yourselves the cream of English society while you sit in judgment on others. You imagine me brought low by a rustic," he continued. "You relish the idea, yet I know that I couldn't be brought low by any young lady, rustic or otherwise. I've been low. I couldn't sink any lower. After searching the width and breadth of England for love, I've found myself the grateful recipient of it. I haven't been brought *low,* I've found my wings. . . . Love doesn't limit," Jarrod said. "It expands. You should all be so fortunate."

"Nicely done," Griff congratulated him as they passed through the main room and into their usual one and found Barclay and Courtland waiting. "If you do half as well with Miss Eckersley, you're home free."

Barclay and Courtland rose to their feet and greeted the other Free Fellows cordially.

"Glad to see you hale and hearty this morning," Barclay told him.

"Thank you." Jarrod wasted no time in starting the meeting. "Did you hear anything about Sussex?"

"No," they answered in unison.

"But we heard you had a spot of trouble at Lady Garrison's last night," Barclay said.

Jarrod lifted an eyebrow.

"It's all over town," Courtland said. "Everyone was talking about the duel."

"There was no duel," Griff said. "Dunbridge didn't appear."

Barclay bit back a smile. "Imagine that."

Colin narrowed his gaze at the two newest members of the League. "Do you know anything about his failure to appear?"

They tried to look innocent and failed.

"Spill it," Griff ordered.

"He was at Madam Theo's after the ball last night," Courtland told them. "Boasting of his impending duel with you." He nodded at Shepherdston.

"And?" Jarrod prompted.

Barclay grinned. "Madam Theodora turned ashen, then quickly recovered and instructed the girls that as long as Lord Dunbridge remained in the house, the night's entertainment and drinks were free." He shook his head. "It was some party."

Jarrod stared at Barclay's pallor and red eyes and agreed.

"Needless to say, no one wanted him to leave. Every time he attempted to go, someone pulled him back inside and handed him a drink," Courtland continued the story. "After he passed out, in the arms of the new redhead—Mina, I believe her name is—Madam Theo went to Barclay and asked for assistance in removing him. I assisted Barclay." Courtland's grin matched Barclay's.

"Did you harm him?" Colin asked, more out of curiosity than out of concern for Dunbridge.

"Not at all," Barclay said.

"But he will need to replenish his wardrobe." Courtland fought to keep from chuckling at the memory and failed.

"We decided it best not to take a chance on him waking

from his drunken stupor and attempting to keep his appointment at the dueling oak," Barclay told them. "So we appropriated his clothes."

"All of them?" Griff began to laugh.

"All, except a pair of brief drawers," Courtland said.

"What did you do with them?" Jarrod asked.

"Got 'em at my house," Barclay declared proudly. "When the blighter apologizes to Miss Eckersley for causing her so much trouble, I'll gladly allow him to reclaim them."

Jarrod smiled. By the time Dunbridge apologized, Miss Eckersley would be Lady Shepherdston. "Thank you," he said.

"Our pleasure," Courtland answered. "In more ways than one."

"Just one thing," Griffin added.

"Sir?"

"Next time you take it upon yourselves to stop a duel, kindly send word so the rest of us won't be freezing our arses off at daybreak when we could be home in bed."

"Be thankful you didn't have to lug Dunbridge home," Barclay said. "Or pick up all the clothing we tossed out the window."

"Fair enough," Griff agreed.

Jarrod returned to the topic at hand. "Now that we know what happened to Dunbridge, let's turn our attention to Sussex."

The other Free Fellows nodded.

"Since we've heard nothing, we've no choice but to assume the worst and begin our investigation." Jarrod nodded toward Barclay. "He's our blood brother, but he's your cousin. Find out what's happened to him."

"All right."

He related to Barclay and Courtland the details about the letter from King Joseph of Spain that Gillian had deciphered before Lady Garrison's party, then nodded to Griff. "His Grace will be addressing the men at Whitehall about the need for a permanent training facility for cipherers."

Griff grinned.

Jarrod turned to Alex Courtland. "I won't be able to make the next smuggling run for I've other more pressing personal business at hand."

Courtland nodded.

Jarrod continued, "With Sussex missing and Barclay assigned to find him, we'll need you to make the trip to the coast."

"Jolly good," Courtland agreed.

"Grantham and Lady Grantham will continue their work on the cipher codes."

"What about you?" Barclay asked. Shepherdston usually took a lion's share of the work. Barclay assumed Shepherdston's pressing personal business involved Miss Eckersley for he and Courtland had heard the commotion when Avon, Grantham, and Shepherdston entered the club. And a gentleman did what a gentleman must do in order to preserve a lady's reputation, but Barclay found it odd that Shepherdston had neglected to mention the nature of his pressing business.

"Me?" Jarrod queried.

"What's your assignment?" Courtland asked.

Jarrod grinned. "I'm going shopping."

# Chapter 29

*Love knows nothing of order.*
—*Saint Jerome, c. 342–420*

*The gifts began arriving at Ibbetson's as soon as* Sarah returned from Lord and Lady Mayhew's wedding.

She'd been invited to accompany Aunt Etta and Lord Rob to Lord Rob's home for breakfast, but Sarah knew enough about passion and desire to know that three was a crowd when you'd waited twenty years for a wedding and honeymoon.

She had volunteered to return to the hotel and pack up their belongings and Precious and Budgie for the move to Lord Mayhew's home, where she'd be joining them for dinner that evening. She was packing Aunt Etta's black dresses in her portmanteau when the first knock sounded on the door.

She opened it to find a footman standing there.

"I've a delivery for Miss Eckersley."

"I'm Miss Eckersley," she told him. "But are you certain it's not for Lady Dunbridge? I mean, Lady Dunbridge who just married the Earl of Mayhew?"

"No, miss," he answered, handing her a thick cream-colored envelope engraved with the Marquess of Shepherdston's seal.

Her name was written on the front in a thick, bold script. Sarah opened it and read: *Please accept this token*

*of my esteem and my sincerest apologies for forgetting our
anniversary. Jays.*

Sarah was bewildered. She looked up at the footman.
"Thank you for bringing it," she said. "And please thank
his lordship."

"He told me to tell you to look out the window, miss."

Sarah walked over to the only window that faced the
street, pulled back the drapes, and looked down.

A beautiful carriage drawn by a matched set of gray
horses and complete with driver and footman was parked
below. On the seat of the carriage was a huge bow. The
driver looked up and waved. Sarah turned back to the footman. "You can't mean that that . . ."

"Happy anniversary, miss," the footman said.

"It's beautiful."

"It's yours, miss," the footman told her. "As are we. I'm
Edwards. The other footman is Cooper. And the driver is—"

"Mr. Birdwell!" Sarah exclaimed as she recognized the
driver.

"Yes, miss." Edwards nodded. "His lordship asked me
to relay the message that he's trusting you not to leave
London until he can apologize in person."

Sarah beamed. "You may tell his lordship that I'm not
going anywhere until he apologizes in person."

"He'll be by later to do so." Edwards bowed. "Good
morning, miss."

Sarah reached for her change purse, but Edwards shook
his head. "No need, miss," he said. "I've been amply com-
pensated." He withdrew from the doorway and closed the
door after him.

Sarah waltzed about the room, then returned to the window and stared out at her beautiful carriage. She was still
admiring it when a second knock sounded on the door.

She opened it to find a wizened little man dressed in the
Marquess of Shepherdston's livery standing in the doorway. "I've a delivery for Miss Eckersley," he announced.

"I'm Miss Eckersley."

"This is for you, miss." He stepped away from the door, out of her line of sight for a moment, then presented her with a beautiful black leather lady's saddle.

"I don't ride," she said.

"May I?" the groom asked, nodding toward the sofa.

"Yes, of course." Sarah stepped back to allow the groom to deposit the saddle on the sofa.

He carefully placed the saddle on the arm of the sofa, then produced a cream-colored envelope engraved with the Marquess of Shepherdston's seal from inside his blouse and handed it to her.

Her name was written on the front in a thick, bold script. Sarah opened it and read: *Please accept this token of my esteem and my sincerest apologies for neglecting to give you your Easter gifts. Jays. P.S. Look outside your window.*

Sarah rushed to the window and looked down.

The footman, Edwards, stood behind the carriage holding the lead of a beautiful golden yellow horse who wore a big red ribbon tied around her neck. Edwards looked up and waved. Sarah waved back.

"His lordship asked me to tell you your new saddle is worthless unless it has a worthy mount beneath it."

"She's beautiful!" Sarah gushed.

"*He's* an eight-year-old gelding and will make you an excellent first horse, miss. His name is Merlin and he'll keep you safe while you learn to ride."

"I can't wait!"

The groom smiled. "His lordship knew that you would say that. He asked me to tell you that he trusts that you will not attempt to ride off until he can accompany you."

There it was again. The word *trust*. Sarah nodded. "You may tell his lordship that I am most trustworthy."

"Yes, miss." The groom doffed his hat. "I'm Toby, miss," he told her. "I'm the head groom at his lordship's stables and I trust that you will allow me to teach you to ride."

"I'd be honored," she said, softly, awed by the magnitude of Jarrod's generosity.

And there was more. . . .

She accepted deliveries for the next two hours. She received a basket with a male spaniel puppy for her birthday and a soft orange furry kitten to mark the New Year, both of which promptly curled up beside her on the sofa and fell asleep. She received a huge bouquet of hothouse roses and a diamond tiara for Valentine's. A fur muff to mark Epiphany. A box of beautifully embroidered linen handkerchiefs and three silk shawls for Lady Day. A leather-bound set of Shakespeare for Christmas, and a gorgeous porcelain doll for her sixth natal day.

She burst into tears when she read the note that accompanied the red-haired, brown-eyed doll. *Please accept this token of my esteem and my sincerest apologies. I know you no longer play with dolls, but I remembered that you desperately wanted one for your sixth natal day and I was too ignorant and arrogant at the time to purchase it for you. Please forgive me for not realizing how much you meant to me and how much you will always mean to me. Jays.*

She didn't think there was anything else he could give her that would touch her heart as much as that doll and his note, until she answered a knock on the door and found Jarrod's butler standing in the doorway.

"I'm Henderson," he said. "London butler to the Marquess of Shepherdston."

"Yes, I know."

"I have a delivery for Miss Eckersley," he said.

"I'm Miss Eckersley," she answered.

"Follow me." He turned and walked to the suite of rooms next door to hers.

Sarah followed.

"Before I open the door, miss, please allow me to apologize for my rudeness the other evening," Henderson said.

Sarah blushed. "Please don't mention it, Mr. Henderson," she said. "You had every right to be suspect of my outrageous behavior. I'm sorry if I embarrassed you, for it was never my intent to cause consternation to Lord Shepherdston's staff." Her brown eyes twinkled as she added, "Only to Lord Shepherdston."

Henderson forgot himself long enough to smile. "Then, I congratulate you, miss, for you've succeeded far beyond your wildest dreams." He opened the door and motioned for her to precede him, then closed the door behind her.

"I've a delivery for Miss Eckersley."

Sarah turned at the sound of Jarrod's voice. He stood in the doorway between a sitting room and a bedchamber, wearing a black traveling cloak that covered him from shoulders to midway down his polished black boots.

"I'm Miss Eckersley."

"This is for you, miss." He reached in the pocket of his cape and drew out a small black velvet box and offered it to her.

Sarah's hands shook when she opened it. "Oh, Jarrod," she gasped when the opened lid revealed a single flawless heart-shaped diamond set in a gold ring. It wasn't a huge stone by the ton's standards, but the heart shape and the high quality of the diamond made it extraordinary. The fact that Jarrod was offering it to her made it priceless.

Without saying a word, Jarrod handed her a cream-colored envelope engraved with his seal.

Sarah handed Jarrod the ring as she tore open the envelope and read what he'd written: *Please accept this token of my esteem and my sincerest apologies for always taking and never giving. I love you, Sarah. I will always love you. And I will always regret that it took me so long to realize it. Will you do me the honor of becoming my marchioness?*

Tears sparkled on her lashes and ran down her cheeks when she looked up from the note, but she was smiling and Jarrod took that to be a good sign.

"No."

Jarrod was momentarily stunned. But he should have known Sarah wouldn't make it easy for him. Not this time. Not after last night. "Why not?"

"This is all too overwhelming. And your decision to

court me is much too sudden," Sarah told him. "I need time to consider it."

"Sudden?" Jarrod burst out laughing. "You've been courting me for nearly eighteen years! How can this be too sudden?"

"What's sudden is that now you're attempting to court me."

"This is more than an attempt," he told her. "For now, I *am* courting you—in earnest." Jarrod looked at her.

"Why?" she demanded. "Because I know about your precious league? Because you think you can purchase my trust with magnificent gifts? Or is this your way of keeping your promise to Aunt Etta and Lord Mayhew and absolving your guilt because my name has been bandied about White's because of your duel and your wager with Dunbridge?"

"No."

"Then, tell me, Jarrod, why are you proposing to me today instead of yesterday. Why now?"

"Because I didn't realize I loved you yesterday!" he exclaimed. "I was too arrogant and stupid to realize I loved you yesterday. I only realized it this morning when I thought it was too late." He stared into her eyes. "But I *do* love you, Sarah," he said. "I love you with all my heart. I love you because the world is a better place when I'm with you. Because I find myself laughing and smiling and thinking of things I'd like to tell you at the oddest moments. Because you love me warts and all and because you make me feel there's nothing in the world I can't accomplish so long as I have you. Even when I'm trembling in my boots at the thought of marriage, I know I want you beside me for the rest of my life. I want to be your husband as well as your lover and I want you to share my name as well as my bed. I want you to spend your life with me and I want us to sit at home in the evenings and think about the sexes and names of our unborn children." He took a deep breath. "My mother murdered my father and the housekeeper when I was sixteen, then turned the gun on herself. She committed an act of madness and before she died, she told me that I took after her side of the family." He closed his eyes, then opened them again and stared down at Sarah. "I swore never to marry. Never to lose my heart or take the risk of passing that madness on to my children. I swore that the Shepherdston and Blackheath lines would die with me because I was afraid that love and marriage had caused it. But I've learned that what my parents had wasn't love. It was something else. Something twisted and dark that had no place in a loving marriage. I'm not afraid of the dark anymore, Sarah. You showed me what love is, and now, I can't imagine my life without you, because I want to learn more about love and I want to share everything I learn with you." He sighed. "I didn't intend my gifts as bribes. I wasn't trying to purchase your love or your loyalty. I've always had those precious gifts. I was only trying to give you the moon and the stars and my heart." He took the ring out of the box and dropped to one knee. "Will you marry me and make something of this man who is hardly good enough to be your husband and lover?"

She nodded.

"Say it, please," he begged.

"It's the least I can do."

"Sarah . . ."

"It's the least I can do to save the man I love." She smiled at him. "I love you, Jays, and I'd be honored to marry you and become your wife and lover and marchioness."

"Thank God," Jarrod breathed, slipping the ring onto the third finger of her left hand. "I've got a special license. I can send for a vicar right now and we can have a wedding right here and honeymoon at Shepherdston Hall until I have to return, but I thought you might prefer to be married in your father's church in Helford Green tomorrow. . . ."

"I would," she admitted. "But I hate the thought of Reverend Tinsley marrying us and he's the rector now."

"He won't be by the time we reach Helford Green," Jarrod said. "The archbishop wouldn't sell me the benefice, but we negotiated the removal of Reverend Tinsley in exchange for my promise not to withdraw the funds for a new wing of the cathedral in Bath. We decided Reverend Ingram from the village of Ashford would do nicely."

"Oh, yes!" Sarah flung her arms around his neck and covered his face with kisses.

"You won't mind consummating our vows before we take them?" he asked between kisses.

"Of course not," she told him. "I've seen the papers, Jays. I'm already ruined. I might as well enjoy it."

"Good," he announced, "because I've another present for you and I would feel very foolish if you'd decided differently." He untied the cords of his traveling cape and let it fall to the floor, revealing himself to her in all his naked glory—except for his boots. "You came to me in your nightclothes and asked me to be your lover," he reminded her, quickly toeing off his boots and kicking them aside. "I thought it only fitting that I do likewise."

"Oh?" She arched her eyebrow in an imitation of him.

"I've come to give you lessons, Miss Eckersley." He closed the space between them.

"In seduction?" she asked, breathlessly pulling his face down to hers.

"No," he whispered. "In making love."

# Epilogue

*Whoso findeth a wife findeth a good thing.*

—Proverbs 18:22

They were married by special license in the church at Helford Green by the Reverend Ingram two days later, having spent the first night of their honeymoon in London in Jarrod's room at Ibbetson's Hotel.

Sarah emerged from Ibbetson's on the morning of her wedding day, well and truly practiced in the art of making love courtesy of her teacher, Jarrod, Lord Shepherdston.

What had seemed impossible just days earlier, had come to pass.

Sarah Eckersley, the rector's daughter from Helford Green, had become Lord Shepherdston's mistress—if only for the one night before she became his wife. And Sarah loved every moment of her educational, liberating, and wildly passionate fall from grace.

She awoke in Jarrod's arms to find that Henderson had delivered Jarrod's idea of breakfast—coffee and French pastries from Gunter's on Berkeley Square.

They made the journey to Helford Green in record time and resumed their honeymoon at Shepherdston Hall shortly after the wedding.

Other gifts awaited her at Shepherdston Hall. For Jarrod had included the return of her family's furnishings from the rectory in his negotiations with the archbishop over the removal of Reverend Tinsley. And Pomfrey, the butler at Shepherdston Hall, had made a place for all of them in her new home.

Sarah was welcomed home to Shepherdston Hall and greeted as if she had always belonged there.

But their idyllic honeymoon there was necessarily brief.

Although he couldn't tell her everything, Jarrod told her as much as he could. He explained that the Free Fellows League had grown from a secret childhood club to an indispensable secret weapon in the fight against Bonaparte. He explained that while he wanted nothing more than to spend the rest of his life making love to her at Shepherdston Hall, there were lives at stake and he was needed in London. There was a leak of information in the War Office and he was determined to stop it.

The fact that the Duke of Sussex and the Marchioness St. Germaine had disappeared, seemingly without a trace, was also of great concern as well as the news of the assassination plot against Wellington and a list of other prominent leaders. Jarrod was needed to relay the news to Wellington and the gentlemen at Whitehall.

So long as England was at war, there was vital work to be done and, as leader of the Free Fellows League, Jarrod had to return to it.

She understood duty and loyalty and patriotism. Duty called. And Jarrod must answer the call. Her fear was that he would leave her behind at Shepherdston Hall. But Jarrod quickly laid that fear to rest.

"When are you leaving?" Sarah asked, as she lay in the big bed in the master's chamber at Shepherdston Hall, her head pillowed on Jarrod's shoulder.

"*We're* leaving later this morning," he answered.

"*We?*"

"If you've no objections." He pressed a kiss against her soft red curls.

Sarah pushed herself up on her elbow and turned to look at him. "I thought you were going to . . ."

"Leave you behind?" He finished her sentence.

She nodded.

Jarrod frowned. "Why would you think that, my sweet?"

" 'We shall install our wives in country houses and keep separate establishments nearby or in London'," she quoted from a long ago memory.

Jarrod immediately recognized item seven from the Free Fellows League Charter. "Where did you hear that?"

"From you," she answered. "A long time ago when you were home from Knightsguild for Easter. You sat on the bank of the pond tossing rocks and repeating it over and over."

"You were spying on me." Jarrod remembered that Easter. His mother was staying with a gentleman at his country home and his father, never one to give up amusements, had remained in London. Jarrod was alone at Shepherdston Hall and missing Griff and Colin who were at home with their families. He'd spent much of his holiday committing the Free Fellows League Charter to memory to remind himself that he had friends and that he meant a great deal to them. Sarah kept sneaking away from the rectory and the solemnity of Holy Week to follow him around.

"It wasn't that hard," she admitted, "since you were always by the pond tossing pebbles and talking out loud." She glanced around and sighed. "You must have been so lonely here by yourself."

"I was," he answered. "And most of the time I was too proud and stupid to welcome a certain red-haired little girl into my life and into my heart." He reached up, tangled his hand in her hair and gently pulled her down for a soul-searing kiss. "And you can bet I won't make that mistake again."

"No?" she asked, her lips a fraction of an inch from his.

"No," he affirmed. "I may have to leave you behind at times in order to fulfill my duties, but it won't be because I want to." He smiled. "I've been alone enough," he said. "And so have you. I greatly prefer this"—he stopped to kiss her—"to solitude."

"So do I," she agreed.

"Then, it's settled," he said, pulling her atop him and settling her comfortably upon his morning erection. "You're coming with me." He gave her a lecherous wink.

"Soon, I vow."

Sarah laughed, then wiggled her bottom against him. "I'll see what I can do to arrange it, my lord."

Jarrod groaned in pleasure as she set out to do just that. He'd never entertained a thought of leaving Sarah behind at the Hall. He couldn't. She was a part of him now. As much a part of him as the heart that beat in his chest.

She was his wife and her place was by his side.

In London.

Where she would delight in the pleasant task of showering him with love and making his house a home and where he would take great pride in loving her and introducing Sarah into society as his marchioness.

After four gloriously romantic nights at Shepherdston Hall, Lord and Lady Shepherdston returned to London and settled into blissful domesticity that included enough secret missions and adventures to last a lifetime.

And in the years to come, the merchants of Bond Street and the owners of Ibbetson's Hotel would often boast of the Marquess of Shepherdston's penchant for showering his marchioness with fabulous gifts. Each merchant took great delight in claiming that his had been the most expensive or the most unusual or the most charming gift.

But Gunter's, the confectioner's in Berkeley Square, knew the truth. For every year on the anniversary of their nuptials, the Marquess of Shepherdston ordered two French pastries exquisitely decorated with single pink rosebuds on top; and the Marchioness of Shepherdston ordered one long French éclair with vanilla cream, but no icing—to be sent to their London residence in time for morning coffee.

And according to his lordship's household, those French pastries were the only meal they ate, for Lord and Lady Shepherdston remained in bed all day. Making love.

Turn the page for a preview of

# TRULY A WIFE

The fourth novel in Rebecca Hagan Lee's
Free Fellows League series

"*Good evening, Miranda. Fancy meeting you here.*"
Sussex gave the Marchioness of St. Germaine an awkward little bow.

"This isn't funny, Daniel." She glared at him. "Your mother was very surprised and none too pleased to see me. She made it quite clear that my name was not on the guest list."

"Not on *her* guest list," Sussex corrected.

"Your mother's guest list is the only one that matters," Miranda snapped at him.

"Not to me," he countered. "And I invited you."

"Then you should have had the decency to inform your mother because hers is the guest list they use at the front door."

He winced.

Miranda frowned. "You do this to me every year, Daniel, and you know she doesn't like me crashing her party."

It was true. His mother had never liked or approved of Miranda. There was, the duchess always said, something unseemly about a girl Miranda's age inheriting her late father's title and becoming a peeress in her own right. Something unseemly about a young woman who considered herself the equal to male peers. Daniel suspected his mother might be more jealous than disapproving, for the duchess had been born an honorable miss and had gained her lofty title by marrying a duke while Miranda had rightfully inherited hers. So, Daniel invited Miranda to the gala every year knowing his mother had deliberately omitted her name from the guest list.

It began on a whim as a way to right his mother's injustice, but Daniel had continued to invite Miranda year after year because he enjoyed her company. He had wanted to see her again, to hear her voice and resume the verbal sparring they'd enjoyed during their brief courtship—a courtship that had come to a rather abrupt end.

He had been a few months shy of his majority and certain his dream of becoming a member of the Free Fellows League was within his grasp when he met her. Miranda had just inherited her title and Daniel's mother had made her disapproval well known. Although he'd liked Miranda immensely and found her physically and mentally stimulating, he hadn't wanted anything more than a light flirtation, and Daniel had been very much afraid that he was in danger of falling in love with Miranda St. Germaine. So he'd stopped calling upon her and he and Miranda had gone from being would-be lovers to complete adversaries almost overnight.

And their adversarial relationship had continued. Every year he invited her to his mother's society gala and every year, Miranda responded to his invitation. And Daniel was convinced it wasn't just to avoid the humiliation of having everyone else in the ton know that hers was the only prominent name that didn't appear on the duchess's guest list. She enjoyed their verbal sparring every bit as much as he did.

"Yet, you came," he mused.

"I must be as daft to accept as you are to invite me," Miranda admitted. "Because I thought, this time, Her Grace was going to have footmen escort me back to my carriage."

"If she had, it would have marked the end of her gala evening and her role as hostess here at Sussex House."

Miranda glanced up at him. A thin line of perspiration beaded his upper lip and the look in his eyes was hard and implacable. "Daniel, you don't mean that."

Daniel met her gaze. "Oh, but I do. After all, it is my house."

"Your mother has had it longer," Miranda reminded him. "And she is the duchess."

"Dowager duchess," he corrected.

"A duchess all the same." Miranda sighed. "You know I don't like coming here uninvited."

"You didn't."

"How many other guests did you invite?"

"None," he answered truthfully. "Only you."

"Why am I the only recipient of the Duke of Sussex's largesse?"

Daniel smiled at her. "Because I didn't want to suffer alone."

She opened her mouth to speak, but he stopped her with his next words. "Let's not argue anymore, Miranda."

"We always argue," she told him.

"Not tonight."

"What shall we do instead?"

"I'm here," he said, reaching for her hand. "You're here. And the orchestra's here. Why not do me the honor of a dance?" He nudged her onto the edge of the dance floor.

Miranda blinked up at him, not certain she'd heard him correctly. "You're asking me to dance?"

"It would seem so." Lifting the dance card and tiny pencil dangling from her wrist, he penciled in his name for the current dance and all the others that followed, blithely crossing out the names already listed and adding his own. "And it seems I've done so in the nick of time before your card was full."

"You want to dance to this?" She frowned. The orchestra was playing a quadrille and in all the years she had known him, Miranda had never seen Daniel Sussex partner anyone to the music of a quadrille.

"You know better than that." He gave her his most devastating smile. "I despise quadrilles." Turning in the direction of the orchestra, Daniel held up three fingers, then four, designating the three-quarter time of the waltz.

"Daniel, you can't!" Miranda protested as soon as she

realized his intention. "You know your mother doesn't allow waltzing at her galas."

"She'll allow it at this one." Daniel ignored Miranda's protest and signaled for the waltz once again. The orchestra leader glanced at the dowager duchess before giving Daniel an emphatic shake of his head.

Miranda turned to Daniel with a smug I-told-you-so look on her face.

But the Duke of Sussex was undaunted. He lifted his right hand, indicated the signet ring bearing the ducal crest and signaled, once again, for a waltz in three-quarter time. "There, now." Daniel smiled at Miranda as the orchestra leader acquiesced. "See, Miranda, with the right incentives, one can accomplish the impossible."

"As soon as she hears the music, your mother is sure to put a stop to it," Miranda warned.

"Then it's our only chance."

"Chance for what?"

"To escape in each other's arms."

The thought of being held in his arms while they circled the room at a romantically breathtaking pace filled Miranda with pleasure until she caught a whiff of his breath. "Daniel, you're foxed!"

"I am," he confirmed.

"But why?"

"Because I've been drinking."

"Yes, you have." Miranda struggled to keep from smiling, but lost the battle. "My guess is whisky. Quite a bit of it."

"Quite." Daniel nodded, swaying on his feet once again, leaning on her more heavily.

Miranda put out a hand to steady him and felt dampness against his waistcoat. He groaned in obvious pain. "Daniel?"

Daniel glanced down. "Bloody hell," he cursed beneath his breath. "Mistress Beekins won't be pleased."

Miranda's ears pricked up at the sound of an unfamiliar female name. "Who is Mistress Beekins?"

"The lady who sewed me up," Daniel replied, matter-of-factly.

"Sewed you up?" Miranda parroted.

Daniel nodded. "In nice, neat stitches." He frowned. "But it appears to be for naught because I seem to be bleeding again." He fought to keep his feet, leaning heavily on Miranda for balance. "There's the end of the quadrille. Come, Miranda, I want to waltz with you. Now."

"Daniel, you're in no condition to waltz." Miranda looked closely and saw that he was flushed with fever. "You ought to be in bed."

Daniel stared down at her. "I'm doing my damnedest to get there."

"I'm serious," Miranda replied, her tone of voice laced with concern and a certain amount of disapproval.

"So am I." He spoke through clenched teeth. "I'm willing to go to bed—just as soon as you waltz me out of here and into the carriage I hope to God you left waiting."

"But your bed is upstairs."

"Up sixty-eight stairs I can't negotiate," he admitted. "And even if I could get to my bed without anyone noticing, how long do you think it would be before *she* discovered the reason for my absence?"

"She's your mother," Miranda reminded him. "She should know you're injured."

"No." He spoke from behind clenched teeth. "No one can know." He leaned forward, pressing his forehead against the top of Miranda's head. "Except you."

"Why me?"

"Because I trust you," he told her. "And . . ."

Miranda's heart swelled with pride. "And?"

"You're the only woman tall enough and strong enough to manage."

Miranda's romantic dreams died a sharp, quick death. "Thank you for informing me of that, Your Grace." Miranda's reply was sharper than she intended, but she was struggling to keep her hurt and the tears that stung her eyes from showing. "No doubt I needed to be reminded that I'm always the biggest girl anywhere," she muttered.

"Miranda . . ." he began.

"No."

He knew she couldn't refuse him. "Please, Miranda, waltz me out of here. I can't walk out of here on my own and I bloody well can't quadrille out. Waltzing is the only way. We'll head for the terrace."

"The terrace?"

"If I hold on to you, I know I can make it. . . ."

"You're an ass, Your Grace. . . ."

"I know," he answered as the orchestra began the waltz.

"You're lucky I don't leave you bleeding all over your mother's marble floors," she told him, as he took her in his arms and guided her into the first steps of the dance.

Daniel inhaled deeply, gathering his remaining strength. "I know."

Miranda felt the trembling in his arms and carried as much of his weight as she could. "Good heavens, Daniel, you weigh a ton."

He grunted in reply and did his best not to lean so heavily on her. But he was fighting a losing battle and they were both keenly aware of it.

Miranda knew the effort it took for him to waltz so effortlessly and she did the only thing she could think to do to keep him upright and moving. "If you stumble and fall or step on my feet, I swear to God, I'll leave you where you lie and let Her Grace deal with you."

Squeezing his eyes shut against a wave of dizziness, he faltered.

Miranda felt the slight breeze from the open terrace doors and realized victory was within reach. She moved closer, taking on more of his weight as she whispered, "Hold me closer."

"Too . . . close . . . already . . ." He ground out each word. "Your rep—"

"Hang my reputation! You're bleeding through your waistcoat and onto my new ball gown. So, don't give up on me now, Daniel. Because when this is over and you're recovered, you're going to accompany me to my dressmaker's and buy me the most exquisite ball gown anyone has ever seen. . . ."